KT-160-014

rachel vincent

BLOOD BOUND

MIRA

DID YOU PURCHASE THIS BOOK WITHOUT A COVER?

If you did, you should be aware it is **stolen property** as it was reported *unsold and destroyed* by a retailer. Neither the author nor the publisher has received any payment for this book.

All the characters in this book have no existence outside the imagination of the author, and have no relation whatsoever to anyone bearing the same name or names. They are not even distantly inspired by any individual known or unknown to the author, and all the incidents are pure invention.

All Rights Reserved including the right of reproduction in whole or in part in any form. This edition is published by arrangement with Harlequin Enterprises II B.V./S.à.r.l. The text of this publication or any part thereof may not be reproduced or transmitted in any form or by any means, electronic or mechanical, including photocopying, recording, storage in an information retrieval system, or otherwise, without the written permission of the publisher.

This book is sold subject to the condition that it shall not, by way of trade or otherwise, be lent, resold, hired out or otherwise circulated without the prior consent of the publisher in any form of binding or cover other than that in which it is published and without a similar condition including this condition being imposed on the subsequent purchaser.

MIRA is a registered trademark of Harlequin Enterprises Limited, used under licence.

Published in Great Britain 2011
MIRA Books, Eton House, 18-24 Paradise Road,
Richmond, Surrey, TW9 1SR

© Rachel Vincent 2011

ISBN 978 1 848 45047 9

60-1011

MIRA's policy is to use papers that are natural, renewable and recyclable products and made from wood grown in sustainable forests. The logging and manufacturing processes conform to the legal environmental regulations of the country of origin.

Printed in the UK
by CPI Mackays, Chatham, ME15 8TD

6840403466 1 312

RACHEL VINCENT

"I liked the character and l... I look
forward to reading th... in the series."
—Charlaine Harris

"Vincent is a welcome addition to this genre!"
Kelley Armstrong

"Compelling and edgy, dark and evocative, *Stray* is a
must read! I loved it from beginning to end."
Gena Showalter

"I had trouble putting this book down. Every time
I said I was going to read just one more chapter,
I'd find myself three chapters later."
—*Bitten by Books* on *Stray*

"Vincent continues to impress with the freshness of her
approach and voice. Action and intrigue abound."
—*RT Book Reviews*

Find out more about Rachel Vincent by visiting
mirabooks.co.uk/rachelvincent
and read Rachel's blog at urbanfantasy.blogspot.com

Also available from **Rachel Vincent**

The Shifters series
STRAY
ROGUE
PRIDE
PREY
SHIFT
ALPHA

Soul Screamers series
MY SOUL TO TAKE
MY SOUL TO SAVE
MY SOUL TO KEEP
MY SOUL TO STEAL

And look for the thrilling second instalment in
Rachel's new **Unbound** series

SHADOW BOUND

Available in 2012

To #1, who understands that a writer can never really leave her work at work. I live in my own head, constantly distracted from the real world by the ones I make up, and it takes someone special to put up with that. I hope you know how special you are. And I didn't even have to make you up.

LEICESTER LIBRARIES	
BA	
Askews & Holts	21-Sep-2011
	£7.99

One

Only two-thirty in the morning, and I already had blood on my hands. The most messed-up part of that? It was the hour that bothered me.

"You sure it's him, Liv?" Booker swiped one hand over his sweaty, stubbly face as we stared at the lit window on the third floor. The apartment building was long and plain, like a cracker box on its side, and the moonless night only smeared the sides of the featureless building into the ambient darkness.

I nodded, shoving both cold, chapped hands into my jacket pockets. It was warm for early March, but still cold for me.

"How sure?"

My eyes closed, and again I clutched the blood-stiffened swatch of cloth in my right pocket, inhaling deeply through my nose, and the world exploded into a bouquet of scents. Relying on years of training, I sorted through them rapidly, mentally tossing aside those I couldn't use. The metal tang of several huge trash bins. The chemical bite of Booker's cologne. And the pervasive, ambient smells of life east of the river—motor oil, fried food and sweat.

What was left, with those more obvious smells out of the way, was the trail I'd followed all over town, as much a *feel* as a true scent, and a virtual match to the blood sample in my pocket.

I am a Tracker. More specifically—and colloquially—I'm a bloodhound. Given a decent, recent sample of your blood, I can find you no matter where you hide. Officially, my range is about eighty miles—on the high end of average. Unofficially…well, let's just say I'm good at what I do. But not too good. Too much Skill will get you noticed. And I know better than to get noticed.

Booker cleared his throat and I opened my eyes to find myself staring up at the lit window again—the only occupant still awake. "Ninety-five percent. It's either him or a close male relative, and that's the best you're gonna get with a dry blood sample," I said, as water dripped from a gutter somewhere to my left. "Tell Rawlinson I'll send him a bill."

Booker pulled his black ski cap over his ears. "He's not gonna like that."

"I don't give a shit what he likes." I turned and walked back the way I'd come, listening as my steel-toed work boots echoed in the alley. I was exhausted and pissed off from being woken at two on a Friday morning, yet still pleased for the excuse to charge nearly double my usual rate. Office space in the south fork doesn't come cheap.

"Warren!" a deep voice barked from behind me, and I groaned beneath my breath. I turned slowly to see Adam Rawlinson step out from behind a rusty Dumpster, his dark hair, skin and expensive wool coat blending into the thick shadows. No telling how long he'd been there. Watching. Listening.

Travelers—shadow-walkers—were notorious for shit like that. They can step into a shadow in their own homes and step out of another shadow across town a split second later. You never know they're coming until they're already there. It's a convenient Skill—except when it's annoying as hell.

"Hey, Adam. Kinda late for a stroll, isn't it?" Especially considering that his home address was at least two tax brackets above the inner-city grime now clinging to the soles of his dress shoes. "What? You don't trust me?"

Rawlinson scowled, his frown exaggerated by deep shadows. "Ninety-five percent isn't good enough, Liv."

I shrugged, my arms crossed over my dark jacket. "You're not going to get a hundred-percent certainty without a better blood sample or his full name to flesh out the scent."

He nodded; I wasn't telling him anything new. "But you'd know for sure if you had a current sample to compare it to, right? Something fresh?"

"I don't get my hands dirty anymore. You know that." I follow the blood scent, and I can track by name if I have to. But that's where my job ends—no reason for me to be there when the action starts. My life was messy enough without adding blood spatter.

"Booker's here for the takedown. I just need you to get close enough for a positive ID," Rawlinson insisted. "We don't know his name, and we're not going to get a better blood sample. I played hell getting that one out of the evidence room as it is. This is personal, Liv."

Damn it. Booker was working without a partner and Adam Rawlinson had come out to see the show. This one was off the books. "Is this about Alisha?" Rawlinson's daughter had been killed in a carjacking the week before. He'd shown up for work the next day as if nothing had happened. As if her death meant nothing to him.

Here was proof to the contrary. I was almost relieved.

His gaze never wavered. "The cops had a near miss, and one of them winged the bastard last night. The sample's from the passenger's seat he bled all over."

I exhaled, watching him closely. "Why do I get the feeling you're not going to turn this asshole in?" Rawlinson's operation had a rock-solid reputation. Official bounty-hunting in cooperation with bail bondsmen and the proper authorities, all on the up-and-up. He would turn in the target, collect a check for freelance services from the city, then pay the rest of his crew. Which used to include me.

But this time…

"Because you're a very smart girl." He started walking toward the building, and I followed reluctantly. "You know, I'd love to have you back on the crew full-time."

"That's because your new Tracker couldn't find his own dick in the dark." I hesitated, and the night was quiet, but for our footsteps on cracked asphalt. "You know better than to start shit east of the river without a work order, Adam. What if someone sees you?"

"That's why you're here." He met my gaze, and I had to respect his honesty, even if it pissed me off. "Everyone knows you're working for Ruben Cavazos, so no one will think to report this if you're with us."

"I work for *myself*." And myself had to pay rent on a shitty apartment *and* a tiny office, repairs on a car saddled with more used parts than Frankenstein's monster, and interest and principle on student loans for a degree I'd never once put to use. "I freelance for Cavazos just like I freelance for you." And everyone knew that black hats paid better than white knights. "Having me with you isn't going to keep your feet cool while you walk through flames, Adam. You need to let the police handle this."

"We both know there's nothing they can do."

But that wasn't true. They *could* do plenty but they wouldn't. Not as long as the courts refused to recognize Tracking as a legal form of identification and discovery. The world knew about us—the Skilled had been dragged into the spotlight almost thirty years ago—but the government had yet to officially recognize our existence. We were the biggest open secret in history. We had no rights and no protection under the law, beyond those afforded us as natural-born citizens.

What that meant in legal circles was that no government office could officially hire Binders to draft or seal contracts. Nor could they use evidence gathered via Trackers, like me. Everything involving the dozen or so Skilled abilities had to be unofficial consultations and contract work. And completely off the books.

What that meant in criminal circles was the gradual formation of the single most profitable—and ruthless—black-market system in history. Because the government didn't officially recognize our Skills, they couldn't regulate or police them, which left a huge

Rachel Vincent

gap at the top of the power pyramid. A gap that had been filled by various Skilled crime syndicates across the world, but most notably—and locally—by rival black-market kingpins Jake Tower and Ruben Cavazos, who together controlled more than two-thirds of the city.

Think of my city like a giant peace sign, divided by the river. Everything east of the river is controlled by Cavazos, everything west of the river by Tower. And on the south side, cradled by the fork in the river, you can live, eat and breathe without lining the pockets of either organization—but you'll do it at a much higher price, because those who understand the world they live in and can afford the rent *will* pay to avoid picking a side.

"Okay, look. Now that you've found him, you should just watch him until he makes a mistake, then go after him legally. Stick to what you're good at, Adam. Anything else would just be dripping blood into the shark tank."

"Wait for him to make a mistake?" Rawlinson demanded softly, and I nodded, already feeling guilty for the suggestion. "How long will that take, if it even happens? Coming in here once, with you, to take care of business—that's one thing. But if we loiter, just waiting for this bastard to commit another crime… Well, that's just not an option on the east side, is it?" His gaze pleaded with me, and I resisted the overwhelming urge to stare at the ground. "She was my *daughter,* Warren," Rawlinson said, and the rare glimpse of his raw pain made me groan on the inside, even as I spoke the question I shouldn't have asked.

"What do you want me to do? Go in and prick his

finger?" My hand clenched around the stiff cloth in my pocket.

"I don't care how you ID him. Just get close enough to tell for sure, and we'll handle the rest."

"That's going to cost you." Sympathizing with his pain didn't change my bottom line—freelancers don't get benefits, and I was currently without health care, a dangerous position to be in, considering my line of work.

"Fine. Bill me."

Against my better judgment, I led the way into the dark, quiet building with Rawlinson and Booker at my back. Most of the apartments were empty. Rumor had it the city planned to knock the eyesore down as soon as they managed to relocate the last six tenants—and convince Cavazos to sell the building. They probably had no idea there was a squatter on the third floor.

We crept silently up the stairs, the stiff bit of cloth clutched in my right hand, my fingers rubbing over and over the rough spot. I could feel him, so long as I was touching his blood. I could smell his sweat and taste his fear, both manifestations of the smear of psychic energy people leave behind with every drop of their blood.

For me, it's a little harder working from only a name, but it can be done. And it's easiest with both a name *and* fresh blood. But that rarely happens. UnSkilled criminals are much more careful than the unSkilled general population, and in hiding from police forensics labs, they're inadvertently hiding from Trackers.

Even stupid criminals don't want to be found.

The door between the stairwell and the third-floor hall was long gone, so we could see the light pouring from the crack beneath his door the moment we stepped onto the landing. The energy signature was stronger here, but no clearer. I was going to have to see the bastard to confirm his ID.

Damn it.

I snuck down the hall silently with Booker and Rawlinson on my heels until we stood in front of the lit apartment. I gestured for them to give me some space, and they stood to either side of the door, backs pressed against the grimy walls, out of sight from the occupant, unless he actually stepped into the hall.

Then I took a deep breath and knocked on the door.

When I'd worked for Rawlinson, I'd done both the tracking and the takedown, and back then, I would have looked the part—harmless, vapid young woman who needed jumper cables, or a telephone, or a big, strong arm to open a jar of pickles. Anything to get close enough to use a Taser on the target and collect a paycheck.

It's amazing what a few years' experience and the threat of mortal injury with no health insurance can do to change your perspective. Especially with the clock ticking in my ear and the certainty that I had no time to be incapacitated by injury.

Footsteps clomped toward me from inside the apartment and the door squealed open to reveal a tall, thick man with two days' growth on his chin and suspicion shining in his eyes. He was armed—the handheld behind his right thigh was a dead giveaway—probably with the gun that had killed Alisha Rawlinson.

"Hey, sorry to bother you so late, but—" I let my right arm fly, and my fist smashed into his nose.

The target gave a wet gurgle of surprise and pain, and swung his arm up, too stunned to actually aim his pistol as blood poured from his ruined face. I ducked below the gun and smashed his wrist into the door facing as hard as I could. Bone crunched. The target screamed again and his fist opened. The gun thumped to the floor and Booker kicked it down the hall.

I stepped back and let him take over, wiping the target's blood from my face with the tissue Rawlinson offered. "It's him." I handed the tissue back as Booker pounded the target into unconsciousness in the doorway. The rest of this floor was empty, and even if one of the few tenants heard something, they wouldn't come out to investigate. Not on this side of town. Not in the middle of the night.

Not if they had any wish to see daylight.

"Thank you, Liv," Rawlinson said, as Booker dragged the unconscious man into his apartment.

"Don't thank me. Pay me." I peeled off my blood-stained jacket and handed it to him. "And if this doesn't come clean, you owe me one just like it." Then I took off toward the stairwell without looking back, trying to ignore the repetitive thud of fist hitting flesh echoing in the hall behind me.

On the street again, I exhaled, then glanced back at the building behind me. Silence, except for my own footsteps and the highway traffic two blocks away. True to his word, Rawlinson was keeping things quiet.

I crossed the road in a hurry, digging in my pocket for my keys, but froze when I spotted my car—and the man leaning against the hood. He was built of shadows, untouched by the streetlight on the corner, but I'd know that silhouette anywhere.

"Hey, Liv." Cameron Caballero stood, and the past

six years without him suddenly seemed surreal, as if I'd dreamed the whole thing, and now I'd finally woken up to the truth. To how my life should have gone.

But then a car engine started, stalled then restarted in the distance, and my life—the gritty reality—snapped back into place like emotional whiplash, leaving me gasping for breath.

Him showing up like this again wasn't fair. But *fair* had never been less relevant.

"Not tonight, Cam." Mentally steeling myself, I clomped toward him and my car, assuming he'd move when I tried to unlock my door. But instead of sliding out of the way, he stood, inches away now, intentionally invading my personal space. I could step back, but that would be acknowledging that being so close to him still affected me. Or I could stand my ground and make *him* back down.

"You know, someday you're going to have to tell me what happened," he said when neither of us moved, his voice an intimate, familiar whisper. "Why you left."

"Today isn't that day. Move." I wanted to shove him out of my way, but touching him would have been a very bad idea. Maybe the best bad idea I'd ever had. "Don't make me hurt you. I've already broken one face tonight."

"I heard you were breaking faces professionally," he said, still watching me as if nothing in the world existed, beyond whatever he saw in my eyes. "Then I heard you quit."

I didn't know what to say to that, but as always, when I ran out of words, he still had plenty. "Would you really hit me?"

"Would you really make me?" I eyed him boldly and

he sighed, and I could see that spark of possibility—of a rekindling—die in his eyes.

"No one makes you do anything, Olivia," he said, and my chest tightened with the desperate wish that he were right. "A friend wants to see you."

I reached around him and unlocked my car door, but he still leaned against it. "I don't want to see your friend."

He stared down at me from inches away, and I knew his eyes would be dark, dark blue, if they weren't swimming in shadows. "Not my friend, Liv. Yours. She came to me looking for you. I think you should hear her out."

But I couldn't do anything that meant spending time with Cam, for both of our sakes. It was the same every time I ran into him: a jolt of memory, a spark of resurrected heat and a huge dose of regret I was sure he could see. That regret was what kept bringing him back.

It was what still drew me to him, even as I pushed him away.

"I don't give a shit what you think," I said, too late to be believable. I didn't bother asking how *he'd* known where to find me. Cam was a Tracker—the best I'd ever met, other than...well, me. But whereas I was good with blood, he was good with names. Given a full, real name, he could find anyone, anywhere, and his range rivaled mine. And I'd made the mistake of telling him my full name—which no one else in the entire world knew—years ago. When I'd thought we'd be together forever.

That was one of the most foolish mistakes I'd ever made, but one he hadn't given me reason to regret. Until now.

"Last chance, Cam. Move, or I'll move you."

He shoved his hands into the pockets of a snug pair of jeans and gave me this sad little smile, as if he missed me and wanted me gone, both at once, and I knew exactly how that felt. Then he stepped aside and watched while I slid into the driver's seat and slammed the door.

As I pulled away from the curb, I glanced in the rearview mirror to find him still watching me, unmoving, until I turned at the corner and drove out of sight.

I unlocked my office door and shoved it open, then trudged across the small space toward the tiny bathroom. I had no waiting room and no fancy chairs. Just my desk, two cheap, upright cabinets full of my stuff and one old leather couch, stained and ripped, and more comfortable now than the day I took it from an ex's house along with my own things—restitution for the car he'd stolen and nearly a year of my life wasted.

In the bathroom, I pulled off my top and grabbed a clean T-shirt from the cabinet over the toilet. The sun would be up in a couple of hours. I'd crash on the couch until dawn, then get an early start, because if I went home and crawled into bed, I'd lose most of the day to sleep, which would lead to me losing the job I'd just bid on to Travis Spencer, the runner-up, and his two meathead associates.

With a quick glance at my pale, blood-splattered reflection, I ran warm water on a clean rag and scrubbed my face until I could no longer smell the energy signature of the blood I'd been tracking. But as I turned away from the mirror, the squeal of hinges bisected the silence, and my heart beat a little faster.

Someone was in my office. At four-thirty in the morning. Without an appointment.

I dropped the rag into the sink and squatted to pull a 9mm from the holster nailed to the inside of the cabinet beneath the sink. Aiming at the floor, I disengaged the safety and stood, ready to elbow the door open. I wasn't expecting trouble, but honestly, I wasn't surprised by it, either. Spencer had been gunning for me ever since he dropped the ball on the governor's missing mistress, and I picked it up and ran for the goal.

"Once upon a time, four little girls, best friends, took an oath of loyalty," a woman's voice said through the door, and I flicked the safety back on. *It can't be...*

Annika. Cam had sent her alone. Smart man.

We hadn't spoken in six years, but hearing her voice was like peeling back layers of time until my childhood came into focus, gritty and rough around the edges— was I ever *really* innocent? yet somehow still naive compared to what time and experience had since made of me.

"They promised to always help one another, when-ever they were asked," she continued, as I fell through the rabbit hole, flailing for something solid to grab on to. "They signed their names, and—"

"And they stamped their thumbprints in blood." I pushed open the bathroom door to find Annika Lawson watching me, green eyes holding my gaze with the weight of shared youth and the long-since frayed knots of friendship. "That's where those stupid little girls went wrong," I said. "They disrespected the power of names and blood."

And look where it got us—my entire life ruled by one careless promise the year I was twelve.

"We didn't disrespect the power, Liv." Her gaze was steady, holding me accountable for every truth I'd ever tried to hide—that much hadn't changed, even after six years apart. "We just didn't understand it."

Because no one had told us. We didn't know we were Skilled, because our parents thought they were protecting us with ignorance. Insulating us from the dangers of our own genetic inheritance.

In the first years after the revelation, people sometimes disappeared. Government experiments or eager private industry research, no one knew for sure, but the disappearances terrified already worried parents into a perilous silence. They could never have known that Kori's little sister was a Binder, or that at ten years old, she'd be strong enough to tie us to one another for the rest of our lives.

"Well, the power understood *us*." And our ignorance didn't make that binding any less real. Or any easier to undo. We'd bound ourselves together so tightly that as we grew up, the bonds chafed, wearing away at our friendship until nothing was left but resentment and anger.

I pulled the bathroom door closed and sank into my desk chair, fending off a battery of memories I'd thought buried. It felt weird to see Anne in my office, out of place in my adult life when she'd been a central figure of my youth. Part of me wanted to hug her and get caught up over drinks, but the stronger part of me remembered what went down that night six years ago, the last time we'd all four been together.

A reunion wasn't gonna happen. Ever. And not just because Elle was dead and Kori was MIA. Anne had disappeared when I'd needed a friend. I could have tracked her, but why, when a dozen unanswered calls and messages said she didn't want to talk to me? So I'd struck out on my own, and never once looked back at the past. Until now.

"What are you doing here? Is a third ghost from my past going to show up and take me to my own grave?" But that possibility struck a little too close to home, and I had to shrug it off.

She sank onto the couch and her composure cracked, then fell away, revealing raw pain and bitter anger, and suddenly I wanted to hurt whoever'd hurt her. In spite of what she'd done to me—what we'd all done to one another—I wanted to protect her, like Kori and I had looked out for her as kids, and that impulse ran deeper than the oath connecting us. Older. All the way back to the day Anne and I had first met, before Kori and Elle even moved to town.

But it wasn't that simple. I knew what she was going to say, even though it shouldn't have been possible.

"I need you, Liv. Will you help me?"

No! Shock sputtered within me, synapses misfiring in my brain as I tried to make sense of what she'd just said. Of what she shouldn't have *been able* to say.

"How did you...?" But my voice faded into silence as the answer to my own question became obvious. "You burned it. You burned the second oath." *Damn it!* "We swore, Anne. We swore to let it stand."

In spite of unshed tears shining in her eyes, Anne's gaze held no hint of shame or regret. "You're the only one who can help me with this and I couldn't even ask you with the second oath binding me."

"That's why we signed it!" I leaned forward with my

arms crossed on the desktop, and my chair squealed in protest.

That second oath was our freedom. It couldn't truly sever the ties binding us, but it prevented us from tugging on them. In the second oath, Anne, Kori, Elle and I had sworn never to ask one another for help, because once asked, we were compelled to do everything within our power to aid one another. Which, we'd learned the hard way, could only lead to disaster. And resentment. And expulsion from school. And arrest records.

"I'm sorry. I really am," Anne insisted, tucking one coppery strand of shoulder-length hair behind her ear. "I know you probably don't believe that, and I can't blame you. But I truly had no choice. Will you help me, Liv?"

"Hell *no,* I'm not going to help you!" But as soon as I said the words, breaking my oath to her, the pain began. It started as a bolt of white behind my left eye, shining so bright that everything else seemed dim by comparison. When I closed my eyes, the light sent pain shooting through my skull, and in less than a second, it was a full-blown migraine. Then came the muscle spasms—a revolt of my entire body, the consequence of going back on an oath signed voluntarily and sealed in blood by a child who'd turned out to be the most powerful Binder I'd ever met.

Defaulting on an oath sealed by an amateur—or even a weak professional—could put you in the hospital. Defaulting on an oath sealed by anyone with real power and/or training could kill you.

First, your brain sends warnings in the form of pain. Migraines. Muscle cramps. General abuse of the body's pain receptors. Then it starts turning things off, one by one. Motor control. Bladder and bowel control. Sight and scent. Hearing. But never the sense of touch. Never the nerve endings. They remain functional so you can feel every second of your body's decision to self-destruct.

I'm a little fuzzy on the order of betrayal by my own internal organs, but among the first to go are the kidneys, liver, gallbladder, intestines and pancreas, any one of which would probably kill you eventually. Then the big guns. If you hold out long enough, you'll lose respiratory function, then circulatory. And without those, of course, your brain has only minutes—*minutes*—for you to try to think through the pain and humiliation and decide whether you're going to stick to your word, or die breaking it.

Most people never get that far. *I've* never gotten that far, as evidenced by the fact that my heart continues to beat, in spite of several times I would have declared it broken beyond repair. But everyone has a limit. A point past which you can't be pushed.

"Please don't do this, Olivia," Anne said, when my fingers began to twitch on my desk. A second later, my legs began to convulse, banging against the bottom of the pencil drawer, but I only stared at her through the ball of light in the center of my vision, breathing steadily through the pain. "I'm not going to take it back, Liv," she insisted, leaning forward on the couch. "I can't. Not this time. Will you help me?"

Her repetition of the original request escalated the process, and I gasped at the pain deep in my stomach. I couldn't identify it, but I knew what that pain meant. One of us would have to back down in the next few minutes, or the last thing I saw would be her bright green eyes, full of tears and regret, and her stubborn lips sealed against the sentence that could make it all go away.

"*Please,* Liv," Annika begged, and this time her voice came from behind me. Water ran in the bathroom. A second later, she leaned my chair back and laid a cold, wet cloth over my eyes and forehead, and my hands twitched violently in my lap. "You don't even know what I need you to do."

"Doesn't matter," I gasped, helpless to keep the rag from slipping down my face. Until I gave in to the compulsion to help her, I would feel nothing but the systematic shutdown of my entire body. But still I fought it. She had no right to make me do something I didn't want to do, no matter what stupid mistake we'd made as children! The compulsion was like having my free will stripped. It was humiliating, and infuriating, and it was the reason we'd all gone our separate ways after high school without even a glance in the rearview mirror. "The point—" I growled through a throat that wanted to close around my words "—is that I...have...no... choice."

Leather creaked as she sat on the couch again, and the hitch in her breath said she was fighting sobs. "I'm sorry, Liv. If I could ask you without compelling you, I would, but I don't have that option."

She was right—her very request triggered the compulsion—but that didn't help. And neither did the regret obvious in her voice. "What do you want?" I whispered with all the volume I could manage, as pain ripped through my stomach again, and my arms began to contract toward my torso.

"I need you to find someone."

No surprise, considering I was a Tracker, both by birth and by profession.

The rag slipped from my eyes and I saw her wipe tears from her cheeks with an angry stroke of one hand. "I need you to find the bastard who killed my husband and return the favor."

Two

For a moment, I could only stare at her, and as my re-sistance began to fade in the face of surprise, so did the pain, though it wouldn't completely subside until I'd said the magic words.

"Whoa, you got married?" I couldn't picture it, and I hadn't even noticed the wedding band that now seemed glaringly obvious on her left hand. Did she have a house in the suburbs? A mortgage? A dog in the backyard?

I frowned and sucked in a deep breath, relieved to feel the convulsions in my arms downgrading to mere spasms.

"Yes. Then I got widowed," she said, and more tears fell, even as her jaws clenched in some powerful com-bination of rage and devastation. "I need you to track the murderer and kill him."

"That's…that's not really what I do, Anne," I said, careful not to refuse—so soon after that last refusal, anyway. I stared at her, surprised by the vengeful im-pulse in a woman who, when we were kids, was a turn-the-other-cheek kind of girl. "I just find people. That's it."

Anne blinked, as if she hadn't heard me. As if she didn't *want* to hear me. Then she plucked her purse from the center couch cushion and dug through it with trembling hands. "Here." She produced a wallet-size photo album and flipped to the second page, already pulling a picture out before I realized what she was going to do.

"No, don't..." *Show me a picture of your dead husband...* That was a low blow. But before I could finish my sentence, she'd leaned forward and slid the photo across my desk. I looked at it, against my better judgment, and found a handsome Asian man with a nice smile, one arm around an obviously happy Anne.

It was like staring at a ghost, though I'd never even met the man.

"His name was Shen Liang. He was thirty-four, and the nicest man I ever met. He wrote proprietary software for a company here in the city, but they let him work from home. I can't imagine why anyone would want to kill him." The tears were back, and I stared at my desk to avoid seeing them.

"What did the police say?"

"They're investigating. But, Liv, his killer was Skilled. A Traveler. The police aren't going to be able to find him, and even if they could, without traditional physical evidence, they can't make the charges stick. You know what they're up against."

Yeah. I knew. Nearly half my business came from victims trying to catch people the cops couldn't identify. "I'll find him for you." I had no choice about that. "But the rest..." The killing... "It's not that simple." Even if I found the suspect, and even if I was one-hundred-percent certain that he was guilty of cold-blooded murder, I couldn't just kill him—not if I valued my own life—until I knew for sure what his connections were. Who, if anyone, he was bound to.

"We have a daughter."

"No..." I shook my head when she started digging in her purse again. *No more pictures...*

"Hadley." More tears, and when her jaw began to quiver, something inside me twisted painfully. "She's five years old, and tomorrow I'm going to have to tell her that her daddy is dead. I can't let her grow up knowing the man who killed her father is still out there. You have to help me. I need you to find Shen's killer and kill him. I'm asking you, Olivia."

I groaned out loud. Those were the magic words. This had gone beyond a general request for help: it was now a specific request that I commit murder, regardless of the cost to me, personally. Now, unless I could somehow talk her out of it without actually refusing to do what she'd asked, I'd have to either kill her husband's murderer or die fighting the compulsion. Or die when the police caught up to me. Or *wish* I'd died if the murderer turned out to be connected and his connections caught up to me.

Motherfucker!

"Annika, I'm asking you to rethink this."

There. Two could play that game. Or—technically— four, since there were four bloody thumbprints on that old oath, wherever it was.

Anne flinched, and her hand twitched. She was resisting, and I could practically see how badly she wanted to rub her own forehead. So I tossed her the cool rag.

"Fine. State your case." She leaned back on the

couch and placed the folded rag over her forehead and tear-swollen eyes.

I took a deep breath, but was careful to keep it silent. I didn't want her to know how important it was for me to get out of the assassin part of the favor she was asking. "I don't have a problem with your husband's murderer dying for his crimes." The state would give him the death penalty anyway, if they could prove his guilt. "And I'm perfectly willing to find him for you. But once he's found, you need an expert for...whatever comes next. And I'm no assassin, Anne."

I was an amateur at best....

She sat up, clutching the rag in one hand. "Olivia, I don't need you to cut his throat with a scalpel and frame the governor's personal physician. I don't need the best. Hell, I can't *afford* the best. Proficiency will suffice, and from what I've heard, you're more than proficient."

What? "I don't care what you've heard, I do not kill people for money!" *Much.* Anymore.

Not *just* for money, anyway.

My head throbbed again, but this headache was stress-induced. She wasn't backing down, and I couldn't tell her why I needed her to. And thanks to the original oath, I couldn't just ask her not to ask me to kill someone. Noelle had called that the no-wishing-for-more-wishes clause—like a contractual paradox. It couldn't be done.

Anne frowned. "But you work for Ruben Cavazos."

"Freelance. I *freelance* for Cavazos." Which was precisely why her request was so dangerous for me. "And for Adam Rawlinson, and for anyone else who can pay." Except for Jake Tower. Working for both sides of the Skilled black market would be like putting a bullet in my own head—only more prolonged and painful. "But all I do for them is find people." Usually. "What the client does with the target after that is their business. I don't get involved with that side of it." Not without a very good reason—and money doesn't count.

"So Cavazos doesn't…own you?" She blinked through her tears, watching me carefully, and if I hadn't known her most of my life, I might not have realized what she was doing. What she was looking for in my eyes.

Anne was a Reader—a human truth detector—born with an ability most law enforcers worked years to develop. Only her Skill was virtually infallible, and it couldn't be turned off. Which was why she hadn't dated much in high school—turns out sometimes ignorance really is bliss. Or at least temporary consolation. Shen must have been the most honest man on the face of the planet.

"Say what you mean, Annika." I *knew* what she meant, of course, but… "If you're going to come in here and pull on the strings of a fifteen-year-old oath, you could at least have the guts to ask me what you really want to know."

"Fine," Anne said, and I recognized the rare flash of temper in her eyes. "Olivia, are you bound to Ruben Cavazos? Because that's what they're saying about you out there." She nodded toward the window overlooking the street below. "They're saying you quit Rawlinson's team because you're bound to Cavazos and he's taking a cut of your freelance fee—along with whatever else he wants from you."

My temper burned like indigestion, and I fought the

need to stand in defense of my reputation—the only real asset a freelance Tracker has. "Who's saying that?"

Anne glanced at her hands again, stalling. Then she looked at the door I still hadn't locked. I followed her gaze as the glass panel swung open and Cam stepped in from the hall.

Damn it!

"Lurking in dark hallways?" I said, my hands hidden in my lap to hide how tightly they were clenched. "Isn't that a little cliché, even for a stalker—I mean Tracker?"

"You wouldn't have heard her out if you knew I was here," he said calmly, and I couldn't argue.

"You told her I'm bound to Cavazos?" I had to force my jaw to unclench as I stood, leaning with both palms flat on my desktop. "You used to be above spreading unsubstantiated rumors."

"Those with Skills live and die by the word on the street, Olivia. Especially in this city."

Yeah. It was that dying part that worried me.

"Look, I may be country mouse in the big city," Anne started, still seated while Cam and I stood, "but I'm not stupid. I know Cavazos is selling blood and names on the black market, and I know he has his homegrown army out there doing the dirty work."

But if that was all she knew, she really *was* country mouse.

"He's not the only one. Jake Tower has this city by the balls, and everyone west of the river's so afraid of his men—"

Anne stood, interrupting me smoothly with that same quiet confidence I'd envied in childhood, then hated in adolescence. "What I need to know from you is whether you're part of that army. Is Ruben Cavazos pulling your strings, Liv?"

"Right now, *you're* pulling my strings." And pushing all the wrong buttons. "You need to back off, Annika. Before I have to push you back."

"She has a right to know what you're tangled up in, Liv," Cam insisted quietly, and I exploded, as always, the roaring fire to his smooth, hard ice.

"*Screw* her rights. What about mine? You two can't just ambush me, *make* me work for you, then question me like a criminal so you can be sure none of my dirt's going to rub off on you."

"Ask her to pull her sleeve up," Cam said to Anne, though his gaze never left mine. "To see if she's marked," he added, when she hesitated in obvious confusion.

Anne sighed, but even the weary grief that had moved me earlier couldn't calm me now. "Are you going to make me ask?" she said softly.

Hell no. I wasn't going to give her—or anyone else—any more power over me, if I could possibly help it. "You wanna see?" I spat, gathering the hem of my T-shirt in both hands. I jerked the material over my head and dropped it into my chair, then stood watching them both, in only jeans and a bra. "Fine. Look."

Cam swallowed thickly—the only outward sign that the sight of my bare skin still affected him—then his focus zeroed in on my arm automatically. "Cavazos's first mark is a small black ring on the left bicep. She's clean."

I was clean? As opposed to *dirty?* "Fuck you!"

Cam flinched, and I recognized the regret that flickered across his expression before he could hide it. "That's not what I... I just meant..." He closed his eyes while I tugged my shirt back over my head, glad for the half second it shielded me from their scrutiny and judgment.

When I sank into my chair, dressed, but still pissed, Cam settled onto the arm of the couch. "I made Anne promise to let you out of this if you were bound to one of the syndicates." Because, having lived in the city almost as long as I had—I was pretty sure he'd followed me there—he understood how dangerous and complicated her favor could make things for anyone sworn to serve on one side of the black-market divide.

It was very...compassionate of him, and it took real effort for me to deny the sudden rush of my own pulse. Because compassion was the last thing I needed from Cam Caballero. "I don't want your pity, or sympathy, or whatever this is."

"Fortunately, it looks like you don't need it," he said, with another glance at my now covered arm. "So let's move on."

Irritated that he seemed to be taking control of things, I turned back to Anne. "I'll find your husband's killer, and I'll take you to him. But you can kill him yourself," I said, careful not to actually refuse to do the second part of her request.

Anne paled, and Cam stood, scowling at me across my own desk. "No, Olivia."

"What, she's brave enough to come in here demanding vigilante justice, but not brave enough to do the job herself?"

Anne glanced back and forth between us, her purse trembling in her grip, but Cam answered before she could even open her mouth. "She's never even held a gun. Even if she had any chance of actually pulling this off, can you really send her back to her half-orphaned daughter with blood on her hands?"

His point was subtle, but it still stung. Anne wasn't like me. We'd started on the same path, sure. Parents, school, friends, college. Then Anne had continued down that path toward a respectable career, civil responsibility and family, while I had jumped the track entirely and derailed my own life with violence, under-the-carpet jobs and solitude.

If I made Anne take the shot herself, I'd be dragging her from her mostly tidy suburban life into the gritty reality of my own existence. Most people can't commit murder then go on living their lives, even if that murder was actually justice. And I had no doubt Anne was one of those people.

But I was not. And Cam obviously knew that.

"Fine. I'll do it." I sighed, finally fully resigned to her request, and the last of the resistance pain faded. "You have a name or a sample of his blood?"

"Well, he didn't leave a business card," she snapped, her anger currently winning the battle against grief. "But I can get you several blood samples from the house." She sniffled, then visibly swallowed tears. "They found Shen holding a bloody knife, so I'm hoping at least one of the blood samples will belong to his killer."

But that made no sense. Why would a Skilled killer—especially a professional—leave his own blood at the scene? Maybe he was interrupted?

"The police left a huge mess, and obviously I haven't had time to have it cleaned yet," she continued.

Obviously? "Annika, when did he die?"

"Tonight." She frowned and glanced out the window, where the first rays of daylight had changed inky black to deep, dark blue. "Last night, I guess."

"Last night?"

"Around eight o'clock"

"Your husband's been dead for less than ten hours?" I rubbed my forehead, then let one hand trail though my hair. "Don't you think you might be reacting before you've had a chance to really think about this?"

"No." For the first time since she'd walked into my office, Anne looked at me as if she didn't even know me. As if I was just some stranger she'd hired from an ad in the phone book. "And I would rather have this whole thing over with before I go pick up Hadley. I don't want to have to think about this while I'm trying to decide how best to explain what happened to her father without scarring her for life."

"Okay." I didn't know what else to say—I wasn't sure rationality would have had much attraction for me, either, in her position. I opened my mouth to name my one condition, but she beat me to the proverbial punch.

"Liv, there's one more thing…" Anne hesitated, and I knew I wasn't going to like whatever else she had to say. "I want you to work with Cam."

I sucked in a long, slow breath, hoping she would deliver the punch line to the world's worst joke before I had to actually say something. But she only watched me, waiting. "No," I said finally. "No way." I turned to Cam for support, but could find no resistance to the idea in his expression. Instead, I found…satisfaction. "This was your idea, wasn't it?" I demanded

He crossed both arms over a still-broad chest. "Does

it matter? Is it going to kill you to work with me on one job? For Anne?"

Yes, it just might kill me. Or him. But there had never been a less appropriate time to explain why I'd left him. Why working with him could be more dangerous than hunting and killing a murderer on my own. And it didn't help that while my brain protested on the basis of logic, the rest of me *ached* for this excuse to be near him again, if only in a professional capacity.

But that was a bad idea. The key to resisting Cam Caballero lay in avoiding temptation—a concept he seemed to personify for me more with every glance I avoided, every memory I buried.

"No." I turned back to Anne, wearing my business face. The one that got me the rates and bonuses I demanded. The one that usually kept creeps off me when I followed criminals down dark alleys and through abandoned buildings. "No. That's a deal-breaker."

"There are no deal-breakers when you're bound," Cam pointed out calmly, and suddenly I wished I'd hit him when I had the chance. "You'll do it, or you'll die trying to resist the compulsion."

"I haven't actually asked you yet," Anne reminded me, echoing the infuriating calm that Cam exuded like radiation—a slow, vicious poison. "But I will if I have to. Your choice."

"So, I either work with him because you're asking me to, or I work with him because you're threatening to ask me to. What kind of choice is that?" I demanded.

"It's better than the choices I'm facing right now. The rest of my day includes picking out a casket and a black suit."

Another low blow. "Why Cam?" I asked, hoping to

talk her out of it before she caught on and actually compelled me.

"Because I'm short on cash but rich on resources, Liv." Meaning the two of us, of course. "But if you're willing to subsidize this project financially and you know someone better than Cam, then by all means..." She extended one arm toward the window and the city just now waking up. "So...do you know anyone better than Cam?"

Damn. "Other than me? No."

Cam laughed out loud. "Still arrogant..."

"Confident," I corrected. "And willing to back that confidence up with results."

"Good." He nodded, in what may have been the first look of respect I'd seen from him in more than six years. "Let's go."

"Um..." I hedged. "I have something to take care of first, and we'll need those blood samples before I can get started." I glanced at Anne with both brows raised, and she nodded, already standing. "So, I'll meet you here at noon?"

"Liv, I really want to get this over with," she repeated.

"I know, but I have a previous commitment." I hesitated, dreading the next part. "Oh, and...um...I'm going to need a retainer."

"What?"

"You're going to *charge* her?" Cam demanded, and that respect I'd seen was long gone. "She's your friend."

I bristled, even though I'd expected—and understood—his reaction. "A friend who's compelling me to work for her." *And* with *you.* I hated what they probably thought of me now, but I had no choice—a state of events I was starting to truly resent. "You need my help? Fine. But I need a retainer. It doesn't have to be much. Five or ten bucks. Just…something to make it official."

Anne looked as if I'd just danced on her dead husband's grave, but she dug in her purse without a word. Something snapped open, and she handed me a five-dollar bill. "I don't carry much cash, but I can get you more, later," she offered, in spite of the hurt clear on her face.

"Don't worry about it. This is plenty." I paper-clipped the bill to a blank invoice and stuffed it into my desk drawer. Never in my life had I been more relieved to lose sight of a payment.

As they left my office, Cam glanced at me with a look of confusion and disappointment so strong it burned deep in my chest. But all I could do was stare back and hope he wouldn't decide to put into words what his gaze was accusing me of.

I hated how he saw me now, and I hated knowing that his opinion of me would only worsen, if I kept my secrets. But my secrets kept him safe, and that was more important than what he thought of the life I'd chosen.

His safety was more important than anything to me. Even if he would never know enough to understand that.

Three

"Well, did that go how you expected?" Anne asked, as Olivia closed and locked her office door behind us.

"Nope." I sighed and dug my keys from my pocket. "I figured it'd be worse. Do you believe her? About the Cavazos syndicate?"

"Yeah." Anne dug her keys from her purse with still-trembling hands. "She's hiding something, but that's not it. She's not a syndicate member."

I shrugged, trying not to show how relieved I really was. "Yeah, I'm guessing that if he owned a piece of Olivia Warren, he'd want everyone to know it." And she'd do everything she could to hide it.

The Liv I'd known and loved was beautiful and passionate, with a backbone of steel and a fiery temper. This new Olivia was everything my Liv had been and more. More steel. More fire. She couldn't truly bend to someone else's will—Anne had *convinced*, as much as she'd compelled—and those who wouldn't bend could only break.

It would kill me to see Liv broken, even after what she'd done.

"You sure you wanna do this?" Anne asked, as I held

the stairwell door open for her. "It sounds like she's pretty good at what she does."

"So am I. This'll be easier and faster with us working together."

But as much as I wanted to help Anne—to know without a doubt, for once, that I'd be taking a murderer off the streets—that wasn't my primary motivation.

Olivia was the goal.

Sometimes I thought about that night and the months afterward, and I hated her. Then I hated myself, for still wanting her. She was pissed at me for making her show her arm—for making her do *anything*—but my relief at the sight of her smooth, bare arm was like nothing I'd ever felt. Part joy, part memory and part aching possibility. I couldn't stand the thought of someone else's hands on her, much less some asshole's mark of ownership.

But she wouldn't talk to me voluntarily, and that left me no choice but to corner her, which Anne had unwittingly helped me do. Now Olivia couldn't just hang up on me or close the door in my face. Now she'd have to listen to me. She'd have to talk. She'd have to tell me to my face why she'd ruined my life and stolen my future....

"What happened between you two?" Anne asked, clicking a button on her key chain to unlock her car doors. She slid into the driver's seat and I settled in next to her.

"I don't know. But I'm damn well going to find out."

New Year's Eve
Six years ago

"Remind me what we're doing here again." I *wrapped my arms around Olivia's waist, watching the*

*party over her shoulder. She smelled like vanilla, and
I wanted a taste.*

"It's New Year's Eve. Stop being so antisocial."

*"Oh, I want to socialize—on a very selective basis.
I want to be very, very social with you." I ducked into
the warm space between her neck and her hair and
dropped a kiss beneath her ear, where the scent of vanilla was strongest. She shivered and twisted to face
me, winding her arms around my neck.*

"You just don't like my friends."

*It wasn't that I didn't like them—I didn't know most
of them. "In the three years since I met you, you've
hardly even mentioned them, and never once introduced me to anyone but Anne. Why would you want to
spend New Year's Eve with people you haven't seen in
years, instead of with me?"*

*"I am with you." She kissed me to punctuate her
point. "But they're my best friends."*

"From high school. That was years ago."

"Some bonds last forever, Cam."

I was kind of hoping she'd say that.

*"Thanks for coming." She turned to pick up her
drink from the corner of an end table. "Even if you do
look like you'd rather be skinned alive."*

*"Not skinned..." I muttered, as she returned a greet-
ing from some tall, fair-haired guy I didn't recognize.
"But maybe shot." The last-minute party invitation had
derailed my plans for the evening, but I had a backup
plan—an empty room, a quiet moment and the small
but clear diamond in my pocket. I kept touching it, to
make sure it was still there, and every time I thought
about it, I got a little queasy and a little high on adrenaline.*

I glanced at my watch, and that adrenaline surged again. Half an hour to go...

She would say yes. I wasn't worried about that. I'd planned and I'd waited, to make sure everything was right. We'd both finished college. Her parents liked me. She was still waiting tables and I was still selling tools, but I had a big interview scheduled, and her prospects were endless. The real jobs would come, and until then, we'd call our tiny apartment cozy and joke that we could make our own warmth when the car's heater gave out again.

But all that was icing. She'd say yes because she wanted me as badly as I wanted her. I could see that every time she looked at me. I could taste it in every hungry kiss and feel it in every fevered touch. This was right. We were right.

"That's Kori's brother, Kristopher," she said, as the blond guy saluted us with an open beer. "This is his house."

Had he looked at her a little too long? Smiled a little too much? My arms tightened around her before I realized what I was doing. "Were you two a couple?"

"Kris?" Liv laughed and twisted to whisper into my ear. "You jealous?" *She bit lightly on my earlobe.*

"Mmm... Should I be?"

"Nah. When I was fifteen, we made out in his basement once, for, like, two minutes. Then Kori found us and threatened to kick the crap out of us both if she ever saw that again."

"Which one's Kori?" *I asked, looking over her shoulder again when she turned and pressed her back against my chest.*

"The one in the corner."

I followed Liv's gaze to an athletic woman with white-blond hair, pouring from a bottle of vodka as if she'd started waaay before her last birthday. "I like her already."

Liv laughed. "Yeah, that'll last until the first time you piss her off. Noelle, though—you'd like Elle."

"The brunette? She seems like fun." She sat surrounded by a crowd, cracking them up with some animated story I couldn't hear.

"She is. Elle's supersmart, but she skipped college in favor of travel. I was always kind of jealous of that." Liv sighed. "She always said she wanted to live life instead of learning about it."

"But if you'd skipped college, we never would have met," I pointed out. "Then we'd both be miserable for the rest of our lives, with no idea why."

Liv laughed. "Another tragedy averted by the lure of a state-school education."

"What's up with Anne tonight?" I asked, as the redhead—the only one of Liv's friends I'd spent any time with—staggered past us with a full plastic cup.

"Another breakup. It must suck to know when people are lying."

I shrugged. "I guess. But it'd be convenient to know when they aren't, right?"

"After hearing Anne cry, I'm starting to think that doesn't happen much anymore." Her frown deepened. "And I kind of want to break some asshole's face."

I held her tighter, just because I could. Because she was fierce, and beautiful, and mine.

"After the countdown, let's go outside. Kris has a telescope, and there are no clouds tonight..."

"It's freezing out there."

Liv smiled. "I'll keep you warm."

"I'll let you." Outside was fine with me. The party was too crowded for my taste anyway.

I glanced at my watch again. Eleven forty-eight. My pulse rushed so fast I spent the next few seconds mentally tallying my drinks. But it wasn't the alcohol, and it wasn't the party. It wasn't the wintertime freeze or even the way Olivia felt in my arms, as if nothing could go wrong as long as I was holding her. It was the look in her eyes, as if there was no one in the room but me.

And in twelve minutes, that would be true. In twelve minutes, our lives would change for the better. Forever.

"Hey, looks like you're out." I looked pointedly at her plastic cup.

"No, I'm—" she began, glancing down into the dark liquid.

I snatched the cup from her and drained it in one swallow, barely tasting the whiskey mixed with her soda. "Now you are."

She shoved me, but couldn't quite pull off a frown. "You owe me a refill."

I grinned. "Be right back."

I headed toward the makeshift bar until I was sure she'd lost sight of me, then veered toward the front door, dropping her empty cup in the trash on the way. Outside, the wind cut through my sweater like needles and my feet slid on muddy slush.

Three cars down from the crowded driveway, I unlocked my trunk and carefully unwrapped the spare blanket to reveal a bottle of champagne—the best I could afford—and two tall glass flutes.

It had to be perfect. This would be the beginning of the rest of our lives, and I wanted to get it right. We would count down toward midnight together, then I'd show her the ring when the party crowd shouted the number three. I would ask her to marry me at the stroke of midnight, and then every year after, no matter what time zone we were in, we would celebrate the New Year at that exact moment. Because we wouldn't just be celebrating the beginning of a new calendar year—we'd be celebrating the beginning of our lives together.

The ring and the wedding ceremony were formalities, to make everyone else happy. The promise was for us. Our word. Our binding. Our future.

Carrying the champagne in one hand, the glasses in the other, I ducked into the house as someone else was coming out, ignoring the raised eyebrows and whispers as I made my way through the crowd, scanning the faces to make sure Olivia wasn't watching.

She wasn't. She was talking with her friend Noelle—evidently the only sober friend she had—and they both looked upset. But that wouldn't last long. No longer than the next ten minutes, by my guess...

At the end of the hall, I pushed open the door to the home office I'd scouted out earlier. The only other choice had been Kris's bedroom, which would have been weird, at best. I set the champagne on the computer desk and arranged the glasses on either side of it. Then I closed the office door and made my way back to the party.

Noelle walked off as I approached, and I couldn't interpret the look she gave Liv.

Olivia was crying.

"Hey, what's wrong?" I tried to pull her close. But she stepped out of reach, tears standing in her eyes.

"This isn't going to work, Cam."

"I know. I just set up a little private party for us, back there..." I tried to guide her through the crowd but she wouldn't move.

Liv wiped tears from her face and blinked up at me, and people were watching now. Kristopher What's-his-face stepped forward, puffed up like a bulldog, as if he thought whatever was wrong with her was my fault.

"No." Liv crossed her arms over her chest. "I mean us. This isn't going to work. I don't...I don't want this anymore, Cam. I'm sorry."

I couldn't process what she'd said. It just didn't make sense. And by the time the truth sank in, Liv was halfway across the room, on her way to the front door.

"Olivia!" I started after her, but Kristopher and three of his friends stepped into my path.

"She wants to leave. Let her go."

I didn't have the coherence to form words, but my fists flew on instinct. I'd bloodied Kristopher's nose and laid one of his friends out cold before the other two managed to toss me onto the front porch. But by then, Liv was gone. Along with our car.

I sank onto the steps, colder inside than out, reeling from what she'd said, but I still hadn't truly heard. She'd dumped me. In the middle of a party full of people I'd never met. Ten minutes before I was going to ask her to marry me.

It didn't make any sense.

The front door opened behind me, and I shifted to make room for whoever wanted past.

"You okay?" Liv's friend Anne sat next to me on the top step, tucking a strand of red hair behind her ear. "I saw what happened."

"Then you know I'm not okay."

"Liv took the car?"

And everything else that had ever mattered to me. But I could only nod.

"Want a ride?"

"No, I want a drink. Lots of them."

Anne nodded, as if she could taste the truth in my words. She probably could. "There's a Hudson's half a mile from here." She stood, wobbling on her feet— she'd probably already had too much. "That's where I'm headed. You're welcome to come."

I stared up at her, and I could see the pain on her face. Whatever this asshole had done to her had hurt her. A lot. I could sympathize—there was now a gaping hole where my own heart had been minutes earlier.

"I'm driving." I pulled the keys from her hand, and she only smiled and led me to her car. I started the engine as the guy on the radio counted down the last three seconds of the year.

"It was a shitty year anyway." Anne punched the radio power button. "Maybe this one will be better."

"Not likely," I mumbled, as I pulled away from the curb. "Happy fucking New Year."

Four

"Hey, Liv," Tomas said, as I pulled open the heavy back door before he could push it open for me. You'd think he'd quit trying. "You're late."

"Yup. Passive resistance." I put my hands behind my head and spread my feet so he could pat me down, then clomped across the kitchen, my boots echoing on the marble tile.

"He doesn't like it when you're late," Tomas called out from behind me, unwilling—or maybe disallowed—to leave his post at the back door.

I turned to face him, walking backward as he rubbed the row of three interlocking blue rings tattooed on his exposed left bicep, indicating his midlevel rank in the organization and his position as syndicate muscle. "Exactly."

Tomas shook his head slowly, half amused, half worried, and I wondered how much shit he'd had to take because of my twenty-minute tardy. East of the river, the concept of not shooting messengers was unpopular at best. I felt kinda bad about that. Really.

I crossed the foyer and ignored the main staircase

in favor of the dim hallway beyond, where two of the three doors were closed. Bypassing the open guest bathroom, I stopped in front of the only door on the left and paused for a deep breath. The kind of breath you take before you step into the sewer, hoping you won't have to inhale again before you're out. But you *will* have to, and every breath you take will remind you that you're standing knee-deep in someone else's filth, and that no matter how hard you scrub afterward, you're never going to feel truly clean again.

Then I pushed the door open and walked in without knocking.

Confusion sparked in the disconnect between my eyes and my brain, before comprehension was rerouted through my ears. It was the heavy breathing that finally clued me in. There was a girl in his lap, behind his desk, nibbling—or maybe sucking—on his neck. Or maybe his ear. And the rhythmic rise and fall of her body said that kissing wasn't the extent of this little demonstration.

They knew I'd come in, but the show didn't stop—a consequence of those twenty minutes I'd made him wait—and it *wouldn't* stop until I officially acknowledged that I'd seen. But the joke was on him. I didn't care who he screwed, and the sight of him being ridden by the nanny, or the maid, or whoever it was this week wasn't going to improve my punctuality. Quite the opposite, in fact.

But since I was already there…

"Ahem." I cleared my throat loudly, one hand still on the door handle. They both froze, pretending to be surprised, and the girl lifted her head, tossing long, straight black hair over her shoulder. And that's when I saw her arm.

Oh, shit.

Beneath the usual interlocking rings, two in this case, her left bicep was tattooed with three beautifully lettered words in a golden band all the way around her arm—a sealed oath and a symbolic wedding ring she could never take off.

Fidelitas. Muneris. Oboedientia.

Fidelity. Service. Obedience.

Michaela. *Shit, shit, shit!* He wasn't fucking the staff, he was fucking his *wife*.

That was new.

Ruben Cavazos peered at me over her shoulder, dark eyes shining. He looked at least a decade younger than his age—his early fifties—yet easily a decade older than his wife. "Olivia. Join us?"

I raised one brow. "Is that an invitation or an order?"

"It is an option."

"Then this is my refusal."

He laughed, and Mrs. Cavazos scowled in profile at the room in general. He couldn't actually order me to sleep with him—or *them*—a fact I reminded him of often. But I wasn't sure if his wife knew that.

He patted her thigh, bared by the skirt hiked up to her waist and trailing between his legs. When she only leaned down for another kiss, his expression hardened, and the next slap was hard enough to make me wince.

Michaela stood, and her skirt fell to her knees, covering the fresh red splotch from his hand. She straightened the blue gauzy material as she turned to me, dark eyes blazing with a fury she probably had no idea we shared. "You're late," she spat, by way of greeting, excuse, explanation and a general "fuck you."

"Mea culpa." I didn't hate her like she hated me. I'd tried, over and over, and failed every time. Instead, I pitied her, and that just pissed her off even more.

"Meika, bring in a glass of Scotch for Ms. Warren," Cavazos said, and his wife stopped two feet from the door, glaring at me openly.

"Ruben, it's ten in the morning," I said, then glanced at her, trying not to let pity leak into my expression. "Coffee's fine."

She stomped past me, muttering angrily in Spanish, too fast for me to pick up anything more than *bitch*. I heard that one a lot.

Cavazos laughed. "Close the door," he called after her, and she slammed it hard enough to shake the framed photos on the wall—a gallery of Ruben Cavazos, pictured with every city official and national and foreign dignitary he'd ever met.

He stood, zipped his black slacks and circled his desk to sit on the front corner.

I dropped into one of the leather chairs in front of his desk. "She hates me."

"With a rather colorful intensity." He chuckled again. "Do you blame her?"

"I blame *you*."

More laughter. His good moods were scarier than his anger, at least to those who knew him well. "Think of her hatred as a compliment."

I thought of it as a problem. Michaela followed orders, just like everyone else bound to her husband. But she also took full advantage of every moment that wasn't governed by an order and every possibility she wasn't specifically ordered not to take. If she got the chance, she'd kill me. Or die trying.

Either way, she had my respect.

"What happened with the apartment in Florida?" he asked, all traces of humor gone.

"I got hold of the superintendent two days ago. It's still rented to a woman named Tamara Parker, and she's approximately the right age, but the description doesn't fit. And he's not with her, Ruben. She lives alone."

"A landlord never really knows how many people live in a unit. And looks can be changed."

"Yes, but unless your Tamara Parker gained two hundred pounds and changed her skin color, I think we've hit another dead end. She gave you a fake name, and she's not using it anymore."

His sigh was so frustrated he almost sounded human. But I'd been fooled by that too many times to let my guard down now. "What about *him?*"

"Nothing new." I shrugged. "I get a faint tug from the middle name, but without more to go on, I can't even tell what direction he's in, much less how far away he is. He could be across the country, or across the street. We're going to have to approach this from another angle." *Damned if I know what angle, though...*

"Agreed." Ruben blinked, then met my gaze with fresh determination, and I realized he was about to change the subject. "Why were you on High Street in the middle of the night?" he asked.

He was like a damn spider—his eyes were everywhere. "I was on a job. Got time and a half."

"From Adam Rawlinson?"

"Yes."

His frown deepened, and suddenly I wanted the laughter back. "I don't like you working for him."

"I don't give a flying fuck what you like."

His hand flew, and pain exploded in the corner of my mouth. My head rocked to the side and I tasted blood. But it was an openhanded blow, intended to make a point, not to truly hurt me. "Respect, Olivia. It's what this syndicate is founded on."

Funny, I thought the syndicate was founded on *money*. And blood. And ironclad bonds of indentured servitude.

I tasted the cut on the inside of my lip. I could hit him back—I'd certainly done it before—but if I left a mark, he'd have to beat the shit out of me so everyone else could see what happens when you disrespect Ruben Cavazos. And I was done being an object lesson.

"If I didn't respect your abilities, you wouldn't be here," he continued, and the irony in that fact stung worse than my lip. Was this the reward for being good at my job? Ruben crossed his arms over his chest and stared at me like he might a crossword puzzle beyond his vocabulary. "But I don't know why you bother with these penny-ante jobs."

I rolled my eyes. "You don't know a lot of things."

"I know you haven't set foot in your apartment in more than a year."

"It's *your* apartment. Mine is the one *I* pay rent on." On the south side. In a building owned by one of the few men in the city who owed loyalty to neither Tower nor Cavazos. The south fork was as close as I could get to Switzerland.

"I understand that you threw away every cent in your bank account."

"*My* bank account is fine." If a little malnourished. "And the account you set up wasn't thrown away. The money was donated in your name." I'd withdrawn the five-figure balance in cash and given it to the Catholic-run homeless shelter around the corner from my office. "Sister Theresa thanks you for your generosity."

His grip tightened on the edge of his desk, and I held my breath. I was poking a lion with a stick, and one of these days he would bite me in half. I knew that. But I wasn't going to just roll over and play dead for him.

That was his wife's job.

Besides, as long as he still needed me, he wasn't going to kill me, and we both knew it.

"Olivia…" he warned.

"I'm not going to stop working, and you can't make me."

Cavazos stood and pulled me up by one arm. I didn't bother resisting—the sooner we got this over with, the sooner I could start Tracking Shen's killer. With Cam. But thinking about him must have shown on my face, because Ruben's grip tightened and he pushed me around the chair.

"You want to work? Fine. I have a job for you." He kept walking—kept pushing—until my back hit the darkly paneled wall. "One of my staff Binders is missing," he whispered, leaning toward my neck. "Along with the contracts he was working on. I need them back. *Rapido.*"

"Can't," I said, as his warm lips brushed the skin just below my earlobe. "I just booked a new client. She's already paid the retainer." *Thank goodness.*

"This is important. And it pays well."

It took most of my concentration to ignore how good his mouth felt, and that pissed me off. I didn't *want* him to feel good. "I don't want your money." I wedged my hands between us and shoved him back. "I don't want anything from you."

"You want me to keep my word, don't you?" he taunted, and my heart pounded painfully, though I recognized the empty threat.

"You don't have any choice about that."

He leaned into me again and slid his hands beneath my jacket, pushing it off my shoulders and halfway down my arms, until they were pinned by the material. "And you don't have any choice about this."

I'd had a choice, once. A year and a half ago. It was a tough one. No good options at all. I'd chosen the lesser of several evils, but in that moment, with his hands pushing my jacket off, his mouth on my skin, the evil I'd chosen didn't feel very lesser.

I closed my eyes and tried not to react, not to feel, and when that didn't work, I pretended. I'd gotten pretty good at that in the past eighteen months. At pretending they were someone else's hands, and lips, and eyes. Pretending it was okay to enjoy it, because I was with someone I wanted.

Those were the only moments I let myself think about Cam—about what I'd walked away from—because those were the only moments when remembering the past hurt less than living in the present.

The door flew open, and so did my eyes. Michaela stared at us, shaking in a fury so strong the coffee mug clattered against the full pot on her tray.

"Out!" Cavazos thundered, whirling to glare at her

while I stared at my jacket on the floor, mortified, and pissed off, and struggling to breathe.

She set the tray on the credenza, then backed into the hall and slammed the door. I flinched. "Why do you do this to her?" I groaned. "*You* told her to bring me a drink."

"She delayed her entrance on purpose for dramatic effect."

"Well, can you blame her?" I enjoyed throwing his own words back at him, but he didn't seem to remember saying them. He just turned back to me with that hunger in his eyes, edged with an anger that seemed to serve as fuel for the fire.

"My marriage is complicated," he whispered into my ear, his cheek brushing mine. "She punishes me, I punish her, and the cycle continues."

"What do you punish each other for?"

"For living."

"That's screwed up, Ruben." I tried to push him off again, but this time he wouldn't go. "Did it ever occur to you that she might prefer a less complicated marriage?"

"*Fidelitas. Muneris. Oboedientia.* She knew what she was signing when she married me...." he murmured, fumbling with the buttons on my shirt.

That was the part I couldn't understand. Why would someone as smart and fierce as Michaela sign a marriage oath promising fidelity to a husband who wasn't bound by an equivalent clause? Was the lure of money and status really worth a husband who screwed around right under her nose? In her own house? Right in front of her?

But then, who was I to judge? The specifics of my

involvement with her husband weren't exactly pretty, so maybe the same was true for her.

"Your people are starting to talk, Ruben."

He shook his head and reached for my waistband, and I let him push the button through the hole. Because I couldn't stop him. He hadn't hit that brick wall yet. "My people are bound by privacy clauses. All except you."

"I'm not yours."

"Yet." He stroked the unmarred skin of my left bicep with his thumb. If he had his way, my arm would look just like Tomas's.

And then there'd be no escaping him.

"Well, *someone's* talking." More than one someone. And whoever they were, they didn't have their facts straight.

He knelt to unlace my boots, then slid my jeans over my hips and let them crumple on the floor. Then he wrapped his arms around my waist, pressing one stubbly cheek against my stomach. "The best way to silence the masses is to cut out a single tongue," he whispered against my skin. Then he stood slowly and his fevered gaze met mine. "I could set something up. You can use my best knife if you let me watch."

"You're a sick bastard." I bent for my pants, but he pulled me back up by one arm.

"Stay."

"I have to work."

"Stay as long as you can…." he insisted. I tried to walk away from him, but again, he pulled me back. "That's an order."

Damn it!

"Not today," I said, and agony exploded behind my

forehead, bright white and unbearable. I staggered and he picked me up. Several steps later, he lowered me onto the leather couch, cold against my bare legs, and knelt on the floor beside me.

He stroked hair back from my forehead while the pain raged behind my eyes and my hand twitched on the center cushion. "Why do you do this to yourself? You know you can't win."

"That's exactly why I fight," I groaned through clenched teeth.

Ruben ran one hand down my leg. "Let me see it," he whispered.

My temper flared at his touch and I shook my head. The pain radiated toward the back of my skull and my left foot began to jiggle. My whole world was agony.

"Stubborn little bitch..." he whispered. "Let me see it."

That time I didn't fight. I'd made my point—he could never truly rule me, no matter what he made me do—and we both knew I wasn't going to win in the end. So I didn't resist when he slid one hand beneath my left knee and bent my leg to expose my bare thigh.

He traced the small black ring tattooed there, and my skin tingled beneath his finger, recognizing his touch. Because the ink was infused by his blood. A year and a half ago, when the needle spilled my blood, he rubbed it with his pricked thumb and sealed the binding.

"You're mine, Olivia," he whispered, leaning closer. His lips brushed the black ring, and I gasped as it burned hotter. Fortunately, he'd finally hit the brick wall—that was as far as he could go without breaking his word and suffering the same pain I'd brought on myself. But that didn't make his next words any less true.

"Until you find and deliver what you promised, I own you, head to toe. And I won't ever let you forget that…"

Five

"You're late," Cam said, as I unlocked the office door and held it open for him.

"Yup." I'd left with just enough time to get there by noon—Cavazos had to let me go to work for official clients, but didn't have to leave me any spare time—but I'd stopped by my apartment first to shower. I couldn't stand the thought of seeing Cam again with the feel of Cavazos still crawling on my skin.

Not with the memory of him calling me "clean" still echoing in my head.

I tossed my scuffed satchel onto the couch and headed straight for my desk.

"You really think that's the best way to start this working relationship?"

"Nope." I dropped into my chair and pulled open the bottom right-hand drawer, pawing through the contents as I spoke. "If you wanna work with someone else, I fully support your decision." In fact, that was the only way I could get out of a direct request from Anne.

"You're not going to get rid of me again, Liv. Unless you have a new vanishing act you'd like to try out."

My fingers brushed smooth glass beneath a tangle of holster straps and receipts I'd really meant to file, and I pulled out a half-empty bottle of cheap whiskey. The shot glass in my pencil drawer had eraser shavings in it, so I tapped it upside down on my desk until they fell out, then poured myself a shot.

I threw it back and closed my eyes, half wishing the alcohol still burned. I'd tried drinking before my weekly report to Cavazos once, and once was all it took. Turns out I don't really want to be relaxed around him after all.

"What's wrong with you?" Cam demanded, sinking onto the couch with his elbows on his knees.

"I had a rough morning, and based on your presence in my office, my afternoon isn't looking much better."

His blue eyes narrowed in anger, and I had to swallow my own regret before it surfaced as an apology—I couldn't afford to let him in again. "When did you turn into such a bitch?" he growled, and my urge to apologize dried up and blew away.

"About a year and a half ago." I poured another shot and pushed the bottle toward him.

Instead of taking it, he watched me slowly turn the shot I'd poured for myself, staring down at the contents. "Are you going to be like this the whole time?" he asked.

"Nope. Sometimes I'll be irritable and unpleasant." I downed the shot and reached for the bottle again, but he pulled it out of my reach.

Cam tilted the bottle to read the label, then set it on the desk again with a disgusted look. "I guess you really don't work for Cavazos. He pays better than this."

"What, you're too good for my whiskey?"

"Yeah, and so are you. When this is over, I'll buy you a real drink." His arched brows were a challenge, but his eyes were serious, and so was the question he hadn't really asked.

"I might let you. Because I like whiskey."

He leaned back on the couch, crossing both arms over his chest. "Is that the best I'm going to get?"

"From me? Today? Yes." I screwed the lid on the bottle and put it back in the drawer. "Where's Anne?" I asked, when the fact that I was alone with Cam became too much to think about.

"You were late and she had to pick up Hadley. She left these for you, though." He picked up a plastic grocery bag I hadn't even noticed and tossed it onto the desk. I opened it and looked in to find several clear plastic bags, each smeared with blood on the inside from their contents.

"She took these herself, didn't she?" I asked, trying not to be horrified by the thought of Anne on her hands and knees, taking samples of blood from the scene of her husband's slaughter.

"She wouldn't let me help." Cam glanced at the floor between his knees. "She seemed to think she owed it to him personally."

Damn.

I spread the bags out on my desk, looking for some kind of order, but they weren't numbered or labeled, as police evidence bags always were. There was a swatch of cloth that might once have been plaid, an uneven square of excised carpet, a patch of stained denim and a formerly white athletic sock.

"Have you tried any of them?" I asked, turning the first bag over to examine it.

Cam shook his head. "You're the blood expert." Which is what had brought me to Cavazos's attention...

I unzipped the first baggie—the plaid cloth—and reached inside with my bare hand. The blood was room temperature and still sticky. Fresh enough to be viable, and readable from a decent distance.

As the metallic scent of blood filled the room, I pulled the cloth from the bag and closed my eyes, fingering the material, focusing on the feel of the blood between my fingers, and the feel of it in my head. That mental scent. The energy signature of whoever'd spilled it.

It came from a man. Gender was easy to discern, but race and age took more experience—exposure to and study of a variety of samples. Fortunately, I'd had plenty of experience.

The blood came from a man of Asian descent. I couldn't pin down his age without a fresher sample, but I know two things for sure. The blood held no power, which meant its owner was not Skilled. And the blood held no pull—no psychic thread connecting it to the man who'd spilled it, through which I could Track him. Which meant the owner was dead.

"It's Shen's," I said, resealing the cloth in its bag.

Cam sat straighter. "How sure are you?"

"As sure as I can be, without having met him. It's either his, or another dead Asian man with no Skill." Which could easily have been one of about a billion other people—if we didn't already know Shen's killer was a Traveler.

I stood without touching anything and crossed into the bathroom to wash my hands with the bar of lye soap on the left side of the sink. It was hell on my skin, but lye destroys blood, which would keep me from confusing one sample with another.

In my chair again, I opened the second bag—the denim—and knew almost immediately that the blood in this one was also Shen's.

Another hand scrub, then I opened the third bag. The carpet. And that one was interesting. Shen's blood was there, but it wasn't alone. Two people had bled on the carpet, and the second person's blood held both power and pull. He was both Skilled and alive. But with the samples so thoroughly mixed, I couldn't tell what kind of Skill it was, nor could I get any specific direction from the pull. I didn't even know for sure that the owner was male.

I sealed up the carpet and washed my hands again, then sat down with the last sample—the sock. "The carpet, I understand. But how the hell did Anne get bloody clothes from a crime scene? Why didn't the police take them for evidence?"

Cam sighed and leaned forward with his elbows on his knees. "The house was locked up tight when Shen was found, and his keys weren't missing. The cops know the killer was a Traveler, and they know they'll never find him with only county resources." He shrugged. "It's no surprise they're not dedicating much time or effort to a case they know they can't solve."

And there were more of those every day, it seemed. Sure, some cops were Skilled, but the police department couldn't legally use resources that weren't officially recognized by the government, which meant they were crippled in the investigation of any crime obviously committed by a Skilled perp.

Victims and loved ones who could pay would come

to people like me for answers the cops couldn't give them. Some independent Trackers—like Spencer and his associates—also offered vigilante justice, of the variety Anne had requested, for a huge fee.

Those who wanted justice but couldn't afford it in monetary terms would turn to either Tower or Cavazos, who were happy to take payment in the form of an IOU—a dangerously vague contract sealed by one of their own Binders. And just like that, one by one, private citizens fell into debt to one syndicate or the other, signing away their souls—or at least their free will—for one short moment of visceral satisfaction.

What they didn't know was that half the time, the very syndicate they turned to for help was responsible for the crime they wanted avenged. I'd seen it happen. If Cavazos wanted a Traveler or a Reader who refused to sign on, he'd have the target's spouse or parent killed—never a child, thank goodness—then sit back and wait for a desperate knock on the door.

And people kept falling for it, devastated and naive in the face of engineered tragedy.

I held up the bloody sock, mentally crossing my fingers that what had happened to Anne was nothing of that sort. That this was something we could put an end to without making powerful enemies. Then I closed my eyes and inhaled.

Score.

One bleeder, with both power and pull. This blood almost certainly matched the second bleeder from the carpet, and with only one scent to concentrate on, I was able to pin down some details.

"Male, and he's a Traveler." Just as Anne had guessed. I'd found the killer. Or, at least, I'd found his blood, and since it hadn't completely dried, the pull from it was strong.

Cam sat straight again and glanced from the sock to my face. "Anything else?"

"A general direction."

He was already on his feet, keys in hand. "I'll drive." I glanced at him, my gaze narrowed in suspicion, and Cam scowled. "What, you don't trust me? Don't you think it should be the other way around? How do I know that you're not just going to ditch me again and move to another city, without even a goodbye?"

"You don't know what you're talking about." I snatched my worn satchel from the couch and filled it with supplies from the cabinet behind my desk so I wouldn't have to look at him.

"Well, then, why don't you tell me?" he demanded, and when I didn't answer, he grabbed my arm and tried to turn me around. "Why are you so angry? You're pushing people away. People who care about you. What happened to you, Liv?"

I jerked my arm from his grasp and met his gaze reluctantly. "Nothing I can't handle." *Yet.* But he didn't understand that, and I couldn't explain it. "Fine. You can drive. It'll be easier for me to concentrate on the blood that way anyway." Which was probably the reason he'd offered in the first place.

The last thing that went into my satchel was a spray bottle of ammonia, then I zipped the bag and set it on the desk. I shrugged into my good holster and pulled my jacket on over it, then checked the clip and the safety on my favorite 9mm and dropped it into the holster. I sealed the sock back into its bag and shoved it into my right jacket pocket. With my phone in the opposite pocket and my satchel over one shoulder, I shooed Cam out the door and locked it behind us.

"It's good to see you again," he said, following me down the narrow staircase at the end of the hall. "Even if you're not talking to me."

"I *am* talking to you." I pushed open the door at the bottom of the stairs and stepped into the bright parking lot, squinting against the glare of the sun. I'd rather work at night, when there were fewer of Cavazos's eyes around to see me with Cam, but Anne's blood sample wasn't getting any fresher.

"You're talking, but you're not really saying anything," Cam insisted, digging his keys from his pocket.

"You're doing enough of that for both of us."

His car—the one he'd tracked me down in the night before—was parked near the end of the front row, and as we approached, he unlocked it by remote.

"What do you want me to say?" I asked, dropping into the passenger's seat.

"It's been six years, Liv. I don't even know you anymore." When I didn't know how to respond, he sighed and started the car. "Is this what you do now? Freelance Tracking?"

I nodded, and the knot of tension inside me eased just a little. Work questions, I could handle. "I was on Adam Rawlinson's team for three years. They taught me to shoot and fight—Rawlinson himself trained me on the nine mil—and I quit last year and went into business for myself."

Cam stopped at the parking-lot exit, the car's V8 rumbling all the way into my bones. "Which way?"

I set the sock on my lap and opened the bag, then ran my fingers over the damp, sticky material and closed my eyes. "West." *Shit.* Tower's side of town. Not a promising start to the afternoon.

"What happened with Rawlinson?" Cam asked, turning left onto the street. "You didn't like the company?"

"No, it was nice." Good money, decent benefits and an upstanding boss. Rawlinson had a sterling reputation and got the bulk of the business from anyone who didn't want to get tangled up with either Tower or Cavazos. Including a lot of unofficial police "consultations."

"So why'd you quit? You obviously took a cut in pay...."

I laughed, and it almost felt good. "Is that a dig at my liquor cabinet?"

Cam smiled. "That wasn't liquor, it was swill. And that wasn't a cabinet, it was a drawer."

"The money will come, once I get my name out there." For too many years, I'd been known only as Rawlinson's top Tracker, "You know, that girl." I'd almost started answering to the unofficial title.

"So you quit over money?"

"No." I glanced at him, looking for judgment in his eyes, because there'd been none in his voice. "I wanted to be my own boss."

The irony of my lie stung. Good thing I wasn't bound to tell the truth.

I'd quit my job after Cavazos inked his mark on my thigh and ruined my whole life. I did it to keep Rawlinson and the rest of his employees safe. He would have fired me anyway if he'd found out. No syndicate-bound employees—that was both company policy and common sense. Never hire someone whose loyalty belongs to someone else. Especially someone with the power not only to kill you, but to make the world forget you ever existed. And that was only one of the reasons I had to keep my binding secret.

"Well, then, I guess you got what you wanted."

Hardly. I stared at my lap. I hadn't gotten a damn thing I'd wanted since that night six years ago.

When the road curved to the right, I looked up. The blood wanted us to go straight. "Take the next left and veer toward the market district," I said, staring out the window to avoid looking at him. Being with Cam was harder than I'd thought it would be. Some things hadn't changed—he still smelled like good coffee and cheap shampoo—and some things were totally different. Like that dark, scruffy stubble, as if he hadn't gotten a chance to shave. And maybe he hadn't. The stubble made him look older, and at first that had bothered me, because it reminded me how much had changed since we'd been together. But now that stubble was kind of growing on me.

Wonder what it feels like...

I'd actually pulled my hand from the plastic bag before I realized what I was doing, and when he glanced at my bloody fingers, I felt myself flush.

"What's wrong?" he asked. "Did you lose the pull?"

"No." I shoved my hand back into the bag and ran my fingers over the stiffening material, staring straight out the windshield. He couldn't guess at my thoughts if he couldn't see my face. "Just keep heading west." Deeper and deeper into Jake Tower's side of town...

"So...how long have you been bound?" Cam asked, when I motioned for him to take the next left.

My heart jumped so high I could practically taste

it on the back of my tongue. "I told you, Cavazos doesn't—"

"I meant Anne. How long have you and Anne been bound to the others?"

Oh. Yeah.

I tried to relax, but that was hard to do, considering I was clutching the bloody evidence from a murder scene, riding into the territory of a man who'd kill me as soon as look at me and sitting next to the man I'd thought I'd spend the rest of my life with. "Fifteen years. Since I was twelve."

Cam whistled, as if he was impressed. Or horrified. "So, the whole time we were together, you were bound to your three best friends?"

"And vice versa."

"Why didn't you tell me?"

"After high school, it didn't seem to matter. We hardly saw one another."

"Anne said it was an accident...?" he prompted, and I wondered how much else she'd told him.

"Yeah. We didn't know what we were doing. Some guy at school made Anne cry, so Kori made *him* cry. Then we went back to Kori's house to comfort Anne with junk food, and we wound up swearing lifelong loyalty and assistance instead."

"How do you *accidently* sign and seal a lifelong binding?"

"We didn't know it was a binding." I twisted to half face him, and only then realized how comfortable that felt. How easy talking to him had become—again—as if we could just pick up right where we'd left off.

But we couldn't. Ever. And forgetting that would get one of us killed.

"It was different then, you know?" I made myself stare out the window to avoid looking at him. "The revelation was still recent, and our parents hadn't told us we were Skilled. They were afraid that if we knew, we'd be in danger. Turns out ignorance is more dangerous than the truth."

"It usually is," Cam said, and suddenly my throat felt thick. He was talking about his own ignorance, about all the things I still couldn't—*wouldn't*—tell him.

"We were just being kids. Best friends standing around the kitchen, making promises we probably never would have kept, just to make Anne smile. But then Kori's little sister, Kenley, came in and overheard us, and she wanted to help. She said it wouldn't be official unless we wrote it down."

Cam's brows rose halfway up his forehead, and he looked away from the road long enough to make me nervous. "Kenley Daniels was your Binder? Sixteen years ago?"

I nodded. "If we'd known that ran in her family— turns out her mother's a Binder, too—we probably would have realized what she was doing, even if *she* didn't."

"Displaying the first instinctive manifestation of a very serious Skill?"

I couldn't resist a smile. "Good guess."

"How old was she?"

"Ten."

"Damn. It doesn't usually show up so early."

"I know." I'd met more than my share of Binders since that day fifteen years ago, and not one of them had displayed a stronger Skill or instinct than Kenley

Daniels had at ten years old. Without even knowing what she was.

"So…she what? Scribbled a promise in crayon and told you to sign it?"

I laughed again, but more out of nerves than amusement. He wasn't far off. "It was pink glitter pen, actually. And after we signed, she said it still didn't feel right. She said it wouldn't be 'real' unless we used blood."

The four of us had been losing interest by then, but Kori had perked up when she realized that meant she'd get to use her knife. And I have to admit, I was curious—perhaps the beginnings of my own talent with blood.

"Oh, shit!" Cam glanced at me again, then back at the road. "Kenley's a blood Binder? I thought she worked with signatures…."

"Actually, it turns out she's a double threat."

Blood binding was a much rarer Skill than name binding—binding a written oath with a signature—and those who could do both were rarer still. And someone with the power to do both at such a young age was almost unheard of.

"So, I'm guessing that contract is ironclad…?" Cam said, flicking on his turn signal when I pointed toward a side street ahead.

"Yeah. And what's worse is that she had plenty of Skill, but no training. It was really more an oath than a contract. Just a promise that we would help one another whenever asked. There was no expiration date, no stipulations and no exceptions. There weren't even enough words to form a decent loophole."

"Why didn't you just burn it?"

Burning it to ashes was the only surefire way to destroy a blood-sealed contract, which is why certain notorious crime lords had started sealing their employee bindings in the flesh—literally—with tattoo marks as a fail-safe in case the corresponding written contract was destroyed. Fortunately, Kenley hadn't foreseen that advancement. I wasn't even sure she was capable of flesh binding, not that any of us knew what that was fifteen years ago. Her first sealed contract could easily be destroyed—if it could be found.

"By the time we realized what we'd done—the first time Kori's grandmother had to pick her up from the police station—the oath was gone. We looked everywhere. Our parents got together and tore the Danielses' house apart, and when it wasn't there, they searched their own houses. But we never found so much as a scrap of powder-blue paper or pink glitter pen."

"You think someone took it?" he asked, and I could only shrug.

"It didn't walk off on its own. But I have no clue who could have taken it. Or why. Until Kori got arrested, only the four of us knew about it—Kori, Anne, Noelle and me. And Kenley, of course. And we all wanted it destroyed." *Badly,* by the time we got to high school. "We explored different theories over the years. A parent trying to teach us a lesson. Kori's brother, Kristopher, being a pain in the ass. Their dog burying a new prize. But no one ever admitted anything, and Anne didn't know she was a Reader yet, so it never occurred to her to look for a lie. And every time we tested it, the binding was still intact, which meant that the oath was still whole, wherever it was. And obviously it still is now,"

I said, gesturing to the entire car to indicate our current vigilante mission.

"That sounds like a total pain in the ass."

"Worse. We started hating each other. Even the most offhand, ridiculous request became a geas—a compulsion that had to be obeyed, to the exclusion of everything else. We wound up cheating, and lying, and stealing, and starting fights for one another. We got hurt, and arrested, and kicked out of school. And the cycle was self-perpetuating. Anne would get pissed at Kori for making her help cheat on a test, so she'd ask Kori to go to the drugstore and shoplift only hemorrhoid cream and Vagisil, knowing that when she got caught, she'd be humiliated."

Cam laughed. "When I met them, the four of you seemed to get along pretty well."

"Part of that was the fact that we rarely saw one another after high school. The rest of it was the second oath."

"There was a second oath?"

"Yeah. My senior year, Kenley got tired of all the bitching and backstabbing. And I think she felt guilty, because she was the reason for the trouble in the first place. So she conned us all into the same room long enough to show us a new oath she'd penned, which basically made us swear never to ask one another for anything."

"So, did you sign?"

"Hell yes! We fought over who got to sign first. After that, everything was fine. We weren't best friends anymore, but we didn't hate each other, either. We just kind of…left each other alone. That New Year's Eve party six years ago? That was the first time we'd spent more than an hour together since high-school graduation. It was also the last time I saw any of them. Until this morning."

"Because Anne burned the second contract?"

I scowled. "You were eavesdropping?"

He shrugged. "I could only hear bits of it from the hallway."

After a moment of hesitation and concentration, I motioned him through the next red light, but I could tell his thoughts were no longer on the drive. "So, why did you guys let Anne keep the second oath?"

"We didn't," I said. "It didn't seem fair for any one of us to have it, so we let Kenley keep it. She was the only neutral party, and she *was* the one who sealed it."

"Well, Anne must have gotten ahold of it somehow, if she burned it."

My hand clenched around the bloody material. I hadn't thought of that. "And she must have gotten to it quickly...." I mumbled, mentally counting the few hours between Shen's murder and the moment Anne showed up in my office. And she'd found Cam even before that. "Maybe she's still in contact with Kenley...." I began, then realized that we'd rolled to a halt three cars back from a four-way stop.

"Which way?" Cam asked, and I forced my mind back to the energy signature I was tracking.

I closed my eyes and placed my hand flat over the tacky sock, inside the bag. The pull was still there, but fading as the blood dried. "Straight," I murmured. "But slightly to the right..."

"There's no *slightly* to it," he said, and I opened my eyes as we rolled through the intersection to find the street sandwiched by tightly packed rows of buildings—mostly neighborhood businesses and apartments.

"Slow down." I closed my eyes again and let the blood guide me. The pull was getting stronger, but not definitively so. "Stop," I said at last, when the blood began to pull me from behind. "We passed it."

He backed into the first available parking spot on the curb and turned off the engine. "Up there, maybe?" he said, twisting to peer through the rear windshield at the building on the right. "In one of the apartments?"

"That's my guess." I pulled a packet of wet wipes from my satchel and started cleaning blood from my hand. Again. The wipes wouldn't work as well as lye, but they were portable and didn't make me want to peel my own skin off to stop the burning.

Cam glanced at the slight gun bulge beneath my jacket as I stuffed the used wipe into a plastic sandwich bag in the side pocket of my satchel. "Are you really going to do this?"

"I don't have any choice. Or did you forget what *compelled* means?"

"I haven't forgotten anything, Liv," he said, and I realized we were having two different conversations. "Do you have a silencer for that thing?"

"No, I don't have a silencer. Because I'm not an assassin." I dug through my satchel for a thin box of surgical gloves and plucked two from the slit on top, then shoved them into my right jacket pocket.

"Well, that's too bad, because this is an assassination."

"No, this is an execution."

"The difference would be…?"

"Assassination is murder. Execution is justice." I

pulled a small, folding blade from my back pocket and flicked it open, then folded it closed again, satisfied that it was still in working order.

"So now you're an executioner?"

"No, I…" Too late, I caught the hint of a grin and realized he was teasing me. I scowled. "Are we going to sit here and argue until he comes out and begs to be shot, or you wanna go in?"

"Honestly, arguing sounds like more fun. And on that note…you sure have a lot of weapons for not-an-assassin."

I shoved the knife back into my pocket and met his gaze, the butt of my gun digging into my side. "Do I look dead to you?"

His grin grew. "You look all pissed off. It's kind of hot."

It took serious effort for me to stay focused when I realized he wasn't joking. "I don't know about your line of work—" I wasn't even sure what he did for a living, come to think of it "—but most of the people I track don't want to be found, and people who don't want to be found are usually armed. And dangerous. And on hair triggers. So yeah, I'm armed. Because I don't want to die."

"If you're the muscle, that must make me the brains of the operation."

I rolled my eyes. "You're the chauffeur. Here's the plan—find him, kill him."

Cam laughed out loud, and my teeth ground together. "That's not a plan. It's not even a complete sentence."

"You got something better?"

"How 'bout this?" He pulled back the right side of his jacket and showed me his gun. It was bigger than

mine. And it was fitted with a long, barrel-shaped silencer in what had to be a custom-made holster.

"Nice," I admitted, and his grin was back. But I
couldn't help wondering why the hell he even owned
a silencer.

"I had a feeling you'd appreciate the reminder that I
come well equipped."

"I'd appreciate it more if I thought you knew how to
use that," I said, without thinking. His eyes lit up, and
that's when I realized I was flirting. We'd fallen back
into that old familiar pattern as if the past six years had
never happened.

"What, you don't remember?" he teased, while I silently cursed myself.

"This isn't going to happen, Cam."

His good humor faltered, then resurged. "The execution?" He was as stubborn as ever.

"No, *that's* going to happen. Then you go back to
your life and I go back to mine."

His grin vanished. "What life?" Cam demanded
softly, his gaze holding mine like the earth holds the
moon captive. "What could you possibly have now
that's better than what you left behind?"

Nothing. I had nothing now but the knowledge that
I'd made a tough choice for us both, because I couldn't
live with the alternative. And neither could he. But
that knowledge did little to ease the hollow ache in my
chest or warm the empty half of my bed, and admitting
regret now would only make the whole thing worse.
So I closed my mouth, opened the car door and got out
without a word.

Turning away from him this time hurt no less than
it had the time before.

Six

Liv opened the passenger's side door and stepped onto the sidewalk without acknowledging my question. She might think she could sweep me under the carpet again when this job was over, but she was wrong. I'd given her time. I'd given her space. I'd given her every opportunity in the world to find someone else and start a family, or at least start a life that included more than just the job she obviously lived and breathed. The closest she'd ever come was moving in with some asshole who cheated on her—*I'd* tracked him, even if *she* hadn't thought to—then stolen her car.

I could see the truth as well as any Reader could have. If she really didn't want me, she would have gotten serious with someone else. She wouldn't grimace every time she told me to go away, as if the words tasted bad. She wouldn't still look at me like she used to, when she thought I wasn't watching.

Olivia still wanted me, just as much as I wanted her, but something was holding her back. Something she couldn't move past. I could take care of that obstacle for her—I'd tear down *anything* standing between us—but

I couldn't destroy what I couldn't even see. She'd have to show me the problem. I'd have to *make* her show me the problem.

Bolstered by fresh determination, I fell in at her side, and we headed for the entrance without even a glance around the neighborhood.

Rule #1 in tracking: don't look like a Tracker.

It's always best to go unnoticed. Even near my own neighborhood.

Especially with Liv at my side.

Even if she wasn't marked or bound, word on the street was hard to overcome, and most people thought she was sleeping with Cavazos at the very least, which meant that Tower's men would see her either as a trespasser to be booted from this side of town, or a prize to be offered up to the boss.

No easy outs, either way.

I jogged up the front steps and she followed me into a tiny, dusty entryway leading into a long hallway lined with doors and apartment numbers. "Well?" I said, relieved to have her off the street and out of sight.

Liv reached into her pocket to feel the bloody sock again. Then she nodded toward the staircase, and I followed her up the first flight of stairs. On the second-floor landing, she reassessed, then started down the hallway, eyes half-closed, obviously letting the energy signature pull her.

She had told me once that the blood pull was really more of a feeling than a scent, and though I had little blood-tracking skill myself, I knew she was right. But as she worked her way down the hall, she sniffed the air softly, like a real bloodhound, though she didn't even seem to know she was doing it.

About halfway down, she stopped and turned to me. "It starts to fade here…." She stepped back toward me, then stopped, closed her eyes and nodded, as if she was sure of something. "And it's strongest here." She stood directly between two apartment doors. "Is that 208 or 210?"

I glanced at the end of the hall, toward the first door, then followed the pattern to where we stood. "Two-ten," I whispered, and reached for the doorknob. But then her hand landed on my arm, warm against my bare skin.

"Let me," she insisted. "Men are still less threatened by women than by other men. I'll have a better shot of getting in there without causing a scene."

I nodded and stepped back from the door, not because I agreed with her—I didn't—but because I could still feel her hand on my arm, and the surprise of being touched by her again had yet to fade.

She may not have looked scary, with her big blue eyes and jacket that hid her gun but not her curves, but Liv could track better than any man I'd ever met, and if word on the street could be believed, Rawlinson had turned her into a damn fine fighter. Over the past six years, living and working in this city had turned the funny, charismatic girl I'd loved with every cell of my body into a jaded, hard-edged loner I still couldn't look at without catching my breath.

I'd never felt more alive, watching Liv prepare to charm—or maybe force—her way into some stranger's apartment. Olivia was a wire wound too tight, always about to snap, but she lived on excitement and thrived under pressure. Being with her was like holding a bomb in both hands, watching the numbers tick back toward zero. I knew she'd eventually explode, and this time it might kill me.

But it was hard to care about the potential for collateral damage when just being near her again felt so good. So I pressed my back against the wall to the right of the door, gun drawn and ready in a two-handed grip. Liv's gun was still concealed, but I had no doubt she could get to it in a hurry. She knocked on the door, but no one answered. There was no sound from inside.

Liv knocked again, but again got no response. "The pull's still strong, which means he's home but not answering. Or, he's lying unconscious and near death from whatever wound Shen managed to inflict before dying." She glanced up at me, brows raised in question. "Plan B?" she whispered, and I nodded.

B always stood for breaking and entering.

She stepped aside and pulled her gun while I holstered mine. I took the doorknob in both hands and twisted sharply. The lock broke with a metallic snap that seemed to echo much louder than it should have. But the door didn't swing open.

"Dead bolt," I said.

"Is that a problem?"

I gave her a disappointed look. "It's like you don't know me at *all*.... Step back."

She stepped away from the door hesitantly as I dropped into a deep squat to stretch—which is when she figured out what I had in mind. "Wait, don't...!" she whispered, but I was already in motion. My foot slammed into the door just beneath the knob and wood creaked loudly. Liv cringed over the noise, then shrugged. "May as well finish it now...."

I kicked again, and the interior frame gave way with

the loud splinter of wood. Maybe not the most subtle entry, but definitely the fastest.

The door swung open, and I lurched to the right, watching her from across the doorway with my gun already drawn. For one long second, neither of us moved.

I couldn't break Cam's gaze, and my own breathing was heavy in anticipation. We shared that single, taut moment of expectancy until we realized that if the target was in there, he wasn't coming out.

Finally, I nodded at the ruined door, reluctantly impressed by the damage, and lifted both brows in question. Cam gestured for me to go first. Which I liked.

I rounded the door frame and into the living room, gun aimed at the floor, scanning the room with my gaze and the entire apartment with whatever sense it is that feels the pull of blood. That pull was still there, but not as strong as it should have been. Not as strong as it would have been if the target were in the apartment, even if he wasn't bleeding.

Cam came in behind me and pushed the front door closed, but it swung open a couple of inches again, because of the busted lock. I heard him checking behind doors and under furniture while I opened all the kitchen cabinets big enough for a man to crawl into.

"I think it's clear," I said, flicking the safety on my 9mm. But I kept the gun out, just in case. "Damned if I understand it, though."

"Maybe he just left." Cam kicked open the bedroom door and glanced beneath the bed, then in the closet, checking both potential hiding places gun first. "He is a Traveler, right? So he probably just stepped into a shadow and out of the apartment the minute he heard us."

Which was why tracking a Traveler could be a real bitch. The only way to catch one was to trap him in a room with no shadows big enough for him to walk through. And that's a lot harder than it sounds. Kori was a shadow-walker, and her grandmother had given up on grounding her when she was fourteen.

But...

"That shouldn't matter," I said. "So long as he's alive, his energy signature should lead to *him,* not to his apartment." Which Cam would know if he were a bloodhound—name-tracking works a little differently, and Cam was no better with blood than I was with names. "But the pull still feels like it's coming from... here."

"Here...where?"

I closed my eyes and clutched the sock in my pocket again, through the plastic bag. The energy signature was fainter now, as the sock continued to dry, but I could still feel it. Eyes still closed, I turned until I faced the direction of the pull, and when I opened my eyes, I found myself staring at the open bathroom door.

"There."

Cam crossed the room in a heartbeat. He pushed the door open all the way with one hand, then scanned the interior with his gun aimed and ready. He'd had training. The same kind of training I'd had. And he was good.

For a moment, I wondered if he was a cop. Was that why Anne had wanted us to work together? Was Cam actually using his criminal-justice degree, while I'd let my B.A. in philosophy rot in a drawer?

And if not, how *was* he making a living?

A second later, he took two steps into the bathroom and pulled the shower curtain back in one swift movement. It rattled on the rod, but revealed an empty — if filthy—tub. There was barely space for two people in the room, but I squeezed in with him anyway, already half suspecting what I'd find.

Sure enough…

I dropped the toilet lid—the bowl was no cleaner than the tub—and sat, then pulled the wastebasket in front of me, between my boots. Inside was a pile of blood-soaked rags, tissues and bandages.

"Shen must have got him good." Cam sank onto the edge of the tub.

"I guess. But why would he leave them here?" Every Skilled person I knew carried a bottle of ammonia—or at least bleach—in their car, and most of us had an entire collection of chemicals that would destroy blood in our homes.

Leaving blood around like this was beyond careless. If found by people with the right Skills—or people who had access to people with the right Skills—fresh blood samples could be used to track the donor, or bind him to…well, anything. At least for a while. Blood not freely given wouldn't bind someone forever, unless the Binder was extraordinarily gifted. But it would work long enough to compel the donor to turn himself in, or keep him from going to the authorities, or whatever the Binder wrote into a contract and sealed with the stolen blood.

This wasn't the kind of mistake anyone with Skill would make. In fact, fewer and fewer of the unSkilled were leaving viable blood samples undestroyed, as the truth of our existence persevered despite the lack of official recognition from the government.

Any government.

"Something's wrong here, Cam." I glanced around the bathroom for something to prod the trash with, and didn't find so much as a plunger. So I donned the latex gloves from my pocket and used them to lift bandage after bloody bandage from the trash can. They were all the same.

"Fresh…" I said, laying the first piece over the edge of the tub next to Cam. He stood to make more room. "He's only been gone an hour. Maybe less. And you're right, he's hurt pretty badly." Based on the amount of blood alone. "But why would I be drawn here, instead of drawn to him? Whoever he is?"

"Maybe he's dead," Cam suggested, leaning over the sink to pull open the medicine cabinet.

"If he were dead, his blood would have no pull. He's still alive, somewhere, and leaving his own viable blood around like he *wants* to be found, whoever he is."

"Eric Hunter." Cam held a prescription pill bottle down for me to see. "Three of them, and they're all prescribed to the same man, at this address. Antibiotics, antidepressants and anti-inflammatories." He set the bottle back on its shelf and closed the cabinet. "Mr. Hunter, you were obviously depressed, inflamed and… biotic. But why did you kill Shen Liang?"

"My guess is that he was hired. But who would hire someone to kill a work-at-home husband and father?"

"Maybe something to do with his work?" Cam suggested. "Did Anne mention what kind of software he designs?"

I shook my head. We were no closer to the why,

but the how was obvious. The killer was a Traveler—a shadow-walker, capable of stepping into one shadow and out of another one, anywhere in the world, if he were powerful enough. Certainly anywhere in the city, based on the strength of the blood sample Anne had brought.

"And why did he leave his blood...?" I thought aloud, staring at the mess he'd left. And that's when I realized why the whole thing felt so weird, beyond the presence of so much viable blood. "It's fading."

"What's fading?" Cam asked. "Is it drying already?"

"Not the blood, the power. The Skill." I stood, stunned by what shouldn't have been possible, but was quite obviously happening anyway. "Feel this." I thrust a blood-soaked dish rag at Cam and he took it reluctantly in his bare hands. "Do you feel it?"

He shook his head slowly, and his blue eyes widened. "I'm not as good with blood as you are, but I should be able to feel *something*. If he's Skilled."

"Exactly." I pulled off my gloves and laid them over the edge of the tub. "I can still feel it, but it's nowhere near as strong as it was. As it *still* is, in this sample." I pulled the bagged sock from my pocket. "But it's definitely the same blood. Which means that somehow, his Skill was stronger when he bled on the sock than when he bandaged the wound here at home, about seventeen hours later."

Cam ran water over his hand to rinse away the blood. "How is that possible? How can Skill fade?"

"I don't know." And I still couldn't figure out why I'd be pulled to a trash can full of bloody rags, rather than to the man who'd left with even more of it in his veins.

The squeal of hinges froze us both, and Cam laid one finger over his lips, warning me to be quiet. As if I didn't already know.

"Who's in there?" a male voice called, and I shoved the sealed sock back into my pocket with one hand while I drew my gun with the other.

Hunter? I mouthed to Cam, but he shook his head, and I read recognition on his face.

"Nick, is that you?"

"Who's that?" the voice from the living room called.

"Cam Cabellero. We're coming out."

"Who's we?"

Cam motioned for me to put my gun up and follow him out of the bathroom. I holstered my pistol, but left my jacket open so I could get to it in a hurry.

Nick turned out to be in his early twenties and un-Skilled, with a thick build, dark hair and a black Glock 9mm, which he was shoving barrel first into the waist of his pants when I stepped into the living room. His eyes widened when he saw me, but in surprise, not recognition. So far, so good.

"Lady next door said someone kicked in the door to 210. I'm guessing that was you and…" He glanced at me expectantly, waiting for me to fill in my name.

"Liv Warren," Cam said reluctantly, when I remained silent. I could have punched him. Why the hell had he given out my real name?

"Liv…?" Sudden comprehension wrinkled Nick's forehead and when he crossed his arms over his chest, one of the short sleeves of his dark T-shirt rode up, revealing a single thick, rust-colored link of chain tattooed on his upper arm. He was one of Tower's grunts—no surprise, considering the neighborhood.

Like most of Tower's men—and more than a few
women—he'd probably grown up on the west side and
discovered after high school that his employment options consisted mostly of greasy fast-food service and
manual labor.

Like the typical syndicate employee, Nick had likely
signed on for a five-year term of service with the potential for renewal and advancement if he proved useful.
But even if he opted not to re-up at the end of his service commitment, he would never be able to work for
another syndicate or work against Tower, thanks to the
lifelong loyalty and noncompetition clauses he would
have been required to sign and seal with his own blood.

"Aren't you on the wrong side of town?" Nick de
manded, staring down at me as if I was worth less than
the crud stuck to the bottom of his shoe.

Nick's single mark said he was in his first term
of service; the cocky grin said he'd been in just long
enough to think he was badass. I was itching to prove
him wrong—to take out some of my unspent anger at
Cavazos on this little prick's face—but I knew better
than to start shit with one of Tower's men in his own
neighborhood. I'd be outnumbered before I could throw
my second punch.

"She's an independent," Cam said, meaning that
I wasn't bound to any syndicate. Which was mostly
true—I worked for Cavazos alone and owed no loyalty
or obedience to any of his syndicate members. "She's
working freelance and I'm helping her out."

"She got a badge?"

"I'm not a cop." Why wasn't he browbeating Cam?
And how did Cam happen to know one of Tower's
grunts?

"Then I gotta check her for marks."

I drew my gun and flicked the safety off with my thumb. "You're welcome to try."

"No, he isn't." Cam met my gaze with a heavy one of his own. "You're going to put the gun away." Then he turned back to Nick. "And you're going to back the hell off. I already told you she's an independent."

Independents were a dying breed in the city, even before I'd defected from their ranks.

"She broke into an apartment, she's armed and I have it on good authority that she's bound to Ruben Cavazos. I gotta check her for marks, Caballero. You don't like it, you take that up with Adler. It's over my head."

Cam's jaw clenched. "My word's not good enough?"

Nick shook his head. "Not this time." He turned to me. "Take off your jacket."

My temper flared. "Go to hell."

"Liv, just show him your arm," Cam said. "You're not marked. What's the big deal?"

"The big deal is that I don't owe him anything." And I was tired of being forced to strip.

"Fine. Then do it for me." Cam frowned, but the lines around his mouth were fear for me, not anger. Something was wrong—beyond the obvious. "You owe me, Liv."

He was wrong about that. I'd already made up for what I'd done to him, several times over, but I couldn't tell him that.

The real question was why he wanted me to cooperate with this arrogant little grunt in the first place.

And that's when I finally understood. "Push your sleeve up."

Cam exhaled slowly, but didn't even try to deny what I'd just figured out. He uncrossed his arms and pushed his left sleeve up with his right hand. And there it was. Not one, but *three* thick, iron-colored links of chain circling a quarter of his upper arm.

"You son of a bitch...." I whispered through clenched teeth. Cam was well entrenched in Jake Tower's infrastructure. Halfway up the ranks. No wonder he'd been worried about my rumored affiliation with Cavazos. We couldn't work together. We couldn't even safely be *seen* together by anyone who knew about our respective bindings.

And that little bit of understanding brought Cam's current predicament into clear focus. He'd brought me—a potential enemy—into his neighborhood and if I refused to prove I had no opposing affiliation, he would be held responsible.

My heart pounding, I holstered my gun and slid my jacket off my shoulders, then let Cam pull my shirt sleeve up to show off the unmarked flesh of my upper left arm.

"See?" he said, as I shrugged the jacket back into place. "No binding."

"That's not the only place she could be marked." Nick's gaze wandered down from my arm before finding my eyes again, his own gleaming in anticipation. "Where does Cavazos mark his whores?"

I stiffened, but Cam didn't hesitate. His fist flew, and a second later, Nick was on the floor, bleeding from either his nose or his mouth—I couldn't tell which, with all the blood.

Out of habit, I pulled the bottle of ammonia from my pocket, but Cam shook his head. "Save it." He plucked a tissue from a box on the coffee table, then knelt next to Nick and wiped the blood from his fist while the grunt pinched his nose, trying to staunch the flow. "You checked. She's unmarked. Your job here is done." He folded the tissue into quarters and held it up for Nick to see. "You ever disrespect her again, and I'll consider it a personal insult." Cam tucked the tissue into his front pocket. "And I'll send this to Ruben Cavazos myself, along with your name and a suggestion of how best to use them both to make your life a living hell. Got it?"

Nick swiped blood from his face with the tail of his shirt—an idiotic move, unless he was planning to burn it later. "Sorry, Cam. I just… That's what I heard…."

"What did you hear?" I demanded, snapping the cap back onto my spray bottle.

Nick hesitated, glancing at me for a second before refocusing on Cam. "I'm not saying it's true, but word on the street is that she's doing Cavazos. And reporting to him. Tower put her on the watch list."

"Based on a stupid rumor?" Cam demanded.

The grunt shrugged. "He don't answer to me. All I know is we got orders to check for a mark if she comes west of the river."

"Since when?"

Another shrug. "Couple hours ago? Maybe less. You didn't get the message?"

Son of a bitch. I'd left Cavazos a couple of hours ago. It *had* to be one of his men.

Cam's frown deepened. "I haven't checked my phone." He stood and shrugged to me. "Doesn't matter, though. You're not marked."

But it wasn't that simple. Eventually someone who

outranked Cam would demand a more thorough search, and then I'd be screwed. We both would.

"We're done here, right?" I asked, already headed back to the bathroom.

"Yeah." Cam pulled the grunt to his feet while I squatted in front of the bathroom sink to check for cleaning supplies. Nothing but an extra roll of toilet paper and a half-empty quart of bleach. But that was good enough.

"What should I report?" Nick asked, still sniffling blood while I stuffed one of Hunter's soiled rags into an extra quart bag from my pocket, then dropped the rest of them in the wastebasket.

"The truth," Cam said. "She's here on a freelance job, for a private party, and I'm assisting. You checked her, she's unmarked, and I'm personally vouching for her. If they want to know any more than that, they've got my number."

He was vouching for me. Shit. I couldn't let him do that—it could get him killed, if something went wrong—but I couldn't make him take the words back without telling him I was bound to Cavazos. And if I admitted that now, Nick would try to haul me in front of Tower, and Cam would try to stop him, and that would lead to more violence and spilled blood, and then we'd both be on the run from the entire Tower syndicate. Which would make it really hard to search for a murderer who lived west of the river.

That slope was slippery, but unavoidable.

Trying to swallow the bitter lump in my throat, I opened the bottle of bleach and poured it into the trash can at arm's length, to keep from splashing my clothes. Then I used the bottle itself to press the whole bloody mess down into the liquid that had pooled at the bottom.

Bleach doesn't erase all evidence of blood, as any crime-scene technician will tell you. But it does destroy the energy signature that pulls a Tracker to it.

I wasn't worried about anyone else looking for Shen's killer—the human police couldn't track like a bloodhound, and Anne wouldn't hire anyone else, with me and Cam already on the case. But if Cam's superiors found out about my mark from Cavazos, it wouldn't be hard for them to deduce that we were tracking Eric Hunter, and they could use his blood to follow our trail.

Thanks to the bleach, though, all they'd have to go on was his name, which cut their chances of tracking him in half. At least.

When I left the bathroom, Nick was gone, and Cam was in the kitchen, labeling the thug's blood sample with a black Sharpie. When he was done, he handed it to me, and I dated Hunter's bloody bandage, then labeled it with his first name and last initial only, for security. It's much harder to find someone—through either traditional or Skilled searching methods—without a last name.

"We need to talk," I said, while he blew on the print to dry it.

"Agreed. We also need to get something to eat and find Eric Hunter. Let's wrap things up here." He shoved the sealed tissue back into his pocket, then brushed past me on his way to the bedroom. "You look for a filing cabinet, I'll check his computer."

"What are we looking for?" I already had a more recent—if weaker—blood sample.

"His full name. Or as much of it as we can find."

Because the Skilled rarely used either of their middle names on official documents. But then again, they also rarely left a pile of bloody rags lying around for someone to find. "Look for documentation. A traffic ticket, an insurance card, an old college ID or even a magazine subscription. It's a long shot, but I've gotten lucky like that before."

Eric Hunter had no filing cabinet, and I couldn't decide whether that meant he was smart enough to store all his dangerous personal information under lock and key elsewhere, or stupid enough not to keep track of it at all. But based on the shoebox full of unfiled receipts under his bed—an organizational method I was well acquainted with, personally—I was betting on the latter.

His kitchen trash—*so* glad I brought a pair of gloves—held an unopened bank statement, a two-week-old copy of *Car and Driver* addressed to Eric R. Hunter, several pieces of junk mail addressed to Resident and…a hospital bill, wadded into a tight, angry ball of crumpled paper.

Hmm… Yet another piece of Eric Hunter's life that didn't fit the profile.

Still wearing my gloves, I took the bank statement into the bedroom, where Cam sat at Hunter's desk, clicking away at his laptop. "What'cha got?" he asked, without looking up.

"Couple of interesting things…" Unwilling to sit on the bed, I leaned against the door facing and unfolded the statement. "One of Eric Hunter's middle initials is evidently R. And until last week, his personal financial crisis made the national debt look like small potatoes." Four bounced checks all with twenty-five-dollar fees attached.

Cam finally looked up. "What happened last week?"

"He received a fifty-thousand-dollar wire transfer. I'm assuming that's the up-front portion of the hit on Shen."

"That must have turned his frown upside down. Where'd it come from?" Cam was already typing again, but the frustrated lines in his forehead said he wasn't having much luck.

I shrugged. "There's just an account number. Can you trace that?"

"Not without a crash course in criminal hacking and a few decades to practice. I might know someone, though...."

"One of your friendly neighborhood gangsters?" I asked, not quite surprised by the accusatory tone of my own voice, and Cam looked up at me again, his expression cautious, and difficult to read.

"I never said I wasn't bound."

"You never said you were, either." I folded Hunter's bank statement and stuffed it back into the envelope. "You made me show you my arm, but you never bothered to mention that you're three chain links up Jake Tower's ass."

"We don't have time for this right now." He turned back to the screen, shoulders tense, forehead drawn low. "Did you find anything else?"

I had to clench my teeth to keep from yelling at him, and I only bothered because he was right—the longer we spent in Hunter's apartment, the better the chance that Nick's report would send one of his superiors our way.

"Just this." I held up the bill, still wrinkled in spite of my best attempt to flatten it. "Hunter went to the E.R.

for a broken arm four months ago and still hasn't paid his bill."

Cam frowned. "Why would he go to the E.R.?"

"Exactly." Skilled people almost *never* go to the hospital, because of the compulsive blood-drawing policies and the staff's utter refusal to let you incinerate your own biological waste onsite. Evidently setting fire to a medical wastebucket is a strict no-no.

Instead, we had our own doctors—certain legitimate private practices with access to all the same equipment as a public hospital, but run by people in the know. People who routinely gather everything you might possibly have bled on into one plastic bag and won't look at you strangely if you take that bag home to burn in the privacy of your own apartment.

For the convenience of certain criminal elements, there were even private practices that were willing to overlook the legal requirement that they report gunshot wounds and other brow-raising injuries– for the right price. Or to comply with the binding that had provided the funding to open that specific practice in the first place. Syndicate-sponsored clinics were all the rage.

"Something isn't right with this guy," I said, and Cam nodded.

"You found more than I did. He pays most of his bills online, but if he keeps a list of passwords, it's either encrypted or saved under a name no one else would recognize. His emails are banal—no smoking gun there, which means we still have no idea who hired him, or why."

"But we do have his first and last name, and one middle initial," I pointed out. "You can work with that, right?"

"Assuming the name's real and he's still anywhere near the city, yeah."

"Good, let's get out of here before we run into any more of your fellow hired thugs." I hated the thought of Cam working for Tower. I wanted to go on thinking that the dirt of the city hadn't touched him. That his hands were still clean. I'd come to the city to protect us from each other, and instead, here we stood, side by side in the muck.

Cam closed Hunter's laptop and frowned at me. "They're not all like Nick, you know. There are some decent men and women working for Tower. Sometimes good people get caught up in bad things, Olivia."

"I know." Better than most. "But I also know that the closer you stand to the monsters, the more human they start to look."

And perspective was something I could not afford to lose.

Seven

"His apartment was empty, but there was blood in the bathroom. His, not Shen's," Liv said into her phone, one boot propped on my dashboard. "We think he was hired. Someone wired a big chunk of cash to his checking account last week."

Anne spoke during the pause, but I couldn't hear much of what she said over the traffic noise as I turned onto Third Street, the main drag and the heart of Tower's empire.

"Not yet. Cam thinks he knows someone who can trace the account, but for now, we're still trying to sniff him out the hard way. Any idea why someone might want Shen dead? Something to do with his work, maybe?"

Anne spoke again, and I nodded through the window to one of Tower's men on the street, his four rust-colored chain lengths showing beneath the rolled-up sleeve of his T-shirt. He nodded back, then glanced at Liv in my passenger's seat. If he recognized her I saw no sign, but being seen with her was good enough. It was proof that I wasn't trying to hide anything. And that she wasn't, either.

"Okay, just let us know if you think of anything," Liv said, and a second later, she flipped her phone closed.

"How is she?" I asked, cruising slowly down the street toward the next checkpoint four blocks away. Tower's eyes were everywhere, and hiding from them would look like guilt.

Liv shrugged and brushed long brown hair off her shoulder. "Fine, considering. I think Hadley was in the room though, 'cause she didn't say very much. It's like she doesn't have the luxury of truly mourning, with the kid around."

"She sounds like a good mother." Though it was hard for me to picture Annika as anything other than the twenty-two-year-old small-town free spirit she'd been when I'd met her. Back then, she'd been more committed to vegetarianism than to any man she'd ever met— holding on to a relationship must have been hard for someone who could taste every lie—but I hadn't seen her since the night Liv dumped me. In the middle of that damned party. It's amazing how much can change in six years.

And how much stays the same.

"How did she get in touch with you?" Liv asked, sliding her phone into her pocket. "If she couldn't find me, how did she find you?"

I exhaled slowly. "I still have the same phone number." Because I wanted it to be easy for Olivia to get in touch with me, should she ever decide to.

Liv suddenly gripped the armrest built into the passenger's side door, as if she hadn't even heard me. "Is this Third Street?"

"Yeah. You still like Greek? There's this great gyro stand on the corner, about a mile—."

Her gaze hardened. "You're headed west. Deeper into Tower's side of town."

"That's where the gyro stand is…." I began, but she wasn't buying it. And she didn't miss my nod to the next sentinel, on the corner.

"You're parading me down the fucking gauntlet."

"I'm taking preemptive measures," I insisted. "If they think I'm hiding you, they'll assume you have something to hide, and you're going to be checked for a mark by every initiate we run into." And if we ran into anyone with more than three chain links, I wouldn't be able to prevent a more thorough search, and we both knew Liv wasn't going to simply submit to one, either. Her trigger finger was looking a little twitchy.

"Which is why we should be heading to the south fork," she said. Toward the only neutral-controlled part of town. Which was where she both lived and worked, in spite of the higher rent.

"Olivia, Hunter lives on the west side, and so does my computer guru. I don't think any of the leads are going to pull us toward the south today," I said, but she looked unconvinced. "What's the big deal? You're unbound, and you must've done work on this side before."

"Yeah, back when I worked for Rawlinson, but I haven't been here since… Since I quit."

"Well, that's too bad, 'cause the gyros are awesome." I pulled into the last available spot at the curb and shifted into Park. "Let's just relax and have some lunch while I track Van down."

"Fine," she said, one hand on the door handle. "But you owe me some answers, and unless you want to give them here, we need to find someplace more private to eat."

I couldn't argue with that, so I texted Van from the line in front of the gyro cart: Got a minute? I need some help.

The response came a minute later, as Liv stepped up to the cart to order: Yr place, 1 hr.

Fifteen minutes later, I parked in a covered space in front of my apartment building and snatched the bulging white paper sack from Liv's lap. She glanced at me in amusement—a good look for her. "What, you don't trust me with the food?"

"Sorry. I'm starving."

She laughed. "I couldn't tell from the four gyros you ordered."

"Don't forget the dolmades." I swung my car door shut and led Liv toward the exterior staircase. "They're the best in the city. Trucked in daily from some restaurant on the east side."

"Yeah. Karagas. The owner's mother makes them every morning. They're best fresh."

I tried on a grin as we walked up the stairs. "What, you won't set foot on the west side, but you'll have lunch in Cavazos's backyard? No wonder people are talking."

Liv scowled. "People are talking because someone's started a smear campaign. The rumors are malicious, and evidently aimed at the west side of the city. Someone's put a target on my head. My guess is Travis Spencer. He's had it out for me ever since I found the governor's missing mistress."

I nearly choked on my own surprise. "That was you?" It hadn't made the local news, of course. Officially, no one was supposed to know that governor was getting some on the side. But Trackers had been rabid over that job, and I'd never heard who finally found the target.

"Yeah. Paid for two whole months' worth of office space. But evidently it also earned me some enemies. Stupid rumor-spreading bastards."

"Relax, Liv. It's just a bunch of idiots talking, and all you have to do to prove them wrong is wear short sleeves." I shrugged. "Besides, I'd go to Karagas for lunch every day if I didn't value my life just a bit higher than good Greek food."

"Maybe if you hadn't signed over your free will in exchange for a paycheck, you could enjoy both your life *and* your lunch wherever the hell you want. Then you could be a part of the solution, rather than the problem. Wasn't that the plan?"

"Plans change." I kicked the door closed and dropped my keys on the coffee table, and when I met Liv's gaze, I was almost bowled over by the pain and power of my own memories. This part of her hadn't changed—this fiery temper threaded with innate goodwill. She would have been one hell of a lawyer, or a child advocate, or a...superhero.

"What happened to the FBI, Cam?" She took the bag from me and pulled out two cartons of dolmades.

I shrugged and took two plates down from the cabinet over the bar, avoiding her gaze. "Last I heard, they're still out there fighting crime. Catching murderers and foiling terrorists."

"And you're here, wasting a degree in criminal justice so you can track losers for a Mafia boss."

"Yeah, well, it turns out the FBI can hold its own

without me." I pulled two forks from the drawer to my right and gave her one while I used the other to slide three dolmades onto my plate.

"What happened to the interview? Did you even go?"

"No, Liv, I didn't go. Okay?" I dropped my fork on my plate, and the clang of metal against glass was louder than I'd intended. "I didn't go on the fucking interview. I didn't join the FBI. I don't fight on the side of truth and justice, and frankly, having been out in the real world for a while now, I can say with some measure of certainty that it was a dumb idea in the first place. Just the stupid dream of a stupid, idealistic kid with a shiny diploma and no clue how the world really works."

At twenty-two, I'd thought I was going to change the world. Or, at the very least, I was going to clean it up. I was going to join the FBI and use my Skill—secretly, of course—to track serial killers and pedophiles, and make the world a better place, one conviction at a time.

"It wasn't dumb," Liv insisted. "A little naive, maybe, but you could have pulled it off. You *should* have pulled it off." She pushed one of the bar stools out with her foot and sat. "So what happened? How did you get tangled up with Tower instead?"

"I got shot."

"What?" Her fork hovered over the open carton.

"I got shot. The week I moved here." I took my first bite while she stared, obviously trying to decide what to ask first.

"How? What happened?"

I shrugged and swallowed, my favorite food suddenly tasteless with the memory. "I don't know. I was walking down Hyacinth, about four nights after I got here, all farm-fresh and clueless—"

Liv frowned. "Hyacinth. That was in my neighborhood."

"I know."

She stabbed a dolma with her fork and the leaf started to come unwrapped as she gestured with it. "Do I even want to know what you were doing two blocks from my apartment?"

"Tracking you. You owed me an explanation—and, frankly, an apology—and I'd come prepared to demand both. But obviously, I didn't find you." Not that night, anyway. "I found the business end of a bullet instead." I stood and pulled up my shirt to expose the small, round puckered scar just to the right of my navel. "I never saw the shooter or the gun. I was just walking down the street one minute, then flat on my back the next, lying in a pool of my own blood. I was trying to hold my guts in with one hand and dig my phone out of my pocket with the other when these guys just showed up out of nowhere."

"Tower's men?" she asked, her food untouched.

"Yeah."

Her brows rose in challenge. "You do know they're probably the ones who shot you."

"Probably." I certainly couldn't prove otherwise. "All I know for sure is that they're the ones who saved me. They took me to one of their doctors and paid the bill. They destroyed all the blood I spilled. Then, when I was released, they took me to Adler's house—he's my direct supervisor now. His wife put me in their guest room and took care of me for weeks, while I recovered. After that, how could I not sign with Tower? I'd come to town with nothing, spent more than I had on a hotel room I never actually checked out of. By the time I was able to get out of bed, I was flat-ass broke, unemployed and—"

"And you didn't have a friend in the world to turn to," Liv interrupted. "Because I wasn't speaking to you."

"That's not what I was going to say," I insisted.

"But we both know it's true."

I couldn't argue. "Anyway, it was only supposed to be for one term. Five years. They'd lost their best Tracker and I needed a job—"

"Convenient..." she noted, peeling the foil back from the first gyro.

"At the time, yeah," I admitted. "It seemed pretty damned convenient." Fortuitous, even.

Liv swallowed her first bite and stared at me with her brows drawn low over those big blue eyes. "You know they set you up, right? They didn't save you. They found you, assessed your potential, then shot you."

"Liv..." I began, but she spoke over me—it almost felt like old times.

"By that point, they had you right where they wanted you. You were incapacitated and in their debt, and they had a *fucking huge* sample of your blood, which is probably on file in a room full of sensitive information somewhere. You didn't really think they destroyed all of it, did you? Please tell me you're not that gullible."

"Of course not." But wasn't I? Liv was sitting in my kitchen, inches away, telling me what a fool I was, and all I could think of was how badly I wanted to kiss her—and not just to shut her up, though that benefit would *not* go unappreciated.

"It was a win-win for Tower from the beginning," she insisted, dropping her gyro onto her plate so she could tick off points on her fingers. "He has you shot. If you die, at least you can't sign on with the competition. If you live, he has a chance to recruit you, albeit through pretty damn vicious means. If you sign on voluntarily, he has one hell of a new Tracker. If you don't, he has enough of your blood to bind you without your consent, at least for a while. Either way, you're his, for the cost of a bullet, some gauze and a round of antibiotics." She leaned on the counter with both elbows, eyeing me with the first sign of amusement I'd seen from her in hours. "You always were a cheap date."

I laughed. "You're one to talk." On our first date, sophomore year in college, we'd split a carnival hot dog and a cherry slushy—which she'd then vomited all over us both on the Tilt-A-Whirl.

"Yeah, I guess I am." Her nostalgic smile lasted as long as it took for me to pull two Coronas from the fridge. "Greek food, Mexican beer. Interesting combination." She reached across the counter to pull the bottle opener/magnet from the side of my fridge, then popped the top off her bottle.

I watched her take a long draft, and when she set the bottle down, she eyed me pensively. Almost reluctantly. "Please tell me you already knew all that. About Tower's unconventional recruiting methods. Because I thought that was just an urban legend until about ten minutes ago...."

"At the time, I didn't know," I admitted, popping the top off my own bottle. Suddenly I wished I'd poured something stronger. "But it didn't take long to figure out. And it's no urban legend." Since my first binding mark, I'd seen two other Skilled members netted the same way, and rumor had it that syndicates in other major cities had caught on to the same recruiting techniques. Certain Skills—and the most talented in *any* Skill set—were in demand, and there was nothing those in power wouldn't do to secure the services they wanted.

Liv took another drink, then stared at me through the half-empty bottle, as if the beer-bottle filter might reveal something she hadn't seen in me before. "So, if you figured it out, why'd you re-up? How'd you get those second and third chain links so fast?"

I studied her for a moment, trying to decide whether or not she wanted the truth. "It's not that bad, you know," I said finally, and she looked at me as if I'd just put a knife through the Easter Bunny's heart.

"It's blood money, Cam," she spat, slamming her bottle down on the counter, and my own temper sparked, part indignation, part denial. "How does it feel to know that your rent is paid with blood money?"

"You tell me," I snapped, without thinking it through. But words can't be unspoken—if I'd learned anything from swearing loyalty to Jake Tower, that was it. "You may not be bound to Cavazos, but you take commissions from him. What do you think he does with the people you find for him? You think he pats them on the head and sends them off to summer camp?"

"I don't..." she stammered, and I'd had enough of her hypocrisy.

"Yes, you do!" I shouted, and some small part of me enjoyed her shock for that instant before it bled into anger. "You work for him, and you take his money, and you use it to pay absurdly high rent on an apartment in the fucking ghetto, just to stand on principle. But you're paying for your principals with the same blood money that pays for this apartment. The only difference is that I can walk down the street without getting shot or mugged."

She stood, practically shaking with fury, and I knew I'd made my point. "The difference," she said through clenched teeth, her voice low and sharp enough to cut glass, "is that you signed on for this voluntarily, but I don't have any choice."

"What does that mean? Why don't you have a choice?" I asked, and her face went as pale as my white Formica countertop.

"I..." Liv blinked, as if she'd confused herself. Or said more than she'd meant to. Then she grabbed her bottle and chugged the rest of it. "I just meant that I have to take whatever work I can get. I'm not exactly rolling in commissions since I left Rawlinson, and yes, I've done some jobs for Cavazos, but that doesn't make me his bitch, or his whore, or anything else."

"I never said it did." But she was already backing across my living room, headed straight for the coffee table on her way to a dramatic exit fueled by something I didn't understand. "Liv, wait," I called, already rounding the countertop into the living room when the back of her leg hit the corner of the coffee table. She went down on one hip, and her bottle smashed against the side of the table, spraying her jacket with the last droplets.

"Shit." She started picking up the sticky pieces of glass and I knelt next to her to help.

"You okay?"

"Yeah. Sorry."

I shrugged. "It's just a little glass."

"I meant about…that whole thing. It's none of my business what you do for a living."

But I wanted it to be. "They offered me a step promotion," I said, dumping the glass I'd gathered onto the coffee table.

"What?"

"When my five years were up. Tower called me in the week my mark would have gone dead, and I would have been free, and he told me I'd become very important to the operation. He said I had two choices—I could sign on for another five years, or I could leave the organization. As incentive to stay, he offered me a step promotion—two chain links for the price of one. Instant seniority." I'd since learned that that offer was seldom extended, and even more seldom refused. "But if I opted out, I'd have to leave the city entirely."

"Was that in your contract? Part of the noncompetition clause?" she asked, staring into my eyes from inches away, and I realized I hadn't been that close to her in years. She hadn't *let* me get that close….

"No. But he wouldn't have had any trouble enforcing it."

"You signed an extension so you could stay in the city?" she said, and I could only nod. "Because of me?"

"There were other factors…." Other people I didn't want to leave behind. "But yeah."

"Cam…" Her voice was more breath than sound, and it echoed in every cell of my body. And suddenly the memories were too much to fight. She was right there, after so many years, and she wasn't pushing me away.

So I kissed her, and she kissed me back, and for several seconds, it was as if she'd never left at all.

Then pain slammed into my chest and I fell backward on my ass. By the time I realized she'd shoved me, she was on her feet, staring down at me. Glaring at me.

"Don't. Touch me." Her voice shook, and she couldn't hide the tremor in her hands, even when she shoved them into her pockets. "This isn't what it used to be. We can't... We can't ever go back to that." She jogged toward the hall, pulling her jacket off as she went, and I only recovered enough to stand when I heard water running in the bathroom.

Anger warred with something else inside me. Something deeper and older. Something that bruised me from the inside out every single time I heard her name, either out loud or in my own head. I followed her down the hall and stopped outside my own bathroom, where she stood with her jacket spread across the counter, trying to scrub drops of beer out of the leather.

"This is bullshit, Olivia."

But she just scrubbed harder, so I snatched the cloth from her and she turned on me, eyes blazing with some dizzying combination of anger and...regret. "Don't do this, Cam. This isn't the time to open old wounds."

"There's never going to be a time, is there?" I pulled the cloth back when she reached for it. "Every time I see you, you tell me to go away, but you look like you want to cry when you say it. You don't mean it, and we both know that."

"I mean it...." she insisted.

"No, you *don't!*" I shouted, and this time she didn't argue. "What happened, Liv? Why are you lying to me? Why are you lying to *yourself?*"

She blinked up at me, eyes damp, in spite of the stoic set of her jaw, and I was nearly knocked off bal-

ance by the storm of conflicting urges raging inside me.
How could I be so furious with her, yet so in love with
her at the same time? How could she be so madden-
ingly closed-off, yet so obviously vulnerable beneath
her shield of denial?

With one breath, I wanted to shake some badly
needed sense into her, but by the next, I needed to protect her. To hide her away from whatever had put that
bruised look in her eyes. And suddenly I couldn't resist.

I stepped so close I could smell her shampoo and
feel her warmth through my clothes. She sucked in a
shaky breath and her fingers curled around a handful
of my shirt, clutching at it, as if she wasn't sure whether
to pull me closer or push me away. Her forehead fell
against my collarbone and in that moment, her defenses
failed. She stood there with me, leaning against me, exposed, her heart so raw and wounded I wondered how
it could possibly keep beating.

I slid one hand past her jaw to cradle the back of her
head, and she held her breath when I leaned down to
whisper into her ear. "Why can't you just admit that
you still want me? We both know it's true."

She took one more uneven breath, and her grip
on my shirt tightened. "Because what I want doesn't
matter. Maybe it never did."

Her defenses dropped back into place with a thud
that jarred my entire existence. She pulled the rag from
my hand and bent over her jacket again, and that's when
I noticed the words tattooed in an arc just below her
neck and above her collar, bared by the hair she'd swept
over one shoulder.

Cedo nulli. Latin for "I yield to no one." It was the
motto of the independents—not a binding mark, but a

promise made to one's self, and a fitting summary of Olivia's entire life. Or maybe it was her battle cry.

Was that the problem? She couldn't be with me because I was bound to Tower? But she'd pushed me away long before I accepted my first mark. No matter what else happened, before the day was over, I was going to know the truth.

Eight

I kept scrubbing my jacket long after I'd gotten the spots out, because my hands needed something to do.

Cam kissed me. And I let him.

That wasn't supposed to happen. I'd spent years pushing him away to make sure that could *never* happen. I'd only let myself think about him when the only other option was to truly experience the present—forced fealty to Ruben Cavazos. The memory of me and Cam together had become my mental refuge. I'd built him up in my mind, inflated my memories of him so that just the thought of him could block everything else out, and I'd never expected the actual man to live up to what I'd re-created in my head.

It shouldn't have been possible.

He shouldn't have had a chance to live up to anything.

But then I tripped, and he was there on the floor with me, and my body remembered what my head was trying so hard to forget—that I wanted him. All of him. That I missed him like I'd never missed anyone in my life.

Sometimes I dreamed about Cam, then woke up

heartbroken and tried to go back to sleep immediately, to recapture the fantasy. The what-ifs. What if I didn't know what I knew? What if I'd never left? What if Noelle was wrong, and I'd spent the past six years running away from the best man I'd ever met—the only one I'd ever loved—and I'd ruined both our lives for nothing?

But Elle wasn't wrong. She'd never been wrong. Cam and I were dangerous to each other, and every second we spent together was a second ticking away on some countdown I didn't truly understand. All I really knew was that when we got to zero, someone would die.

Knowing he was alive but I couldn't have him was infinitely better than knowing I'd gotten him killed because I had the willpower of a nymphet in heat.

What the hell is wrong with me? I was deep in Jake Tower's territory, sporting an intimately located binding mark from his nemesis, which could easily get me killed—or worse—if exposed. Yet all I could think about was the hurt look on Cam's face when I let him kiss me, then pushed him away again. The confusion in his eyes when I refused to explain why I'd left.

It wasn't fair of me to keep that secret from him. I *knew* it wasn't fair. But what if telling him only sped up the inevitable? What if telling him *caused* whatever Elle had seen?

What if *not* telling him caused it?

The doorbell rang, and my head popped up. I saw my reflection—never a good idea after a day of submission, coercion and sneaking around unfriendly territory—and I looked tired. But that was better than looking scared.

After a long, slow exhale, I ran my fingers through

my hair and tossed my damp jacket over one arm instead of putting it back on. Surely meeting Van would be easier if we got this whole mark search out of the way first.

I was halfway down the short hall before I realized something was weird. Cam was laughing, and he wasn't alone. And the other voice sounded distinctly...feminine.

I stood in the living-room doorway for almost a minute before they realized I was there, watching them, surprised and a little disappointed to realize that Van was a girl. I was kind of ashamed of myself for assuming she'd be male, and even more ashamed of myself for wishing I'd been right.

Then Cam noticed me, and when he stood, she swiveled on her chair to face me. And some fragile part of me withered and died. Van was gorgeous. Not just pretty, like I could be, with a day's notice and an hour in the bathroom. Gorgeous like Elle had been—effortless, largely oblivious and completely natural. If she wore makeup beyond mascara, I couldn't tell.

There had to be a reason Cam hadn't mentioned the fact that Van was a woman.

"Van, this is Liv Warren," he said as she stood and offered me her hand. I shook it, and held it for maybe a second too long, trying to decide how threatened I should be.

"You're Van?"

"Vanessa." She pulled her hand firmly from my grip, but offered me a friendly, if cautious smile. "And that's all you need to know."

Smart, for someone unSkilled. But considering that I was evidently the talk of the west side at the moment, it did no good for Cam to withhold my name anymore; I'd just have to be content with the knowledge that—hopefully—my middle names were still my own little secret. Well, mine and Cam's.

"Cam says you need some technical assistance?" She wore a long, filmy black skirt and a green-and-black-patterned tank top beneath a bulky sweater that couldn't quite hide how very well built she was. However, it did cover her markings, which left me no way to judge her rank within the Tower organization, or to guess what her job within it was.

And suddenly I truly understood why Nick had insisted I remove my jacket earlier—so he'd know exactly who he was dealing with. And that point of commonality between us pissed me off.

"Yeah." I reached for the lunch I'd barely touched, then realized I no longer wanted it. "We're looking for a full name and the owner of a certain bank account. But those'll be two different people."

"Which do you want first?" Van bent to pick up a backpack I hadn't noticed and set it on the extra bar stool.

"The name," Cam and I said in unison. If we could find Eric Hunter's full, rightful name, Cam could track him from that, while I made what use I could out of the strange blood samples. We'd come at him from two different angles, and hopefully arrive at the point where they met.

Van set up her laptop and several other pieces of equipment on the kitchen peninsula while Cam told her what we already knew and I…watched them. I couldn't help it. I couldn't be with him—not like I wanted to be—but that didn't make it any easier for me to see him with someone else. And the fact that he still wanted me clearly hadn't stopped him from exploring his options.

They were obviously close—they laughed easily and seemed to share several private jokes no one bothered to explain to me. He knew what she liked to drink, and she knew where he kept the glasses, paper towels and extra notepads.

Conclusion: she'd been over before. A lot.

"Okay, let's see what we can find on Mr. Hunter." Van took her sweater off and draped it over the back of her stool, and that's when I got my first look at her mark. A single greenish chain link. She'd served less than five years, based on the fact that she hadn't earned a second mark yet, and the color green said she worked in some kind of unSkilled staff capacity. That could be anything from bookkeeping to housekeeper, but based on the equipment she'd unloaded, I was guessing Van served in a more technically apt position.

Did Tower have a dedicated hacker?

For several minutes, she clicked away at her keyboard while Cam finished his lunch and I stared at her arm, trying to guess how someone like that—someone beautiful and talented enough to have a zillion other options—had gotten mixed up with Jake Tower.

"Just ask me," Van said, without looking up from her screen, and it took me a minute to realize she was talking to me. "I'd rather be questioned than gawked at."

I glanced at Cam, and he nodded hesitantly. As if he was afraid I'd scare her.

"Okay...how'd you get your tattoo?" I glanced at her arm for clarification, in case she had any more I couldn't see.

"The usual way. Ink and needles." Van looked up

from her screen to smile at me, but her clacking never stopped.

"No, I meant…"

"Why did I sign on?" she finished for me, when I let my question trail off.

Cam shot me an irritated look, but spoke to her. "You don't have to answer that."

Van shrugged. "Everyone else knows anyway." She swiveled away from her equipment and met my gaze. "You want the long version or the short?"

"Whatever you want to tell me." And I knew from Cam's clenched jaw that it wouldn't be a pretty story.

Van stared into my eyes as if she were assessing me. Then she shrugged again. "You look like you can handle the unabridged version. Here goes." But then she turned to Cam, who popped the top from a bottle of Corona and handed it to her. Then he handed one to me. Van chugged half of hers, then glanced at me apologetically. "Goes down better this way." She set the bottle on the counter next to her computer. "I grew up in the south fork. My dad was a gambler and a drunk, and when I was a kid, he lost the rent money once too often and had to borrow from some guy on the east side to keep a roof over our heads."

The east side? That was Cavazos's side of town. I took the first sip of my beer. How the hell had she gotten tangled up with Tower, if her dad was borrowing from one of Cavazos's usurers?

"For a while, my dad made the payments okay, but then he lost his job, and we fell into the red pretty damn fast, and when he couldn't pay, we got a visit from a guy with four interlocking rings on his left arm."

Four rings... "One of Cavazos's thugs?" I asked, and she nodded.

"He brought some papers and said my dad had to pay his debt in blood—either his or mine. My dad was drunk, of course. Maybe it woulda made a difference if he'd been sober. But I doubt it. Either way, my dad sliced my thumb, then slammed my hand down on that contract before I even knew what was happening."

"He *sold* you?" Horror engulfed me, growing deeper and darker with every breath I took. What kind of parent sells his *child* to pay off bad debt?

"Lock, stock and barrel." Van took another swig on her beer, then propped her boot on the next bar stool. "They shot me up with something right there in front of my dad, and I woke up two days later with this." She pulled her long skirt up to reveal a single ring tattooed on the inside of her left thigh, the faded grayish hue of a dead mark. "It used to be bright red."

I could hardly breathe through my own horror and revulsion.

The ring meant she'd been bound to the Cavazos syndicate, a plight I could certainly sympathize with. Together, the color red and the placement of the mark—on her thigh—meant she'd been sold into the skin trade. As a minor. Against her will.

And suddenly I wanted to throw up.

"How old were you?" I whispered, as Van lowered both her leg and her skirt.

"Fifteen."

I could practically taste vomit at the back of my throat. "That can't be right." I took another sip, but alcohol couldn't help me make sense of something that just didn't add up. "Cavazos won't sign underage girls. It's too much of a liability."

"Evidently the profit outweighs the risk," Cam said, blatant disgust dulling the usual shine in his eyes.

I shook my head. "No. I *know* he doesn't take them that young. Did you tell him how old you were?"

Van stared at me as if I'd just lapsed into nonsense. "I never even saw him. Not while I was conscious, anyway. I was just one of dozens of girls, probably nothing more than names and numbers on a profit-and-loss statement to him."

"If he'd known, he would have fixed it." I *had* to believe that. Cavazos was an abusive, lying, murdering bastard. I'd seen him hit his wife. I'd seen him shoot a trespasser through the forehead in the middle of his living room, then complain about the stain on the carpet. He'd done everything but violate our contract to humiliate me. To break me. But he wouldn't hurt a kid. He wouldn't even let someone *else* hurt a kid. That was the only marginally human trait I'd been able to find in him, and I needed to be able to believe in that. Otherwise, I'd lose my mind the next time he touched me. I'd just fall right over the edge of sanity into oblivion.

"Liv, if he didn't know, it's because he didn't *want* to know," Cam insisted. "His men can't lie to him, right?"

I started to nod, then reconsidered. "Well, there are certain exceptions, for plausible deniability…"

"Exactly." He opened another beer for himself and frowned at me over the bottle. "Why are you so sure he'd care, even if he knew?"

"Because he has a kid of his own. A daughter." I closed my eyes and rubbed my forehead, battling a stress headache strong enough to rival the typical breach-of-contract pain. "I've seen him with her. He may be the scum of the earth in every other respect, but he's a good father. As good a father as a felon can be, anyway."

"Charles Manson had kids, too." Van pushed her empty bottle across the counter toward Cam, who dropped it into the trash, then opened the fridge for more.

After several more sips from my own bottle, my stomach had mostly settled, and I turned to Van. "You were bound by force. That shouldn't have been possible. Not for the long term, anyway."

"What do you mean? Why not?"

And that's when I realized how viciously unfair her situation truly had been. She wasn't Skilled. Her family wasn't Skilled. So she'd grown up with even less insight into the way the world really worked than I'd had, and clearly, even after years spent bound to first one syndicate, then the other, she still didn't fully understand the chains she was tangled up in.

"How much do you know about bindings, Van?" I asked. She frowned at me, then glanced at Cam, and when he nodded, I realized what she was doing—looking to him, her superior in the organization, for guidance on what she should and shouldn't say in a situation that wasn't strictly governed by the mark on her arm.

"I know what I can and can't do, based on my mark. Though honestly, some of that comes from trial and error." She shrugged, and I nodded. That was typical. "And I know what I *have* to do, to fulfill my contract."

"Okay, but beyond your specific case, how much do you know about the binding process in general? About how it works?"

"Only what Cam's told me."

"Which isn't much," he admitted. Because he wouldn't be allowed to say anything that might scare her away from extending her contract, whenever it came up for renewal—also typical.

Fortunately, I had no such restrictions.

"Okay, here we go—a crash course in binding." I set her bag on the floor and took the stool next to her. "You know you can be bound to anyone, right?" I began, and she nodded hesitantly. "All it takes is an oath and a seal. Bindings can be as simple as a pinky promise between classmates, or as complicated as a two-hundred-page contract negotiated for a year by attorneys on both sides and eventually sealed by the best binder in the country. Regardless, the key ingredients remain the same—an oath and a seal."

"The oath, I got," Van said, lifting her beer for another swig. "What's the seal?"

"The seal is what makes a binding final and official. Think of it like one of those fancy wax impressions they used to use to seal documents, a couple hundred years ago. It's the metaphysical version of that. And only a Binder can seal a binding, usually by signing it or stamping it with blood. Or both."

"So, those kids with the pinky promise…" She held up one hooked finger to demonstrate. "One of them would have to be a Binder?"

"In that scenario, yes. Because there are no written words or blood, one of the kids would have to actually be a Binder for the promise to hold. Though it's really rare for Binders that young to even know their Skill yet. That was just an illustration."

Van nodded. "I'm with you so far."

"Good. Now, here's where it gets interesting. I know there are probably times when you feel...enslaved. Times when you physically can't say no, even when it kills some vital part of you to just...let horrible things happen."

"More so with the red mark," she said. "It's not so bad on this side of the river."

I shook my head, horrified that she seemed to actually believe what she was saying. "If that's really what you think, it's only because they haven't made you do something you don't want to do yet. But that day *will* come. Jake Tower may not be renting you out by the hour, but he *is* using you for profit, one way or another. As long as you lack the ability to say no to something, you're not truly free. You're his."

She shook her head, visibly frustrated. "You don't understand. You've never been bound like I was," she insisted, and the irony stung all the way into my soul. "For four years, I couldn't say no. I couldn't fight back. I couldn't even complain. I could do what I was told, or die fighting the impulse.

"Now I work with computers, fully clothed, and I'm allowed to take down any bastard who tries to touch me. Which would you prefer?"

I exhaled slowly. "I'd prefer not to need permission to defend myself."

Van blinked, and a single, unguarded thought crossed her expression. In that moment, I could see that I'd gotten through to her. It was like seeing the light for the first time in a decade—so many of us had forgotten the sun even existed.

"But you have a valid point, and I'm not trying to minimize that," I assured her. "The difference between your first binding—the red ring to Cavazos—and your current one is the difference between full-on slavery and indentured servitude. The first time around, you were bound by force, and that's not the way it's supposed to work. In fact, it takes a very powerful Binder to be able to seal a nonconsensual oath. Most of those break as soon as the ink dries. Or the blood, depending on the binding method. Flesh bindings, bonds sealed with a tattoo, are a little more stable, but unless the Binder is a real rock star, all it takes is a couple of intentional breaches—something small enough to survive—and voilà, you have a dead mark, as worthless as the artist who inked it."

Van frowned, obviously confused. "But my mark never died."

"Which means that whoever sealed it was pretty damn badass. But that..." I gestured to the mark on her left arm. "That's the way it's supposed to work. The syndicate doesn't give as much as it takes, but it has to give *something*. Otherwise no one would ever be willing to sign. It's still not a fair trade for *you*—thus the indentured servitude—but at least you're getting something in exchange for your service to Tower, right?"

"Yeah." She looked a little relieved—as if maybe she hadn't made the worse decision of her entire life—and I almost hated to burst her bubble. "I get protection. A salary. A family."

"No." That came out harsher than I'd meant for it to, and she practically jumped. "Protection, yes—at a cost. Salary, yes—because it doesn't do them any good for you to starve to death before you've served your term. But Tower and his men will never, ever be your family." Though considering that her own father had sold her into prostitution as a teenager, the distinction seemed a little less clear than it should have. "They won't even truly be your friends. Not even Cameron."

For a minute, Cam looked as if he wanted to argue. Then he just looked miserable. The truth does that to people.

"I have lots of friends in the syndicate," Van insisted, and I almost felt sorry for her.

"No, you don't, Vanessa. You can't possibly, because any one of them would kill you with one word from Jake Tower, just like you would kill any one of them if he told you to. You can't help it. Obedience is in the boilerplate contract. And since you signed willingly, this one would be much harder to get out of than the first one."

She huffed, a harsh, bitter sound. "I don't see how that's possible, if the last binding was strong enough to hold me against my will."

"How'd you get out of it?" I asked—she'd only served four years of a five-year term. If they were willing to sign her underage, against her will, there wasn't much they wouldn't have been willing to do to keep her, even after her contract officially expired.

"Cam got me out." She glanced up at him, and my heart ached at the look that passed between them.

"How?" That was all I could manage through the bitter jealousy I had no business indulging.

"One night a few years ago, they rented me out to this bad apple. A real asshole. He…" She stopped and drank from a glass of water Cam set in front of her, and he took over the story, when it became obvious that she couldn't.

"I found her on the side of the road, beaten half to

death and barely conscious. I wanted to take her to the hospital, but she begged me not to."

"So he brought me here." Van glanced around the apartment, picking up the thread where he dropped it, and I hated myself for wishing she'd never been in his home. "I was here for nearly a week, but I couldn't give him my name. I wasn't allowed to. But he saw my mark, and he knew...what I was."

Cam nodded, picking up the story again. "We talked, and bit by bit, I realized what had happened to her. How they got her so young. She couldn't tell me who she was, but I finally convinced her to give me the name of the Binder."

I glanced at Van in surprise. "You knew the Binder?"

She nodded. "Not personally, but he was kind of a legend to most of the girls. Like the bogeyman." Which was no wonder, considering he was evidently strong enough to bind people against their will, and to enforce an underage binding past the age of consent.

"So she gave me the name, and I..." Cam broke off with a shrug, part modesty, part shame. "I took care of it."

"He tracked the bastard down and killed him," Van finished, the words lingering on the end of her tongue, as if they tasted too good to let go.

I blinked at Cam. Then I blinked again. "You killed Cavazos's Binder?"

"Yeah," Van answered for him. "Shot him in the groin first, then twice in the head." Cam flinched, but didn't deny it. "Tower was so impressed he offered him a step promotion." She beamed at Cam, obviously proud for him. But Cam looked sick, and I understood that there was more to it than that. Some part of the story that he hadn't told her.

"They gave you a step promotion for killing one Binder?" I said, picking at the seams of his secret.

"It wasn't just a Binder," Van said. "It was Cavazos's *top* Binder. When Cam killed him, he nullified every contract that bastard had ever sealed. Three dozen of the girls went free—at least until a few of them were rounded up again—and Cavazos lost hundreds of thousands of dollars in unenforceable contracts."

And suddenly I remembered. "Lorenzo..."

"Yeah." Van looked surprised, but Cam frowned. "You knew him?"

"No, I..." It was just before I signed with Cavazos. His men were still talking about it—all the money they'd lost, and what they were going to do when they found the bastard who killed Lorenzo...

Son of a bitch! Puzzle pieces fell into place in my head, and the thuds echoed through not just my mind, but my past. And Cam's past. We were tangled, even beyond what I'd known....

"No, I just... I heard about it. Cavazos had Lorenzo brought in from Spain, at a huge expense."

Van's smile was a grim parody of joy. "Good—I hope Cam cost him a fucking fortune. Doesn't matter, though. No amount of money can give any of us back what he cost us." Van drained her second bottle, then stood, looking just a bit unsteady, but whether that was from the beer or the memories, I couldn't tell. "Be right back," she said, on her way down the hall.

As soon as the bathroom door closed, I turned on Cam, pleased to note that my angry face could still make him squirm. "What aren't you telling me?" I demanded in a whisper. "What aren't you telling *her?*"

It was something about his promotion. He'd accepted it because of me. So he could stay in the city. But why had they offered it? It wasn't just because he'd killed Lorenzo. Whatever it was, it had something to do with Vanessa. Something he didn't want her to know.

Then it hit me, like a knife to the chest, disappointment so sharp I couldn't breathe. "You son of a bitch," I hissed, fury burning through me as if my blood was on fire. "You fucking *recruited* her. You didn't get promoted because you killed Lorenzo and freed all those women. You got promoted because you brought the women over with you—straight into Tower's grasp."

Nine

"How many did you recruit?" Liv demanded in a furious whisper, and it took real effort for me not to lie. I'd been lying for so long now, to everyone but her, that telling the truth was hard. It hurt, like facing myself in the mirror—something else I didn't do much anymore.

"I didn't have any choice," I said finally, so low even I could barely hear myself. "I was under orders to recruit Vanessa, then get her to help me track and recruit as many of the others as we could. All I got from her was a list of names, though." I glanced at the bottle between my hands on the countertop, then made myself look at Liv. Just thinking about what I'd done made me sick to my stomach. "I didn't want to involve her in the rest of it."

"Well, she's involved now, isn't she?" Liv hissed. "She's in it up to here." She held one hand at shoulder level, where Van's binding mark would be. "You could have found a way around those orders, Cameron. I've *seen* you wiggle out of things you're supposed to do."

"Yeah, maybe I could have. And maybe it *wouldn't* have gotten both me and Vanessa hauled up in front of one very pissed-off Jake Tower." Though I highly doubted that. "But if I hadn't recruited them, someone else would have, and their methods might not have been quite as gentle as mine."

"Gentle? Is that a euphemism for coercion and outright lies?" she demanded.

"It's an alternative to gunshot wounds and children sold into the skin trade."

"It's all the same, Cam. You can't serve yourself while you're serving someone else."

"Does that make you feel better?" I snapped, pissed off like only Liv could make me. "Standing there throwing stones from your pretty little glass house? Or is that an ivory tower? I can't tell from my lowly vantage point, but I can tell you *this*—no one down here in the gutter has the luxury of principles like you're flaunting. Some of us had to make compromises to survive."

Her face flushed, her fists clenched in fury. "Don't tell me about compromise—" She bit off whatever she'd been about to say and took a second to visibly regroup. "That poor girl was sold by her father, bound by one monster to another monster, then turned out on the street to bastards who beat and raped her for *four years,* and she didn't even have the ability to voice protests no one would have listened to anyway. Then you swoop in and save her, and for what? So you can turn her over to yet *another* monster?"

Again, I opened my mouth, and again she spoke over me, leaving my protests powerless and unspent. "That girl trusts you." Something dark and intense flashed behind the mask of anger Liv wore. Something I recognized… "She *loves* you, and you…"

"She *what?*" I said, forgetting to whisper. Liv blinked, and her confidence faltered. "Is that what you think?"

"I can see it, Cam. I can see it in the way she looks at you. And that's fine. You and I can't be...us...anymore. So you may as well be with her. But that's not the point. The point is what you—"

"Olivia, will you shut up for a minute?" The toilet flushed down the hall, and I spoke over the anger rapidly flooding her cheeks. "She might love me like a brother. Because I took care of her. But she's not in love with me." I hesitated, trying to decide how much of Van's business I was entitled to share with someone else. Then I forged ahead, hoping the truth really would set me free, at least to some degree. "She might like *you,* though."

Water ran in the bathroom sink, and Olivia gaped at me. "She doesn't like...men?"

I raised one brow, mildly amused. The bathroom door creaked open, and I leaned close to Liv to whisper in her ear. "You were jealous," I taunted. She pushed me away, but before she could deny it, Van emerged from the hall, and Liv's mouth snapped shut with an audible click of teeth.

"Okay, let's get this done." Van slid onto her bar stool and moved her finger over her laptop mouse to wake up the screen. "I have to be somewhere in an hour." Then she glanced up, as if something didn't feel right. "Did I miss something?"

"No," Liv said, before I could even open my mouth. And when I saw her watching me out of the corner of her eye, I watched her back, while Vanessa clacked away, largely ignoring us both.

Armed with Eric Hunter's address, the IP address I'd taken from his computer, the partial social security number from his hospital bill and his bank-account number from the statement Liv had found, it took Van less than ten minutes to find Hunter's middle name.

"Ta-fuckin'-da!" She clapped her hands in triumph. "Richard! His middle name is Richard."

"Great." Liv leaned over Vanessa's shoulder to peer at her screen. "Did you find anything on the other one?"

Van frowned. "The other what?"

"The other middle name. Skilled children are always given two middle names."

"They are?" Van glanced at her, then looked to me for confirmation.

"Yeah. One from their mother and one from their father, but neither tells the other."

"Why wouldn't the parents tell each other their own child's name?"

"Two-person integrity," Liv said. "So only the child himself knows his full name. I got one for my sixteenth birthday and the other for my eighteenth."

"You got your own *name* for your birthday? Twice? How lame." Van frowned. "Then again, I didn't even get the day off for my birthday, so maybe that's not such a bad deal after all."

"It's done for the child's protection," Liv explained, scribbling information from Vanessa's laptop onto a notepad while she spoke, hair tucked behind her ears. She'd done the same thing in college, when we studied, and I never could understand how she could say one thing, but write something else entirely. "Names are power, and children aren't mature enough to handle that power responsibly."

"What do you mean *names are power?*" Van asked, and Olivia frowned at me in question.

"There are some things I can't explain to her." Not without breaching my contract with the Tower syndicate. Liv was right about that much—they don't want us arming anyone with knowledge.

"Stupid binding restrictions…" Liv muttered under her breath. Then she stood, pen in hand, and gestured with it while she spoke. She would have made a scary teacher.

"If you know someone's name—even just part of it—you have a certain measure of power over that person. The power to track, or compel, or bind that person to an oath or contract. Or, in your case, the power to hire someone to do any of that for you. How *much* power you have depends on how much of the name you know. And how much of that name is real."

"What do you mean *real?*" Van looked fascinated, and more than a little frightened, now that she was starting to grasp the scope of her own ignorance. "Do Skilled children use fake names?"

"Not really. But kind of." Liv chewed on the end of her pen, thinking. "Were you always called Van?" she finally asked.

"No, Cam was the first to call me that. I was always just Vanessa to everyone else." Van hesitated, and I could see the light go on behind her eyes. "That's why…" She turned to me, and that light brightened. "That's why you told me never to give anyone my full name."

I nodded, but was contractually prohibited from elaborating.

Liv rolled her eyes at my restrictions, but then she

started filling in the things I couldn't say. "Cam probably gave you your nickname for two reasons. One, out of habit. Skilled children are always given names that can be shortened into at least one nickname. To us, full names sound formal, and a little dangerous."

"Like when your mom gets mad and she shouts your whole name?" Van asked.

Olivia laughed. "Kind of. Only Skilled parents would never do that. Anyway, the second reason Cam gave you a nickname was to help protect you. We're taught to shorten our own names and to use friends' nicknames in public, because using your full or even part of your real name in front of people you don't know is like walking around handing out loaded guns to total strangers. Eventually, someone's going to shoot. Just because *you* don't know your name can be used against you doesn't mean it never will be."

Van's brown eyes were huge. "That's pretty damn scary."

Olivia nodded. "It should be. Kids can't grasp the importance of not shouting their names for the whole world to hear. Hell, most unSkilled adults can't even grasp that. Which only fuels the black-market demand for names." She paused long enough to take a sip from a fresh bottle of water I'd set out on the counter—two beers apiece was plenty for three o'clock in the afternoon, and more than enough to lift Liv onto her soapbox. "But my point is that if you tell a child his full name before he's old enough to keep a secret, he'll inevitably tell someone else. And every little bit of his identity that he lets slip gives a stranger power over him. It works the same way with blood."

But Vanessa already knew that. The first thing I'd

taught her was to destroy every single drop of blood she either shed or spilled. She was a fast learner.

"I'm at a serious disadvantage, having only one middle name, aren't I?" she asked, and Liv nodded. "So…how can I get a second one?"

"Do you know which parent gave you the middle name you have now?"

"Yeah." Van frowned, as if she was thinking. "My dad. It was his sister's name. She died when he was a kid."

I knew exactly what Liv was going to say next, and I'd been itching to tell Vanessa myself—to give her one more way to defend herself—but I couldn't. I wasn't allowed. But hearing Liv say it was almost as sweet. "Then your mother can still give you a middle name."

"She's dead," Van said, and her frown deepened into worry. "Does that mean I'm screwed?"

"Quite the opposite." Liv grinned for the first time since we'd been reunited. "That means you have the power to name yourself. Just…decide on a middle name, and keep it to yourself. Don't write it down, and don't tell anyone."

"It's that easy?"

"Yup," I said, pleased to be able to add something to the conversation. "But think about it carefully—when you decide on a name, it becomes part of your identity, and you can't change your identity, even if you change your name legally. But once you have a second middle name, you'll be that much harder to track or bind." And as long as Tower didn't know she had a second middle name, he couldn't order her to divulge it.

"Awesome." But she looked distinctly less than thrilled. In fact, she looked kind of scared. "So, if you

Skilled people have this much power over names, and blood, and oaths, and contracts, why aren't you ruling the world? I mean, why haven't you guys just kind of… taken over?"

Liv glanced at me, and when I shrugged, she returned Van's somber gaze with one of her own. "What makes you think we haven't?"

Vanessa's eyes went so wide she would have looked funny if she hadn't looked so stunned and terrified.

"Not us personally," I clarified. "Liv and I have no more power over the rest of the world than you do. But the people in political power have a lot more at their disposal than just a lot of money. Why do you think that not one single country's government has been able to officially recognize—and thus claim the ability to regulate—Skills?"

Van blinked. "Because somebody in Washington doesn't want that to happen?"

"More than one somebody," Liv said. "And more than one somebody in Ottawa, and London, and Paris, and Berlin, and Mexico City, and Beijing, and…"

"I think she gets the picture, Liv," I said, before she could recite the seat of government in every country in the world. And before Van's eyes could bug out of her head.

"So it's a conspiracy?" Van whispered, and that time I wasn't even sure if she was talking to us.

"It's a way of life," Liv corrected. "It's a game of misdirection. It's the wolf dressed in lamb's wool, holding a filibuster on the senate floor. You'll hear what he's saying, and you may even see his sharp teeth peeking out of the disguise, but you'll never know what he's trying to distract you from with all the noise and the political controversy."

I scowled. "Well, now that you've scared the shit out of her, how 'bout we return to the job at hand, and let D.C. run itself into the ground without our help?"

Vanessa glanced at her watch, then turned back to her laptop screen, obviously relieved to have something else to think about. "Well, if Mr. Eric Richard Hunter had a second middle name, it's not on anything I've been able to find online."

I rounded the corner of the peninsula to join Liv in looking over Van's shoulder. "What worries me is that his first middle name was so accessible."

"Why does that worry you?" Van asked, cracking the top on her water bottle.

"Because we don't actually use our middle names," Liv said, before I could answer. "That would defeat the entire point of having them. They don't go on our birth certificates, or any other official paperwork. That's like handing out the key to your house every time you fill out a routine form."

"So, wait a minute," I said, going over the facts in my head. "Hunter left large amounts of his own blood in his bathroom, and the power from it is fading faster than the blood itself is drying? He went to a public hospital, and his middle name is on records accessible to the public?"

"Well, maybe not accessible to *most* of the public," Van amended.

"Okay, but my point is that this doesn't sound like the behavior of any Skilled person I ever met."

"Nor does the Skill fading from his blood make one

single bit of sense," Liv added. "I don't know what to think."

"Does that mean you can't track him?"

Liv grabbed her jacket from the back of an armchair and dug into her pocket, presumably for the most recent blood sample. "It still has some pull. Which means we can and will track him. Especially now that you've found his middle name for us." Because for all we knew, the pull from his blood might just lead us to another pile of bloody bandages instead of to the man himself. Which was why we'd stopped to look for his name—our tracking plan B.

"What about the bank account?" I asked, and Van turned back to her computer as I slid Hunter's bank statement across the counter toward her.

"I'll see what I can do, but I'm going to need some privacy. My methods are kind of…supersecret, proprietary knowledge." Van picked up her laptop and gave me a sly smile. "Should I take the bedroom, or would you two like it?"

I laughed, and deferred the matter to Liv, who looked as if she wanted to boil me alive. "You go ahead," she said finally. "We're not going to need it."

Vanessa shrugged and hauled her stuff down the hall to my bedroom, the only other room in the apartment, except for the bathroom. I took my water bottle to the couch and sat, amused when Olivia just stood in the middle of the room, glancing between the couch and the bar stools. "I promise I won't bite," I said, gesturing at the two unoccupied couch cushions.

She considered for a second, then dropped onto the opposite end of the couch. "If memory serves, you're all bark anyway."

"I think we both know better than that. And if *my* memory serves, I have a couple of bite marks that prove you're not, either."

Liv laughed, and my mission in life became making that happen again. When she laughed, she looked like the Olivia I'd known, and if I closed my eyes and listened closely, I could almost pretend the past six years had never happened. I could pretend she might not hate me for signing my life over to a man and an organization she detested. An organization we *both* detested, if I were being completely honest—which I couldn't do aloud.

"Can I see your tattoo?" I asked, and her smile died a sudden, brutal death. "On your back. You don't have to take anything off," I clarified. What had she thought I meant? "You don't have a mark from Anne and the girls, right? I thought that was a paper binding."

"It is. Blood bound and name bound, but on paper. Thank goodness." She relaxed a little, but I couldn't forget the severity of her original reaction. What did it mean? Why was she so touchy on the subject of marks?

And then the guarded look in her eyes gave me sudden insight: she had another mark somewhere— one she clearly didn't want anyone else to know about. It was probably a dead mark—the statement tattooed on her back clearly stated her position on the subject of ownership—but I couldn't help wondering who she'd been bound to. What she'd been bound to do—or not to do?

Instead of answering the questions I hadn't asked, she twisted away from me and folded one leg beneath herself on the couch. Then she slowly swept her long hair over one shoulder, baring the small black script echoing the neckline of her shirt, between her shoulder blades.

And there it was. *Cedo nulli*. The script taunted me. It said that, even if she'd been bound before, she'd gotten out of it with her principles intact. She answered to no one.

Well, no one but the women she'd sworn to help, and none of them would ever make her do what I'd had to do for Tower and the syndicate.

I reached out without thinking, drawn by the pull of the words and the purity of soul they represented, and traced the first letter with my finger. Liv's whole body tensed. She pulled away from my touch, and the ever-present ache in my chest widened into a chasm I couldn't climb out of. My sigh was an exhale of pain.

But then she relaxed a little—an obvious effort for her—and leaned back until her skin touched my finger again, at the base of the calligraphic *C*. I held my breath as I traced the rest of the letters, treasuring the warmth of her skin. I don't know why she let me touch her this time, when she'd been pushing me away for years, but I wasn't going to question it.

I'd just finished the last letter—acutely aware that once I'd started breathing again, her breathing synced with mine—when my bedroom door opened and Vanessa clomped down the hall toward us with her backpack over her shoulder, equipment already stowed.

"Any luck?" I asked, as Liv swept her hair back over her shoulder to cover the words, as if she had never let me touch them.

"I'm sorry, Cam, but I can't help you." Vanessa walked past the kitchen on her way to the door, and

Liv was up in an instant. She grabbed Van's arm and pulled her to a stop before I could get between them.

"What do you mean? Why not?"

Van tugged free from Liv's grip, and I pulled Olivia back, in case she was tempted to reach out again. Vanessa didn't like uninvited touches.

"Let her go," I said, recognizing the frustration and fear cycling in a never-ending loop beneath Van's sudden mask of disinterest. "If she says she can't help, she can't help."

Liv whirled on me, confused and angry. "She found the account! You know she did. She knows who hired Hunter to kill Anne's husband, but she's not telling. That is in *no way* okay with me."

"I'm sorry." Vanessa backed toward the door, the strap of her bag clenched in a white-knuckle grip. "I just can't." She was upset—I could see that much. She liked Liv, probably because of what she'd told Van that I couldn't. They could have been friends, if not for that damned Tower binding.

Liv was right. No one bound to a syndicate could ever really have friends.

She reached for Van again, and again I pulled her back, and Van slipped out of the apartment and into the hall. When I wouldn't let Liv go, she spun into a right hook that caught me square on the jaw.

"Damn it, Olivia!" I rubbed my face with one hand and held her arm in the other, forced to tighten my grip until it probably bruised. "Just let her go."

"She knows who paid him!"

"That's exactly why she can't tell you!" I shouted, hoping—*wishing*—that she would just calm down long enough to draw the obvious conclusion, a fact I wasn't allowed to outright divulge. "I can't tell you this, Liv. You're going to have to think it through for yourself."

And finally she stopped struggling, and her arm went limp in my hand. "It was there all along, and we didn't see it." She swallowed thickly, and suddenly looked sick to her stomach. "It was Tower. Jake Tower hired Hunter to kill Anne's husband."

Ten

"Tower." Stunned, I sank onto Cam's couch and closed my eyes. But that didn't make it any less true. "Are you sure?"

Cam sat next to me. "If that money had come from anywhere else in the world, she'd tell us. But she can't say anything that might incriminate the syndicate, so it has to be from one of Tower's accounts."

I frowned at him, confused. "Are you allowed to say that?"

Cam shrugged. "Now that you've already guessed, I'm not divulging incriminating evidence."

"Is she going to get into trouble for this?" I felt sick, knowing I might have made things worse for Van, after everything she'd already been through.

"Not unless someone asks her a direct question. And that can't happen unless someone finds out what she was doing here. So, obviously, don't tell anyone."

I nodded absently, but my brain had already moved on. "Why the hell would Jake Tower want to kill Anne's husband? I can't imagine him being tangled up with the syndicate without her knowing about it." And if she'd known about it, surely she would have told us—not telling us would only make it harder for us to find Shen's killer.

"It's probably not actually Tower," Cam pointed out. "It could be anyone with access to a syndicate bank account."

But that wasn't really true. "It'd have to be someone high up enough to have access to the account, *and* the clout to spend funds autonomously. Maybe even anonymously, right?" I had no personal knowledge about the Tower syndicate, but I knew how Cavazos ran his operation, and I was willing to bet my unmarked left arm that their day-to-day operations had a lot in common. "I'm guessing that's no more than a handful of people, right?"

Cam nodded, looking distinctly uncomfortable, and I took that to mean we were getting close to a line he couldn't cross.

"I'm also guessing you can't tell me who those people are, can you?"

"No," he said, and my sigh sounded almost as heavy as it felt. "But I swear, Liv, I had no idea the syndicate was involved until Van came out of the bedroom."

I believed him. I don't know *why* I believed him; he'd lie to protect the syndicate if the situation required it. But when I looked into his eyes, I believed him, and I felt a ghost of his touch on my back, tracing the words I wanted so desperately to be true. For both of us.

"Okay. I can get those names on my own." Most of them, anyway. I wasn't without resources. "But first we need to update Anne. And she needs to know about your binding, Cam."

"I know." He took my hand and pulled me closer,

and I let him, against my better judgment. "Maybe you should let me talk to her. Alone."

"Why?" I didn't even bother screening suspicion from my voice. I hated knowing that even though he still loved me—I had no doubt about that—I couldn't trust him. As long as he bore a live mark, *no one* would be able to fully trust him. Not even the syndicate. They may have had his service and obedience, but they didn't have his heart—maybe they never had—and that meant he would use whatever loopholes he found.

But I still couldn't trust him.

Cam looked up at me from the couch, and I let him pull me forward until I stood between his thighs, my knees brushing the front of the couch cushion. "Olivia, if you go up against the Tower syndicate, I can't help you. And if Anne asks you to, you'll have to do it. So it seems to me that the only way to avoid being asked to go up against the syndicate is to let me deal with Anne."

I pushed aside the ache I got every time he touched me—the overwhelming urge to lean into his touch, rather than pull away from it—and made myself focus on his words. Because they made sense—up to a point. "Cam, I can't avoid Anne. Even if she weren't a friend, I'm *working* for her." And unease was already crawling beneath my skin—the very beginnings of resistance pain—because I wasn't actively pursuing her husband's killer in that moment. "But she's not going to ask me to go up against Jake Tower. She won't do anything to put her daughter in danger, and going after Tower would do just that."

"She's in mourning, Liv. You can't expect her to react rationally. And you'll be bound to whatever suicidal, impulsive revenge she asks for." He frowned, and

I recognized the stubborn set of his jawline. "I can't let you put yourself in that kind of danger."

I stepped out of his reach, crossing both arms over my chest. "That's not up to you."

"I'm just trying to protect you, Liv." He frowned up at me from the couch, elbows resting on his knees.

"I don't need your protection. But I could use your help. And for the record, you're not giving Anne enough credit—I think she's holding things together pretty well. Besides, I owe her an update, and she deserves to hear the facts in person."

Cam gave in with a heavy exhale and a single nod. "Six years has only made you more stubborn."

But he was wrong about that. The past six years had also made me faster, meaner and less willing to believe in the inherent goodness of any species that could include Jake Tower and Ruben Cavazos among its numbers.

"I take it this little emergency meeting means you haven't found him yet." Anne's hand shook as she spooned sugar into her coffee, and I wondered if she'd had any sleep at all in the twenty hours since her husband was murdered.

Cam and I had not.

"Not yet. But we know where he lives, we have most of his name, and we found a fresher sample of his blood." And we had tested the pull of Hunter's energy signature using both his blood and his name on the way to meet Anne. Both were very strong signals, leading deeper into the west side. Hunter was still alive, and he almost certainly knew someone was after him. Yet he hadn't left the city.

The fact that he'd stayed made me nervous, and it was one of the biggest factors in our decision to update—and question—Anne before going after Hunter again.

Anne sipped from her mug and watched us from across the table, oblivious to the Friday-night dinner crowd just starting to filter in at the end of the nine-to-five shift. "So what's the problem?"

I glanced at Cam to see if he wanted to take the lead—he was the one bound to Tower, after all—but he gestured for me to go ahead.

"Anne, was Shen involved with the Tower syndicate?" I whispered, leaning across the table to make sure we wouldn't be overheard. "In any way at all?"

She choked on her coffee. "No," Anne croaked, blotting her mouth with a paper napkin. "Absolutely not."

"Are you sure?" Cam asked. "If he was, he might not have been allowed to tell you. Did you ever see him with anyone who had a chain link tattooed on his arm. Or her arm?"

Anne leaned closer, brows drawn low over eyes shining even greener than usual with exhaustion. "Living in the suburbs doesn't make me an idiot. I know Tower's insignia, and I would know if my husband were working for him. Or meeting with someone who worked for him."

Cam gave her an awkward little grin, obviously trying to soften the coming blow. "You might not." He slid his right hand beneath his left sleeve, as if he had an itch to scratch. "I'm a third-tier initiate." He lifted the hem of his sleeve quickly and subtly, just long enough for her to get a peek at his marks, then let the material fall.

Anne set her coffee down carefully, deliberately, but she couldn't hide the tension in her grip. "You work for Tower." It wasn't a question. It was a stunned statement of new facts, spoken to try to convince herself of the reality.

I knew exactly how she felt.

"He's being modest," I said, unable to keep the bitter edge out of my voice. "He's actually Jake Tower's top Tracker. Even got a step promotion last year. Isn't that *swell?*"

Cam's jaw tightened, but just because he didn't like the truth didn't make it not true.

Anne focused on him with an iron glare, and I realized she was about to make me proud. "I'm going to forgo the whole 'what the hell were you thinking?' speech in favor of something even more obvious," she snapped in a harsh whisper. "You should have told me that up front. I *never* would have involved you in this if I'd known!"

"That's why I didn't tell you," he said, with a meaningful glance at me. "I wanted to help."

Anne took a deep breath and another sip from her mug. "So, what does this mean? Why are you asking about Shen in relation to Tower? You think someone killed him because they thought he was…one of you?" she asked, with a censuring glance at Cam.

"Not exactly…" he mumbled, and I exhaled slowly.

"Anne, someone in the Tower syndicate paid to have your husband killed."

In the silence that followed, the ambient restaurant noise seemed to close in on us, amplifying Anne's shock and denial, Cam's obvious confliction, and my own kaleidoscope of anger, fear and dread.

"Why?" she said, when she'd recovered the ability to speak. "Why would they want Shen dead?"

"I don't know." And I wasn't sure I *wanted* to know. "Are you sure he never had any business with the organization? Could he have been working with or for someone you didn't know about?"

Red hair tumbled over her shoulder as Anne shook her head slowly, clearly giving it serious thought. "We both worked from home. We shared an office. There's no way he could have kept something like that from me. No way he *would* have."

"Then I don't know," I repeated. "Cam, any insight? Why might your brothers in crime have a suburban software engineer capped?"

He scowled at me, but didn't even try to deny the illegal nature of most of his employer's business. "It could have been anything. To stop him from working on whatever he was working on. Or, if they wanted him to do something and he refused, this could have been a reprisal. It could even have been intended to scare someone else he worked with into falling into line. Or it could be completely unrelated to his job. Maybe he saw something he shouldn't have. Maybe he borrowed money he couldn't pay back. But based on the amount of money someone put out for this, and the fact that they hired someone outside of the organization, I'm guessing this was both personal and important to someone pretty high up. And that's all I can say. But for the record, it's also all I know." *This time.*

He didn't say that last part, but we all heard it.

"This doesn't make any sense." Anne still looked so stunned I was surprised she could form complete sentences. "He didn't owe any money. We're not wealthy, but our savings are intact. And he didn't see anything unusual—he would have told me if he had." I started to argue that he might not have, to keep her safe, but she amended her own thought before I could. "Or maybe he wouldn't have told me, but I would have known if he was upset about something. But everything was *fine*." Anne closed her eyes and visibly paled. Her hands shook as she pushed straight red hair back from her face.

"What's wrong?" I asked, though the answers seemed too numerous and obvious to be stated.

"I just realized that Hadley could have been home when it happened. Any other Thursday night, she *would* have been. She would have seen him die. Or worse."

"What was unusual about yesterday?" Cam asked, and I leaned closer to listen. Any variation in their normal routine could hint at why Shen was killed.

Anne picked at the fingernails of her left hand. "It was Hadley's best friend's birthday. I dropped her off at the party on my way to the gym. Any other night of the week, we all three would have been home. Any other Thursday, Shen and Hadley would have been home together."

I laid my hand over hers on the table. "Okay, I think you should focus on the fact that she *wasn't* home. Neither of you were. Focus on that and be grateful. And leave the rest of it to us."

"You're still going to…finish this?" Anne's eyes shined with feverish hope. Dark desperation.

"We can—and will—still go after Hunter," Cam said. "He's not a member of the syndicate, so I have no official conflict of interest. But that's as far as I can go. I can't take any action against the organization, and I can't know for sure that either of you are going to, or I'd be obligated to stop you. So please take this seriously—do *not* move against Tower." He turned to me then, as somber as I'd ever seen him. "And if you choose to ignore that warning, as I'm fully aware that you will, do *not* discuss it in front of me. Wait until I'm gone."

"We're not moving against Tower," Anne insisted. "That would be suicide. Just get Hunter—that's all I have any right to ask."

"Wait…" I turned to Cam, choosing not to point out that Anne didn't actually have the right to ask for Hunter's life, either—she was neither judge nor jury. "How do you know Hunter isn't syndicate?" Surely Cam didn't personally know everyone bearing Tower's mark.

"An initiate wouldn't have been paid like that—he would just have been ordered to make the kill. He might have gotten a bonus after the fact, if he really rocked the execution, but it wouldn't have been even half what Hunter got paid. Someone hired an independent to keep this from being traced back to the syndicate."

"But we traced it back to you guys pretty easily," I pointed out.

"No, *Van* traced it back to Tower. Because she works on the business side of things and is already familiar with the accounts. An outsider would have had a bitch of a time finding the source of that money, I'd bet you anything."

"Okay, I think the best thing for you to do is to go back home and be with your daughter. And forget about the Tower syndicate," I said to Anne, pushing my own mug toward the middle of the table while Cam dropped a twenty-dollar bill next to his. "We'll call you when it's done."

Anne nodded, still gripping her mug.

I glanced back at her from the front of the restaurant as Cam pulled open the door. She still sat there, staring at the table. Shaking. Gone was the steel-spined widow who'd walked into my office demanding justice. Things had changed. She was in over her head.

And so were we.

Eleven

"Why would he stay?" I asked, as Cam flicked on his left blinker. At the moment, the pull of Hunter's name was stronger than the pull from his blood, so I was letting him take the lead in tracking, so long as his path didn't contradict the pull I felt. And so far, it hadn't.

"If he were an initiate, I'd say he's being shielded—Tower put the word out that he's not to be touched. Or maybe he put Hunter in a safe house. But he's not a member, and I would have heard about him being shielded. Thanks to Nick, the organization knows you and I are working together, and that we're looking for Hunter. If the syndicate had any problem with us killing him, they'd have already stopped us."

We were still on the west side, but headed east now. *Huh*. Hunter was on the move.

"So, what, they don't care if we kill him, because then they don't have to drop the second half of his payment?"

"Maybe." Cam shrugged and took another left, and I verified our direction privately with another feel of the stiffening bandage in my pocket. "Also, whoever hired him is probably happy to have us clean up loose ends for him."

I would have been much more comfortable if those loose ends weren't winding through the center of Jake Tower's territory. The blood pull of Hunter's energy signature was very strong now, and based on the confidence with which Cam navigated the streets, the name pull was even stronger. Which didn't make much sense. Even if he'd died in the three hours since we'd found blood in his apartment, the blood pull should have been just as strong.

"Do you know this neighborhood?" I asked, as Cam slowed the car to a crawl and the setting sun blinded me in the side view mirror. We were close now. Close enough that we'd overshoot it if we weren't careful.

"Yeah, and so do you. We were here this afternoon."

We were? I sat straighter, glancing around for something I recognized, but saw only a narrow backstreet— an urban alley bordered by rear garage entrances and tiny backyards fenced with chain link. "This doesn't look familiar."

"The back of his building's about half a mile ahead. We're coming at it from another direction. I know this way better."

His sudden glance out the driver's side window told me there was something he wasn't saying. So, of course, I asked. "Why are you familiar with a residential neighborhood backstreet, when you live in an apartment on the main drag?"

"I used to know a girl who lived in that house." He pointed to a small, run-down, white-sided house with a big dog fenced into a small yard. "But I don't think she lives there anymore."

I swallowed the bitter taste on the back of my tongue at the thought of him with someone else. It was inevitable. Six years is a long time, and Cam...he wore it very, very well. Of course other women would want him.

"Was she syndicate?" I asked, and he glanced at me with a look I couldn't quite interpret. Was he surprised that I'd ask? Or that I cared? Or that I thought he might go out with someone outside of the organization? Or the opposite?

"No. I don't...socialize with coworkers. That's too complicated. And dangerous."

"You'd give up on a relationship because it's dangerous?" Maybe he *would* understand why I'd left...

But he mistook my hope for a criticism.

"Not a relationship," he clarified. "Sex. No momentary pleasure is worth the risk that she might be looking to sleep her way up the tiers. Or that she might think I am. Or that she may be bound to someone who outranks me, but she's unhappy with his performance. And it's even worse if *she* outranks *me,* because then I'm tiptoeing through a minefield where orders and requests get confused."

My stomach churned. "It sounds like you've learned through experience."

"Six years is a long time." He turned left onto one of the major streets, then met my gaze. "Are you jealous?"

"No," I answered too fast.

"You never used to lie to me."

Speaking of minefields... I exhaled slowly and made myself hold his gaze. "I shouldn't have asked. It doesn't matter whether or not I'm jealous. Do I like thinking about you with other women? Of course not—"

"Then why'd you ask?"

"Because..." *I'm an idiot. A masochist.* "I don't know why I asked."

"I do." He exhaled, then shifted into Park right there in the street, sitting idle at a stoplight. "Would it help to know that I tracked down and beat the shit out of the asshole you moved in with a couple of years ago? The one who stole your car."

I felt my jaw drop open, but words wouldn't come. I could only gape at him. "Are you serious?" I asked at last and he nodded solemnly. "Over a *car?*"

He blinked, but his gaze held mine captive. "It had nothing to do with the car, Liv."

"Did you... Is he...?"

"He lived." Cam shifted into Drive again when the light changed and we rolled through the intersection. "But I don't think he'll be looking either of us up again anytime soon."

"I can beat up my own exes, thank you."

He laughed. "Not like I can."

"That's not the point."

"You're right." We cruised slowly past two more buildings, headed for the next traffic light. "The point is that I was jealous, just like you were jealous. And *you* were jealous because you still want me."

"No..." I said through clenched teeth. "The point is that we have a job to do, and that job has nothing to do with who either of us has slept with or pounded on since we broke up."

"We didn't break up, Liv. You ran out on me, right before..." He stopped, staring out the windshield at the city as we rolled through it slowly enough to annoy the cars trapped behind us.

"I'm sorry." I glanced at him, but his gaze never left the road. "I don't think I've actually said that yet, but I'm sorry for…the way it happened. But none of that matters anymore. What matters is that for some reason, Eric Richard Hunter went home again, and we need to make sure he never leaves."

I could see his building now, and for a second, I worried that I might be tracking the same cold trail that had led me there earlier—the pull of his spilled blood. But then I remembered that I'd destroyed what he left. And that the name pull Cam was tracking could only lead to the man himself.

Cam parked in the unlit lot behind Hunter's building. As the engine cooled and ticked, he watched me in the last dying rays of light, painting his dashboard red. "Sorry isn't good enough."

"What?" I frowned, trying to ignore the discomfort buzzing beneath my skin, now that we were so close to the goal, yet not actively pursuing it. "Good enough for what?"

"Not good enough for me. Not good enough for us. For what we still have, even if you're too damn stubborn to admit it. You owe us better than a half-assed apology, six years too late."

"I owe you…?" My words expired on a cloud of disbelief.

"No, you owe *us*."

Itching to get going, I pulled my 9mm from the holster and released the clip to check it, though I already knew it was full. "There is no us, Cam. Not anymore."

"The hell there isn't." He twisted in his seat to face me. "You can keep saying that if you want. You might even convince Anne. But you're not going to convince me, and you're sure as hell not going to convince your-self. You've had years to forget about me and move on, but you haven't done it."

"Yes, I…"

"No, you haven't!" he thundered. His anger seemed to echo in the confines of the car, and that time, I didn't bother arguing. "If you had, this wouldn't be so hard for you. And I can see that it's hard. I don't know why you're still trying to push me away, but it obviously isn't because you want to."

My next breath hurt. It ached in my lungs, as if my heart was bruised. "You're right," I admitted, but the truth didn't set me free. It felt like a whole new set of chains. "This isn't how I want it, but this is how it has to be."

"Why?" he demanded. "Why are you doing this? I need to know, Liv. You owe me that much."

He was right. Hiding what I knew when I could just walk away from him was one thing, but now that we were stuck together? Keeping my secrets—this one, anyway—was too much for us both. "Fine. But it's a little complicated, and we need to move on Hunter now." Before the buzzing beneath my skin ushered in full-scale resistance pain. Before Hunter stepped through a shadow and we lost his trail again.

"You swear?" Cam wasn't happy, but was obviously willing to delay full satisfaction if he had my word.

"On my life. When this is over, I'll explain why I left. Why I had to."

"Fine. For now. But don't think you can just disap-pear on me again. I know how to find you, and there's nothing stopping me from showing up everywhere you go, until you tell me what I want to know."

Actually, Cavazos would have been happy to stop Cam from showing up everywhere I went. But that was one secret I couldn't give up. What little self-respect I still had would bleed into humiliation if Cam found out I was bound to Ruben. I didn't want him to know what I'd agreed to. I didn't want him to know about the things I couldn't say no to, or how much worse it would be if—*when*—I couldn't fulfill my contract.

I didn't want him to know that the words on my back were just that: words. An ideal I'd failed to live up to.

"Are you ready?" I asked, one hand on the door handle. He nodded stiffly, and I pushed the door open and stepped into the parking lot. It wasn't fully dark yet, which meant my gun would have to stay holstered for the moment. People on the west side almost never spoke to the police, but their silence wasn't my license for carelessness.

Cam followed me across the lot and through the rear door, which opened into the opposite end of the long, dark hallway we'd entered from the front earlier. After a second to check the pull from Hunter's blood, I pointed to the rear staircase with my brows raised in question. Cam nodded, confirming that the target's name was pulling him upstairs, too.

We took the steps quickly and quietly, and I let him lead. This was his neighborhood and the residents would be less likely to interfere with or report us if they recognized him. But both the stairs and the hallway were deserted, either because it was dinnertime, or because the occupants sensed that something was going down. TV applause and canned laughter rang out from behind some of the doors, and muffled conversation from others, but no one came out to investigate our soft footsteps.

On either side of Hunter's door, we drew our guns, and I attached the silencer Cam had lent me. A seam of light showed around three sides of the frame—it was still broken from when Cam had kicked it in. I heard movement from inside. A scrape of something against the floor. Light footsteps. A quiet curse.

Hunter was alone, and he wasn't happy.

I lifted one brow at Cam, and he nodded. So I knocked on the door frame.

Silence from inside. Then two more footsteps, and the floor creaked. I could practically hear his heart beating. His brain racing. Should he answer? Or just wait? Would he have time to go out the fire escape? Or simply step into a shadow and disappear?

Cam nodded, and I nudged the door open with one foot while he knelt in the open doorway, below typical firing height, gun aimed and ready. He held that pose for a single breath, then rose smoothly to his feet.

I peeked into the apartment. The living room was empty. But Hunter was still in there. I could feel the pull of his blood, stronger than ever. Yet somehow *different* than it had felt before.

Cam stepped inside and I followed him, then pushed the door closed. Or, as close to closed as I could get it, because of the broken door frame. I checked the right half of the room while he checked the left, silently clearing the possible hiding places and turning on lights to banish the shadows one by one. You can never be too careful about shadows when tracking a Traveler.

The living room and kitchen were both clear, the only remaining shadows too small for a man to fit through. The bathroom was open, the shower curtain pulled to one side to reveal the empty tub. That only left the bedroom. But surely Hunter wasn't in there. Why *would* he be, when a Traveler can leave a room just by stepping into a shadow?

Yet his blood pulled me toward the closed bedroom door.

I tossed my head toward the door and gave Cam a questioning look. He closed his eyes for a second, meditating on Hunter's full name, then nodded. Every tracking instinct we had said that, in apparent defiance of logic, Hunter was still in his room.

Possible explanations ran through my head while fear and doubt prickled my skin. Was this a trap? Had Tower found out about my mark and hired Hunter to kill me? If so, this would be the easiest hit in history—I'd actually tracked the man contracted to shoot me.

And what about Cam? Did Tower consider him a traitor? Was he on the chopping block, too?

Or was there a simpler explanation for why a Traveler would stay in an apartment with two people intent on killing him? Was his bedroom somehow devoid of shadows? Was he too weak from blood loss to travel? Could that have something to do with why the level of Skill in his blood had dropped between the sample Anne had provided and the one I'd found in his bathroom?

We took positions on either side of the bedroom door, and again, I knocked on the frame. "Eric, come on out," I said.

Harsh laughter from the other side of the door, followed by a man's voice. "They sent a girl. I'm not sure if that's insult to injury, or a gift from above."

I glanced at Cam. Hunter thought I was alone, which gave us the element of surprise. I chose to ignore his misogynistic underestimation of my abilities, but who were the "they," who'd supposedly sent me? "I just want to ask you a couple of questions."

Yes, I was lying. But considering I was about to commit vigilante murder, a half-truth felt pretty insignificant.

"Yeah, right." Hunter laughed again, but this time sarcasm exposed his nerves. "Because you guys are known for asking questions first."

You guys? I mouthed to Cam. Who did he think I was?

Cam pushed up his left sleeve and tapped the chain links on his upper bicep.

Oh, shit. Hunter thought the Tower syndicate had sent someone to kill him. But why? Had he assumed that our break-in earlier meant the syndicate would rather kill him than pay him? Or had he actually given Tower a reason to come after him?

Was he running his mouth? Demanding more money? Threatening to turn state's witness?

"So you know why I'm here?" I said, playing along, hoping for more information.

"Unless they're sending singing telegrams now instead of mercenaries—in which case you should start warming up—I'm gonna have to assume you're here to kill me."

Funny. We might have been friends, if he weren't a hired killer. But then, considering I was standing outside his door with a loaded gun, maybe we had more than sarcasm in common.

"Look, I know you got your orders, and I know I

fucked this up. But how 'bout, instead of killing me, you take him a message from me instead?"

Cam and I shared a look of mild surprise. The killer had messed up? "And what would that message be?" I called through the door.

"Tell him that if he kills me, he's just going to have to hire someone else to clean things up. Or he can let me fix my own mistake—at no additional charge, of course."

The man had balls—I had to give him that. But if I were under orders to kill him—and I was—going back to beg for mercy on his behalf wouldn't even be a possibility. I'd be physically incapable of leaving until I'd done my best to kill him. Did Hunter really not know that, or was he speaking from desperation?

Cam looked as puzzled as I was.

"Why the hell should I put my ass on the line for you?" I asked.

"Because it wasn't my fault. I didn't do the recon," Hunter insisted. "*Your* guy did that. How was I supposed to know she wasn't going to be there?"

She?

With that, my mental fog lifted, revealing the truth in stark, devastating clarity. Hunter wasn't after Shen. He was after Annika. He thought Tower wanted him dead because he'd missed his target. Which might well be the case—was that why the syndicate seemed content to let us go after Hunter? Because we were saving them the trouble?

"You should have known exactly who was in the house before you went in," I said, the facts and implications still tumbling around in my head.

"Fuck you, I did my job," Hunter snapped. "I'm not

gonna pay for someone else's mistake. You come in here, and you won't go back out."

I tossed my head toward the door. Cam stood and kicked it.

Wood splintered—as usual, the door frame was weaker than the lock—and Cam lurched out of the line of fire as the door swung open. A bullet split the air between us and I dropped into a squat, peeking carefully around the door frame. A suitcase lay open on the bed, already too full to close. Hunter was going to run.

So why was he still there?

"Okay," I said, scanning what I could see of the bedroom for any sign of movement. "You have a valid point. Why should you be held responsible for someone else's screwup?"

I waited out the quiet that followed; I couldn't pinpoint his location until he moved or spoke. And finally, he gave in to the urge to fill the silence—most people can't stand a vacuum.

"Especially when I'm offering to repair the damage for free," he said, and my gaze found the narrow space between the bed and the dresser, just a few feet away from the window and the fire escape he could have climbed down—if the window weren't obviously painted shut, a fire-code violation he was probably kicking himself for now.

Except that a Traveler shouldn't be bothered by a window that won't open.

The sun was down and Hunter's bedroom faced an alley. Very little light shone through his window, and the room was lit only by a single dim bulb overhead. There were small shadows everywhere, and the floor beneath his bed should have been an endless, gaping void for a Traveler. He should have been able to roll into the darkness and roll out of another shadow somewhere else. Anywhere else he wanted to be, depending on how strong his Skill was.

So why the hell was Hunter cowering on the floor with nothing but a couple of mattresses between him and the barrel of my gun?

I was missing something. I had to be.

Careful not to compromise my aim, I slid one hand into my pocket. I took a silent breath, touching the stiff bandage in my pocket, and concentrated on the pull of Hunter's blood. Every single drop of it called to me, drawing me like a magnet as long as I touched the sample in my pocket. The closer I got to him, the stronger the attraction.

And suddenly I realized what was wrong. I wasn't the one missing something; *he* was. Hunter's blood— the part still flowing in his veins—had no power at all. Somehow, incredibly, he was completely without Skill, though he'd been a Traveler only hours before. The blood sample in my pocket proved that, as did the one Anne had brought.

"So what's the plan, Eric?" I let go of the bandage and aimed with both hands again, still squatting. "You were just going to…what? Get on a bus?"

Cam raised one eyebrow at me in question, but I couldn't explain about Hunter's mysteriously disappearing Skill. Not even if I wanted to—it made no sense.

"That was the plan."

"So which is it going to be? Run, or fix what you messed up?"

"Does that mean you'll deliver my message?"

I pretended to think about that for a moment. "Fortunately for you, I like your idea. And I really like the part where I get to be the bearer of good news. So why don't you come out and tell me who really screwed the pooch. That way you can go work on damage control and I can go make a very powerful man smile."

A second or two of silence passed while he thought about my offer, and I held my breath, waiting. Surely he wasn't stupid enough to fall for that my karma wasn't that good.

"Aren't you under orders to kill me?" he asked at last, and I was almost relieved. If he'd given in that easily, I'd have assumed it was a trick. "That means you don't have any choice, right?"

"Smart man," I said, hoping he was unfamiliar with verbal irony. "But actually, I was ordered to kill the one responsible for the fuckup. If that turns out not to be you, then killing you would put me in breach of my contract, wouldn't it?"

Another moment of silence, and I measured his ignorance with each second that passed. With each mistake I could tick off on mental fingers. He'd left viable blood in the trash can He'd gone to a civilian hospital. He'd put his real middle name on government documents. He'd trapped himself in his bedroom rather than escaping into the shadows. These were not the actions of a man who understood my world.

"Yeah, I guess it would. But I'm gonna need some kind of reassurance. A guarantee."

"Such as...?" I shot Cam a questioning glance, but he looked even more confused than I felt—he didn't know about the powerless pull of Hunter's blood yet.

"Your word. If you promise you won't kill me, you'll be bound to that, right?"

Was that a trap? Was he using something he knew to be false to test my honesty? Or was he really that ignorant? The blood in the trash can suggested the latter, but I flavored my lie with a little truth, just in case.

"That's not the only way to bind someone." And unless the person swearing was a Binder it was about as reliable as crossing your fingers and making a wish. "But yes, a verbal oath is certainly one kind of binding."

"Swear, then," he said, too quickly to be anything but eager impulse. Which meant he believed it, right? "Swear you're not going to kill me, and I'll come out."

I glanced at Cam for an opinion. He shrugged, leaving it up to me, but looked far from convinced. But the standoff couldn't last forever. My thighs were on fire from squatting, and my arms were already aching, which would soon compromise my aim. Did Hunter know that? Was he counting on it? Or was he just trying to get out of this alive?

Cover me? I mouthed to Cam, and he nodded, a silent vow of ironclad support. "Okay, I swear," I called into the bedroom. "You can come out now."

"Be more specific," Hunter insisted, and I had to admit he wasn't a *total* moron. "Swear you're not going to shoot me. Or kill me in any other way," he amended.

I rolled my eyes. "Fine. I swear I will in no way harm you. Now grow some balls and stand the hell up. If I have to track someone else down tonight, I'd like to get going."

That last bit did it—that touch of authentic weariness and impatience convinced him I had no more time to waste on him. Hunter stood slowly, and I stood with him, each of us still aiming at the other.

"Put the gun down, Eric," I said. Cam waited on the opposite side of the door, gun pointed at the ground, a fraction of a second from taking the kill shot. But he wouldn't do it while Hunter still had me in his sights.

"You first." Hunter had a wide stance and a steady, two-handed grip on a Beretta 9mm, and I couldn't tell whether or not the safety was engaged. But I was betting it wasn't. He may not know how to destroy blood or walk through shadows, but he knew his way around a gun.

"I can't shoot," I insisted. "I just swore I wouldn't."

"Then you shouldn't mind putting the gun down."

Too late it occurred to me that I should have made him swear the same oath. If he believed it would work on me, he'd believe it would work on him, too, right? Had I just been played?

Shit. If I didn't lower my gun, he'd know I wasn't bound, and he'd shoot me. But if I lowered my gun, he'd shoot me anyway.

Sometimes having no good choices brings things into crisp, clear focus.

I lurched to one side and squeezed the trigger. The gun *thwupped* loudly and the recoil threw my arms up, because I was already in motion. I stumbled. Blood sprayed from Hunter's right shoulder. His gun flashed in the dim room. Something slammed into my left arm, throwing me off balance again. My knees crashed into the ground.

Cam's silencer *thwupped* from behind me. Hunter fell against the wall at his back, then slid to sit on the floor, gurgling with each breath. A thick trail of blood led up the wall behind him.

Cam stepped over me and fired twice more. Hunter's gurgling stopped.

"Damn it!" I twisted to sit on the floor, but the impact ache in my knees was still vicious as I glared up at Cam. "You couldn't let him make a dying confession? I had more questions for him!"

Cam thumbed the safety, then dropped the gun, silencer and all, into his custom holster. "I just saved your ass. You're welcome."

"Thanks." I flicked the safety on my own pistol, then tried to unscrew the silencer, but stopped at the sudden sharp, hot pain in my left arm. "But he wasn't after Shen, he was after Anne, and we need to know why." I tried to push myself to my feet, but my left arm was reluctant to move. In fact, my fingers were oddly numb. But the rest of me felt fine. Better than ever in fact. With Hunter dead, the geas from Anne was gone, and I was once more free from compulsion.

"Well, we're not going to find out from him. But on the upside, you're still breathing." Cam knelt next to me and gently peeled my fingers from the gun, then set it to the side.

"If Tower—or whoever—sent one man after her, he'll send another," I insisted. We'd have to hide her somewhere. Would Cam even be able to help me protect her, or would that mean breaching his contract to Tower? Should I let him help me, even if he could? If he knew where she was, he could be forced to tell Tower. Why the hell would Jake Tower want Anne dead, anyway?

"I know. And as soon as we get you taken care of, we'll call and warn her. But right now, I need you to stand up and try not to move your arm."

I frowned, irritated by his lack of concern. "Cam, your boss is trying to kill one of my best friends." Or former best friends. Or whatever. "Couldn't you act like that bothers you, just a little bit?"

Cam blinked at me, blatant surprise brightening his eyes. "Of course it bothers me. But right now, I'm a little more worried about *this*." He lifted my left arm by my bent elbow, and pain shot through my bicep. When I looked down, I was surprised to see blood staining my shirt and welling through a hole in the material. "You've been shot, Liv."

Oh. How the hell had I missed *that?*

Twelve

"Well, the good news is that the bullet went in one side and out the other," I said, dropping the bloody hand towel onto the table with the bandages I'd found beneath the bathroom sink, all of which were now soaked in Liv's blood.

"How is that good news?" She flinched when I pressed a folded paper towel against the front of the bullet hole. Between his own previous injury and Liv's gunshot wound, Hunter's first-aid supplies had been thoroughly exhausted.

I set the paper-towel roll on the table and tried not to think about the fact that Liv had to be *shot* to let me touch her for more than a couple of seconds at a time. "Through 'n' through means I won't have to dig the slug out of your arm." I placed her right hand over the makeshift bandage. "Press and hold."

The dinette chair had no arms, so she rested her elbow on the tabletop, watching while I folded another makeshift bandage. "What's the bad news?"

"I'm going to have to find the slug and destroy every drop of blood you lost. Quickly." All three of the guns used had silencers, so the noise wouldn't have echoed beyond Hunter's apartment. That would cut down on the chances that someone called the police—as would the fact that we were on Tower's side of town, in a building he owned. But someone had probably called in *somebody,* and hanging out at the scene of a crime you've just committed is never a good idea. "Unfortunately, Mr. Hunter isn't very well equipped for triage."

"Or basic housekeeping," Liv added, as I pressed the second wad of paper towels to the back of her arm and reached for the duct tape with my free hand. We'd used Hunter's entire supply of bleach that afternoon, and so far, we'd found nothing else capable of destroying blood, other than a box of matches in one of the kitchen drawers.

"I have emergency supplies in my trunk." Using my teeth, I tore off a length of gray tape and dropped the roll on the table, then wound the tape around her upper arm, careful not to let the bandages slide out of place. It didn't have to be perfect. It just had to keep her from dripping blood until I could get her back to my apartment.

Duct tape and paper towels. No one who has any idea what can be done with a viable blood sample would ever keep an apartment so empty of supplies. And if Liv were right about the fading power in his blood, something really strange was going on.

"Okay." I stood while she examined the makeshift bandage. "I'm gonna grab the stuff from my trunk. Could you gather up everything you bled on and throw it in the tub?"

"Sure," she said, and when I started to leave, she grabbed my arm. "Thanks, Cam." She looked as if she wanted to say more, but when nothing else came out, I shrugged.

"You got lucky. It's barely gonna scar."

I jogged down the stairs and into the parking lot, where I grabbed the plastic tub of emergency supplies from my trunk. On the way through Hunter's hallway again, I listened for any unusual noises—or any unusual silences—from the other apartments, but everything sounded pretty normal. People watching TV. The soft buzz of conversations I couldn't quite make out. The occasional shout from a fighting couple.

It was kind of disturbing to realize we could commit murder without even bothering the neighbors who shared the victim's walls.

In the apartment, I pushed Hunter's broken front door shut and shoved an end table in front of it to keep it closed. "Liv?"

"In here," she called from the bedroom. I glanced into the bathroom on the way and saw that she'd thrown the used bandages and discarded tissues into the tub, along with her own bloodied shirt.

I stopped in the doorway to find her kneeling next to the body, only her head and bare shoulders visible over the bed between us, and for a moment, my breath froze in my throat. I hadn't seen anything more intimate than her forearm in six years, and now she'd taken her shirt off in front of me twice in twenty-four hours.

With my next breath—a conscious effort—I set down the supply box and pulled my T-shirt over my head. It would be huge on her, but that was better than nothing, at least in public. "Here." I held the shirt out and she stood, and I tried not to stare.

Her eyes widened, and *she* stared, and I couldn't

resist a grin, in spite of the circumstances. "What?" I knew what she was looking at, but I wanted to hear her say it.

"You've...um...changed." She took the shirt, but flinched when she tried to lift her arm over her head. "You got...bigger."

I took my shirt back and gathered the material, then slid the sleeve over her injured arm, acutely aware that very little stood between us now. "As it turns out, tracking is kind of a worthless skill, if you can't bring down the target."

"So you trained." She slid her other arm through the second sleeve, and watched me for a moment over the material sagging between us. "Like a soldier."

"Yeah." Only I didn't believe in the war.

I tugged the shirt over her head carefully, then let my fingers trail slowly over her ribs and the hollows of her waist along with the material, waiting—fully expecting—for her to yell at me, or step out of reach.

Instead, she closed her eyes and exhaled slowly, and only met my gaze again when my hands rested on her hips. Her mouth was open, as if she wanted to say something, and I wanted to kiss her to show her that sometimes you don't need words. Sometimes they only get in the way, and you end up talking yourself out of things you need. People you want.

She inhaled, and her warm hand found my chest and trailed toward my stomach, and I almost forgot we were supposed to be fleeing the scene of a crime.

Then she blinked and snatched her hand away, and though I knew it was for the best—this wasn't the time—I missed both the warmth of her hand and the heat in her gaze.

Liv turned around, and the moment was over, and I knew that if I called her on it, she'd deny that moment ever existed. But she'd be lying. She'd been lying for six years, and that's why I hadn't given up on her. Why I *couldn't* give up on her, even when she was with someone else, and I was with someone else. I couldn't give up because I could still feel her.

All I had to do was think of her name—her real, full name, which no one else in the world knew—and I could feel her, all the way across the city. Hell, I could feel her all the way across the state. I couldn't tell what she was doing—tracking didn't work like that—and with anyone else, someone I didn't know as well as I knew Liv, I wouldn't have gotten anything more from the pull of her name than a direction.

But with Liv, it was different. I knew her name, and I knew *her,* and when I thought of her, sometimes I could feel what she was feeling. And all too often, that was pain. Physical pain. Emotional pain. Anger. Humiliation and degradation. Olivia wasn't happy, and maybe it was egotistical of me to think that I could fix that—that being with me again would make her happy like we used to be happy—but ego or not, it sometimes took every single ounce of self-control I could muster to keep from tracking her and killing whoever was hurting her. Whoever was making her hate herself.

In the end, when my restraint wavered, the only thing that kept me away from her was knowing that she'd hate me for interfering. For wounding her self-respect by ending whatever abuse she couldn't—or for some reason *wouldn't*—put an end to. Even if it killed me to let her suffer.

In Hunter's room, Liv knelt next to the body again,

putting a clear end to whatever had almost happened between us. "I can't figure this out." She scowled at Hunter, as if he might open his eyes and submit to questioning. "He's not Skilled. There's no trace of it in his body. But the blood in my pocket is still humming with power—a low level, like his bloodline is diluted. Then there's the sample Anne brought us—that one felt as Skilled as *your* blood. He *was* a shadow-walker. And now he's not. It doesn't make any sense."

"Well, staring at him isn't going to change that. Come on, we need to get going. Find something to wipe down the guns with. And put these on." I reached into the supply box and tossed her a set of surgical gloves, then I pulled on a pair of my own and scanned the wall opposite the bed. There it was, just above elbow height on me—a small round hole in the Sheetrock. It would have been just below shoulder height on Liv. In the center was the slug, smashed flat from impact with the fire wall.

I took the folding knife from my pocket and flipped it open, then carved the bullet out of the wall, along with a two-inch-wide disk of the surrounding Sheetrock. Then I soaked the resulting hole with the spray bottle of bleach solution from my box of tricks, just to be safe.

"Where's your gun?" I turned, expecting to find Liv wiping down the pistol I'd lent her—mine were unregistered, filed free of serial numbers and equipped with silencers; an advantage of working for the syndicate—but she still knelt on the floor next to Hunter's body. "Liv, we have to get out of here before the cops show up or you start bleeding through your bandages." Or worse.

She didn't even look up. "His cell's in his back pocket. We need to know who he's been talking to, if we're going to find out who's behind the hit. "

I twisted the Sheetrock and smashed the bullet into a paper towel and dropped the tiny, incriminating bundle into the plastic tub. Then I rounded the bed into the narrow space Liv had wedged herself into. But I stopped cold when I saw what she held between gloved fingers.

"It was with his phone." She lifted the photograph for me to see, but I pushed her hand away. I didn't want to see the blue-eyed, dark-haired little girl smiling at me from some happy moment frozen in time. And I certainly didn't want to dwell on the fact that I'd killed her father—even if he was a murderer.

"Don't think about it." I reached down to help Liv up by her good arm. "He couldn't have been much of a father—there's no sign that a kid's ever even been here. He probably hardly ever saw her."

"She's not his," Liv said, and I recognized both the angry set of her jaw and the stunned distance in her eyes. "This is Hadley."

"What? How do you know?"

She flipped the picture over and showed me the back, which read Hadley, Kindergarten Class Photo. "It's Anne's handwriting, Cam. Anne wasn't the target, and neither was Shen. The bastard was after their daughter."

My denial surfaced as confusion, and suddenly ignorance seemed like a blessedly blissful state. "Why the hell would Hunter want to kill a five-year-old?"

"Because that's what your boss *paid* him to do."

I ground my teeth over yet another reminder that she

considered me a part of the problem. "You're assuming Hunter was hired by Tower himself?"

Liv's brows shot halfway up her forehead. "Hell yeah, I'm assuming it, and until we come up with some reason to discount that theory, I'm going to *keep* assuming it, because Tower's at the top of the pyramid. No one beneath him would spend this much money and order a hit on a five-year-old—a PR *nightmare,* even if it only got around by word of mouth—without his blessing. And that's not all. Look at this." She slid the photo into her own back pocket and dropped into a squat next to the body.

I glanced at the man I'd killed, then looked away again. Yes, he was a murderer, and yes, I'd probably saved Liv's life by taking the bastard out. But staring at the evidence of yet another of my own crimes—at the very vivid illustration of the sanctioned violence my life had become—brought reality into sharp focus for me in that moment. And it hurt to see it all laid so bare.

"What am I supposed to be looking at, exactly?"

Liv huffed in exasperation, then grabbed Hunter's limp right wrist and pulled his arm up as far as it would go without actually moving the body. I bent for a closer look and finally saw what she was getting at, there in the crook of his elbow.

"Track marks."

"*Fresh* track marks," she corrected.

"Some of them, yeah." I shrugged. "So he was a junkie." I rounded the corner of the bed and picked up my tub of supplies.

She followed me into the living room and when I shoved a clean shop towel into her gloved hand, she started wiping down her gun at the table. But a minute later, she set the gun down next to the one I'd cleaned and pulled the photo from her pocket. "Why would anyone want to kill a five-year-old?"

"Silencer, too," I said, trying not to think about the little girl who could have died. Who could *still* die if Tower sent someone else after her. I needed to think about cleaning up our current mess and getting us both the hell out of there. We couldn't be caught with guns the cops could match to bullets from Hunter's body, so the guns would have to stay at the scene—without our fingerprints. Mine weren't on file—yet—but hers would be, because she'd worked for a licensed bail bondsman.

Liv pulled the silencer from her pocket, wincing at the movement from her injured arm as she wiped it clean, still staring at the photo she'd laid on the table. When she finished, she set the silencer down and grabbed the picture again, and a second later she turned to me, sudden excitement firing like sparks in her eyes. "She isn't Shen's!"

"What?" I set my clean silencer down and frowned at the photo she held up.

"Hadley isn't Shen's daughter. Not biologically. She can't be. Look, there isn't a drop of Asian blood in her!"

Reluctantly, I glanced at the photo one more time—then couldn't look away. Liv was right. Hadley had curly brown hair and deep blue eyes. But… "That might not mean anything. Genes are complicated. I've seen a bunch of kids who look nothing like their parents." And that was the case here. It had to be, because if Hadley wasn't Shen's daughter…

No. I did the math in my head, my heart pounding so hard it echoed in my ears.

Hadley was five. I wasn't sure how close she was to turning six, but either way, if Anne wasn't already pregnant at the party—the one six years ago; the night Liv left me and never looked back—then she got pregnant very soon afterward. Maybe even that very night...

No.

No.

I'd know if I had a kid. Anne would have told me. She would never have hidden something like that from me, even knowing how I felt about Liv.

No!

"We have to get out of here." I plucked the picture from the table and slid it into my own pocket, then shoved a plastic canister of antibacterial wet wipes at Liv. "Wipe down the bathroom. Faucets, toilet, sink. Anything either of us might have touched. I'll be there in a minute with the alcohol."

Olivia looked at me as if I had brain damage and it might be contagious. But she took the wipes. While she worked on the bathroom, I did a quick, thorough job on the kitchen and the table where we'd worked on Liv's arm. Then I dumped everything that had her blood on it in the tub and doused it with alcohol, which would destroy the blood as well as fuel the flames. Finally, I smashed the smoke alarm with one fist. Then I lit a match.

It was a brief, beautiful blaze of glory, and once I was sure the blood couldn't be identified by the police or tracked, I turned on the shower to put out the flames. Then I dropped Hunter's laptop into my plastic tub and followed Liv out of the building. But I didn't relax enough to breathe normally until we pulled out of the parking lot, unassailed by police, local criminal elements or neighborhood vigilante mobs.

Two blocks away, I made the call from a pay phone—a dying resource, still favored by criminals everywhere. I kept it quick and simple: Hunter's address and apartment number. When the police arrived, they'd find the body and do the cleanup we hadn't bothered with. We didn't care if they ID'd him, and with any luck, we hadn't left any viable traces of ourselves for them to find. And if anyone had seen us, our descriptions would be reported to Tower's men—de facto neighborhood security—rather than the police.

Behind the wheel again, I glanced at Liv. "How's your arm?"

She lifted her elbow and glanced at the makeshift bandage in the glow from a passing streetlamp as I turned left onto a side street. "Starting to bleed through."

"I have real bandages at home. We're only a couple of minutes away."

"I have everything I need at my office."

But I didn't want to take her back to the south fork, especially her office, because now that we'd killed Shen's murderer, Liv was no longer being compelled to work with me. She could kick me out of her office—and out of her life—whenever she wanted, and I couldn't let that happen again.

"My place is closer," I pointed out, using logic to justify an admittedly selfish desire.

Liv sighed. Then, finally, she nodded. "But only because I'll be dripping blood all over your car by the time we get to the south fork." She leaned to the left and dug her cell phone from her pocket. "I'm going to call Anne. Want me to put her on speakerphone?"

No. Because Liv would ask her about Hadley's father, and my worst fear in the world at that moment was finding out that I was—maybe—the father of Anne's child. In front of Olivia. That potential complication would put a serious crimp in my efforts to stay in Liv's life, and she should hear it from me.

But not now, when there was so much else to worry about.

"Sure." The most gutless word in the English language. Consent with no real feeling. The antithesis of certainty and determination. But if Liv noticed my lack of enthusiasm, I couldn't tell. She scrolled through the recent calls on her phone and pressed a button, and a moment later, the electronic, bleating ring echoed in the confines of my car and the even tighter space inside my skull.

The ringing stopped with a soft click. "Hello? Olivia?" Anne said over the speaker.

"Yeah, it's me. Cam's here, too." Liv glanced at me, but I couldn't meet her gaze. Not knowing what she was about to find out. "We got him. Hunter's dead."

Anne burst into tears, sobbing and sniffling over the phone. "Thank you. Thank you both so much...." Another wet sniffle. "Maybe I can sleep, now that it's all over."

Liv met my gaze in the rearview mirror, and her disbelief echoed my own. "Annika..." she began, as I braked for a stoplight. "I don't think this is the end of it."

Anne's end of the line went silent, except for a crackle of static. "What do you mean?"

"Are you where you can talk, free from little ears?"

"Yeah." She sounded scared now, and I couldn't blame her. "Hadley's watching TV with my mom." They were staying with Anne's parents, because she couldn't stand the thought of taking her daughter home to the scene of her husband's murder. "What's wrong? Olivia? Cam?"

Liv exhaled slowly. "He wasn't after Shen. He was after Hadley."

For one long moment, there was only silence, as if she'd actually stopped breathing. "No," Anne whispered at last, and I could practically see her shaking her head. "That doesn't make any sense. Why would he want Hadley? How do you know?"

"He had her picture," I said, suddenly almost as desperate to know for sure about Hadley's paternity as I was eager to keep Liv from finding out. "With your handwriting on the back."

"What picture?" Anne's voice was low. Stunned. Pained. And I wondered if I should feel the same way. If Hadley was mine, shouldn't I be terrified for her and ready to kill anyone who even *tried* to hurt the blood of my blood? Or something like that?

"Hadley's kindergarten school picture." Liv glanced at me, and I had to force my jaw to unlock. I couldn't even make sense of the storm of fear and confusion raging inside me. "It was wallet-size, and kinda beat-up. He had it in his pocket."

"Why?" There was a thin thread of panic woven through that one word, and it rang a harmonic chord in me. "Why would a murderer have my daughter's picture?"

"I don't know," Liv admitted, as I pulled into the

parking lot in front of my building. "But someone wants her dead. If there's anything you think we should know about Hadley, this is the time to tell us."

"What do you mean? What would you need to know?" But her voice was missing the confusion her words tried to imply. She was hiding something, and I was afraid I knew what it was.

Liv turned to me, as I pulled into my assigned parking spot, wordlessly requesting my participation, but I shook my head. I couldn't ask what needed to be asked. Not with her listening.

Olivia rolled her eyes at my reluctance and turned back to the phone she'd laid on the dashboard. "Who's Hadley's father, Anne? We've seen her photo. There's no way she's Shen's."

Anne's sniffling grew louder, and for a moment I was afraid she'd hang up. Then she cleared her throat, and her next words were firm, her voice surprisingly steady. "Shen is her dad—the only father she's ever known."

Her obviously unconscious use of present tense verbs made me ache for her loss, and her strength amazed me. I'd seen cold, hard men fall to pieces over the death of wives and children, and I couldn't imagine how she was holding up so well under the extenuating circumstances Liv had just hit her with.

"Okay, I understand that. And I know these aren't the kinds of questions you want to answer right now. But, Annika, someone's trying to kill your daughter, and if you want me to help keep that from happening, I need to know anything and everything that might lead me to whoever wants her dead. Or at least tell me *why* she's been targeted. So who is her father, Anne? Her real father?"

Another moment passed in silence, and my heart beat frantically, almost painfully. I was sure Anne was going to say my name. Or that she'd hang up to avoid having to. But instead, she cleared her throat again—a nervous habit—and springs squealed over the line as she sat down somewhere in her mother's house, in a suburb thirty miles away. "I don't know."

"You don't *know?*" Liv glanced at me, frustration and disbelief lining her forehead and outlining the corners of her mouth, and I could only shrug. My only possible contribution to the conversation was the question I desperately didn't want to ask, and I could see no real benefit of asking it. If I were the father, knowing that wouldn't shed any light on the real question—why Hadley was being targeted. And if I wasn't the father, I'd have just admitted to sleeping with Anne—a drunken, reactionary mistake I'd regretted the moment it was over. And Liv would probably never speak to me again.

Sleeping with random strangers years after we broke up was different from sleeping with her best friend the night Liv left. And at that moment, admitting what I'd done would only hurt everyone involved. Including Hadley.

"I already had her when I met Shen, and he loved her like she was his own," Anne finally admitted. "But no, I don't know who her biological father is."

My grip around the wheel tightened until my knuckles stood out, white in the glow from the parking-lot light overhead. Was she telling the truth, or just trying to avoid outing me in front of Liv? Either way, her silence on the issue was both blessing and curse. If I was a father, I wanted to know it. I wanted to know *Hadley*.

Liv glanced at me again, and I avoided her gaze to keep her from reading the confliction surely obvious in my expression. She picked up the phone and held it between us. "Surely you have an idea. Like, a list, or something, that we could use to narrow it down?"

"Liv…" I began, humiliated for both myself and for Annika.

"No, I don't have a list," Anne snapped. "What I have is a very upset little girl who's just lost the only father she's ever known. She's away from her home and all her things, and she doesn't really understand why her dad won't be coming home again. And now you're telling me that whoever killed Shen will probably be coming back for Hadley, but instead of trying to help keep her safe, you're interrogating me about my past sex life!"

"I *am* trying to help," Liv insisted. "But Hadley's not a random target. Someone planned this, and paid for it, and is probably pissed off that his hired gun misfired. And if I'm going to keep the next guy from succeeding where Hunter failed, I need to know why someone high up in the Tower syndicate wants your daughter dead."

"I don't know!" Anne cried. "She's just a normal little girl. Happy, healthy, friendly. Loved by anyone who's ever met her."

"Is she Skilled?" I asked, without truly thinking the question through. A child of two Skilled parents would inherit the abilities of one or the other, or possibly the Skill of a grandparent. But a child of one Skilled parent had only a fifty-percent chance of inheriting that Skill.

If Hadley was a Tracker, I couldn't rule out the possibility that she was mine.

"I don't know yet," Anne said miserably. "She's still so young...."

"Okay, you need to hide," Liv said, and I could tell from the slump of her shoulders that she'd given up on the paternity angle, at least for now. "Take Hadley and your parents, and go somewhere random. Someplace you have no connection to. Pay in cash and don't tell anyone where you're going." That was so she couldn't be easily found through traditional means. But what neither of us wanted to say aloud was that if Tower sent another Tracker, they'd eventually be found, no matter what.

"Leave your cell phones behind," I said, glad to finally have something helpful to contribute. "You can get prepaid ones on the road. And don't use your real names." That part was obvious, but couldn't be stressed enough. "If you have access to a car you don't own, use it." Tower had contacts in the police department, and if he wanted Hadley badly enough, he'd use them. "And don't tell us where you're going." Because then Tower could use me against Anne without even making me track her.

"But check in with one of us every hour," Liv added, and in spite of the circumstances, that tight feeling in my chest eased a little. She wasn't trying to get rid of me—yet, anyway.

"Okay..." Furniture springs groaned over the line again, and Anne's footsteps echoed on a hard-surface floor. "I'll call you back in an hour, from the road."

"Good luck," Liv said. Then she hung up and turned to me, gaze heavy with the weight of what we'd stumbled onto, and what had yet to be said. "I need to do something about this...." She held up her injured arm. "Then, I guess I owe you an explanation."

I nodded and opened my car door, then sucked in a deep, cold breath. Yes, Liv owed me some information, but I wasn't the only one in the dark about what had really happened that night, six years ago, and if she showed me hers, I'd have to show her mine. That was only fair.

But I couldn't think of a single good way to tell the woman I wanted to be with more than anything in the world that I'd slept with her best friend.

Thirteen

I followed Cam into his apartment and he closed the door behind us. The scrape of the dead bolt sliding home sounded louder and more final than it should have—a reminder that I was somewhere I shouldn't have been, doing something I shouldn't have been doing, even though I was no longer being compelled. Anne had never officially asked me to help protect Hadley. But I couldn't just let a five-year-old—not to mention the family hiding her—get slaughtered. And I couldn't protect Hadley from the Tower syndicate without whatever information Cam would be able to give me about his own employer.

And that was assuming I'd be any good to them at all. At the moment, with an open, bloody wound, I was a walking target for any blood Tracker. My arm stung, and ached, and throbbed, and every movement pulled the makeshift bandage, which tugged on the wound itself.

"Have a seat, and I'll get my stuff." Cam pulled out a bar stool on his way past the kitchen, and I sat, resting my arm on the counter. He opened the front closet and hauled out the huge duffel bag taking up most of the floor space, then hefted it onto the bar with a solid *thunk,* while I surreptitiously studied the way his arms and still-bare chest bulged with each movement.

Training agreed with him. A lot. So much, in fact, that I had to focus on the pain in my arm and the duffel bag on the counter to keep from staring. Again. He was going to *have* to put a shirt on.

"That's your first-aid kit?" I glanced at him in amusement. "You could fit a body in there."

"Most of one, anyway," he said, and it took me a minute to realize he was joking. Cam unzipped the bag and started pulling out supplies. Alcohol, gauze, medical tape and several small bottles I didn't recognize. "There's some extra bandages and splints and stuff in the bathroom."

"Do you really need all this?" Or had *somebody* turned into a hypochondriac?

Cam's brows rose in amusement. "My job's a little more adventurous than your average nine-to-five."

So was mine, but my first-aid kit would have fit in a bread box. Of course, I was free to turn down the jobs most likely to get me killed, but Cam wasn't free to do much of anything.

"Okay, let's take a look…." He sat on the stool next to mine and gently peeled the duct tape from my arm. The paper towels had started to stick where the blood was drying, and I winced when he carefully tugged them free. "It looks like the bleeding's mostly stopped. Which is good. But we have to clean it, so it might start up again, a little."

Blood had saturated both sides of the makeshift bandage, and he set the entire mess on a paper plate, which would be easy to dispose of along with the bandage.

He leaned over the counter to pull a clean dishrag from the top drawer, then laid it across the counter beneath my arm. "This is gonna sting, but it'll help prevent infection." Cam unscrewed the lid from a bottle of alcohol, then poured a thin, clear stream directly into the front of the wound.

Flames lapped at my arm and I hissed, then bit my lip against the pain. Tensing made it worse, so I tried to relax, but there was no way to relax with Cam this close. Even if he was only touching me to clean the wound inflicted by a syndicate hit man hired by his boss to kill a mutual friend's young daughter.

Yeah, no stress there.

"First bullet wound?" He twisted my arm carefully, then held the towel beneath it to catch the alcohol as he dribbled it down the back side of my arm, over the exit wound.

"Yeah. Had a couple of knife wounds and two broken hands, though."

Cam blotted the drips of alcohol, then laid the towel on the counter and started digging through the duffel again. "So you've had stitches before?"

"I am familiar with the concept, yes. But I'm not a fan."

"Don't worry." He set a sealed hypodermic needle next to a small bottle of clear liquid capped in rubber. "I'm going to give you a local. You shouldn't feel anything but some tugging."

"Are you…um…qualified for this?" I asked, trying not to squirm as he stuck the needle through the rubber cap and drew liquid into the syringe.

"Six years' experience in battlefield triage. Of sorts." He tapped the syringe, just like nurses on TV. "Because some injuries you don't want to have to explain, even to very discreet doctors."

Even with the anesthetic, getting stitches sucked, mostly because seeing my torn flesh held together only by surgical thread was vaguely nauseating. But to his credit, Cam's stitches were small and even—almost as good as the professional sutures my last knife wound had required. And, as usual, the worst part was having to sit still.

When I was stitched, rebandaged and still pleasantly numb, Cam set a glass of water and a pill on the counter in front of me.

"No painkillers." I pushed the pill back across the counter toward him, careful not to move my left arm. "It doesn't hurt that bad." It would hurt like hell when the local wore off, but I couldn't afford to be foggy-headed while we tried to figure out why someone high up in the Tower syndicate would want Hadley dead.

"It's an antibiotic. To keep the wound from getting infected." He set a large, opaque pill bottle in front of me and I squinted at the print. An off-brand of penicillin. "You're not allergic, are you?"

"No." I took the pill with a couple of sips of water. "Why do you have a bulk bottle of penicillin?"

"I actually have about a dozen of them." He pulled a smaller bag from the huge duffel and unzipped it to show me more big white bottles. "Standard issue, from one of half a dozen pharmacists bound to the syndicate."

"Because you're no good to Tower if you die of infection?"

"Yeah." Cam started loading supplies back into the duffel, but he left the pill bottle on the counter. "I don't suppose you have a change of clothes in there?" He nodded toward the satchel I'd dropped on his couch.

"Nope. Had one in my trunk, though." I *knew* I should have driven….

"I have something you can wear for now." He piled everything my blood had touched onto the paper plate, then rolled the sides of the plate up like a big, bloody burrito and carried the whole thing down the hall. "Can you bring the syringe?" he called back over his shoulder.

I grabbed the disposable syringe, careful not to poke myself, and followed him toward the bathroom. But I missed whatever he was saying, because staring at the needle reminded me of the track marks on Hunter's arm, and I couldn't get that image out of my head. Something about it didn't make sense.

In the bathroom, Cam pulled the shower curtain all the way back and set the paper plate in the middle of his tub. I sat on the closed toilet seat while he squatted in front of the cabinet beneath the sink, inches away, and I started a conversation about work to stop myself from asking why he ever bothered wearing clothes at all.

"So, what's your theory on Hunter's track marks?" I said, as he set a gallon-size bottle of rubbing alcohol on the floor.

"My theory?" He opened a drawer and set a pair of scissors and a box of matches on the counter. "I theorize that he's a junkie who takes contracts most people wouldn't touch—for instance, the murder of a five-year-old—to pay for his habit."

"But that doesn't add up," I insisted. "Some of those needle marks were very fresh, but he didn't act like any junkie I've ever met. He was coherent, and not too bad a shot, considering his view was partially obstructed, and his target was moving." I lifted my arm as proof.

Shooting isn't as easy as the movies make it out to be. Any decent-size gun packs a hell of a recoil, and aiming on the fly takes practice. An arm shot—a few inches from my chest—wouldn't have been possible for anyone who maintained the level of high indicated by the number of tracks on Hunter's arm.

Cam closed the cabinet and sat on the edge of the tub with the scissors in hand. "Okay, so he's a very *high-functioning* junkie."

"There's no such thing." I shivered as he slid the cold lower scissors blade beneath the bloody sleeve of the T-shirt he'd lent me. Since we'd have to destroy the clothes anyway, to keep viable blood samples from ever being used against me, it was easier to just cut the shirt off and avoid moving my injured arm any more than necessary. "And anyway, we tore his place apart looking for first-aid supplies. Did you see anything that even resembled drug paraphernalia?"

Cam frowned as he cut my sleeve up the outside, clear through to the collar, careful not to snag the fresh bandage. Or touch me, which was somehow both a relief and a severe disappointment.

"So he doesn't shoot up there." Cam shrugged. "Or maybe it's not heroin. Maybe those are from his hospital visit. Allergy shots, or insulin. Maybe that's why he goes to the public hospital."

My ruined sleeve flopped forward, and I clutched the material to my chest, acutely aware how close Cam was, and how fully dressed he wasn't. "You don't go to the hospital for allergies unless you're in anaphylactic shock, and if you're *that* allergic to something, you keep one of those adrenaline needle pens on you all the time." You'd think someone whose first-aid kit could supply a small country would know that. "But Hunter doesn't have anything like that. Also, allergy shots go in your upper arm. Insulin can be given in your upper arm, stomach, hip or thigh, but *not* in the crook of your elbow."

Cam frowned at me in the mirror as he moved to my other side. "How the hell do you know all that?"

"I have a television and I pay attention. How do you *not* know?"

"No time for TV." He cut up the side of my right sleeve, quicker this time, since there was no bandage to work around. "You're reading too much into the damn track marks, Liv. Maybe he just donated blood."

My right sleeve parted down the middle and peeled back in either direction, leaving me to clasp the top of the shirt to my chest. Which was kind of pointless, considering he was about to cut the rest of the material off anyway. "No way," I insisted, as Cam squatted next to me and took the hem of my T-shirt in one hand. Skilled people can't donate blood. It's a shame, from the perspective of the medical community, but a necessity from any other angle. We can't risk leaving even *drops* of our blood lying around—imagine what entire *bags* of it in the wrong hands could do?

Samples of it could be distributed to an entire army of Trackers, who could find you in no time. That much fresh blood would give even a mediocre Binder the ability to bind you against your will, at least temporarily. You could be compelled to do just about anything.

"You said it yourself—he's not Skilled." Cam cut up the right side of my shirt, and I shivered as the dull side of the cold lower blade brushed my side. "And he clearly has no idea what can be done with a drop of blood."

"But he *was* Skilled," I insisted, as he lifted my good arm for better access to the material. And that's when the epiphany hit me, like a bolt of lightning straight to the brain, and suddenly the whole thing made horrifying, earthshaking sense. "Holy shit." I grabbed Cam's chin, rough with pale stubble, and lifted his head to force eye contact. "What if he wasn't giving blood? What if he was getting it, instead?"

He blinked in surprise and the scissors went still against my skin, but he made no move to pull his chin from my hand. "Liv, he looked like a human pincushion. That adds up to a lot of blood transfusions, and he didn't look very sick to me."

"He's not sick." I let go of his face, but Cam's gaze never left mine. "He's not Skilled, either. But a few hours ago he *was.* And a few hours before that, he was even *more* Skilled—before the power began fading from his blood…."

It took a second for my implication to sink in, but when it did, he sat down on the bathroom tile, stunned, leaving the last couple of inches of my shirt unclipped. "No, that can't be right." The scissors clattered to the floor and he stared up at me. "Is that even possible? Gaining Skills from a blood transfusion?"

"I don't know." I'd certainly never heard of it. "But

that's the only thing that explains the dropping Skill levels in his blood. That's what would happen as the new blood cells die out or are absorbed by his body."

Cam picked the scissors up again and lifted my arm to snip the last bit of material. "So it doesn't last."

"Which would explain the whole pincushion-arm thing." With my good hand, I pulled the T-shirt off and dropped it into the bathtub with the other bloody materials, and I was then nude from the waist up, except for my bra. "You'd have to keep doing it over and over to maintain the Skill."

"No wonder he didn't know better than to leave viable blood all over the place—he's new at this." Cam stood. "Fortunately, we're not." He gave me an efficient once-over, and I was suddenly very aware that I was half-naked. And that he didn't seem to have noticed. "Your bra and jeans have been compromised. Throw them in the tub, and you can wipe the blood off your skin with these." He held up a packet of antibacterial wipes.

"My bra and jeans are *compromised?* So...what? They agreed to share and play nice?"

Cam's mouth twitched in an almost-grin. "You know what I mean." He set the wipes on the counter. "I'll find something else for you to wear." Then he was gone, and I was alone in the bathroom, trying not to be offended by the fact that his gaze hadn't lingered.

What did it matter? I winced at the pain in my arm as I unhooked my bra, then dropped it into the tub. We couldn't be with each other anyway, so we were both better off not looking at what we couldn't have. But knowing that didn't make his ironclad restraint any easier to take.

I took off my boots, then unbuttoned my jeans and pushed them to the floor one-handed, while metal scraped metal from down the hall—Cam sorting through the clothes hanging in his closet, by my best guess. I emptied the contents of my pockets—a convenience-store receipt and a handful of change—onto the counter, then dropped my pants into the tub. *What a shame.* They were my favorite pair.

Fortunately, my underwear looked "uncompromised."

I gave my left side a once-over with one of the wipes, then dropped it into the tub, too.

The hangers went still, and a moment later, Cam's footsteps echoed from the hall. Trying to ignore the throbbing in my arm, I sat, arms crossed over my chest, legs crossed in a vain attempt to look normal, while sitting on a toilet in my underwear. And as he rounded the corner into the bathroom, wearing a clean shirt and critically eyeing the one he carried, I glanced down at myself self-consciously and noticed the black ring tattooed on my left thigh.

Shit!

As he looked up, I recrossed my legs in the other direction, covering the tattoo. My heart raced from the near-catastrophe. He couldn't know. Ever. I'd rather cut the mark out of my own skin than ever let Cam know I was bound to Ruben Cavazos.

"Van left these here after she…" Cam blinked, and his next words were lost to us both as he stared. He hadn't seen the mark, but he was seeing everything else. Finally.

For both of our sakes, I shouldn't have let him look. And I certainly shouldn't have *enjoyed* letting him look.

But mistakes are just another kind of choice, and saddled with two bindings, I'd had precious few choices lately. So I let him look, for several long seconds.

"After she...?" I prompted finally, fighting a smile at his reaction, and at the fact that I could still provoke it.

Cam blinked again, and I could practically see the return of upper-level reasoning as blood was diverted back into his head from...wherever else it had been. "After she got her own place," he finished, glancing at the clothes he held to avoid looking at me. "You guys are about the same height, so this should work until you can grab a change from home."

And there was nothing stopping me from doing that. I could throw on Van's clothes and make Cam take me back to my office right then. I could even explain why I'd left him in the car. But I didn't want to go. Once this was over, I'd have to leave him again, but until then, I had a justifiable excuse for hanging around. And a dark spot of guilt on my soul for not entirely hating the circumstances that had brought us together.

"Here." Cam handed me a black baby-doll-style T-shirt. On the front was a beautifully detailed golden dragon clutching a human skull with one clawed foot. The crinkled, gauzy black skirt was ankle length, and heavier than it looked. It wasn't something I would ever have bought for myself, but I couldn't afford to be choosy, considering the alternative.

But there was no bra.

"Thanks."

When he turned to give me privacy—which I would have found pointless, if not for the mark on my thigh—

I stepped into the skirt first and didn't fully relax until it was tied at my waist, my secret safely hidden.

"Okay, assuming you're right about these transfusions, where's Hunter getting the blood?" Cam asked, as I carefully pulled the shirt over my head.

"I don't know. But the implications of this are beyond terrifying." I tugged the shirt into place, trying to ignore the pain reawakening in my arm, then tapped him on the shoulder. Cam turned and met my gaze in the mirror as I ran my hands through my hair, trying not to look at the rest of me. Blood loss and exhaustion were *not* good looks for me. "I mean, if the resources are there, men like Hunter—or anyone else—could be Travelers one day, Blinders the next and Seers the day after that. Men like Tower could hire one thug and get a whole series of Skill sets. Maybe even more than one at a time. Though I'm not sure how that would work."

I wasn't sure how *any* of it would work, but the concept alone was staggering. It was world-changing. And if the government couldn't even officially recognize the existence of Skills, it would never be able to regulate the renting of them.

Rented Skills, like everything else private industry couldn't legally provide, would be offered up to the black market on a silver platter. And presumably, those who could provide the rarer Skills—Seers, Bleeders and Jammers—and those with extraordinary ability in any of the more common Skill sets would be in high demand.

And worth even more to the syndicates than they already were.

"Okay, let's not get ahead of ourselves. Let's clean this mess up, then we can figure out our next move."

Cam doused the contents of the tub with rubbing alcohol while I took a match from the box. When he was done, I lit the match and tossed it onto the pile.

Flames erupted immediately, and the fire burned hot and fast. Cam flipped on the ceiling vent to suck out the smoke, and when the flames started to threaten the shower curtain, I pulled the plastic liner out of reach. Thank goodness for porcelain tubs—fiberglass would have burned right along with the clothing and bandages we needed to destroy.

When we were sure all the blood was destroyed, Cam turned on the water and aimed the handheld showerhead at the base of the flames. The blaze was out in seconds, leaving only the soggy, charred rubble in the tub and another layer of smoke on the ceiling— a common sight in most Skilled households.

Before he moved out, Cam would have to repaint the entire bathroom. As would I, in my own apartment.

I grabbed a contractor bag—a big, thick black garbage bag, like building contractors use—from beneath the kitchen sink while Cam dug up a couple of pairs of thick dishwashing gloves, and I held the bag while he scooped the wet rubble into it, so I wouldn't have to move my injured arm too much. Then he walked the trash to the apartment complex's Dumpster while I used the high-pressure setting on the showerhead to spray the remaining tiny bits of char and ash down the drain. After a final scrub with a disposable sponge and some bathroom cleaner, the shower was fit to use once more.

"Thanks for doing all this," I said, settling onto a bar stool while Cam pulled open the fridge.

He glanced at me over the open door. "I'd do more, if you'd let me."

I didn't know what to say to that. So I said nothing.

"You hungry?" Cam asked, pulling two bottles of water from the fridge. "Fajitas wouldn't take long...."

"Shouldn't we focus on finding out who's trying to kill Hadley? Or who's selling Skilled blood transfusions to known criminals? Or both?"

Cam closed the fridge and eyed me across the counter, his hands flat on the tile. "You were just shot. You need rest, water and food."

"I don't have time for any of that." The monster who wanted Hadley dead wasn't going to put his horrific mission on hold just so I could take a nap.

"Okay, then, you grab my laptop, Hunter's cell phone and his bank statement, and see if you can't find out where he got this super-Skilled blood transfusion while I make dinner. Because I'm starving."

I considered arguing that with his help, the detective work would go much faster. But I wasn't entirely sure that was true—too many cooks in the proverbial kitchen. Also, he'd already started pulling beef and vegetables from the fridge.

And I was a *little* hungry...

"Laptop's in my bedroom, on the dresser," he said, when my lack of objection seemed to indicate surrender.

"Fine. But make it fast." I waved one arm at the spread of colorful peppers, tomatoes and red meat now covering the kitchen peninsula. And only then did it occur to me that he hadn't pressed for the explanation I owed him. I wasn't sure why he'd forgotten—could that be attributed to the sight of me nearly naked?—but I wasn't going to remind him.

I stopped in his bedroom doorway, surprised to realize that even after six years and at least one move, he still had the same furniture we'd shared for two of our three years together, in college. Same scarred upright chest of drawers, which he was still calling a dresser. Same weight bench in the corner, ancient free weights stacked by the wall. Same simple iron-frame headboard with stupid decorative balls topping the posts. I wondered if the mattress still squealed, or if he'd replaced it.

Curious, I almost sat on the bed to test it, but then my gaze found the laptop and its cord on top of the chest of drawers, and I remembered why I'd come in the first place. And it wasn't to try out Cam's mattress. No matter how hard memory and nostalgia tried to argue otherwise.

At the peninsula again, I plugged in the laptop and dug Hunter's phone and bank statement from my satchel.

I started with the statement. I'd been over it several times before, but this time I was looking for a big expense, not a big deposit. I wasn't sure how a Skilled blood transfusion would work but I was sure it would be expensive, and I was sure it would have to have been done—and thus paid for—very recently, considering how quickly it had faded from his blood signature.

Unfortunately, the period covered by the bank statement ended the week before—the payment from the Tower syndicate was literally the last entry. Which meant that any transactions made in the past eight days would go on the next reporting cycle, and until then, they'd be accessible online only.

"Hey, you said Hunter paid most of his bills online, right? Did you notice whether he has online access at his bank? Statements in his inbox, or something like that?" Though he clearly got printed statements, too…

Cam looked up from the peppers he was chopping. "Yeah, I think so. But you can't log in without his password."

"Fortunately, we have his account number…." I held up the bank statement, then set it on the counter and crossed the room to grab Hunter's laptop from the box of supplies Cam had brought in to restock. "And if he's anything like the rest of the country, he probably uses one password—or variations of one password—for most of his accounts. I'm guessing he's smart enough to use something random, but not smart enough to keep all the variations straight. Which means he probably keeps a list."

Cam scraped the peppers from the cutting board into the skillet. "Well, if it's on his hard drive it isn't called 'top secret keys to invading my privacy,' or anything else convenient. And I didn't find a notebook or calendar, or anything it could have been written on."

I set Hunter's laptop on the bar next to Cam's and pressed the power button. "Nobody writes anything down on paper anymore. But what's the one thing people never leave the house without?"

Cam looked up from the skillet, challenging grin intact. "Underwear. Or would you like to prove me wrong?"

I rolled my eyes and logged in to Cam's wireless network. "Cell phone. Most of them have a notepad feature, and you know what most people keep on it?"

"I'm guessing passwords?"

"Yup. And grocery lists, and reminders, and anything else they need access to. Although, personally, my phone calendar is much more incriminating than my notepad."

"So, if I want to know where you'll be this Friday night, all I have to do is steal your phone?"

"Well, that, and figure out the code to unlock it. But his phone isn't locked." I opened a browser on Hunter's computer, then clicked the drop-down menu listing his favorites. And sure enough, after three listings for what could only be porn sites, he'd bookmarked the power company, the water company, his mobile service provider and...his bank.

I clicked on the bank link, and while the page loaded, I scrolled through his cell-phone notes for anything resembling passwords. There weren't many choices, and the third one, titled FNB, consisted only of a seven-digit alphanumeric code with a pound sign at the end.

"First National Bank. Got it." Hunter turned out to be no smarter than the average bear.

I typed his account number into the bank site, then his password, and when the site had "verified" my stolen identity, I clicked on My Account. Where I discovered what I already knew—until the week before, Mr. Hunter had been in dire financial need, even more so than I. But his banking activity since the big deposit was sparse.

The bank had auto-removed the overdraft fees he owed, and he'd paid a couple of utilities online. But other than that... "Nothing." I looked up to find Cam chopping peppers on a plastic cutting board. "There are no big withdrawals. His bank balance is just over $49,500. Nothing in savings." I frowned as he scraped the peppers from the cutting board into the skillet. "So, what? The transfusions were free?"

"Or he paid by credit card."

"There were no credit cards in his wallet, and based on his banking history, I'd say that's because his credit is less than stellar."

"So maybe the transfusions were free for *him*."

"Someone else paid...." *Shit.* The only reason someone else would pay for Hunter's superpowers was to help him carry out a job they'd commissioned. Which meant... "The Tower syndicate paid for Hunter's upgrades. They didn't just hire the monster—they created him."

Fourteen

"Did you know about this?" Liv watched carefully for my reaction, obviously fully aware that my body language might say things my mouth wasn't allowed to.

But this time, I had nothing to hide. "Nope. Whatever Tower's up to, it's above my pay grade."

She looked as if she wanted to believe me. As if she was working really hard to convince herself that I could be trusted. But we both knew I couldn't be. Not so long as my enforced loyalty to Tower trumped everything else in my life. Including her.

But I was telling the truth.

Frustrated, I set my butcher knife on the counter and met her suspicious gaze with an open one of my own. "Liv, if there's something I can't tell you, I just won't say it. But I'm not going to outright lie to you." That much, at least, hadn't changed.

"Unless Tower tells you to. You'd have to lie then, right?" Her brows rose in challenge, and suddenly I hated Jake Tower more than I'd ever hated anyone in my life. Including previous incarnations of my own hatred for him.

"Yes. If he told me to lie to you, I'd have to. But unless he got really creative with the orders, I wouldn't have to make you believe it. I'm not going to go out of my way to make him happy, after what he's done to Anne and her family."

She almost smiled, and some small bit of tension inside me eased. "So, you're working under protest now?"

"Silent protest. But yes." Because open protest would only get both of us killed. "And anyway, I haven't had any communication from Tower directly or indirectly all day." Which was interesting, considering the fact that I'd been seen all over the west side of town with her.

"What do you think that means?"

I shrugged and resumed chopping. "I think it means that we were allowed to track and kill Hunter because that benefited the syndicate—we were cleaning up their mess. But if we step over whatever line they've drawn for us, they *will* redirect my attention to something Tower considers more worthy. More syndicate-spirited." And Liv's interest in syndicate business would be noted. And monitored.

Nothing good ever comes from being monitored by the Tower syndicate.

"That means we've hit a dead end on the money trail for now, then?" she said. "Because if we keep digging into their involvement, they're going to hit your manual reset button."

I laughed. "Pretty much." And the reset button, for the record, was the back of my skull. I set the spatula down and met Liv's gaze, letting her see that I was serious. "But I'm not saying we should give up on the money trail *or* the transfusions. I'm just saying that if we dig for clues directly beneath the syndicate, we're going to come up right under Tower's feet. And he's going to stomp on us."

"So we should approach them both from another angle? Pursue leads that don't originate within the syndicate?"

"Exactly." While the skillet sizzled behind me, I picked up Hunter's phone. He hadn't gotten a single call since his fortunate demise, which was no shock, considering he'd only been dead a couple of hours. "I suggest we start with this. Maybe someone he knows can tell us where he got the transfusions, or who actually hired him. Even if they don't know what they're really telling us."

I slid the phone across the counter to Liv and plugged my food processor in on the peninsula as she scrolled through the entries on the phone.

"He only got eight calls in the last week, two of them from the same number. And he only made three calls. Not exactly a social butterfly." She pulled my laptop closer and started typing. "With your computer, my credit card and an online reverse phone book, I should be able to put a name with most of these numbers."

"Wouldn't it be easier and cheaper to just call them?"

"Definitely." She glanced at me over the screen. "And calling his friends, relatives and 'professional' associates would also be the easier, cheaper way to raise a bunch of red flags, put Tower's men on our tail and get us both shot for our troubles." I stared at her, and Liv laughed. "New to this part of the game, huh?"

"Yeah." I dug three tomatoes from the vegetable drawer and rinsed them in the sink. "Most of my work involves name-tracking, not computer snooping. I usually call in Van for that kind of thing."

Liv's fingers attacked the keyboard, rapid-fire clacking, as if she could pound the answers from the internet by force. "I think we should leave Van out of this, for her own safety."

"Agreed." I cored the tomatoes on the cutting board, then dropped them into the food processor and started on the cilantro. "Any luck?"

"Yeah." More clacking, then she picked up the notepad and spoke as she scribbled. "One of the outgoing calls was to his bank, on the day of the big deposit. I assume he was calling to make sure the money landed safely."

I nodded and scooped the leftover onion into the food processor with the cilantro and tomatoes.

"The second call went to a man named Gavin Payne, no address listed." Liv glanced up when I started chopping again. "I hate jalapeños. They're all heat but no flavor."

I kept chopping. "This is a smoked poblano. You'll like it. Trust me."

She looked skeptical, but went back to her typing with no complaint. I ran the food processor, and a few minutes later, I poured fresh salsa into a bowl shaped like a hollowed-out red pepper.

Liv looked up when I pushed the bowl toward her. "Okay, I can't find anything on the third number, even on four different sites claiming to have access to unlisted landlines and cell-phone numbers." She picked up a corn chip from another bowl and dipped it into the salsa. "Wow." She finished the chip and dipped a second. "When we were together, it was all takeout, all the time."

"I've had some free time lately."

"Well, it's paid off." She turned back to the screen, crunching into another chip. "Of the numbers that called Hunter's phone, two look like they're from his mother, calling once from her home phone and once from her cell. I wonder if Mrs. Hunter has any idea that her little boy grew up to be an attempted murderer of small children?"

I shrugged and turned off the stove. "I blame the parents."

"Me, too." Liv snagged another chip while I pulled the steak from the skillet to slice on a fresh cutting board. "The repeated incoming number was Gavin Payne, and the one that called most recently was the same unidentifiable number Hunter dialed last night. The other three incoming calls were from his building superintendent, his pharmacy and a telephone survey company."

"Bastards. They always call during dinner."

Liv laughed as I slid the sliced steak onto a platter and topped it with the sautéed vegetables. "Forget crime lords and corrupt politicians—telemarketers are the root of all evil."

"Now you're getting it." I took a twist tie off a bag of flour tortillas and set a clean plate in front of her. "So, unless he's in cahoots with Walgreens or his landlord, the only real possibilities are this Gavin Payne and the unknown number."

"Yeah. But I still have to check his texts."

"Let me." I took the phone from her and replaced it with her empty plate. "You eat."

Liv hesitated, then reached for a tortilla.

Hunter hadn't sent any texts in the past week, and he'd only received one, a couple of days earlier. An address. "Shit."

"What?" Liv looked up from her empty fajita, and I turned the phone around for her to see.

"That's Anne's address," I said, when she showed no recognition. "I was there with her this morning when she gathered the blood samples." Was that really less than a day ago? It felt like a week.

Liv took the phone from me and compared it to the notes she'd taken. "It's from that same unidentified number. Let me see your cell," she said, her dinner already forgotten.

"Why?"

"Because I know you're not allowed to tell me if you know whose number that is. But if you do, it might be in your phone. Right?"

Smart girl. "In theory. But I actually don't know that number."

"And you won't care if I verify that, right?"

I handed her my phone. "Do you mind if I eat while you openly distrust me and invade my privacy?"

"I'm sorry, Cam." But she pressed a button to wake my phone up, without hesitation. Not that I could blame her. "Password?" she said, eyeing me expectantly.

I piled steak and peppers onto a tortilla and answered without looking up. "Zero-one-zero-four."

Her finger hovered over the last digit, and I could practically feel her gaze on me. "That's my birthday."

"Huh. Weird." I dropped a glob of sour cream on my fajita, then folded the tortilla over its contents and took a bite without waiting for her response. Not that she had one, other than a slight flush not caused by the spicy food.

I watched as Liv navigated her way through my phone menus. She never looked up at me, which was how I knew she really wanted to.

After less than a minute, she held my phone up so I could see my own contacts list, and the only number listed there. "How the hell did you get my personal number?"

I took another bite, then spoke around it. "It's listed."

"No, it isn't. And I change it every year, to make sure it isn't just floating around out there, through random people I called years ago."

I shrugged. "It's listed *somewhere,* or how else could I have it?" Of course, it wasn't in any *public* listing I'd found, but I knew people—like Van—who knew how to get things.

Liv frowned. "Is that it? What about all your syndicate buddies? What about Van?"

I slid the meat platter toward her, and she finally picked up the tongs. "We're not allowed to program syndicate numbers. They all have to be memorized. And we delete the recent-calls list daily." All to keep from incriminating one another, of course. It was part of my nightly routine.

Set alarm. Brush teeth. Purge the call lists from my phone...

"And you're sure you don't recognize this one?" Liv spun the notepad around so I could see the unidentified number she'd jotted down. The one that had called Hunter, been called by Hunter and later had texted Anne's address to him.

"Nope." I took the tongs from her and loaded her tortilla myself, since she obviously wasn't going to. "But that doesn't mean anything. I don't have the personal phone numbers of every initiate in the city." Thank goodness. And since most of my work was done at Tower's personal request, very few of the other initiates had my number, either. "Check my recent calls, if you don't trust me."

I tried not to be hurt when she only hesitated a second before taking me up on my offer. Then she slid the phone back to me, having obviously learned what I already knew, that in the past twenty hours—as far back as my current call list went I'd only called Van and Anne.

"Do you know Jake Tower's personal number?" she asked, picking up the fajita I'd rolled for her.

"One of them—and that's not it. But I'm sure he has at least a couple. There's no way the number his wife and kids call is the same one his employees use. And that probably goes for anyone in the top tiers."

"Great. Another dead end."

"What about Payne?" I said while she chewed. "It sounds like he's either a professional associate or Hunter's only friend."

Liv wiped her mouth with a paper towel—I rarely wasted time, thought or money on napkins. "I did a search for him, but all I'm finding is an announcement of his arrest in one of the local papers."

"What was he arrested for? Is there a picture?" I may not know the personal phone numbers of every syndicate initiate, but I'd recognize most of them on sight.

She stared at the screen again, scrolling with the mouse pad while she chewed. "Armed robbery." More scrolling. "The police pulled him over for a traffic violation and smelled pot, so they searched the car and found twelve thousand dollars worth of jewelry in the trunk, all taken during a B and E reported the night before."

"How much time did he get?"

Liv read a little further, then her eyes widened. "None. He was found innocent, when nearly twenty different people claimed to see him at a party eighty miles away at the time of the robbery."

"He's a Traveler?" If that were the case, he could step into one shadow at the party and out of another one anywhere else within his range—including the jewelry owner's house—in less than a second. Then he'd be back in no time, establishing his own alibi.

Liv shrugged. "Or maybe he had a transfusion, too. Maybe that's how he and Hunter know each other." She set down her half-eaten fajita. "I'm going to call him. From Hunter's phone. Maybe he doesn't know Hunter's dead yet."

"And you think he's just going to confess to robbery, and perjury, and the use of black-market superpower injections?"

Liv smiled, and my pulse raced a little faster. "This ain't my first rodeo, cowboy."

She returned Payne's last call while I dribbled salsa onto a fresh tortilla, and he answered on the third ring. Liv pushed the button for speakerphone and warned me to be quiet with a *shh* finger against her lips.

"Who the hell is this?" Payne barked over the line. His voice was low, but not unusually so, and had no discernible accent. I'm pretty good with voices, and I'd never heard his before.

"Hey. Um...my name is Grace," Liv said, and I was

amused to see that even her mannerisms changed with the character she was playing. "I found this phone on the sidewalk and I'm trying to find the owner. Your number was in the recent-calls list, so can you, like, tell me whose number I'm calling from?"

It was everything I could do not to laugh.

"Where'd you find the phone?" Payne asked. Which meant he either wasn't buying her Good Samaritan act or he wasn't willing to give out his friend or coworker's name to a stranger. Either way, he was smarter than I'd hoped.

"In front of the deli on Fourth." Which was right next to Hunter's apartment building. "Why? Do you know the guy it belongs to?"

"How did you know it was a guy?" Payne demanded, and Liv rolled her eyes over the obvious suspicion in his voice, still in character.

"It's in a gunmetal-gray case and the wallpaper is a picture of muddy girls in bikinis playing soccer. Let's just call it a good guess." She waited, but Payne made no reply. "So, do you know the guy or not?"

"Did you call any of the other numbers?" he demanded, and I lifted one brow in interest. Payne obviously knew something, and he obviously wasn't going to give details to some random chick from the block.

Liv seemed to debate her answer for a second, then she shrugged, though only I could see her. "No, yours was the first one listed." She huffed in feigned frustration, then let a little impatience leak into her voice. "Look, I lost my cell last month and this guy down the street returned it instead of running up my bill, so I was just tryin' to pay it forward, you know? But if it's gonna be some big hassle, I'm just gonna—"

"Now hold on!" Payne snapped, and Liv grinned at me. *Now* we were getting somewhere. "If you bring the phone to the deli, I can get it back to its owner." Someone knocked on a door in the background—three short, sharp taps—and the ambient noise changed as Payne crossed the room, presumably to answer the door. "Just a minute."

Hinges creaked over the line and unease flared in my chest like heartburn. Those knocks meant business. Something was wrong.

"No, wait!" Payne cried, and Liv obviously thought he was talking to her until her eyes went wide at the familiar *thwup* of a silencer over the line—the term is a bit of a misnomer; it still makes noise. Then there was a loud crash and a thud that could only be a body hitting the floor. Payne's body, almost certainly.

I stretched for the phone, but Liv pulled it out of reach. She looked shocked by the lethal development, but determined to hear it out. Something scraped against the phone softly, then we heard nothing but the deep, steady breathing of whoever had picked up Payne's phone.

Liv opened her mouth, probably to ask Payne if he was okay—the reaction you'd expect from a clueless Good Samaritan—but I shook my head. I didn't want whoever'd killed Payne to hear her speak.

"Who is this?" a new voice demanded, and I closed my eyes. *Shit.* I knew that voice.

That time when I reached for the phone, Liv let me have it. I flipped it closed and dropped it on the counter, and Liv stared at it as if it might bite her fingers off if she got too close.

"You recognized that voice, didn't you?" she asked, watching me closely. "Who was it?"

"Adler." I ran one hand over my face, then through my hair. "My direct superior."

"So what does this mean?"

"It means they're cleaning up. Clipping all the loose threads. Payne obviously knew something, and whatever he knew just died with him. But now they know someone has Hunter's phone, and they'll trace it."

"They can do that?"

"You can do anything with enough money and the right connections. It'll probably take a couple of hours, but as long as Hunter's phone is transmitting a signal, they can trace it."

Liv sank onto a bar stool and leaned with her good arm on the counter. "Okay, but does that really matter? They already knew we killed him. And by now, they probably know Anne hired us."

"Yes, but when they trace the phone back to us, they'll know our involvement didn't end with Hunter's death, and they'll know we're looking into the syndicate's involvement."

Liv shrugged. "So we destroy the phone. We already have everything we can get out of it anyway. Got a hammer?"

"Even better." I opened the drawer to my left and took out a two-pound stainless-steel meat mallet, hefting it to get a feel for the weight. Then I wrapped Hunter's phone in a hand towel and set the bundle on the counter. I could have just snapped the SIM card, but swinging the meat mallet felt great—a cathartic release of primal rage at Tower, for targeting a child. At myself for signing with him in the first place. At Olivia, for running off to the city for no reason I could fathom, leaving bloody bits of my own heart like a bread-crumb trail for me to follow.

The crunch of plastic was muted by the towel, which kept electronic shards from raining down on our dinner, but the destruction was obvious, and so satisfying that I did it again. And again, grunting with each release of pent-up fury.

After several swings, I couldn't even see lumps beneath the top layer of towel. I unfolded it and searched through the debris for remnants of the SIM card—it was in several pieces—then shook the towel over the trash can. The pieces that tumbled out were too small to even identify, much less trace.

"Wow," Liv said, when I dropped the mallet back into the drawer. "That looked like fun. I call dibs on the next over-the-top destruction of evidence." She tried on a smile, but couldn't quite pull it off.

I didn't even try. "Obviously that won't keep them from suspecting we took the phone, but at least now they can't confirm that with a trace."

Liv stared into the bowl of salsa, slowly stirring it with a corn chip. "How much trouble are you going to be in?" Because it wasn't a question of whether or not Tower would find out what we were doing, but a question of *when* he'd find out.

I shrugged, but she wasn't buying my nonchalance. "I haven't actually broken any of the rules yet." Which meant precisely nothing. Exploiting the loopholes would only piss off Tower, and we both knew it.

"What's the drill, Cam?" She dropped the soggy chip onto her plate and eyed me steadily. "What would he do to someone else in your position?"

I exhaled, long and slow. "You don't want to know." And neither did I.

"Okay." Liv nodded decisively, as if she'd come to some sort of decision. Then she closed both the laptops and slid off of her stool. "I want you to take me back to my office, then I need you to come straight back here and forget about all of this."

"Liv, wait…" I said, but she was already gathering her things.

"Every second I stay here is another second you are closer to death, or dismemberment, or whatever torture Tower saves for employees who plot against him."

"Olivia." She'd misunderstood the true threat.

I rounded the counter and grabbed her good arm before she could zip up her satchel, and she turned on me, ready to pull free from my grip. But she stopped with one look at my face. "Tower still needs me. He's not going to kill me or do anything else that'll affect my ability to do my job." I hesitated, dreading the part I had yet to say.

"What does that mean?" Liv asked softly, and suddenly I was hyperaware of her arm in my hand, and of the warm smoothness of her skin. But that time, even touching her couldn't distract me from the brutal truth—she needed to understand what was at stake.

"If he finds out what we're doing, he'll punish me by hurting the people I care about. And the only people in the world he's going to be able to connect to me are you, Van and Annika."

Liv's face paled, and her eyes narrowed in protective rage. She was thinking of the risk to Anne, but had yet to consider the danger to herself. Cavalier heroism was as much a part of her as her thick brown hair or bright blue eyes.

"I can take care of myself, Cam," she said, finally pulling her arm gently from my grip. "And I can take care of Anne and Hadley, too. So you worry about yourself and Van, and we'll all be fine." She frowned, as if something new had just occurred to her. "If I leave now, Tower may never know you were involved in this beyond helping me find Hunter. Especially if I take what's left of his phone with me, so they can't find it here." She tried to step around me, heading for the kitchen trash can, but I stepped into her path.

"He'll know because he'll ask, and I'll have to answer. And I don't *want* you to go." I lifted her chin until her gaze met mine—I needed her to see how important this was. "We're of more use to Anne and Hadley as a team than we are on our own, and Van's safer not knowing what's going on. Plausible deniability is the best defense."

"No, a loaded gun is the best defense." She settled her satchel strap over one shoulder and reached for Hunter's laptop. "Well, that and a good head start. So I have to go."

"Please stay." I grabbed the computer before she could reach it and held it against my chest. "If not for me, then stay for Anne and Hadley. We really are better for them as a team."

"That might be true if we could trust each other. But we can't." She sighed and I reluctantly let her pull the laptop from my grip. "If he can hurt us to punish you, then he could just as easily make you into the weapon that does the hurting. Then I'd have to defend myself, and Van, and Annika, and we'd all be hurt."

Or worse. She didn't say it, but we both heard it.

"And I can't let that happen," Liv concluded.

But there was more. There was something she wasn't saying, and I could practically see it dangling from the end of her tongue, but she swallowed it. And whatever it was, it obviously tasted horrible.

"I gotta go. If you won't drive me, I'm taking your car." She glanced around for my keys, but I knew better than to leave them lying within reach. Olivia was an established flight risk.

For one long moment, I watched her, weighing the options and impossibilities in my head. What I was considering would never work. Mere determination— no matter how strong—could never overpower an oath willingly taken and sealed. Just trying it would probably kill me. But at least then I couldn't be used against Liv, or anyone else.

"If you could trust me, you'd stay?" I said, staring straight into her eyes, trying to see past her defenses and distractions to the truth. "For good?"

Olivia frowned and seemed to think about it for a second. Then she shook her head slowly, wincing, as if her answer actually hurt. Or maybe it was my question that hurt. "No fair posing hypotheticals, Cam. What-ifs have no place in the real world. And I have no place in your life so long as Jake Tower is pulling your strings."

But again, there was more she wanted to say. I could see it peeking out at me from behind the truth she wielded like a sword and hefted like a shield.

"This isn't a what-if." I stepped closer and she held her ground as the space between us disappeared.

"I don't…" She cleared her throat and started over, staring up at me, each breath fast and shallow, as if she couldn't get enough air. "I don't know what that means."

"It means that I'm with you, Liv. Screw Tower." A brief bolt of pain lanced the center of my forehead at the minor mental infraction of my loyalty clause, but it was gone the instant the words left my mouth. Actual breach of contract would hurt a hell of a lot worse, I knew, but this first step felt invigorating. Liberating, as if I'd just taken back the reins of my own life, however briefly.

And that was just the start, of both the pain and the progress.

"I'm done with Tower. I'll do whatever it takes to break my binding to him, even if it means carving these damn marks out of my own arm." I lifted my sleeve for emphasis.

"If it were that easy, you'd have already done it," she said. "*Everyone* would have. But removing the evidence of an oath doesn't unseal that oath. It doesn't work like burning a contract. Please tell me you understand that."

I forced a grin. "Yeah, but it makes an impressive gesture, right?" But she didn't even crack a smile. "Olivia, I *will* break this binding. I swear. I'll find the original contract and destroy it, even if I have to burn down an entire building in the process."

"Cam, it won't work…." she insisted, warily backing toward the door. "And even if it did, it could take you months just to *find* your contract, and even if you were able to destroy it, Tower would never let you live. You know that."

I shook my head. "You're getting tangled up in the details, and I don't give a damn about the details. We'll make it work. I'll take a new oath, like you took as a kid. Right now. Write something and I'll sign it. Write whatever you want—write that I'll never leave your side again—and I'll call a Binder right now so we can make it official."

"It's not that simple." She shook her head, but her eyes were shiny and red with unshed tears. "It won't work, Cam. It can't."

"Yes, it can. But I can't make it work on my own. If you really want to leave, then leave. But don't go just because you're scared, of Tower, or anything else. *Cedo nulli,* Olivia. If you yield to no man, why should you yield to fear?"

"I'm not yielding to fear and I'm not running away. I'm facing facts. We don't have any choice about this."

"I have choices," I insisted, refusing to break eye contact. "We both do. I may have to make mine carefully, and make a few compromises along the way, but I have a choice. I choose you."

Fifteen

Liv wiped tears from her face with the back of one arm and retreated until her leg hit the arm of the couch. "I can't do this."

"Then you're a coward." It took effort for me to unclench my jaw and loosen my fists. "I'm willing to risk my life to break my contract with Tower and you can't even risk your pride to tell me it won't be for nothing."

"This has nothing to do with pride." Her blue eyes blazed, and I could practically see her temper flare. "And yes, I'm afraid, but that fear isn't just for me." She had one hand on the doorknob, but made no move to turn it. "I'm leaving to protect us both, and that's the same now as it was six years ago. I left then because I had to."

"You had to," I repeated, and she nodded, holding my gaze. "You *had* to get up and leave in the middle of the party? You *had* to go right home, pack everything you could fit into two suitcases and drive straight to the city?"

She hadn't just left me. Hell, she hadn't even just left the party. She'd left the whole damn town. Her parents didn't know why. Anne didn't know why. If Kori or Elle knew, they wouldn't say.

Liv nodded, looking miserable, but her regret now was nothing compared to what she'd put me through. It couldn't be.

"Why?" I shouted, fed up with the lies, and the silence, and the secrets. I could feel the end of my patience flapping in the wind, like the last bit of kite string about to slide through my fingers, and no matter how I clutched at it, I couldn't quite catch it. "Why did you run, Olivia?"

I saw the secret crack inside her, like a dam under too much pressure, and the truth came gushing out in a painful jet of words she seemed to regret before the last syllable even fell from her tongue. "Because you would've killed me!" she shouted. "Or I would have killed you. If we'd stayed together one of us would have killed the other. I left to stop that from happening, and if I stay now—if I stay with you—it *will* happen, and I can't live with that, no matter which way it unfolds."

She sagged against my front door, as if there was nothing left to hold her up, now that her secret had leaked out, and I could only stare at her.

"What the hell are you talking about?" I felt as if I'd just stepped into bright sunlight and couldn't bring anything into focus, least of all Liv. "I would never hurt you, and I can't believe you'd ever intentionally hurt me." Physically, anyway.

"Six years ago, I couldn't have imagined myself killing anyone. But things change. I *have* killed, when I had to, and dealing with that wasn't as hard as I expected it to be. As I *wanted* it to be." Liv watched me through haunted eyes, and I realized that it wasn't me she was scared of. It was herself. "We don't know who we're going to be in another six years, Cam. Hell, *I* don't know who I'm going to be in another six *months*. I don't know anything about the future except that if we stay together, one of us *will* kill the other. Elle told me, that night. At the party." Liv exhaled, long and deep. "She said that if we stay together, one of us will kill the other."

"Kill, like accidently hit with a car, or serve something with food allergens?" I said, still trying to understand what made no sense.

"No. Kill, like homicide. Murder-most-foul. She was very clear on that point. The only way to prevent it is to stay apart. So I tried. I've been trying for six years, Cam." She sank onto the arm of the couch, still near the door, but no longer determined to leave. I'd asked for the truth, so she was going to give it to me.

"You followed me to the city, and I could have run again, or maybe I could have made you leave, but I didn't want to. I thought that this way, I could still see you sometimes, and I'd know you were okay, even if you thought I hated you." She shrugged, arms spread to include our current disaster. "You can see how well that worked."

I settled onto the edge of the coffee table, staring straight into her eyes, hoping she understood how crazy the whole thing sounded. "Liv, I'm not going to kill you."

"I know. But that only makes it worse. If you're not going to kill me, that means I'm going kill you, and I'd rather die first. I don't want to kill you."

"Oh, come on." I grinned, trying to lighten the mood. "I bet *sometimes* you want to kill me..."

"This isn't funny!" She stood and started pacing angrily.

"Okay, calm down." I grabbed her hand and she let me hold it for a second before pulling away. "Just because Elle saw something years ago doesn't mean it's necessarily going to happen. Or that it'll happen exactly like she saw...whatever she saw."

"She's never been wrong."

"How do you know that? Have you personally verified every prediction she's ever made? Hell, you haven't even seen her in six years, right?"

"She's dead, Cam. I tried to track her. I've tried over and over, and I get nothing. If she were just out of my range, I'd at least get some faint hum of life, but I get nothing. She's dead, and she's been dead for years, and as far as I know, what she told me that night was the last prediction she ever made."

I blinked, stunned. I'd only met Elle once and hadn't thought about her in years, but hearing that she'd died after making a prediction about my own possible demise—left this strange numb spot in my chest. "Are you sure? I could try name-tracking her."

Liv shrugged. "Go for it. I hope you find something. But I'm not holding my breath. If she's still alive, she's been connected at the hip to a world-class Jammer for the past six years, and that's just not possible."

"Anything's possible with enough money and the right connections." I thought we'd established that. "Most Skilled celebrities keep a Jammer on staff 24/7, to prevent them from being tracked by Skilled paparazzi, and the president probably has a whole *team* of them."

"Right, but Elle doesn't have any money, and if she

had connections, she hid them pretty damn well." Liv
scrubbed her face with both hands again, then pushed
her hair back and met my gaze. She looked exhausted,
and not just from the very long day we'd both had;
Liv looked as if she hadn't slept well in a year. "Elle's
dead, Cam. And she was right about us. She wouldn't
have said anything about it if she weren't one-hundred-
percent sure. That was kind of her policy."

That ache in my chest spread until my heart felt like
a vacuum, desperately sucking at everything in a vain
attempt to fill the void. To feel something that wasn't
pain and shock. "Why didn't you tell me?"

"Because I was afraid you wouldn't believe me and if
I gave you a chance, you'd talk me out of leaving. Then
one of us would die. I was trying to protect you."

"You were trying to *protect* me? By not telling me
about the most horrible thing my future is rumored
to entail? How the hell is that protecting me?" I demanded, and my pain sounded a little too much like
anger. Felt a little like it, too.

"This is hell, Cam," Liv said through clenched teeth,
as if she was trying to physically hold back more tears.
"I think about it all the time. I hide it. I run from it. But
every time I close my eyes…every time I let my mind
relax—there it is. One of us is going to kill the other.
Not in a wreck or an overly enthusiastic hug. Murder. I
dream about it—nightmare after nightmare. I look for
it over my shoulder. I try to imagine what could possibly turn us against each other, and in my head, the sce-
narios leading up to murder are almost worse than the
outcome itself. I didn't want you to have to go through
that, too. I thought it'd be easier for you if you didn't
know."

She was serious. I could see it in the tears still standing in her eyes. In the closed-off, self-defensive way she crossed her arms over her chest, as if she was hugging herself.

"So you carried that all by yourself?" I didn't understand her willingness to suffer in silence—to suffer *alone*—but I knew what it meant. How hard it must have been. "How long did you think that could go on?"

She shrugged miserably. "I was half hoping you'd find someone else and forget about me. Then I could leave without worrying that you'd follow me, and we'd both live."

"With other people." Why did just saying it out loud sound like a death sentence? I swallowed thickly and made myself meet her gaze. Promising myself I'd accept the truth of whatever she had to say. "Is that still what you want?"

"Cam, that was *never* what I wanted," she said, and my relief was like a pardon from the governor. "It's what I thought we both needed." She glanced at the floor, then took a deep breath and looked right into my eyes. "But seeing you—touching you after so long— makes leaving again *so* much harder. The thought of walking through this door hurts worse than any resistance pain I've ever felt. Like I'm resisting a compulsion from my heart." Her tears finally fell, and my chest ached fiercely. "I understand something now that I couldn't come to terms with before."

"What?" My question was more breath than voice.

She wiped her face with both palms, then looked straight into my eyes. "I realized that I'd rather die with you than live with someone else."

I don't remember crossing the room, but the next

thing I knew, she was in my arms, so real, and solid, and just like I remembered. I couldn't resist anymore. So I kissed her.

Sixteen

I shouldn't have said it. I meant every word of it, but I shouldn't have said it, because it wouldn't work out. It couldn't. Just because I was willing to risk my life to be with him didn't mean he should be willing to risk his.

Then he was kissing me, and everything else just kind of melted away. It was as if I'd never left. As if I'd never lost him, or my friends and family. As if I'd never worked as a Tracker, or been stabbed on the job. As if I'd never even *met* Ruben Cavazos and lost a good chunk of my free will.

But it wasn't real. We were both six years older, and about a century wiser and more jaded. The world had kept turning in my absence and slung us onto opposite poles, though Cam didn't know it yet.

What we wanted didn't matter. What mattered was what we'd sworn. What we couldn't undo.

"Wait." I pulled back, but couldn't quite make myself step out of his arms. They felt too good. Too familiar. Cam stared down at me expectantly, and I forced out more words I didn't want to say. "I just...I need to know that you understand what you're getting into."

He grinned, and his hand slid over my hip. "I think I remember how this part works…." He leaned down for another kiss, but when his lips trailed down my neck, I stepped back reluctantly.

"I want this as badly as you do," I insisted, but he shook his head, reaching for me again.

"That's not possible…."

"But we're making a choice here," I continued. "And I need to know that you understand that. We're choosing a short life together, rather than potentially long lives apart." I was weak. He felt too good. And at the moment, theoretical death seemed too distant and vague a concept to worry about. But death *would* come, and I didn't want either of us to regret our decision when the end came.

"Olivia, I'm not going to kill you. Okay?" he demanded softly, and I could only nod. "And you're not going to kill me. There isn't a single doubt in my mind about that. Why would you go to all this trouble to keep us safe, only to turn around and kill me down the road? Our future is whatever we make of it, and that's nothing to be afraid of."

I wanted to believe him. I wanted to silence that cynical voice in my head and embrace the cheesy optimism Cam had always been prone to spout when he got emotional. But he didn't know about the mark on my thigh, and he didn't know what would happen if I failed to fulfill my contract with Cavazos. "It's a nice sentiment. It really is. But it's just not practical. Didn't you ever read *Oedipus Rex?* Trying to avoid our fate could damn well be what causes it."

"This, coming from the woman who's been trying to avoid it for six years."

I shrugged. "I didn't know what else to do. Doing nothing felt like slow suicide. Or homicide. But my point is that no matter how good this feels now, it isn't going to have a happy ending. I need to know that you understand that."

"No, I don't." He took me by the shoulders, careful of my bandaged arm, and stared down at me with that infuriatingly stubborn hopeful streak. We used to argue opposite sides of the same coin all the time—usually waxing pathetic on the state of human kindness—and I was always the skeptic. I used to think that was because he was gullible. Not quite naive, but just a *little* too trusting of people in general. But if that were the case, the Tower syndicate would have beaten the optimism out of him years ago.

No, Cam was neither gullible nor truly optimistic. He was desperate. He needed to believe that there was some kind of greater good out there to give his life meaning. Even when his life was currently chained via blood to one of the largest, most dangerous Skilled crime families in the country. And that desperation—that need to believe—was what stared down at me, when I was ready to die for him, and he was ready to live for me.

"No, Liv," he repeated. "Don't give me any of that 'cruel fate' bullshit. I don't believe in it, and neither do you. We don't know if Noelle was seeing the etched-in-stone future, or just one possibility. There aren't enough Seers around for us to really know any of it for sure."

He was right about that. Seers were so rare the Skill often skipped entire generations. Elle was literally the only Seer I'd ever met, and the only other one *she'd* ever known was a dead grandmother on her father's side.

"There's so much we don't know. So much we may *never* know. But I do know this—we can make this work. We *will* make this work. And all you have to do is stay. That's it, Olivia." He eyed me expectantly, his heart not merely on his sleeve, but in his entire bearing. In every breath he took, and in the one he held, waiting for my answer.

So I kissed him.

Then I kissed him again with everything I had stored up from six years without him. With all the love, and fear, and parts of myself I'd kept boxed up and thought I'd never feel again.

And suddenly kissing wasn't enough. I didn't realize I'd taken off his shirt until it fell from my fingers. Then his chest was warm beneath my hands, and I realized all over again—feeling the differences I'd only seen earlier—that he'd changed. He was stronger. Harder. And I hoped with every breath I had left that those changes were limited to his physique. Was it possible that the syndicate could have made him this tough on the outside, yet failed to harden him on the inside?

Then my fingers found sudden roughness among the smooth, hard ripples low on his stomach. I pulled away from his kiss and looked down to find the round, puckered scar. "You got shot looking for me." I traced the thick scar again.

"That doesn't make it your fault," he insisted, pulling my chin up until our gazes met again. But *didn't* that make it my fault?

"If I'd never left, you wouldn't have come looking for me."

Cam groaned. "Don't start playing the what-if game, Liv. That one never ends, and it'll drive you crazy." I must have looked unconvinced, because he grinned like he used to when we had plenty of time and nothing to lose. "I know a much better way to drive you crazy...."

Crazy had never sounded so good.

We wound up on the couch, making out like college kids. Like we had all through our first year together, when no touch was ever enough, no taste ever quite satisfying. We'd weathered the drought, and now we danced in the rain. And it felt good.

I left my shirt on to keep from aggravating my wounded arm, but his hands wandered beneath the material, and they were so warm, and just rough enough to feel real. I ran my fingers over his chest and arms, exploring the new planes and ridges, while his hands slid beneath my borrowed skirt. And that *did* drive me crazy, just like it used to, only worse. I mean, better. Had I just forgotten how good he felt, or had he learned a thing or two in the past few years?

I had one bitter moment to wonder who he'd learned *from,* then I pushed that thought aside. Just as he pushed my skirt up and slid down the length of my body. My head fell back in anticipation, and too late I realized the problem. Too late, I sat up and pushed the borrowed material back into place.

But he'd already seen.

"What. The *fuck.* Is that?" he demanded, voice low and hard, anger and betrayal dulling the shine in his eyes.

"Nothing," I lied out of habit, stretching the material so that it covered not just the mark on my thigh, but both of my legs, now curled beneath me. My pulse raced so fast my vision was starting to go weird, but there was nothing I could do. I couldn't take it back. Couldn't make him unsee what he'd seen. And I sure as hell couldn't get that mark off my thigh just by wishing.

"Nothing!" Cam threw the copious, gauzy material back and grabbed my left ankle, then pulled my leg out straight so that I slid onto my back, my stenciled secret bared once again. "That is not nothing! That is hypocrisy, and lies, and fucking *betrayal*. Are you spying for him? Or recruiting? Is that what this is?"

I tried to pull my leg free and when he wouldn't let go, I kicked him square in the chest with my other foot. Cam fell back against the arm of the couch, grunting in pain and surprise. I rolled onto the floor on my knees, gasping at the pain in my arm, and was on my feet in an instant, backing across the room. "Don't you ever touch me like that again. Not *ever*." I used the anger burning bright inside me to dry up tears I couldn't let fall. "I may have to take that from him, but I don't have to take it from *you*." And if Cam didn't think I could defend myself, he hadn't been watching me closely enough. If I weren't contractually prohibited from seriously injuring Ruben Cavazos, I'd have ripped his balls off and fed them to him a year ago.

Cam stood, his expression a tangle of horror and remorse. And anger. "I didn't… I would never…"

"I know." I closed my eyes and took a deep breath, fighting for calm. Cam wasn't the enemy. He would never even *try* to hurt me. In fact, he'd kill to protect me. But lying on a couch, on my back, forced to bare my mark… It all felt too familiar. And I'd never wanted so badly to take back a single minute of my life. Not the moment I'd bound myself to Kori, Anne and Elle. Not the moment I'd left Cam. And not the moment I'd signed with Cavazos. Hell, taking that one back would make things sooo much worse than they were now....

Which was only one of the reasons I'd never wanted Cam to see that mark.

"Cedo nulli..." He laughed harshly, and I wanted to die, just a little bit. "What is that, a joke? 'I yield to no one.' It's *bullshit!*" he roared. "You yield to the fucking enemy!"

"It's not bullshit, and it's not a joke. It's a goal." I took a deep breath, grasping for calm. "I'm sorry, Cam, but this is really none of your business. So you need to just let it go."

"None of my *business?*" He crossed his arms over his chest, and I got my first glimpse of what he must look like when Tower used him as muscle. He was solid and broad. A brick wall. Or maybe more of a hammer. Either way, I couldn't imagine anyone messing with him, armed or not. But I had no choice.

"Yes. It doesn't have anything to do with Anne or her family, or with...us." At least, us as we'd been a few minutes earlier. Us, as I wanted us to be.

"You sure considered *my* marks *your* business this afternoon."

"Yours are standard syndicate marks, binding you to obey Tower's every word," I said through clenched teeth, trying to decide whether I even owed him an explanation. After all, I'd never actually said I didn't work for Cavazos, had I? And I wasn't bound to the syndicate—not the way Cam was bound to Tower's, anyway. "My situation is completely different."

But he wasn't buying it. "How exactly is you having a mark different from me having a mark?"

"It's different because I hate every minute of it. Every single second. I feel like I've rolled around in the mud and it's oozed into my nose and ears, and other places I can't even reach, and I'll never get clean. I feel filthy. I fight the binding with every breath I take. But you've been bound to Tower for six years and until today, I bet you never even *thought* about trying to get out of it. Hell, you reenlisted and took an early promotion! That's the difference, Cam."

"That's not a difference—it's like looking in a mirror. You think I want to be bound to Tower? Or to anyone else? Believe it or not, I don't like marching in their little rows, following orders like a tin soldier. But I don't have any choice, and from where I'm standing the only difference between your situation and mine is that at least I'm serving on my *feet*."

I felt my cheeks flame and fought to turn humiliation into anger, because then at least I'd be in control of my own emotions, if nothing else. "You don't know what you're talking about. This isn't what it looks like...."

Cam stood, all puffed up with fury, but I could see the fear and pain in his eyes. He was hiding behind anger, just like me. "Well, that's good, because it *looks* like that's Ruben Cavazos's live mark on your thigh!"

"Okay, that part's what it looks like, but it doesn't mean what you think it means. I'm not in the skin trade. This is nothing like what happened to Van. And I'm not spying on you, nor am I trying to recruit you. You and Anne came to *me,* remember?"

"Olivia, Tower's men *shot* me, just so I'd need their help, then be in their debt. I know how this works. I

know what the syndicate—*either* syndicate—will do
to get whoever they want. And I know what a mark on
the thigh means. If he's not turning you out, he's keeping you in." His voice cracked on the last words, and
my heart felt as if it was cracking along with his, one
excruciating inch at a time. "You're his personal whore,
just like Nick said."

"No, I am *not*." Pain and anger coiled so tightly
inside me that I could no longer tell the difference between them. "And don't you *ever* say that to me again."
I stomped across the room toward him and propped one
bare foot on the coffee table, then pulled Van's skirt up
so he could see the mark again. "Take a closer look," I
demanded, but his gaze never left mine, his eyes shiny
with unspent, angry tears. "Look at it!" I shouted, and
finally he did. One quick glance.

"It's not red, Cam," I pointed out. "I'm not his whore,
or anyone else's. In fact, that mark is like a fucking
chastity *force field*. Thanks to our contract, he can't
go past it without my permission. Which he has never
had, nor will ever have."

Cam exhaled, his relief almost palpable. Then he
frowned. "If you're not…sleeping with him, why the
hell is his mark on your thigh?"

"Because if you give him an inch, he'll take the
whole damn planet. Cavazos wanted the mark on my
arm, but I told him I wouldn't wear it where anyone else
could see it. His compromise was that he got to pick the
unseen location—and ink the tattoo himself. I consider
myself lucky it's not on my ass."

Cam blinked, and the momentary confusion cleared.
"He's a Binder?"

I nodded slowly and lowered my leg. "He's not very

good with a verbal or written seal—though his staff is top-notch—but he's a damn strong flesh Binder. Didn't you ever wonder what his Skill is?"

Cam shrugged. "I just assumed that was privileged information. Tower would kill anyone who leaked details about what he can and can't do. Not that any of us could actually blab, thanks to the binding."

Hmm. Maybe that was in Cavazos's boilerplate, too. Good thing my contract was custom…

"Flesh binding is how he got his start," I said. "In his twenties, a couple of years before the revelation, he conned a few of his friends and cousins into signing unfavorable bonds of loyalty to him, and he inked the marks into their flesh himself. And the syndicate grew from there. He takes a cut of everything, and he still does some of the marks himself. His organization is older than Tower's, you know." According to Cavazos, his was one of the oldest Skilled syndicates in the country, and I'd found no reason not to believe that.

I sank onto the edge of the coffee table and Cam sat on the couch in front of me. "So what do you do for him?" But he still looked as if he didn't really want the answer.

"I don't do anything for him on a regular basis. This is a one-shot deal. He needs someone found and once I fulfill my part of the deal, the mark goes dead, and I'm done with him. No extensions. No noncompete clauses. Nothing complicated."

"If it's so simple, why the binding? Why didn't he just hire you, like everyone else?"

"The contract is simple, but he's not. Ruben likes to own things. Specifically, people. Especially women. I needed to win this particular job, and he knew it, which gave him the upper hand. He wouldn't hire me without a binding."

"But you negotiated, right? You must have, to get out of the standard clauses."

"Yeah. Under the terms we both agreed to, he can't tell anyone I'm bound to him, or what I'm doing for him." That one turned out to be a mistake on my part, because it meant he couldn't tell Meika what his business with me really was, leaving her free to draw the obvious conclusions.

"But he can't...touch you?"

Shit. This was the part I *really* didn't want Cam to know. "He gets to...um..." I closed my eyes, trying to remember the exact wording. "'Physically express either his pleasure or displeasure with my performance.'"

"Which means he gets to feel you up and hit you." Anger bled into his features and the couch groaned beneath him as he leaned back.

"Yes, up to a point. But I get to hit back." Also up to a point.

"Damn it, Liv!" Cam stood and stomped across the room, a spring coiled tight and ready to burst free. "Why would you agree to that?"

"Because he had the advantage and I *needed* the job." Worse than Cam would ever know. "At the time, I thought I was being smart for insisting on limits, but it turns out I'm not as good with contract language as I thought I was."

"I hear *some* people spend years in law school studying that very thing."

"Yeah, well, I didn't have years and I don't know any lawyers. But I think I did pretty well, consider-

ing what I had to work with. He can't make me sleep
with him or with anyone else, and he can't use weapons
against me or do any permanent damage. Those were
my deal-breakers."

"I'd like to break *him*." Cam pulled me up and
wrapped his arms around me, speaking into my hair.
"I can't stand the thought of his hands on you."

That made two of us. And that part would only get
worse—if he knew Cam and I were together again,
Ruben would get possessive and start pushing boundaries, just to demonstrate his own power. But Cam didn't
need to know that.

"And he has to let me make a living, even while
the mark is live," I said, to redirect the conversation.
"That's why I needed a retainer from Anne. Without
it, she's not an official client, and he can call me away
from this little project anytime he wants, to put me back
on his."

"Oh." Cam's brows rose in an almost-grin. "If I
didn't think it'd offend you, I'd offer to pay for your
time permanently, just so he'd have to let you see me."

I laughed, in spite of the circumstances. "As insult-
ing—yet sweet—as that is, it only works with tracking jobs. I can track for other people, as long as they're
paying me."

"Funny you should say that. I just happen to have
lost touch with my kindergarten teacher. And my girl-
friend from fourth grade. And the obstetrician who delivered me. In fact, I'm pretty sure I could keep you
busy—and officially employed—for the rest of your
life."

I laughed again, and it felt *good*. "You're just stupid
enough to try it, too, aren't you?"

"I think the word you're looking for is *brilliant.* I'm *brilliant* enough to try it. And yes, I told you I'd do whatever it takes. Knowing about your mark doesn't change that."

I leaned forward and kissed him. And it felt so good, I did it again. And when he pulled me onto the couch with him, I went willingly, sparing a moment of pure gratitude for the fact that this stolen moment was even possible, in the midst of the violence and chaos defining both of our lives in general, and this job for Anne in particular.

"How long have you been bound to him?" Cam lay on his side against the back of the couch, and I lay on my back next to him. He ran his fingers slowly up and down my left arm, just brushing the lower edge of the bandage.

"A year and a half."

His hand went still on my arm. "You've been looking for one person for a year and a half?"

"It's pretty…complicated." To say the very, very least.

"It's busywork, Liv," Cam insisted, frowning down at me from inches away. "He's playing you. Whoever you're looking for is dead. That's why you can't find him. Or her."

I shook my head against the couch pillow, wishing we'd never have to move past that moment in time, with him pressed against me and the worst six years of my life rendered a distant memory, even if that meant having to talk about my work for Cavazos for eternity. "It's a him. And he's alive. Every time I try, I get just the faintest pull from his paternal middle name."

"You're *name*-tracking? Why would you even

bother?" Cam asked. Then he realized what he'd said, and how I might take it, and shook his head, backtracking with an apologetic smile. "Not that you *can't* track by name. But you're so much better with blood..."

The story of my life...

"Unfortunately, we don't have a blood sample, and even if we did, it'd be too old to be of much use. All we have to go on is one middle name."

Cam stretched to prop himself on his elbow. "Liv, that's crazy. I don't know that *I* could find someone based only on a single middle name. How can he expect you to?"

He expected it because I'd sworn on my liberty that I could deliver within two years. "I'll do it. I have to." Because I wasn't the only one who would pay if I defaulted on my contract.

"I don't think he really wants you to," Cam insisted. "He put his mark on your thigh and he's obviously been pushing the boundaries of what he's allowed to do to you." He looked as if the mere thought made him want to vomit—as it did me. "He wants you to fail, so he can keep you indefinitely. He's probably counting on you wanting to renegotiate down the road, when you realize you can't find whatever obscure goose he's picked for you to chase."

"No, that's not it." But *damn,* did I wish it was. "He's desperate for some legitimate news. I have to report to him every week and he always grills me about my progress first thing. It's personal, and he's very, *very* serious about this tracking. It comes before everything else."

"Is that where you were this morning?" he asked, and I nodded. "Then the whiskey shots in your office...?"

"A time-honored ritual and proven coping mechanism."

"And I'm guessing you can't tell me who he's looking for?"

"Nope. Though I'm free to tell the whole world that I'm working for him in some unnamed capacity. In fact, he *wants* me to." Because he wasn't allowed to openly discuss our connection.

"So, I guess this mark is the source of the rumors that you're bedding the boss...." Cam looked so relieved to have found a logical explanation that I almost hated to disappoint him.

"Nope." I shook my head firmly and felt the couch material snag in my hair. "I can't figure out where those are coming from, because no one's seen the mark."

"No one? You haven't...?" He let the question fade into implication, flavored by the blatant hope in his eyes.

I propped myself up on my good arm and faced him eye to eye. "Didn't we already agree not to ask that question? I don't want to know who you've been with since me, and you don't want the details of my personal life, either. But none of that matters anymore, right?" I said, and he nodded hesitantly. "All I'm saying is that no one's seen the mark."

I hadn't been nude in a lit room for almost eighteen months. And I hadn't had sex at all in nearly a year. Since word—inaccurate, of course—got out that I was working for Cavazos, everyone I might have considered going home with seemed more interested in proving or disproving the rumors. And no one would press past what they thought to be evidence of Ruben's claim on me.

No one I'd want, anyway. Anyone willing to cross that mark was just in it to prove he wasn't afraid of Cavazos.

Anyone but Cam.

"So, what you're saying is that no one's seen this—" his hand slid down my stomach and over the gauze material covering my thigh "—in a very long time."

My breath hitched. No one had touched me like that in years. That was the touch of a man interested in more than a quick fix for us both. More than a story about sleeping with a woman who may or may not belong to one of the most powerful men in the country.

"Just you…" I breathed. And Ruben. But he didn't count. In fact, he'd never counted less.

"I like that," Cam whispered, sliding down next to me on the couch. "Say it again."

"Just you…" I murmured, reaching up with my good arm to pull him closer. His mouth brushed mine, and I lifted my head for greater contact, pulling his lip into my mouth. Tasting him.

A thousand times I'd imagined this, blending memory and imagination to keep from thinking about what was actually happening—who was actually touching me. And now it was real. *Cam* was real, and this moment was real; surely the pain in my arm proved that. A gunshot wound was better than a self-inflicted pinch any day of the week, and the pain was minor compared to how good everything else felt. His hands. His lips. The rough stubble on his chin, catching in my hair when his kisses traveled over my jaw toward my ear.

Being with him was better than I remembered.

Better than I'd imagined. The moment would have been perfect, except that...

"Wait. We can't do this." I put a hand on Cam's bare chest and he stared down at me in amusement.

"Speak for yourself. I'm ready."

And boy was he. But... "That's not what I mean. We don't have time for this right now." We were supposed to be saving lives. Finding murderers. Making the world a better place, one mob boss at a time...

"According to you and Noelle, one of us will be dead soon. So if you think about it like that, we don't have time to wait."

"Don't joke about death."

"I'm joking about sex."

"Cam, this isn't funny!"

He sighed and propped himself up on one elbow, running the fingers of his other hand lightly over my stomach. "Olivia, neither of us is going to die anytime soon. I'm not going to let that happen, so worrying about it is pointless. As for the rest of this..." His hand slid lower, and I caught my breath. "I make time for the important things, and you're the most important thing in the world to me." He leaned closer and whispered against my skin as he dropped kisses down my throat. "Besides..." Kiss. "Anne texted ten minutes ago." Kiss. "They're all fine." Kiss. And when he reached my collarbone, I threw my head back. "That gives us fifty minutes to play with." Kiss. "And I can do a lot in fifty minutes...."

His hand slid lower, and I arched into his touch. My body was alive every place my skin met his, and I craved more. And for the first time in six years, I could have more. I could have *all* of him. It might not be smart. It might even be the last time we'd be alone together, if whatever Elle had seen was related to this new working relationship. But no matter what had come before or what we would be made to do next, these stolen moments belonged only to us, a victory of faith and second chances.

I pulled Cam up for a kiss I never wanted to end, then he helped me get my shirt off without aggravating my injury. I lifted my hips so he could slide the borrowed skirt down my legs, trailing his fingers the whole way. His touch gave me chills, yet somehow stoked a growing flame inside me, and the conflict of fire and ice amplified every touch. Magnified every sensation.

I squirmed out of my underwear while he stepped out of his jeans, and then there was nothing between us. Nothing but memories, and the desperate hope that there'd be time to build a few more.

For one long moment, Cam stood in front of the couch staring down at me. Looking at me as if he was trying to memorize the sight. I looked back, aching to touch him, and treasuring that moment of anticipation, when possibilities abound and reality promises even more.

Then the moment was over and I had to touch him.

I pulled Cam onto the couch with me and indulged my greedy hands, my selfish lips. I wanted to touch all of him, and his desires mirrored my own, and the blaze between us burned so hot anyone standing near would surely have been scorched.

When I could stand no more teasing, no more promises without payoff, I arched into Cam's touch, aching for more. Demanding it. His laugh was soft and deep in my ear, and his hand played a little deeper. A little rougher. "What do you want?" he whispered, and I groaned, overwhelmed by the possibilities. By needs I couldn't put into words.

"You."

"Anything more specific?" His lips trailed down my neck again, and I closed my eyes when he lifted my breast. My back arched when his mouth closed over my nipple, pulling gently, sending waves of heat to echo lower.

"You. Now."

"Not yet…" he murmured, and I groaned. His tongue trailed down the center of my stomach slowly, leaving a hot, wet trail as he crawled down the length of my body. I writhed beneath him and sucked in a sharp breath when his hands slid beneath me, lifting my hips. His stubble scratched my thighs and I opened wider, breathing heavily, anticipation a wild blaze consuming me from inside.

With the first stroke of his tongue—fire given rhythm and form—his hand slid up my side and over my stomach to cup my breast. I gasped and arched into him, lost in need building with every pause, cresting with every touch. Pleasure coiled, so hot and fast nothing else existed in that moment.

"Wait!" I gasped. But he only pushed my hand away when I tried to pull him up. The strokes came faster, hotter, and I clenched the couch cushion beneath me. Then that single point of heat spilled over, and my entire body rocked with wave after wave of pleasure.

Cam groaned, and for a second, the air was cold where he'd been. Then his weight settled over me and I pulled him closer, clutching at him as the muscles in his back shifted beneath my hand. He slid inside me in one stroke, then stayed there, moaning, while after-shocks of my own pleasure clenched around him. Then he was moving inside me, and that heat built again with every stroke.

So familiar, yet so much better than I remembered, and the whole world funneled around me until there was only him, and us, and the rhythm that defined our reunion. And in that moment, as pleasure built between us, racing toward a conclusion I needed, yet was desperate to delay, it felt possible that there might never be anything else. That we could live like this forever. That I could subsist on Cam Caballero alone and never want for a thing in my life.

Then the rhythm changed. The strokes deepened. And I fell right over the edge of need into a wordless, thoughtless convulsion of pleasure. Cam groaned in my ear, and my legs tightened around him, and we rode the last waves together until electric aftershocks gave way to a pleasant numbness, and he collapsed on the couch beside me, his body stretched down the length of mine.

His hand splayed over my stomach, damp with our combined sweat, and his lips found my ear one more time. "I love you, Olivia," he whispered, and my heart ached as if it would break in half. "You think we'll die if we stay together, but I've been dying slowly for the last six years. I'm taking my life back, Liv. Our life together. And this time, I'm not going to let you go."

Seventeen

My phone rang in the dark, interrupting my first sleep since I'd been called out for Rawlinson's job at two the previous morning. I glanced at Cam's alarm clock, glowing red from his nightstand. Eleven o'clock at night. Shen had been dead twenty-seven hours. I'd been asleep for three.

My nap was just a tease, and I knew before I even glanced at my phone that it was over.

Groaning, I twisted away from Cam to free my good arm, then reached toward the nightstand to unplug my cell from the travel charger. Cavazos's private number flashed on the screen.

Son of a bitch... What the hell did he want?

"Don't answer it," Cam mumbled, trailing one finger down my arm as I turned on the lamp. "You've earned a nap. Hell, you've earned a coma."

"No choice." When Cavazos called, I had to answer. I sat up, and Cam's warm arm wrapped around my bare waist. "Can you...not talk?" I turned to give him an apologetic smile, and he nodded. But he wasn't happy.

I pressed the accept-call button, and Cavazos was

talking before I even had the phone at my ear. "What are you doing, Olivia?" He was pissed. I could tell by how smooth and low his voice was—the calm before the storm.

"Working."

"You're working? Right this minute? Getting paid?" he said, and my internal alarm sputtered to life and tried to wail.

"Yes." I knew the lie was a bad idea even as I said it, but no matter what he thought or wanted, Cavazos didn't rule my life, and he had no right to monitor every second of it.

Then the pain hit, right behind my eyes, and the room wobbled around me. And that's when I understood. We'd found and disposed of Shen's killer. My job for Anne was technically finished, and since she hadn't paid a new retainer, I was no longer officially working for her.

I hadn't just lied, I'd lied about my state of employment, a minor breach of my contract with Cavazos.

Shit, shit, shit!

"If you're getting paid for whatever you're doing with Caballero, you've expanded your services since our agreement," he said, and my heart dropped into my stomach with an almost-audible plop.

He knew I was with Cam. Had one of his men seen us together?

I took a moment to weigh my options: feign ignorance, or unleash honest anger? I went with the best of both worlds: feigned angry ignorance.

"What the hell, Ruben?"

"Get dressed. There's a car waiting for you downstairs. If you're not in it in five minutes, I'm sending them in after you."

Fuck. *Fuck!* He knew where we were. "You had me followed?"

"No, I had you tracked."

Motherfucker! I stood and headed into the living room, in search of my clothes.

"What are you…?" Cam asked, standing naked in the doorway, but I silenced him with a look as I stepped into my underwear, the phone pinned against my shoulder, wincing at the fresh pain spawned in my arm by the movement.

"Is that him?" Cavazos said into my ear, sounding almost…eager. Hungry. He wanted a fight.

"Leave him out of this," I said, pulling up my borrowed skirt.

"Leave me…?" Cam sputtered, and I scowled at him again, shoving my good arm into Vanessa's T-shirt.

"Leave him out of this?" Cavazos said. I had to take the phone away from my ear to pull the shirt over my head, and I could still hear him yelling. "If your ass isn't in that car in—" he paused, and I pictured him looking at his watch "—three and a half minutes, I'm going to pull him so far into this he'll wish he'd never even met you. No piece of ass is worth the pain you're bringing to his doorstep. Are you hearing me, Olivia?"

I sat on the couch next to Cam and pulled on my left sock, then shoved my foot into my boot.

"I said, are you hearing me?"

"Yes!" I shouted into the phone. "I fucking hear you! Three minutes." Then I pressed the end-call button and dropped the phone on the coffee table. *Damn it!* Pissed beyond all control, I kicked the table with my booted foot and it skidded across the room, launching my phone into the wall. It hit the floor undamaged, unfortunately.

"Cavazos?" Cam righted the table as I pulled my second sock on, and I could see the flare of temper in his eyes.

"Yeah."

"He called you in?"

"Yeah." I shoved my foot into the last boot and laced it up like my fingers were on fire.

"Don't go. You don't have to go."

I stood and met his gaze. "Anne's no longer paying me. I have to go."

"But you already reported to him this week."

"Doesn't matter." I headed back into the bedroom to unplug my phone charger, and Cam followed, arms crossed over his chest. "He can request additional reports, at his convenience." Or he could offer me side jobs, which I had to take unless they conflicted with existing work.

"That didn't sound like a request to me. Did he say there's a car outside?"

"Yup." In the front room again, I picked up my satchel and shoved my phone charger inside, then bent for my phone, glancing around to make sure I wasn't forgetting anything. I'd have to leave everything related to Shen's murder—I couldn't take anything I wouldn't want found in a search. Which meant my gun would have to stay, too.

"How the hell does he know you're here?"

"Sometimes he has me watched. This time he had me tracked."

"You're serious?" Cam said, and I glanced at him

with both brows raised in answer. "He wants more from you than a tracking job, Liv."

"I'm aware. He just wants what he knows he can't have—a pretty standard obsession for the rich and spoiled. But that doesn't invalidate the importance of the work I'm actually doing for him."

Cam stepped between me and the front door. "The Liv I knew would never jump just because some abusive asshole told her to."

I exhaled slowly. "The Liv you knew didn't have to jump. This one does." He started to argue, but I put my whole hand over his mouth. "Stay here, Cam. I'll be back as soon as I can. Just…stay in the apartment. Please." He shoved my hand away, but I spoke over whatever he'd been about to say. "Swear."

"Hell no. If you're going, I'm going with you."

"You can't." I tried to pull him away from the door, but he wouldn't move. "Cam, you have three marks from Tower on your arm. If you come anywhere near Cavazos's house, they'll kill you…."

"They'll *try*."

"They'll succeed. You can't fight his entire security detail by yourself," I insisted, and Cam tried to interrupt, but I spoke over him again. "And after you've tried and failed, Ruben's going to take it out on me, for bringing you."

Cam's mouth closed, and his protest died. But he stayed in front of the door. "If he touches you, I'll kill him."

I sighed, hyperaware of the seconds ticking away while we argued. "He's going to touch me. He's been touching me for a year and a half, and there's nothing either of us can do about that." Except plot his ultimate destruction in new and sadistic ways.

"We can kill him."

"Yeah." I nodded. "Maybe we can." If I could sneak a weapon in and kill him with one blow. My mark would die along with Ruben, so there'd be no resistance pain—in theory, that was as close as I could get to an easy out. However, if I couldn't kill him with one blow, I'd wish I'd died instead. "But even if we manage to kill Ruben, we'd never make it out of there alive. I have to go, and you have to stay here until I get back. I'll be fine."

Cam took me by both arms, below my bandage. "Olivia, you're not listening." He stared straight down into my eyes. "I can't stand the thought of him touching you. At all. I can't just sit here and wait for you to come back, imagining him all over you. Or hitting you. I can't."

I pulled free from his grip, wincing over the fresh pain in my left arm, and returned his steady, pained gaze. "I'm only going to say this once—get over it. If I can deal with the reality, you can survive imagining it. Now move. I have to go." This time he let me pull him away from the door. I kissed him one more time, then stepped out of the apartment and closed the door.

Cam's wordless shout of anger and frustration followed me into the hall, chased by the crash of something heavy hitting the wall.

I stomped down the stairs, cursing Ruben beneath my breath the whole way.

The car was a shiny black sedan, a stereotype on wheels. It was also double-parked and idling. As I stepped onto the curb, the back door opened and Tomas climbed out. He grinned. "I almost didn't recognize you in a skirt."

"That makes two of us," I said, sliding into the backseat. He sat next to me, and the car was rolling before he'd even fully closed the door. "I didn't think he ever let you out of the house."

Tomas laughed. "I think he was trying to find a messenger you'd hesitate to kill."

"Smart man." I had a soft spot for Tomas, because he'd never leered at me, taken liberties while patting me down or made innuendos about my relationship with his boss. But that only went so far. "I'd have killed you in a second if you laid one hand on Caballero." Assuming Cam didn't do it himself.

Tomas laughed. "I believe you'd try."

"You better believe I'd do more than that."

He looked as if he just might.

Twenty minutes later, the driver parked behind Cavazos's fortress, and Tomas patted me down in the driveway, while the driver went through my satchel. "A year and a half, and I've never once tried to sneak in a weapon," I said, as the driver handed my bag back to me. "You know that, right?"

"Just followin' orders," he said.

I could swear he used to call me "ma'am."

Tomas relieved the man covering the back door for him, and I continued through the kitchen to the back hallway. Cavazos had never received me anywhere but his office. In fact, I'd only seen a total of four rooms in the huge house—one of them a bathroom—and I'd never been above the first floor.

Exhausted, but even more pissed off, I stomped down the unlit hall, mining my own anger for enough stamina to get me through this unexpected tête-à-tête. I was so focused on the rage I was nurturing that I didn't realize someone had stepped out of the darkened bathroom as I passed until a hand wrapped around my throat and shoved me backward into the wall.

"What the hell are you doing here in the middle of the night?" Michaela Cavazos's piquant accent was thick with anger, and her words practically floated on a tequila cloud. She was drinking alone on a Friday night, while her husband was having me tracked.

When I tried to push her away, something cold and sharp poked my neck.

Shit. She'd finally lost it. My heart jumped so far into my throat I could practically taste it.

"I don't know." I swallowed, trying to ignore the blade poking me just below my jaw, praying it wouldn't break my skin and give her access to even a drop of my blood. "Command appearance."

"I know you are fucking him, and you *will* pay for it," she slurred.

"I'm not..." The knife trembled in her grip, and my pulse raced so fast I could hear it whooshing in my ears. "I swear, Meika, I have never slept with your husband. And I never will."

"Lying bitch."

I exhaled slowly. "You've seen my mark. You know it's not red."

"That doesn't mean he's not fucking you. It just means you don't have to let him." The knife left my throat, though her hand did not. "The apartment. The bank account. The mark on your thigh. Those do not add up to innocence." The cold blade lifted my left sleeve to bare the bandage she could probably barely see in the dark. "Fresh ink?"

"Unrelated injury. No ink at all."

"So it's just the one mark, whore?" she whispered, and I gasped when she used the blade to lightly drag the material of Van's skirt up my left leg. "I'm going to cut it out of you, and cut your cancer out of my marriage...."

"For the last time, *I'm* not the problem in your marriage. And if you don't put that damn blade up, I'm gonna start yelling, and *you* can explain why you're holding one of his employees at knifepoint." Normally I hate a tattletale, but then, I also hate being threatened with a knife, and she sounded drunk enough to forget there would be consequences for stabbing me.

Her blade stopped just above my femoral artery. Guess she wasn't *that* drunk. "Shout, and I will cut you. Whatever comes after will be worth watching you bleed out on my floor."

And I had no doubt she'd do it. She could slice my artery before Cavazos even made it out of his chair. "I'm *not* sleeping with him. If you don't believe me, why don't you take this up with your husband?"

"He is a man, and men are fools. This is a matter for the women." The blade tugged my skirt higher, then we both froze at a shuffling sound from my left.

"Mommy?"

I turned my head to find Cavazos's four-year-old daughter—Isabel—standing at the end of the hall clutching a stuffed giraffe, backlit with light from the kitchen.

Michaela hid her blade lengthwise in the folds of my skirt, pressing both her knife and the fist holding it between my thighs. I gasped, then bit my lip. "Go back to bed, *niña*. I will be there in a minute."

Isabel stuck her thumb in her mouth, then tottered off again without a word. Probably half-asleep.

"I know you are sleeping with him, and I know who you are tracking for him, and I will *not* let you bring that bastard into my house."

A door creaked open and light flooded the hall. "Michaela."

She froze at the sound of her husband's voice, and I looked up to find him standing in his office doorway, a silhouette backlit from within.

"Go upstairs," Cavazos growled.

Still glaring at me, she stepped back and folded her knife with one hand, then turned and walked down the hall without a word to—or a glance at—her husband. I only exhaled in relief when she disappeared around the corner.

Cavazos's gaze traveled over my attire and his brows rose in approval. "A skirt. I like it."

I made a mental note to apologize to Van in advance for burning her skirt.

He gestured with one outstretched arm for me to go inside, then he closed the door behind us.

"Would you please tell your wife that you and I aren't sleeping together?" He couldn't tell her what we were doing, but he could tell her what we *weren't* doing.

He frowned. "Where would be the fun in that?"

"The fun would be the part where she doesn't stab me to death in my sleep. Your wife is psychotic." I leaned against the back of a chair, hoping if I stayed standing, he'd subconsciously be less tempted to drag this out. It was a long shot, but I was desperate.

"Michaela is just angry. Anger does fascinating things to a woman—no two react the same."

"Yeah, well, she's *over*reacting. With a knife."

He nodded with a small, almost nostalgic smile. "It was my wedding gift to her. The handle is ivory."

Sick bastard. "Well, at least my murder weapon will have sentimental value."

"That's actually an honor, you know."

"I'll keep that in mind as my life flashes before my eyes. She knows who you're looking for, Ruben."

He perched on the edge of his desk, watching me. "That was inevitable, and it changes nothing. Nor is it the reason you're here. Why have you spent the entire day west of the river?"

"Working."

"With Cameron Caballero?"

"The job required the assistance of a name-Tracker, and he's the best in the city." Which Cavazos damn well knew.

"Required? So the job is complete?"

Shit. Careless phrasing had been the downfall of more than one fool attempting to stonewall Ruben Cavazos, and if I weren't so tired, I never would have made such a novice mistake. "Um...yeah. The first phase. But that led to —"

"Have you fulfilled your obligation to the client?" he said, waving off my attempt at damage control.

"Yes."

"Then you will say *adiós* to Mr. Caballero and return to your work for me."

I had no choice about working for him—at least until I could get a new retainer from Anne—but... "You can't keep me away from Cam."

"Are you sleeping with him?"

"That's none of your business."

Ruben stood, stalking closer, and I stubbornly held my ground. "Everything you do is my business—I have a right to protect my investment. I want you to stay away from him, Olivia."

"Then you should have written that into my contract."

His fist flew. My face exploded in pain. I stumbled back from the blow, tripped over the clawed foot of the chair and went down hard on my right side. "You know how this is going to end. The game never changes, yet you keep playing." He dropped into a squat in front of me and tilted my face up to inspect the damage while I ground my teeth together, breathing through the pain. It was bad, but not as bad as it was about to be. "Why do you do this to yourself, Olivia?"

"That's what I was going to ask you." I shoved him with my good arm. He went down on one hip, and I relished his ungainly fall and rare loss of poise. I pushed myself to my feet and kicked as hard as I could. My boot slammed into his ribs. He grunted in pain and I kicked again, then backpedaled when he made a grab for my leg. He was on his feet in an instant, storming after me, eyes alive with fury. Some sick part of him liked it when I hit back.

So did I.

"Are you trying to make me kill you?"

"Nah." I backed around the corner of his desk and out of reach, adrenaline surging through me like tiny bolts of lightning. "But you were right—anger does interesting things to women."

"So do I." He lunged around the desk, holding his

ribs where I'd kicked him, and I backed up until I hit the wall. But then there was nowhere else to go. Ruben was there in an instant. I tried to dodge him, but his fist slammed into my stomach and another breath was ripped away from me. I choked and half collapsed, but he held me upright.

When I could breathe again, I pushed him away and took another swing at his ribs—an angry afterthought that exposed the bandage on my arm. Ruben dodged the blow and grabbed my left arm, pulling me closer, squeezing my injury mercilessly.

I screamed as his fingers dug into both the entry and exit wounds, through the bandage.

"Done?" he asked, in a whisper against my ear.

I could only nod. There was still plenty of fight in me, but I'd had too little sleep and lost too much blood to give it my best, especially considering that he had the greater size and strength, and he could command me to stop whenever he tired of the game. I was never going to get the better of him without a weapon.

"What happened to your arm?"

"Got shot," I gasped through the brutal pain he'd re-awakened.

"Sit." He hauled me toward his desk and shoved me into one of the chairs in front, where I sucked in a deep breath and held it, riding out the worst of the pain in my stomach and my arm. All in all, I'd seen better days.

"I want you back on my case, full-time," he said, picking up our ongoing business discussion as if there had been no hiatus. "What's your next step?"

"I don't know yet. The name she gave you was fake. All of it, as far as I can tell. And you don't even have a picture of her."

"It was eight years ago. I was trying to *hide* her from Michaela, not provide evidence of our affair." Though clearly his policy on extramarital recreation had changed at some point. "And that was before I realized the only women who can be trusted are woman under surveillance."

"Fine." I shrugged. "But without her blood, or her real name, or a photo, or proof that *anything* she told you about herself was actually true—including her fucking age—she can't be found. She disappeared, Ruben. All I have to go on for your son is the middle name you gave him. I don't know what else you want me to do."

"I want you to find him!" Ruben roared. "I don't care about her—I don't even need to see her—but I want my son. You will find him for me, or you will be in breach of contract, and I *will* execute the consequences of that breach. Do you understand?"

Of course I understood. I'd thought of little else in the past year and a half. "There's one other possibility, but you're not going to like it," I said, holding my arm, though that did nothing for the pain.

"No." He gave his head one short, sharp shake for emphasis. "You're not getting a sample of my blood."

"Ruben, this may be your only shot. Other than the mother, you're his closest relative, and since you're both male, your blood's going to be the closest in energy signature to his. I wouldn't need much, and you'd have to be out of my range, so I wouldn't be pulled to you instead. But at the very least, I should be able to tell if he's alive, and if he's within my range, I might get a general direction."

He scowled. "Do you really expect me to give you a

sample of my blood, then leave the city with it in your possession?"

I eyed him in challenge. "Do you really expect me to find your son?"

He closed his eyes and exhaled, and when he met my gaze again, suspicion rivaled determination in his eyes. "You'd have to take another oath, swearing to destroy the sample when you're done and never, under any circumstances, use my blood for any other purpose."

"Paper only," I said. "No more marks."

He nodded. "I'll have something drafted in a couple of days—the contracts department is backed up at the moment, with my top Binder missing."

"Fine. Are we done here?"

"For now. My driver will take you home."

"My office," I insisted.

"Good." He nodded, and I decided to let him think I was heading to the office to work on his case. "Stay away from Caballero," he called, as I headed for the door. "Or I'll call you right back in."

"Bite me," I said, and he laughed, already picking up the phone to give instructions to the driver.

I closed the door behind me and had made it halfway down the hall, clutching my bruised stomach, before I realized I wasn't alone. Again.

"You are never going to find her," Michaela said, and I stopped in the middle of the hall, groaning on the inside.

I let go of my stomach—never advertise weakness— and turned slowly to see her leaning against an open doorway behind me. "Find who?" Feigning ignorance seemed like my best bet at the time.

"Tamara Parker. She is dead." Michaela sauntered toward me, and I took a step back.

"Do I even want to know how you know that?"

Meika shrugged. "I had her killed years ago. For sleeping with my husband."

Oh, *hell*.

"Please tell me you didn't have the baby killed, too...."

Another shrug, and a small, callous smile. "I would have, but he wasn't with her."

"Does Ruben know?"

She shook her head slowly. "I'm saving the announcement for a special occasion."

"You're sick." I turned my back on her and started down the hall again, but froze at her next words.

"Did you have fun on the west side today? Were you searched for Ruben's mark?"

I turned slowly. "You...?" I demanded, and her cruel smile grew. "You started the rumors? Is that how you got rid of Tamara?"

She laughed, a brittle, delicate sound. "No, I had her shot. But he watches you too closely for that, so I had to get creative." Her gaze narrowed on me. "Did anyone find the mark? Because they will keep looking, you know. They won't let Ruben Cavazos's spying whore wander in their midst, and when they find the mark, they *will* kill you."

"They'll have to kill me to find the mark," I corrected, and she shrugged again.

"You'll be dead either way."

Eighteen

I didn't truly relax until I'd closed and locked my office door, locking the rest of the world out in the process. I called Cam from my cell and poured the first shot of whiskey while the phone rang in my ear.

"Liv? Are you all right?" He sounded near panic. I knew how he felt.

I tossed back the whiskey and slammed the shot glass down on my desk, my eyes squeezed shut until the burn in my throat faded. The burn was a relief, even if I only felt it because Michaela had bruised my throat with her grip.

"Yeah. I need a favor."

"What? Where are you?"

"At my office. Alone. I need you to bring me everything I left at your place. Including my gun. And on the way, can you stop and pick up one of those prepaid phones and have it activated?"

"Do I even want to know why?"

"Probably not." I poured another shot, and he must have heard me swallow.

"Put the whiskey back in the drawer, Liv," he said,

and over the line I heard a zipper being opened as he packed my stuff into a bag.

"I'm done." After one more shot. "See you in a few?"

"Be there as soon as I can."

After that, I called Anne and asked her to send me another five-dollar retainer online, officially hiring me to track whoever wanted her daughter dead. Immediately. She sounded confused, but agreed and assured me that she, her parents and Hadley were all fine. But I wouldn't let her tell me where they were.

When her payment came through, I printed the receipt and filed it, then exhaled in relief as I stowed the whiskey in my bottom desk drawer. I could now legally and officially tell Cavazos to go fuck himself. With that taken care of, I headed into the bathroom to assess the damage to my face.

My left cheek was turning purple—I'd already suspected as much, based on the reproachful shake of his head Tomas had given me when I'd left. The second bruise forming on my stomach was fainter and less defined, but very tender to the touch.

I'd had worse.

When Cam knocked on the office door, I lowered my shirt and let him in. He took one look at my face and dropped his duffel on the couch to take my chin in hand. "That black-hearted *bastard*... I'm going to break every tooth in his head."

"Get in line."

"Did you at least hit him back?" He let go of my chin and unzipped his bag.

"Hell yes. I may have cracked his ribs."

"What set him off?"

"Does it matter?" I sank into my desk chair and dug a bottle of ibuprofen from the middle drawer.

Cam looked up, noting my reluctance to answer. "It does now."

I sighed. "He wanted me to stay away from you, and I refused."

"He hit you because of me?" Cam's fist clenched around the duffel strap and his brows dipped low.

"No, he hit me because I refused an order he had no right to give. He doesn't own me like he owns everyone else in his life, and he hates it that I can say no." To some things, at least. I was a threat to his manhood, or his authority, or whatever, and he struck out to reassert himself. And he left visible bruises so everyone else would know I wasn't getting away with anything. "He wouldn't do it if I did everything he told me to." But that just wasn't in me. I'd rather be bruised than acquiescent.

"Yes, he would. I had a run-in with him once, Liv." Which I already knew, of course. "I know what he's like."

But he was wrong there.

"Here's the phone." He handed me a slim slider phone with a full keyboard. "I activated it in the car—the number's in your contacts list, and I already programmed mine. And here's your gun."

"Thanks." I dry-swallowed the painkillers, then emailed Anne the new number. Then I tossed my old phone to Cam, who caught it one-handed.

"What's this for?"

"Nothing, anymore."

"So, what do you want me to do with it?"

"What I can't." What I couldn't even actually ask

him to do. I was contractually prohibited from doing anything to avoid getting Cavazos's calls or messages, which I was obligated to answer at the earliest possible moment.

Comprehension bloomed on Cam's face in the form of a satisfied grin. He threw the phone at the floor and stomped on it. The crunch of plastic was clean, and violent, and cathartic, and I really wished I could have been the one to do it.

I would pay for that later, but for the moment, I was grateful to have a loophole to exploit. Fortunately, no contract is ever truly ironclad.

Cam dropped onto my couch and looked at me across my desk. "Okay, so now what?"

"Now...we figure out why Tower wants Hadley dead, without using any of your syndicate connections or letting Tower know what we're up to. And we figure out where Hunter was getting those injections, still operating under those same constraints, while simultaneously avoiding all contact from Cavazos."

"So basically, we're working against the syndicate I'm bound to while hiding from the one you're bound to."

"Technically, I'm bound to Cavazos, not to the syndicate. But yes. Also..." I sighed and leaned with both elbows on my desk, fighting the seductive lure of sleep. "We should probably steer clear of the west side entirely."

His eyes narrowed. "Agreed, but why do you say that?"

"It turns out that Meika Cavazos is the one who started the rumor that I'm her husband's bound concubine-slash-mole. She's not allowed to kill me, so she's hoping to have me hung as a spy. Or whatever the modern equivalent of that is."

"The modern equivalent would be systematic dismemberment, followed by a bullet to the brain." And I could tell from the way he said it that he'd actually seen the floor show. And that it left an impression.

"Wow. Tower puts some serious thought into his executions."

"They're as much preventive measure as punishment. He's big on public consequences. Speaking of overkill, that's quite a complicated murder plot Cavazos's wife has cooked up."

"Evidently I'm taxing her creativity." I shrugged. "She just had the first girl shot."

"The first girl?"

"Ruben's first mistress. At least, I assume she was the first. Not that I'm sleeping with him, but Meika *thinks* I am, and she and logic don't exactly share closet space these days."

"Sounds like she and sanity aren't on very good terms, either."

I was still laughing when my new cell phone rang. I glanced at it in surprise, then snatched it and pressed the button to accept the call. Only two people had the new number, and one of them was sitting on my couch.

"Liv, we're headed your way." Anne's voice was tight with panic, and I recognized street noise and the rumble of an engine in the background.

"What? No. Tower wants to kill your daughter. The city's the last place she should be. You need to hide her."

"I *did* hide her, just like you said, and they found us."

"They?" When I noticed Cam trying to eavesdrop,

I put the call on speakerphone and set the new cell on the center of my desk.

"Just one, really. Another Traveler. But there will be more. He's not going to give up."

Cam and I exchanged a glance, then he returned his attention to the phone. "Okay, Anne, I need you to calm down and tell us what happened."

Anne took a deep breath, and in the background, a little girl said something I couldn't understand and was answered by an older man. She had her parents with her. "I put Hadley to bed at about eight-thirty. Then, maybe fifteen minutes ago, I went to check on her and found a man in the hall. He was just standing there, holding a gun. So I shot him, Liv." Her voice splintered into broken, hiccuping half words, and an older woman reminded her gently to watch the road.

"You shot him?" I couldn't believe it. I'd never even seen Anne hold a weapon, much less use one. "Where'd you get the gun?"

"It's my dad's. He brought it so we could protect Hadley, but I didn't think I'd actually have to use it. But I did, and now someone's dead."

"Where?" Cam said. "Where were you?"

"At one of my mom's show houses."

"One of your...?" Cam frowned at me, silently asking for a translation.

"Her mother's a real-estate agent," I whispered. When we were in high school, Anne would sometimes borrow the keys to a show house and let us all in for a private party. The houses were fully furnished—the perfect place for kids to hang out and drink in private. But not a good place to hide from Skilled hit men.

"Why the hell didn't you leave town? That's not running, it's…burrowing."

"A hotel seemed too obvious, and we needed someplace for Hadley to sleep. Someplace that felt like a home and wouldn't scare her any more than she already is."

"Well, scared is better than dead!" I snapped, then immediately wished I could take it back. Anne was a suburban wife and mother, not a trained bodyguard. She was new to all this, and obviously doing the best she could. "How did he get in? You had all the lights on, right?"

"Yes. All of them. There's no way he could have come in through the shadows. He must have actually physically broken in."

"But we would have heard that, Annika," her mother said softly.

"What about the closets?" Cam asked. "And under the beds?"

"We opened all the closets, but…I forgot about the beds," Anne groaned. "We've always used loft beds and captain's beds." To make sure there are never shadows beneath the beds—standard practice in Skilled homes; it's like nailing your basement windows shut so you don't have to remember to lock them. "It's possible he could have come in under one of them…."

I exhaled, trying to control my temper, and noticed that Cam had closed his eyes. He was as frustrated by Anne's survival skills—or lack thereof—as I was. "Okay, Anne…" Cam began, and I leaned back in my chair, happy to let him take over while I tried to gather my thoughts. "I understand that you were thinking about Hadley, but bringing her into the city is a bad idea. That'll just make her easier to track."

"Cam, I don't know what to do. I can't protect her. Liv, I need your help!"

"I know. Give me a minute...." I leaned with my elbows on my desk, forehead in my hands, thinking aloud. "Do they have her blood?"

"No," Anne said, without hesitation. "There's no way they could. We've burned every drop she's ever spilled."

"'Cept the drops in the trash," a young voice said, and chills shot up my spine so fast I broke out in goose bumps all over.

"What?" Anne said, and again her mother reminded her to watch the road.

"I'm sorry, we forgot!" the child howled, then burst into sobs. "I fell and cut my knee yesterday. Daddy burned the tissues, but we...mighta forgot the Band-Aids. I think I threw them away."

"Was there much blood?" I asked, holding my breath for her answer, and based on the silence in the car, I think they were all doing the same thing. But the child didn't seem to know how to answer, so her mother rephrased my question.

"Hadley, honey, how many Band-Aids did it take?"

"Three!" she cried, half choking on her tears, and my sympathy for her was the only thing rivaling my fear and frustration at that moment. "I'm sorry! I didn't mean to forget!"

"It's okay, sweetie," Anne said, and in the background, I could hear her parents comforting their granddaughter.

Cam looked as if he was holding back a string of

profanities with sheer will. "I don't suppose you know whether or not anyone actually found the blood, do you?" he asked, with more patience than I could have mustered.

"I have no clue," Anne moaned miserably.

"Okay." Another breath, while I waited for my thoughts to fall into some kind of coherent order. "We'll have to assume they did, just to be safe. Which means they can track her. So we need to hide Hadley someplace where Tower can't find her."

"Is that even possible?" Anne asked.

Cam shook his head, though no one over the line could see it. "No. Short of putting her on a plane—and you can bet they're watching the airport—there's no way to get her out of tracking range fast enough for the Tracker to lose the pull of her blood, right?" He glanced at me with brows raised in question.

"Right." Damn it. "Okay, then, what about a Jammer? Does anyone know a Jammer we can trust?" A good Jammer could block Hadley's energy signature, preventing her from being tracked.

"No," Anne said over the line. "I've never had use for one before."

Cam scrubbed his face with both hands. "All the Jammers I know are loyal to Tower. If we hire one of them, we may as well hand her over to him ourselves. Not that we could actually *afford* a syndicate Jammer…"

And, naturally, all the Jammers *I* knew were bound to Cavazos.

I leaned back in my chair, eyes closed, searching the dark behind my eyelids for a stroke of brilliance, trying to ignore the certainty that the metaphorical lightbulb hanging over my head was surely sputtering its very last spark. Then, suddenly it flared to life so brightly I was nearly blinded. I sat up straight, hands flat on the desktop. "If we can't put her somewhere he can't find her, we'll have to put her somewhere he can't *get* to her."

"Where's that?" Anne asked, the first ribbon of hope in her voice battling a darker thread of skepticism.

"I'm not sure yet, but I have an idea." I pushed my chair back, wishing there was room to pace in my office, so I could burn some of my nervous energy. "How far are you from the city?"

"Um…an hour?" Anne said.

I glanced at the clock on my computer screen. It was twelve-thirty. They'd be in town by 1:30 a.m.

"Okay, here's what I want you to do. First, drop your parents off somewhere where they can take a cab or a bus home. They shouldn't be in any danger so long as Hadley's not with them, because she's the one they'll be tracking."

After a moment's hesitation, Anne said, "Okay, then what?"

"Then drive straight to Cam's apartment. Do you know where that is?"

"No," Anne said, so I listened while Cam recited his address and Anne asked her mother to write it down. "But you said not to come to the city."

"Change of plans." I dug through my drawer for a spare box of 9mm shells. "Don't worry, you won't be there for long."

We said goodbye and hung up, and Cam watched me expectantly from the couch. "Well?"

I pulled a spare clip from the bottom drawer and

started loading it, in spite of the tug on my injured arm. "I know where they can stay. Where we all can stay. If we keep all the lights on, Tower's men can't get in through the shadows. And if my plan works out like I think it will, they won't be able to get close enough to break in the traditional way."

Cam's brows rose halfway up his forehead. "Why do I get the feeling this plan is more dangerous than it is clever?"

"I'd call it a fifty-fifty mix of risk and genius." I grinned as I forced the last shell into the extra clip. "You know how Cavazos is having me followed, and Tower's men think I'm sleeping with the enemy, and Ruben wants me to stay away from you?"

"I don't think I like where this is going…"

I avoided his gaze while I shoved the half-empty box of shells into my satchel along with the extra clip. "I'm about to make all that work in our favor. I think I know how to get Ruben's men to protect Hadley and her mom—only they won't know they're doing it."

"I'm listening…."

"Okay, here's how it should go—I'll leave your place and make sure Cavazos's men see me. They'll follow me to my apartment, watch me go in, then hang around to make sure I don't go anywhere. What they won't know is that you, Anne and Hadley will already be there waiting for me. With Cavazos's goons hanging around, Tower's men won't be able to get close enough to break in." I shrugged, then pulled on my shoulder holster. "It's not a permanent solution, but at least it'll keep Hadley safe while we plan out our next move."

Cam nodded slowly. "I like it. But why did you send

them to my place? Why not send them straight to your apartment?"

I perched on the edge of my desk, in front of the couch where he sat. "Because we're not going to my real apartment in the south fork. We're going to one on the east side—deep in Cavazos's territory. It's only a mile from his house and it's crawling with his initiates. Even once Tower's men track Hadley there, there's nothing they can do. They'll be spotted and run off by Cavazos's men. And no one will be able to get in through the shadows, because there won't *be* any shadows. You and I can make sure of that."

Cam blinked at me for nearly a minute, and I would have given anything to know what he was thinking. Then, finally he asked, "You have an apartment on the east side? Since when?"

"Since about a year ago. It's not really mine. It's Ruben's. In one of his buildings. I've only been there once, but I have a key because he...kind of...gave it to me. Did I not mention that?" I smiled, trying to lighten the moment, but Cam wasn't buying it.

"You seem to be forgetting to mention a lot of things, Liv."

"Okay, I'm sorry. But there's no good way to tell the guy you *want* to be with that the guy who's rumored to own you gave you an apartment. You would never have believed that I'm not sleeping with him." Just like Meika.

Cam gave me an open, expectant look I wouldn't have bought from anyone else. "I believe you now."

"But would you have earlier? Before...your couch?"

He sighed, then met my gaze again, reluctantly. "Probably not."

"Well, now you believe me, and now you know about the apartment. So back to the plan. The only real problem is figuring out how to get the three of you inside. You can't just walk up with my key and let yourself in. Everyone in the building knows whose apartment it is, and even if they don't stop you, someone will call Ruben, and this whole thing will fall down around us."

"Do you leave the lights on all the time?" Cam asked, and I could see the early spark of an idea glinting in his eyes.

"No... Like I said, I've never even been there, except the time he first showed it to me. I thought he was showing me a target's apartment."

"So someone could get there through the shadows now, before you actually arrive and turn on all the lights?"

I shrugged. "Yeah. If one of us were a Traveler." But, obviously, we weren't.

He glanced at the ground, his foot tapping the floor nervously. "What if one of us *knows* a Traveler?"

I shook my head. "Cam, we can't trust any of your friends."

"Not my friend. Yours. And she may be the only person in the world we can all trust right now."

"You mean Kori?" She and her brother were the only shadow-walkers I knew, and Kris wasn't obligated to help me if I asked him to—not that I knew how to get in touch with him. But now that Anne had burned the second oath, getting Kori's help would be as easy as calling her up and asking her for it. Except... "I don't know how to get ahold of her, Cam. We lost touch years ago." When I'd left town. Just like I'd lost touch with everyone else. "I guess I could track her, but I'm not sure we have the time. I don't even know if she's in the city…."

"She is. And I have her number."

He said it casually, as if it was no big deal. But if it was really no big deal, he would have already told me. There was something he wasn't saying. Something important.

I'd given up my secrets—sure, a couple of them had to be dragged out of me—but Cam was obviously still hiding a couple of his own….

Nineteen

We took separate cars back to Cam's apartment, and I stopped on the way for some cheap sleeping masks at a local drugstore. I always carried one for myself, of course—they come in handy when you sleep with the lights on—but knowing how scattered Anne's thoughts were, considering she was running for her daughter's life, I figured we'd need some extras.

By the time I pulled into the parking lot of Cam's building, I'd decided I *had* to know. If we were going to give this another shot—if we were willing to risk our lives to be together—secrets weren't going to cut it. He knew mine. Reciprocation was only fair.

On my way into the building, I glanced around the lot, looking for Ruben's men. I couldn't see them, but I knew they were there. Watching. And for once, that would actually help, rather than hinder, my plans.

I knocked on Cam's third-floor apartment door, then tapped my foot impatiently for the fifteen seconds it took for the door to open. "Okay, why do you have Kori's number?" I asked, before he could even invite me inside.

His brows rose in amusement, and he visibly fought a grin. "I wondered how long that would take."

"You don't have to look so smug." I stomped past him when he stepped back to let me in.

"Are you kidding? I'm surprised you resisted this long."

"So?" I set the convenience-store bag on his counter and my satchel on a bar stool. "Why do you have her number?"

Cam closed the door and crossed both arms over his chest. "I think the real question is why don't you? Most people don't leave their friends just because they leave town."

Ouch.

"I didn't mean to lose touch with everyone. I just… I needed some time to myself." To process the fact that I was suddenly without Cam, under threat of death. "And by the time I felt like getting back in touch, Elle had disappeared. I tracked Anne and Kori just to make sure they were alive, but by then…so much had changed I was afraid I wouldn't even know them anymore." And they wouldn't know me.

"Well, now you're getting a second chance. You ready?"

"Yeah." Though being ready didn't really matter. Anne and Hadley would arrive in half an hour, and we needed to be ready for them. "What's her number?"

Cam recited and I dialed. Then the phone rang. And rang. And rang. Then my call went to a voice-mail system answered by a computer-generated voice.

I hung up.

"She hasn't recorded a voice-mail message," I said, scowling at my new phone as if it had personally be-

trayed me. I hadn't expected Kori's message to provide her real name, but hearing her actual voice would
have been nice. "How do I even know I have the right
number?"

"It's the right number. She doesn't usually pick up
if she doesn't recognize the incoming number. You'll
either have to bug her until she answers or call her on
my phone."

I hit Redial. I hadn't spoken to her in six years—I
didn't want to know she'd only taken my call because
she thought it was Cam. I got her voice mail again, but
when I called back a third time, she answered on the
first ring.

"Who the fuck is this?"

I smiled. It was good to hear her voice, and from the
sound of her greeting, Kori hadn't changed a bit.

"Five seconds, then I'm hangin' up and blockin' your
number," she snapped.

"Kori, it's Liv—willyouhelpme?" I ran the words
together in my rush to be heard before she could hang
up.

Silence. Then a deep intake of breath, and I flinched,
knowing what was coming—I'd been pissed, too, when
Anne asked for my help. "You *bitch*..." Kori mut-
tered, and I smiled again, surprisingly nostalgic over
Korinne's all-purpose greeting/curse/compliment.
"How did you get this number?"

"Hey, Kor," Cam called, by way of explanation.

"You soft-skulled, marble-balled motherfucker. I'm
going to kick your ass next time I see it."

Cam laughed. "You know, my grandmother always
said no woman with a decent vocabulary would resort
to profanity."

Kori huffed. "*My* grandmother said, 'Get the hell out of my house, bitch, before I throw you out on your ass.'"

"Well, you did set the kitchen on fire. Twice. With her in it." Kori had slept on my couch for two weeks before her grandmother finally took her back the second time.

Another impatient huff from over the line. "I fail to see how the facts are relevant here."

"Don't you want to know why I called?" I asked, leaning back to prop my boots on Cam's coffee table, over scarred marks in the wood, proving he'd obviously done the same thing.

"I figure you'll get to it eventually."

I grinned at Cam—if I were speaking to anyone else, I'd have felt guilty for how much I planned to enjoy tugging on Kori's binding. "I need help. Will you please come to Cam's so we can talk?"

"Hell no—oww, *fuck!*" she cried, and I could practically see Kori clutching her head from the unexpected pain—proof that our original oath was still intact. "What the hell, Liv?"

"I'll explain when you get here. Will you come, please?"

"Like I have any choice."

A second later, the bathroom door squealed open and I turned to find Kori stomping toward me from the darkened hall, still holding her cell. She flipped the phone closed and shoved it into the pocket of her ripped, artfully ratty jeans—like us, she was fully dressed and obviously wide-awake at one in the morning—and propped both hands on her hips in the living-room doorway.

"You better tell me what the hell is going on, or I swear I'll kill you just so I don't have to listen to you."

I laughed. "Good to see you, too."

She shoved wavy, white-blond hair back from pixie-ish features twisted into her usual angry scowl. "I'm not fucking kidding."

"Me, neither." I'd actually missed her crass, sarcastic affection. Kori only yelled at people she liked. She didn't bother with anyone else. "It's been too long."

"No, it hasn't been long enough. What the hell happened to the second oath?"

"Anne burned it." Cam tossed her a beer and Kori caught it one-handed, without even looking. She'd always been eerily well-coordinated, though I could find no correlation between that and her Skill as a Traveler.

"That mousy little *bitch*..." She twisted the top from her bottle as she crossed the room, then tossed the cap onto the coffee table and dropped onto the couch next to me. "Make this quick."

"Okay, the short version..." I couldn't quite escape the feeling of déjà vu. We'd sat just like that—with Anne and Noelle —all the time as teenagers, sharing an honesty everyone else in my life seemed to have outgrown.

Everyone except Kori.

"On Thursday night, Anne's husband was killed. She asked us to track and kill the murderer, so Cam and I did. But it turns out he was after her daughter, not her husband. Somehow, the Tower syndicate is wrapped up in this...." I said, and she glanced briefly, pointedly at Cam. Did she know about his binding? "But we're not sure how, or how far up it goes, except we have reason to believe that whichever high-level initiate hired the killer also paid for him to have some kind of blood transfusion—of Skilled blood."

Kori blinked. Then she took a long, long chug from her bottle, and I couldn't help wondering if she was just stalling until she could come up with some clever, curse-riddled response. "Do you always jump right into the deep end?" she said finally. "What happened to wading in a little at a time?"

"Wading into what?"

"Into trouble, Liv." Kori set her bottle on the coffee table and gave me a half amused, half exasperated look. "You're swimming with the fuckin' sharks, and you're too stupid to even know it. Those fins circling you? Those are warning signs. Take heed, and get the fuck out of the water before they eat you alive."

"I didn't jump in, I got pushed," I insisted. "And I can't just crawl out. We're talking about Anne's *child,* Kori."

"Anne has kids?"

"One. A daughter. She's five."

Kori shrugged. "Well, she musta been an accident. Last time I saw Anne, she was in grad school, taking a bunch of sociology and psychology classes, talking about how pointless it was to bring another kid into the world, when there were already thousands of them in this country alone who didn't have homes, or a fuckin' thing to eat."

"Clearly a direct quote…" Cam said, not bothering to hide a smile.

"Well, things change. *People* change." I shrugged. "Now Anne has a daughter, and Jake Tower is trying to kill her."

Kori leaned back and crossed her arms over her chest. "Okay, first of all, if Tower wants Anne's kid, it's not so that he can kill her. It's so he can keep her."

"*Keep* her?" The horrifying conclusions that accompanied that thought were too awful to fully focus on, so I pushed them aside for the more immediate question. "How do you know what Jake Tower does or doesn't want?" I wasn't sure I really wanted the answer, but I was suddenly absolutely *convinced* that I needed it.

She downed the last third of her beer, then waved the empty bottle at Cam, wordlessly demanding another. "Okay, look," she said finally, turning back to me. "I take this little command appearance to mean that I don't have any choice but to help you with this."

"That's right," I said, as Cam twisted the top from a fresh bottle and handed it to her.

"Fine." She took the bottle and drank the neck in one gulp. "The truth is that I won't hate doing what I can for Anne and her unlikely progeny. If we're keeping score, I probably owe her anyway."

In fact, if we were keeping score, Kori would be in debt up to her hair follicles to me and Noelle, too. If Elle were still alive.

She took another gulp, then continued. "But before you start officially asking me for help, you need to understand that there are certain requests I can't carry out, and making those particular requests would be like pushing my self-destruct button. I'll implode, like the fuckin' Death Star."

"Um, point of fact, I believe the Death Star *ex*ploded," Cam said, leaning back on a bar stool, his elbows propped behind him on the counter. "Twice."

"Congratulations. Your official super-nerd badge is

in the mail," Kori said, but I couldn't get past the part about me accidently pushing her self-destruct button.

Shit. *Shit, shit, shit!* "Please tell me that doesn't mean what I think it means...."

Instead of answering, Kori shrugged out of her jacket and twisted to show me the two black chain links inked on her upper left arm.

"Son of a bitch!" The pressure building inside me had no outlet—I felt as if the top of my head was going to blow off. "Both of you?" I glanced at Cam, and as I'd expected, he showed no sign of surprise. "Why didn't you tell me?"

No wonder he had her number memorized and she knew where he lived...

"It's not my place to tell you about Kori's marks. That's up to her." He glanced at her and shrugged. "Or not, if she chooses."

Kori rolled her eyes. "Like I had any choice but to show her."

She didn't. And I didn't. And Cam didn't. We were fresh out of choices, and probably running out of time. Working with them was like playing Marco Polo, with all the Polos gagged.

"Does Tower know you're bound to me and Anne?"

"No, but only because he hasn't specifically asked. I was searched for marks when I signed on and forbidden to take on any more while I'm in his service. But so far, he's assumed his are the only bonds I have."

But if he asked, she'd have to tell him.

Beyond frustrated, I scowled at them both. "How the hell am I supposed to be any use to anyone if neither of you can do what I need done or tell me what I need to know?"

Kori shrugged, and the gesture looked well-worn. "Work around the bindings."

I'd been working around my bindings to Cavazos for a year and a half, but I rarely had to work around anyone *else's* marks....

Cam lowered himself onto the coffee table in front of me, and I didn't miss Kori's look of surprise when I let him take my hands. "Yes, our bindings to Tower complicate things. But your own professional life isn't exactly simple at the moment."

"My ties to Cavazos are nowhere near as restrictive as yours to Tower. And Ruben isn't trying to kill a five-year-old!" Though if I failed to find his missing son in the next six months, I was going to wish he'd killed *me*.

"Wait, what? She's bound to Ruben Cavazos?" Kori's eyes widened dramatically, then she grinned and grabbed her beer. "You two take the concept of *star-crossed* to a whole new level."

"So glad we amuse you," I muttered, trying to refocus my thoughts and work around her chain links. "Okay, instead of just flat-out asking you to do some things, which would *compel* you to do them, I'm going to ask you if you *can* do what I need done." I'd rather her help us of her own will anyway.

Kori nodded. "Greatly appreciated."

"Okay, here goes. When Anne and Hadley get here, can you take them and Cam through the shadows to an apartment if I give you the address?"

"How far away is it?"

"About six miles. Less, as the crow flies." *Much* less, as the shadow-walker travels...

"No problem. Anything else?"

I inhaled, debating my next request. "I don't suppose there's any way you could...not tell your boss where she is, or that we have her?"

Kori frowned at me. "Have you really been here for years, 'cause you sound like you just fell off the truck, fresh from the fuckin' farm."

I rolled my eyes. "I'm not green. I was just hoping you might be able to...work around your own bindings."

"I'll do what I can," she said. "But if Tower asks me a direct question, I'll have to answer."

"I know. But we'd appreciate any sidestepping you're able to do." I shrugged and sipped from my bottle of water. "Hopefully, though, it won't matter either way. We're putting her deep in the east end, and I can't see Tower making a move for her there, considering he'd have to physically break into the apartment once we get all the lights on."

"So, what's the plan after that?" Kori wore skepticism like some women wore jewelry. "Cower under a desk and hope nothing falls on your head? You can't hide from Tower forever. Trust me."

"I know. This is just to keep her safe while we figure out why he wants her and how to stop him. I don't suppose you could help with any of that?" I watched Kori closely, expecting to learn as much from what I saw on her face as from whatever she'd actually say.

But her expression gave away nothing. It was carefully guarded and practically blank, which told me she knew something. Something big.

"I don't have any knowledge of Anne's kid specifically," she said. "But I know that Tower's working on a big project and that it requires a lot of...resources. Which may be why he wants her."

Resources? Project? What kind of project could be so important, so top secret that he'd need a five-year-old to... To what?

"What big project?" Cam demanded, his irritation bordering on anger.

Kori shrugged. "If you don't know, it's because he doesn't want you to know."

"*I* want me to know," he insisted.

"Well, then, it's too damn bad you don't have your *own* mark tattooed on your arm, instead of his," Kori snapped. "You know how this works, Cam. I don't make the fuckin' rules."

"I also know you don't mind breaking them whenever possible." His frown deepened. "Or whenever it benefits *you*."

"Look, I would tell you if I could." Kori set her empty bottle down on the coffee table. "But I'm strictly prohibited from talking about the project. And there's not a damn thing I can do about that."

But if I caught her off guard with a good guess, her surprise—or lack thereof—might say as much as her silence.

"He's selling Skills, isn't he?" I asked, making a sudden, mental leap between two pieces of the puzzle we hadn't yet connected. And her surprise—then quick poker face—was like a little gold star for my internal score card. "We thought Tower just paid for Hunter to have the procedure—whatever it is—but actually, he's the one who *provided* it."

"No." Cam shook his head firmly. "It's not possible. There's no way Tower could be up to something that big without me hearing about it."

Kori laughed out loud. "I'm not sure if you're overestimating your own abilities or underestimating Jake's, but you're—" she hesitated, evidently running up against a verbal line she was forbidden to cross "—inaccurate, at best," she concluded, her amusement dampened by the restriction.

"And you're saying he wants Hadley for this little project?" I said, while Cam sat in stunned anger.

"I'm not saying a damn thing," Kori insisted, and I ignored her words, again focusing on her expression, which seemed to give a little this time. She looked... pleased.

"Does he want to use her blood for a transfusion?" Cam asked, when he caught on to my game. "She's supposed to be one of his resources?"

Kori crossed her arms over her chest. "I can't answer that." Which was an answer in itself. "Nor can I confirm my own involvement in collecting these resources."

Which was as good as admitting that Tower had made her kidnap people to be used in his new project.

"But that doesn't make any sense," I said, to Cam this time. "Hadley hasn't come into her Skill yet. We don't even know what Skill she'll have. If she even has one." I turned back to Kori. "Anne's husband wasn't Hadley's biological father. Anne doesn't even know who the father is." And again I was struck by how odd that was—Anne just wasn't the type to not know something like that. "It's entirely possible that her father was unSkilled, and that Hadley's not going to inherit any ability at all." And honestly, if she inherited Anne's Skill, she wouldn't be much of a prize. Readers were a dime a dozen. "Why would he go through so much trouble to get her if he doesn't even know whether or not she'll be Skilled?"

Kori's brows rose and she looked right into my eyes. "He wouldn't."

I glanced at Cam, but he looked as surprised as I was. "You're saying he knows she'll be Skilled? How can he possibly know that unless...?" My voice trailed off as synapses misfired in my brain. *Surely not...*

"Unless what?" Kori prompted.

"Unless he knows who her father is." I blinked and glanced at Cam, but he only shrugged, as if he was following my train of thought and reluctant to derail it. "But how could Tower know, if Anne doesn't even know?"

"Maybe she does know." Kori grabbed my water bottle and helped herself to several gulps. "Our binding doesn't prevent us from lying to each other...." She left that reminder hanging in the air while she drank the rest of my water.

And suddenly everything I thought I'd known about Anne and her child was thrown into question. I felt as if I was standing on my elementary school merry-go-round, watching the world spin around me, struggling to identify the now-blurry landmarks I'd known all my life.

I turned to Cam to find him frowning, his grip on his own water bottle tight enough to crack the plastic. If Anne had lied to me, she'd lied to him, too.

"Be right back," Cam mumbled, then set his bottle down on his way to the bathroom.

When the door closed behind him, I turned to Kori, unable to purge my own curiosity. "So, you and Cam work together? How did that happen?"

She shrugged. "We don't so much work *together* as work near each other. I see him all the time, but we've only been paired up for a couple of jobs."

"Was he already bound to Tower when you...signed on?"

"No, but he came on board soon after," she said. I started to ask how the hell she'd wound up working for Tower, but she spoke before I could. "Speaking of familiar faces, you ever hear from Elle?"

I frowned, and she saw it on my face before I could figure out how best to say it.

"She's dead, isn't she?"

"Yeah. I've tried to track her over and over, and I'm not getting even a blip of an energy signature from her name." And I didn't have a blood sample, of course.

Kori nodded. "I had a feeling. Her brother's been looking for her for a while, without any luck." Her petite features betrayed no hint of emotion, but I saw through her mask of disinterest. She and Elle were close once, like Anne and I had been.

Then Kori blinked, as if someone had pressed her reset button, and I knew she was going to change the subject—a tried-and-true defense mechanism. She twisted to face me, one arm resting on the back of the couch, and I should have recognized the look on her face. As if she was bored and ready to start trouble. I should have remembered....

"So, I'm kinda surprised to see you and Cam together again, after what happened at that party. Especially with Anne coming over."

Anne? I shrugged. "That was six years ago. I made a mistake, but that's all over now."

Kori blinked, surprised. "*You* made a mistake?"

"I dumped him in the middle of the party, Kor. He deserved an explanation, at least. Then maybe I wouldn't have lost six years with him. Maybe I wouldn't have lost touch with the rest of you, either."

Kori just frowned at me. "You really don't know, do you?"

"Know what?" Why was my heartbeat suddenly painful? Why did it hurt to inhale?

"Shit." Kori glanced at the ceiling for a second, then met my eyes again. "I didn't wanna be the one to tell you. I figured you knew and just decided to sweep it under the rug. Or whatever."

"Knew *what,* Kori?"

"Cam slept with Annika. That night at the party. I thought you knew. Hell, I thought that's why you walked out." She watched me, waiting for my reaction, but I didn't have one. Her words bounced around in my head and the hollow echo reverberated the entire length of my body. "Six years ago. Do the math, Liv."

So I did the math. And suddenly wished I'd never learned how to add.

Twenty

The apartment was quiet when I stepped out of the bathroom. That should have been my first clue that something was wrong.

"Liv?" I called. There was no answer, and my skin prickled. "Kori?" I ducked back into the bathroom to grab the spare 9mm I kept between the two bottom towels stacked beneath the sink.

"She left to give us some privacy," Liv called. I exhaled in relief and headed down the hall. I should have known better.

"We need privacy?" I leaned against the living-room doorway to find Liv waiting for me on the couch, arms crossed over her chest, gaze hard. "What's wrong?"

"You're Hadley's dad?" Her voice could have cut glass. "When were you going to tell me?"

Every single hope of a permanent reconciliation I'd harbored in the past twenty-four hours died a bloody, violent death and a deep, numbing cold grew in my chest. "No, Liv, it's not like that." *Damn you, Kori!* I crossed the room toward her, but Liv stood and backed away from me, keeping the coffee table between us.

"Really? What is it like, Cam? Is it like you sleeping with my best friend at a party while Elle was telling me you're probably going to kill me someday? Because that's what it sounds like. Is that why Tower wants Hadley? Because he knows she's yours, so she has a fifty-fifty chance of becoming one of the best name-Trackers in the country?"

"No." I tried to round the coffee table, but she backed out of reach again. "Liv, I don't know why he wants her. I don't know anything about his project."

"But she is yours?"

"I don't know. I honestly have no idea." I struggled to hold together the pieces of the life I was determined to reclaim, but they just kept slipping through my fingers to shatter on the floor between us. "I want to believe that if I had a kid, Anne would have told me. Six years ago. But I don't know *what* to believe anymore." And I'd never spoken a truer sentence.

"But there's a possibility that she's yours? And you didn't tell me?" She shook her head, as if she wanted to deny it, but she couldn't shake the thought loose. "*Neither* of you told me?"

"I can't speak for her—I'm sure she has her reasons for not telling either of us, and I'm hoping one of them is that I'm not the father."

Not that I was set against ever having children, but this wasn't the way I wanted that to happen—missing out on the first five years of my own daughter's life. Not even finding out about her until my boss tries to abduct her. I wanted to be a part of my kids' lives. And I wanted them to be *Liv's* children. Not Anne's. The product of our life together, not a drunken mistake.

"But Liv, Anne and I didn't…get together…until

after you left. Not that that makes it okay, but for the record, I didn't cheat on you. I would never have even *thought* about anyone else, if I'd still had you. And I wouldn't have been drunk enough to make a mistake like that if I hadn't just been hurt and humiliated by the woman I loved more than anything else in the world, without even a word of explanation."

"Are you seriously saying it's *my* fault you had sex with my best friend?" she demanded, and I felt her slipping away from me again....

"No. I'm saying I was out of my mind with grief when you left, Liv. I had a plan for that night. I...I had a ring."

Liv blinked, then sank onto the couch, as if her legs wouldn't hold her anymore. "You had a what?"

"A ring. I was going to ask you to marry me. I had this whole cheesy moment planned. There was champagne, and a ring, and I was going to ask you at the stroke of midnight. But then you dumped me in the middle of the party instead, and when you left, you took my whole life with you, Olivia. Everything I ever had, and everything I ever wanted. All of it, gone. I couldn't think straight. Then Anne was there, and she was hurting, too, and she wanted to go to a bar, but she was too drunk to drive. So I drove her and I tried to drink until I forgot all about you. And it worked—for one night."

Liv stared at me in shock. As if she couldn't form a proper sentence, or maybe even a single word. She swallowed thickly and stared at her hands. Then she met my gaze again, and this time when her mouth opened, words actually came out.

"Kori said you two hooked up while I was still there. She thought that's why I left."

I almost laughed at the absurdity of her statement. "Yeah. Because Kori was a pillar of sobriety that night, so her version *must* be accurate."

"She *was* pretty drunk...." Liv conceded, and I grasped at the straw of belief she dangled in front of me.

"Olivia, I'm sorrier than you can possibly imagine for not telling you. I didn't know how to say it. I didn't know *when* to say it. There haven't exactly been many good moments to blurt out, 'Hey, remember when you left me with no warning and no explanation and ruined my entire life? Well, I got drunk and slept with your best friend, and there's a very slight possibility that I might be her daughter's biological father.'"

"Yet Kori found an opportunity," Liv snapped.

"Kori waited until I left the room to throw a wrench into our reunion, and she did it to get back at us for dragging her into this. She doesn't like being forced to do something. *Anything.*"

"That makes two of us."

"That makes *all* of us," I corrected. "I wish you'd stop acting like you're the only one saddled with a mark. At least yours comes with some measure of freedom and a nifty expiration date. I'm stuck tracking for Tower—not to mention whatever else he wants done—for the next four years, minimum."

Liv's face flushed with anger, and I recognized the building storm that was about to wreck us both. "You want to talk about that expiration date? Let's talk about that." She stood, fists clenched at her sides. "In six months, if I haven't found Cavazos's...missing person, I will officially be in default of my contract. Do you know what happens then? Have I mentioned that?"

I shrugged. "A really big headache?"

The look she gave me was so cold my teeth wanted to chatter. "If I default on my contract, I become his. Completely. Exclusively. Without restriction. In six months, unless I suddenly, miraculously develop the ability to track someone through a single middle name or get close enough to use a relative's blood sample, I become the private property of Ruben Cavazos, compelled to obey his every word. Whatever he tells me to do. He can make me kill for him. Maim for him. Kidnap or steal. Or anything more personal and humiliating that strikes his fancy. This boundary tattooed on my thigh? Six months from now it becomes a fucking red carpet. For the rest of my life. So tell me again how I have it so good, Cam. 'Cause right now, that kinda feels like a fairy tale."

For one long moment, I could only stare at her, drowning in a very private horror, and an even more private rage. I got homicidally pissed off thinking about the limited groping rights Cavazos had now. The thought of what he'd be able to do to her—or make her do—in six months sent bolts of protective rage surging through me, obliterating all rational impulses. My teeth ground together. My fists clenched so tightly my hands cramped. But I couldn't find words to express any of that. They were all tangled up in the bitter lump in my throat, refusing to budge.

What came out instead was, "Why the hell would you let him seal a mark like that?" People all over the world were having their free will stolen or sold out from under them, like what had happened to Van. But Olivia had intentionally signed hers away!

Liv grabbed an unopened bottle of water from the coffee table and threw it at me, grunting with fury. I tried to duck, but the bottle hit my shoulder then fell to the ground, leaving a deep throb in the joint. "Why would I sign on for that? Why would I sell him my service, and my body, and my fucking *free will?* I did it to *save your ass!"*

I blinked in surprise. "To save...? What the hell does this have to do with me?" Other than my renewed determination to burn her contract to ashes, even if that meant dousing Cavazos with gasoline and lighting a match.

"You said you had a run-in with Ruben once," she said, her eyes blazing with some toxic combination of anger, fear and some small measure of resentment. "Would that have been about eighteen months ago?"

"Yeah." Confused, I sank onto the nearest bar stool. "Tower sent me to the south fork to pick up some loser who'd flaked on a loan extension. But when I got there, the target was... Well, I don't know where he was. I'd tracked him there, and I could feel him there somewhere. But Cavazos's men were *everywhere.* Evidently I got in the way of something they had going down, and his goons hauled me in." One of them had smashed me over the head with a bat, and I'd woken up somewhere on Cavazos's private property, tied up and bleeding, being questioned by the man himself.

Liv shook her head. "You didn't get in the way— you were set up. Your target knew you were coming for him, so he sold you out to Ruben, in exchange for enough cash to pay off his debt."

I shook my head. "That doesn't make any sense. They messed with me for a while and asked me a bunch of questions I couldn't answer, but then they let me go a day later. If he wanted me badly enough to pay for me, why would he just let me...?" My words faded into silence when she stared at the floor to avoid my gaze. "Liv, what the hell did you *do?*" I stood and tried to touch her, but she backed out of reach again.

"I traded my services for yours. You know how I'm tracking for Cavazos using only a name?" she asked, and I nodded again, stunned when the pieces began to fall into place. "That's why he wanted you. I'd only dealt with him a couple of times, but I'd seen enough to know I didn't want you to have to sign with him." She barked a bitter laugh. "Of course, the joke's on me—I didn't know you'd already signed with Tower. I thought you were freelancing. Like me."

And suddenly the devastating weight of my own un-witting involvement was too much to bear. I sank onto the couch, stunned. "You signed with Cavazos to...?"

"To keep you from having to," she finished for me. "It was my fault you were in the city, and I thought you were freelancing in the south fork to stay close to me. I was...trying to protect you."

She was trying to protect me.

My head spun a little, then the room spun a lot more. "You gave yourself to Ruben Cavazos—with no restric-tions—to protect *me.*" *Son of a bitch!* My fist slammed into the coffee table and an empty water bottle fell over, then rolled onto the floor. "Why would you do that? Why the hell would you ever think I *wanted* you to do that? *I'm* supposed to protect *you.*"

Liv's gaze hardened again. "Right after you drag me

back to the cave by my hair, right? Damn, you can be a real asshole sometimes."

"Then why would you sign over the rest of your life for me?" I demanded, standing, even though the room still felt a little unstable.

"Because I love you!" she shouted, anger flashing in her eyes, as if loving me was some kind of bitter curse. And maybe it felt that way, after everything she'd been through. "Because that's the only way he would let you go. He knows you're better with names, so trading my services for yours didn't benefit him. He wouldn't make the deal without knowing he stood to gain something if I failed. But I still have six more months to find his... missing person, before he can collect on the penalty."

"Can you do it? With this relative's blood sample?" Because I couldn't have. Liv's talent with blood went *way* beyond anything I could have done.

"I don't know. If I'm close enough to feel the pull... probably. Maybe."

"How close do you have to be?" She advertised her services with a range of eighty miles, but she'd been better than that when we were together in college— back when she was still an amateur, not even regularly using her Skill.

Liv hesitated, but only for a moment. "Three hundred miles, give or take."

Holy shit... I sank onto the couch again, stunned. That was nearly double the range of the next best blood Tracker I knew. If Cavazos knew how good she really was, he'd never let her go. He'd find some way to keep her, even if she fulfilled her contract.

She shrugged. "I know it sounds like a lot, but considering that the target could be anywhere in the world, my range could be a thousand miles, and I'd still be useless without something else to go on. I have to narrow down the possibilities before tracking even becomes an option, and I've been trying to do that for the past year and a half with no luck."

"Okay…" I nodded, my brain racing so fast my head was starting to hurt. "But that means we still have six months to destroy your contract."

Liv barked a bitter laugh. "You think I haven't thought of that? I have no idea where he keeps his signed contracts. For all I know, they're not even in the country, and they're most definitely stored in a fireproof vault, under armed guard, and probably shielded by the best Jammers in the world. Those contracts are Ruben's lifeblood. He'd put everything he has into protecting them. We're never going to find them, and even if we did, we'd never get to them."

"The hell we won't. I'm not just going to let him have you, Olivia. And neither are you."

She exhaled slowly. "The only way out of this is to fulfill my contract."

"And you can't tell me who he's looking for?"

She shook her head.

I shrugged. "That'll make it harder for me to help, but not impossible."

"There's nothing you can do, Cam. I can't even give you the name I'm tracking."

Another shrug. "So I'll get it from someone else. You sold your soul for me, and I'm going to help you get it back."

She shook her head, slowly, sadly, and sank onto the couch next to me. "I love you for trying, but it won't work. No one else knows the name I'm tracking."

I felt my brows rise as what she was saying sank in. "No one?" She shook her head, and I frowned. "No one in the whole world? Just you and Cavazos?"

This time she nodded, eyes narrowed as if she'd just stumbled upon my train of thought. "No one knows this name, other than me, except for Ruben Cavazos. He's the *only* one," she said, eyeing me meaningfully.

And the only possible way that Ruben Cavazos could be the only one in the world to know someone's name was if... "It's his kid," I said, and Liv's sudden smile brightened her entire face. "That's why you only have one name. You're tracking the middle name he gave his own kid."

"I cannot confirm that," she said, grinning like a fool. "I can't even discuss it."

"Yet I can't help noticing you're not denying it."

"No, I'm not."

"Then let me follow that path a little farther...." I closed my eyes, thinking. "He doesn't know the rest of the kid's name, so that means he's probably never met him. You said it's a him, right?" I said, and she smiled again. The kid was a son. "And I'm guessing you would have tried tracking the boy's middle name with the last name Cavazos." Again, no confirmation. She couldn't discuss it. "And based on the fact that you're still tracking a single name, I'm assuming the mother—whoever she is—gave her son a different last name. Probably her own."

Liv shrugged and sat on the coffee table in front of

me. "That, I honestly don't know. I have no clue what the mother's real name was—the one she gave Ruben was fake. But I know, as of this evening, that Meika had her killed years ago."

"That's what you were talking about earlier...." When she'd said Cavazos's wife had his first mistress killed. "Which means this son must have been conceived years ago. So why is he just now looking...?"

"He didn't even know—" Liv flinched and one hand flew to her forehead, obviously the source of the pain. "Okay, evidently that's prohibited information."

Yet I could finish most of that sentence myself. Cavazos hadn't even known he had a kid with this other woman until...something. Something Liv obviously couldn't explain to me.

"Just like me..." I whispered, without thinking that through. Then I realized I hated having something in common with Ruben Cavazos. But not as much as I hated the thought of having to share Liv with him.

"You really think Hadley's yours?" she asked softly, from inches away now.

"I honestly don't know. But if there's even a chance of that, I have to admit I understand why Cavazos would be so hell-bent on finding his kid." I hated not knowing whether or not I was a father. And feeling guilty that I might have accidentally abandoned my own child for the first five years of her life. And I was pissed at the thought of how many things I'd already missed, that I could never get back. "I guess that's at least one thing a woman can never understand—if you have a kid out there somewhere, at least you know it."

"Yeah, I guess." She looked as if she wanted to add to that—or maybe argue—but then her phone rang and she dug it out of her pocket to read the text. "Anne's downstairs with Hadley. Will you get Kori while I bring them up?"

I nodded and when she disappeared into the hall, I grabbed my own phone and texted Kori. Get back here, bitch.

A second later, she walked out of my unlit hallway and leaned against the peninsula separating the kitchen from the living room, watching me with undisguised mischievous curiosity. "What'd I miss?"

"Only the chaos of your own creation," I said, and she laughed out loud. "I was going to tell her, you know. I just wanted to do it my way. In my own time."

Kori shrugged. "Your own time should have come a little sooner."

"Mind your own business, Korinne. Or I might decide to tell a couple of *your* secrets."

Her laughter died a sudden, quiet death. "Don't threaten me, Romeo. Our checks may be signed by the same man, but Liv had my back way before she met you, so if I have to choose between the two of you, she'll win every time."

I rolled my eyes at her. "Don't try to sound all noble—we both know you were just making trouble out of habit."

She shrugged and managed a grin. "I'm not sayin' it wasn't fun. But if you'd told her like you should have, *when* you should have, I couldn't have had any fun at your expense, now could I?"

Before I could argue, my front door opened behind

me, and I turned to find Liv leading a child into my apartment.

And maybe into my life…

Twenty-One

Liv led Anne and her daughter into my living room, carrying two backpacks, presumably full of on-the-run essentials. I glanced at Anne, looking for some sign in her eyes to tell me whether or not I was a father. Whether or not my boss was trying to kidnap and drain my own daughter. But she wasn't looking at me. She was looking at Kori.

"Holy crap, it *is* you."

"You, too." Kori's gaze passed over Hadley for a single, fleeting instant. "Plus one."

Liv laughed nervously. "It's a regular reunion. All we need now is Noelle."

"I could go get a Ouija board...." Kori offered. Anne flinched and visibly paled, and I realized this was the first time the three of them had been in the same room since the night of the infamous party.

"We should probably get going...." I said, to nudge things along, and Liv nodded.

"First, brief introductions." Anne held one hand out to Hadley, and the child let herself be pulled forward, huge green-eyed gaze capturing mine. Were my eyes that color, or just a shade darker? Wasn't my skin paler, except during the height of summer? Or was I looking for dissimilarities that weren't really there?

"Hadley, this is my friend Kori Daniels."

Hadley stared up at Kori, eyes narrowed in suspicion. "If you're friends, how come my mom never talks about you?"

I glanced at Anne in surprise. Hadley was very well-spoken for a five-year-old—not that I had any ruler to measure her by....

Kori started to answer, but I was afraid of what might come out of her mouth, so I stepped in. "They haven't seen each other in a long time," I said. "Since before you were born."

Hadley studied me for a moment, and I wondered if she was seeing those same dissimilarities. Or if she saw something more? Did a kid know when she was looking at her father? *If* she was looking at her father?

Her green eyes peered up into mine. "Who are you?"

Did that mean she didn't recognize me, on a biological, cellular level? Or just that she didn't know my name?

"This is Cam Caballero," Liv said. "Another...friend. The three of us are going to keep you safe until we can figure out what's going on and make all this go away." Hadley nodded solemnly, still clutching her mother's hand, and Liv continued. "Kori's going to take you and your mom and Cam to my apartment. She's going to take you through the shadows. Do you know what that means?" Another nod from the child, and this time I thought I saw a slight spark of interest in her eyes. "Good. We're going to hang out there with all the lights on for a while so no one else can get in while we figure a few things out. So...you ready to go?"

Hadley nodded one more time, but Anne pulled her back a little. "I think I should go first, so she won't be there alone."

"Let me," I said. "So neither of you will be."

Anne glanced at me in surprise, and again I tried to read whatever lay beneath her expression, but either she was really good at hiding her thoughts, or there was truly nothing to hide. "Thanks," she said at last.

"Okay, Romeo, you're up." Kori slapped my shoulder, then headed for the darkened hallway. I grabbed a backpack full of prepacked emergency supplies and started to follow her, then felt Liv's warm hand on my arm.

"Wait," she said, and I turned just as she wrapped her arms around my neck. Her lips met mine, demanding, and I gave everything I could, a little worried by the intensity of her goodbye. I'd see her again in half an hour. "Don't turn any lights on," she said, pulling away reluctantly. "And stay away from the windows. No one can know you're there, even once I get there."

"Don't worry." I let my forehead touch hers. "I'm not afraid of the dark." I glanced at Anne, then smiled at Hadley, who was staring at us. "See you two in a few minutes." Then I followed Kori down the hall to stand in front of the unlit, windowless bathroom.

"You remember how?" she asked, and I nodded, though I wasn't sure if she could see that in the dark. I'd shadow-walked with her a few times before, for work. It was faster and quieter than driving. "Good. Nothing's changed. Just hold my hand and take three normal steps forward when I tell you to. I'll do the rest."

"You know where we're going?"

"Yeah. Liv gave me the address, and I checked it out when I left here, 'cause I'm that fuckin' pro." She glanced over her shoulder, where I could hear Anne talking to her daughter in the living room, explaining what was going to happen and that it wouldn't hurt at all. "Okay, start walkin'," Kori said, taking my hand. So I stepped deliberately into the bathroom, and she walked with me. Three steps later, her hand tightened around mine. "Stop. We're here."

I stood still and blinked, and realized almost immediately that the room we'd stepped into felt much bigger than my bathroom, though I couldn't make out anything other than darkness and the general sense of open space. The air was cooler—obviously the heat wasn't running, and I was willing to bet it hadn't been used since the previous winter.

Kori let go of my hand and I blinked rapidly, trying to bring the dark room into focus. "Give your eyes a second to adjust," she said, backing away from me with confidence while I stood with my arms out to feel for obstacles I couldn't yet see. Kori was accustomed to the dark. She was at home there.

I blinked again and finally found two windows, defined by the weak light leaking in around what could only be blackout curtains, probably hung for privacy by a very optimistic Ruben Cavazos. My blood boiled over the implications, and only when Kori tugged me toward the silhouette of a couch I could barely make out did I realize the room was slowly coming into focus as my eyes adjusted. Familiar shadows took shape against the darkness in the forms of chairs, small tables and a large, sleek entertainment center on one side of the room.

"Sit, and stay out of the way." She pushed me onto
the center couch cushion, and my temper burned a little
brighter when I felt rich, smooth leather beneath my
hands, double stitched and trimmed in what felt like
rivets. Did he think he could buy Liv with nice furniture, when he hadn't been able to command his way
into her pants? I'd never met anyone as strong-willed
as Olivia Warren, and whether Cavazos knew it or not,
he probably hadn't, either.

But in six months, if I couldn't get her out of her
contract, Liv's free will would be reduced to a furious
voice screaming inside her head, while the rest of her
submitted to his every demand. He would break her,
both body and spirit, and I couldn't let that happen.

"I'll be back with Anne in a second," Kori said, pulling me from my inner rage, and though I didn't see or
hear her step back through the shadows, I could tell by
the suddenly empty feel of the room that she was gone.

My eyes continued to adjust in her absence, and less
than a minute later, Kori stepped into existence in the
middle of the room with Anne in tow. "Here." Kori held
Anne's hand out to me in the shadows and I stood to
take it. "Don't let her trip over anything while her eyes
adjust. I gotta go get the kid."

Then she was gone again, and Annika's hand was
tight around mine. "I can't see you, Cam," she said,
and I squeezed her hand to set her at ease, trying not
to think about the last time I'd touched her.

"I know. Your eyes will adjust in a minute. Come
sit over here, though, or they'll walk right into you
when they get here." I led her back to the couch and
we sat side by side in the awkward silence while I tried

to figure out how best to begin the conversation that would reveal Hadley as my daughter. Or not.

But I couldn't find the words, and she didn't seem to know they were missing, so we just sat there in the dark, waiting. And waiting. And waiting.

And finally Anne turned to me, her face a darker silhouette against the dim room. "Something's wrong."

"It's only been a couple of minutes," I insisted, pulling my phone from my pocket to check the time. But that was pointless, because I didn't know exactly when Kori had left us. "Hadley probably just got scared. She doesn't really know Kori, and Kori *can* be kind of scary…." I forced a laugh, but even I wasn't buying it.

"It's more than that," she said in a fragile whisper, and the shaking in her voice worried me. The entire disastrous day suddenly seemed to be illustrated by that one small warbling sound—unsteady, and broken, and a little creepy. Anne was right. It had been too long. "Call Liv."

I unlocked my keypad and was about to autodial when the phone started vibrating in my hand and Liv's new number popped up on the screen. I accepted the call and held the phone to my ear. "Liv?"

"Yeah." Something zipped on the other end of the line, and her footsteps clacked on my kitchen floor. "I'm about to head your way. Is there anything you want me to bring? A change of clothes, or something? I grabbed some easy food from the freezer—hope you don't mind. I'm not sure what a five-year-old eats, so can you ask Hadley if she likes mac and cheese?"

My heart jumped into my throat and Anne leaned closer so she could hear. "Liv, she's not here yet. Kori left, and she never came back."

"What?" The background noise went quiet over the line as Liv stopped rooting through my cabinets, and there was only a heavy, shocked silence as we all came to the same conclusion.

"When did they leave?" I asked, and Anne's breathing became fast and ragged beside me. I put my free hand over hers, trying wordlessly to calm her.

"A couple of minutes ago," Liv said, and I heard the familiar groan of my own couch springs as she sat. "How could they not be there?"

"Where is she?" Anne demanded, breathless with encroaching panic. But I had no answer for her. None that she would want to hear, anyway.

"Kori…" Liv whispered. And as badly as I wanted to deny the obvious conclusion, there were no others to jump to. She'd infiltrated our operation at our invitation, divided our forces at our request and taken off with the prize—with Anne's *daughter*—because we'd just handed the child over, foolishly trusting in the ties of our past, rather than the unbreakable chain on Kori's arm.

I, of all people, should have known better.

"She tried to warn us," Liv continued softly. "She practically told us she was involved in collecting Tower's 'resources,' and she pointed out that her binding to me and Anne doesn't prevent us from lying to one another. She tried to tell us, but we weren't listening."

"No…" Anne groaned, and my hand tightened on hers.

"Anne, can you hear me?" Liv asked over the line, and Anne nodded slowly, clearly in shock.

"She can hear you," I said.

"Okay, good. I'm headed your way. We're going to get her back, Anne. I swear we will." A door closed over the line, and Liv's boots clomped with the familiar echo of my building's hallway. "Cam, you call Kori. If we both call we'll just tie up the line, and she's more likely to answer you."

Though if she'd done what we suspected, mine was the last call she'd accept at the moment....

"Don't panic," Liv said, and in the background an engine rumbled to life, then her car door slammed shut. "I'm going to find her."

Then Liv was gone, and I was alone with Anne and the harsh, whistling breaths she was sucking in like air was in short supply. "Annika, calm down." I twisted to face her on the couch without letting go of her hand, but she just stared at her lap, squeezing my hand so tight it was starting to go numb. "Anne. You're going to hyperventilate. Slow down…"

But I didn't know how to help her. I had no experience with emotional trauma, other than what I'd helped Vanessa through, but that was completely different. That experience wouldn't help me with Anne.

"Why?" she croaked finally, as I dialed Kori's number one-handed. "Why would she do this? Where would she take Hadley?"

What are you supposed to say when the truth will only make things worse?

"Anne…" I began, and she must have heard something in my voice. Something I didn't want her to hear, but didn't know how to hide. She looked up at me, and I realized panic had sharpened her focus, not dulled it. She was stronger than I'd thought, and that really shouldn't have surprised me.

"You know something," she said, her focus shifting back and forth between my eyes, silently demanding answers she had every right to, but I *really* didn't want to give. "What's going on, Cam?" I hesitated, and she squeezed my hand so hard I actually heard my knuckles groan. "Tell me!"

"I will, but I need you to stay calm, okay?" I said, and she nodded eagerly, desperate to hear what I desperately didn't want to say. "Kori is bound to Jake Tower, just like I am. Only she's bound much more tightly. And hers is a much closer, more direct bond."

"What does that mean?" Anne demanded, and I gently pulled my hand from her grasp before she could break my fingers off.

"She works for him directly."

"She…" Anne swallowed thickly, then started over. "Korinne has a direct link to Jake Tower—to the man who's been after Hadley the whole time—and you just handed my baby to her?" She stood and backed away from me before I could pull her back down to the couch or try to shush her.

"Anne, I swear I didn't think she'd…" My words trailed off as I realized our mistake. "We should have compelled her. Her binding to you and Liv is older than her marks from Tower—if she'd been under a geas from either of you, it would have trumped her binding to Tower."

Or, if her binding to Tower was extraordinarily strong, trying to follow both conflicting bindings would have killed her.

We'd been playing nice, trying not to put her under conflicting orders, but Tower *never* plays nice. If he ordered her to take the child and she had no conflicting directive, she'd have no choice but to do what he wanted.

"Call her!" Anne demanded, gesturing to the phone I still held in my lap. "Get that bitch back here with my baby!"

Speechless, I could only nod and finish dialing. A second later, Kori's computer-voiced message system picked up, inviting me to leave a message. So I did.

"Korinne, where are you?" I said into the phone, and Anne's shadowed face gaped at me. I'd considered ranting and screaming like she probably wanted me to, but pissing off the woman who had her daughter—at least, I *hoped* Kori still had Hadley—seemed stupid at best. "You can still fix this, Kori. You can bring her back. You still have time to do the right thing…."

"Give me the phone," Anne demanded, and I started to pull my cell away from her until I realized what she was doing—pulling on strings we should have pulled in the first place.

I handed her my phone and she practically shouted into it. "Korinne, it's Anne. I need you to—" Then she screamed in rage and frustration and flipped the phone closed. The machine had hung up on her.

A single heartbeat later, she flipped the phone open again and hit Redial, and this time she was talking before the beep even faded from my ears. "Kori, it's Anne. Will you please bring my daughter back, unharmed? Immediately," she added as an afterthought. Then she slammed the phone closed and dropped it into my lap.

Anne stood, pacing furiously in front of me.

"You have to calm down," I said, trying to tug her back onto the couch, but she dodged my reach as if my hands were on fire. "Give her a chance to listen to the message. You have to believe that if she had any other choice, she wouldn't have done this."

"No, I *don't* have to believe that." Anne spoke through clenched teeth, and I was sure that if her face weren't layered by thick shadows, her cheeks would have been flushed red with fury and fear. "What I have to believe is that Korinne stole my *child*. My daughter is out there somewhere, with people she doesn't know, in a place she's never been. I don't know if they're hurting her, and if they are, there's not a damn thing I can do about it. I don't know if she's cold, or in the dark, or all alone, or in pain. She's probably crying, calling for *me,* and I'm not there, and she doesn't know *why*."

"Anne, it's going to be okay." That was a lie, and we both knew it, but that lie was all I had to offer her, and I'd never felt so helpless in my entire life.

Anne turned on me, fists clenched in shadows at her sides. "No, it is *not* okay. It may never be okay again. I don't know what they've told her. What if they told her I don't want her anymore? What if they told her this is because of something she did? Some people are monsters, Cam. We both know that, but I've spent the last few years telling her there's no such thing as monsters so she can sleep at night, and now Kori, and Tower, and some husband-murdering bastard have made a liar out of me, and even when I get Hadley back, she's never going to trust me again."

She sucked in a deep breath, then more words fell from her mouth before I could interrupt. "My only function in this whole world is to protect that little girl. It's part job, part moral mandate and part intrinsic maternal urge I never expected and could never even begin to explain. I'm supposed to protect her, and I failed, and she could be dead or dying, or just scared to death, and *I can't help her!*"

Her tears were flowing freely now, and each breath was a hiccuping sob. I tried to pull her close, but she backed out of reach again and banged her hip on an end table. "No. Don't touch me. I don't want your sympathy or your pity. This is your fault, Cam, and you *will* help me fix it." She scrubbed her cheeks with the palms of both hands, then stood straight to wag one finger at me like my grandmother had done all my life. "So you… get Kori back here, and you make sure she has Hadley with her. Or I swear on my own soul, Cam Caballero, I *will* kill you and go after her myself."

Twenty-Two

Cam was sitting on the couch in the dark when I opened the door, hunched over with his elbows on his knees and his head hanging low. He looked up when a slice of light from outside fell over him, and my first thought was that he'd aged ten years in the half hour since he'd walked into the shadows with Kori.

If she weren't dead yet, I'd kill her myself for what she'd done, not just to Anne and Hadley, but to Cameron, too. And to me by extension.

"Any news?" I asked, when I'd closed and locked the door.

"I left Kori two messages—the second much angrier and more demanding than the first—and Anne left one of her own, outright asking her to bring Hadley back, but Kori hasn't responded. I don't know if she's even heard them yet."

I flipped the switch to the left of the door and light from overhead flooded the living room as I set my bags on the floor. "How's Anne?"

For a second, Cam just blinked at me, clearly trying to decide how to say something I wasn't going to want to hear. Then he stood and grabbed the duffel I'd filled with food from his apartment. "I...um..." He set the bag on the table and started pulling out boxes of toaster pastries and mac and cheese Hadley wasn't there to eat. "I had to kind of...sedate her."

"You *sedated* her?" I repeated, hoping I'd heard him wrong. But he only nodded, opening the freezer to shove several still mostly frozen pizzas inside. "With what?"

"Diazepam." He lined up the food boxes on the counter next to the fridge, in descending size order.

"What's that?"

"Valium. Liquid solution, in a glass of Coke," Cam said, and he spoke over me before I could ask where the hell he'd gotten liquid valium. "It's left over from what the doc gave me for Van, when she was...hysterical. But don't worry, it's mild, and I gave her a low dose. She'll wake up in a couple of hours." When I only watched him, silently demanding more of an explanation, he sighed and leaned against the short kitchen bar. "I had to. She was flipping out, threatening to kill me and go after Hadley herself. I couldn't just let her storm out of here and get herself killed. And I was afraid the neighbors would hear her shout."

I closed my eyes and sank into one of four chairs around the small breakfast table. "Okay..." He'd done it to keep her safe, and even if that wasn't how I would have handled the situation, I couldn't fault his intent. "Talk while we work." I bent to pull two rolls of duct tape from my bag and tossed him one. "What's the best way to get to Hadley? Do you have any idea where Tower would keep her?"

Cam shrugged and turned the tape over in his hand,

as if he wasn't quite sure what to do with it. "I assume he'd keep her wherever the project is headquartered, but I have no idea where that is."

"It's for the windows," I said, holding up my own roll. I crossed into the living room and stood on a chair to tape the thick blackout curtains to the wall on first the left side, then the bottom, then the right, leaving the top open, because it was higher than the glass. Cavazos's men wouldn't be able to see anything that way.

"Won't this look suspicious?" Cam asked, moving to help me tape the second living-room window.

"Nah I tape my own windows sometimes, when I know he's watching. They'll assume I just want some privacy."

"You should know I'm fighting an overwhelming urge to pull Cavazos's intestines out slowly, though a small hole in his navel."

I scrounged up a small smile. "You should know I'm fully committed to that same urge."

Together, we taped the small bathroom window and the one in the only bedroom, then started turning on lights. I'd spent a grand total of ten minutes in the apartment before, but I remember thinking when I first saw it that it was perfect for keeping Travelers out. Of course, at the time, I'd assumed I was seeing the home of a target I'd need to track, and that he or she had been hiding from Travelers. But now I'd *become* that resident, hiding from Travelers—yet desperate to get my hands on one shadow-walker in particular.

The only bed, where Anne was cringing in her sleep, was built on a base of drawers, so there were no beneath-the-bed shadows to worry about. All of the closets were equipped with hardwired lights, so eliminating shadows there was as easy as pushing all the clothes—Cavazos had furnished some kind of creepy Barbie dream-date wardrobe for me—to one side. The kitchen cabinets all had glass fronts, which let light in and killed potential shadows. I pulled back the shower curtain and opened all the bathroom cabinet doors— you can never be too careful.

None of the living-room furniture cast a shadow big or dark enough to let someone in, and I'd just turned on the light in the small pantry when Cam spoke up from a bar stool behind me. "Maybe we should leave an opening," he said. "For Kori."

I crossed my arms over my chest, watching him. "You really think she'll just bring Hadley back?"

He shrugged. "She won't have any choice once she hears Anne's message. And even if she doesn't, I don't think Kori wanted to take Hadley in the first place. I think she'll be looking for an opportunity to make this right. We'll have to trust her."

"Like we trusted her half an hour ago?"

"She's in a tough spot, Liv," he insisted, but I could see beyond what he was saying to what he was actually thinking—his inner conflict was clear, from the deep lines carved in his forehead.

"Just like you are."

He looked up, and his gaze was heavier than I'd ever seen it. "If she was given a direct order, she had no choice."

"And you think this hypothetical order justifies what she did?"

His gaze hardened and he leaned forward with both elbows on the counter. "First of all, that order isn't hypothetical, or theoretical, or mythical in the least. We both know Kori would never do something like this if she had any choice. She'd never hurt a child."

Well, I couldn't argue there, even though the facts seemed to be arguing for me.

"And second, no, I don't think orders justify what she did. There's no way to justify that. But I think she's eager to make it right. To make up for it, if possible." He hesitated. "We owe her the chance to do that. Leave her a way in, Liv. We'll work on finding Hadley from our end, but we need to leave Kori a way to bring her back, if she gets a chance."

I thought about that for a second, then nodded. "Fine. She can have the bathroom. But if someone else shadow-walks into this apartment, you better be prepared to shoot."

"I always am...." He smiled and pulled back his jacket to show me the gun in his custom holster.

"Well, now you're extra prepared." I leaned over the back of the couch and picked up the backpack I'd dropped on the center cushion and tossed it to him. He caught it with an "oof," unzipped it, then "oohed" at the contents.

"Okay, this one's mine," he said, pulling his own .45 out, along with a box half-full of the corresponding shells. "But if the rest of these are yours, I have to admit my manhood is slightly threatened here."

"Yeah, but you're a little turned on, too, right?" I sat on his lap to start lining the weapons up on the table. Three extra 9mm guns, a .38—I'd brought that one for Anne—and one truly badass, guaranteed-to-blow-a-hole-right-through-you .50-caliber monster.

"More than a little..." Cam muttered, gripping my

hips from behind. Then he spotted the .50 caliber and I was all but forgotten. "Christmas, already?" He reached for it, and I slapped his fingers.

"Hands off, little boy. That's a very grown-up piece of equipment." Overkill, probably, but you never know when you're going to need a really big gun.

Cam laughed. "Are we hunting *bears?* You got an elephant gun in there, too?"

I twisted to grin down at him, feeling guilty for the moment of levity, even as I seized it. "I like power—when I'm wielding it."

"Mmm… I like it when you're wielding it, too." His lips found my neck, and I indulged in one more moment of pleasure before pulling away to bring us both down to earth.

"Okaaaay, back to work." I slid out of his lap and onto my own chair while he started loading extra clips. "I assume you've actually been to Tower's house. Or… estate, or whatever…?"

"Yeah. It's not as…overdone as Cavazos's address, but it's a good-size property."

"Big enough to hide an operation like this Skilled transfusion thing?"

"I honestly don't know." He shrugged. "It's not like they let you just wander around the grounds. Well, not like they let *me* wander. Kori might have wandering privileges."

"Speaking of which…" I jogged into the bathroom, where I turned off the light and pulled the door halfway closed, leaving more than enough darkness for Kori—and hopefully Hadley—to make a triumphant return.

In the kitchen again, I grabbed two sodas from the fridge—no telling how long they'd been there—and set one in front of Cam. "The way I see it, we can sit here and wait for Kori to bring her back—" which wasn't going to happen, no matter how hard we wished or how many happy thoughts we threw out into the universe "—or we can track Hadley ourselves."

We could have tracked Kori—I'd certainly done it before—but we had no way of knowing that Hadley was still with her. For all we knew, she'd turned over the child, then been reassigned. If she heard Anne's message, she'd have to respond, but we couldn't afford to sit back and wait for that. What if she never checked her voice mail, or had been ordered not to listen to messages from us?

Cam popped the top on his can and took a long chug. "The real question isn't whether or not we can find Hadley, but how do we get her back, once we've found her. We can't just go ring the doorbell."

"You're crossing bridges we haven't come to yet. First, let's find her. We'll worry about the rest of it then." I kicked out the chair between us and propped up my feet. "For the moment, at least, we don't have a blood sample for Hadley, so we'll have to start with name-tracking."

"For the moment?"

"Anne may have one." I'd been thinking about that for the past hour. Some Skilled parents kept blood samples of their children—under lock and key, of course—like normal parents kept their kids' fingerprints and current picture. As a precaution, for the worst-case scenario. "But if she does, we can't get to it until she wakes up. Fortunately, we have Hadley's name, and that should be enough, right?"

"Assuming they haven't put her on a plane? Yeah."

Cam took another drink from his can, then set it aside. "Do we have her middle names?" he asked, and I shook my head. Anne hadn't mentioned them, and it would have been rude to ask. Though now that we officially needed it, she would be more than willing to divulge the necessary information—once she woke up. "Okay, then, we'll start with first and last." He closed his eyes, blocking everything else out to aid his concentration.

"Hadley Liang." Cam whispered her name, and I couldn't help wondering if he felt anything, beyond the normal tracking senses. Would he know it, if he were tracking his own daughter? Would saying her name aloud trigger some kind of primal response deep inside him, even if she did carry some other man's surname?

After a long couple of minutes and lots of slow, careful breathing, he opened his eyes and frowned. "Nothing. It's like she doesn't even exist."

No. I closed my eyes, fighting down nausea at the thought. "Tower needs her. He wouldn't kill her as long as he can use her, right?"

Cam shrugged miserably. "I like to think he wouldn't kill her anyway. She's just a kid. So…I'm thinking we don't have her real name. Not all of it, anyway." Which wasn't unusual, for Skilled adults. Most of us took on fake names or obscure nicknames once we were old enough to have to sign official documents, like drivers' licenses and tax forms. But few children had reason to use a fake name.

Then suddenly I understood what he was saying. "Her last name. Shen adopted her, but his last name won't actually be hers. She's not a Liang, she's a Lawson, like Anne."

"Let's hope." He closed his eyes and whispered

the new version of her name, and again I waited. And again, quicker this time, he sighed in frustration and opened his eyes. "Nothing. If I knew her personally and already had a feel for her energy signature, I might be able to get at least a blip to let us know she's alive. But I only met her for a couple of minutes, and her name... just isn't working. I feel like we're missing something."

Oh, shit. "Try Caballero," I said softly, and Cam's entire frame went stiff. "If she's yours, it's possible Anne gave her your last name."

"Why would Anne give her my name, but not tell me about it?"

"I don't know. To protect her?" From exactly what *we* were doing... Because if Cam didn't know she had his name, no one else would, either. "Just try it, and we can deal with whatever the result tells us later."

Cam closed his eyes again, demonstrating a level of concentration he wouldn't have needed for most other trackings—which just showed how difficult this one was proving. "Hadley...Caballero," he whispered, and I held my breath, not sure how to feel about the possibility that his paternity might be revealed through a routine tracking. I wasn't sure how he felt about that possibility, either, which made my nerves a little harder to control.

But a minute later, he looked at me again, this time with an odd mixture of disappointment and relief. "Nothing. If she's mine, she doesn't have my name." He grabbed his soda again and drank as if he was wishing for something stronger. "How the hell does Cavazos expect you to find his kid with one name, when I can't even find Anne's with two names?"

"When she wakes up, we can get Hadley's middle name." And hopefully a blood sample.

Then I froze as Cam sat straighter, and we both seemed to realize what I'd said at the same time.

"Her middle name..." I mumbled, and he nodded. "If she's your daughter, her second middle name is yours to give. And you haven't named her yet."

"There's no better time..." he said. "Just like Cavazos." And he looked sick over the comparison.

I could have happily lived my entire life without ever finding a similarity between Cameron and Ruben, but if it helped us find Hadley... "So, what are you going to name her?" Though I really shouldn't have asked. It was none of my business, and revealing her potential middle name could put the child in some serious potential danger someday.

But Cam only blinked at me. "I have no idea. I've never even thought about it. I always assumed that when I had a kid, I'd have at least a few months' warning. Time to prepare."

While he thought about it, I started opening the top cabinets we'd left closed in search of something stronger than soda. And finally, above the fridge, I found a small bottle of very expensive whiskey.

"Go easy on this," I said, setting it in front of Cam along with a short, clear glass. "I suspect this is going to be a long night."

"Thanks." He opened the bottle—the seal hadn't even been cracked—and poured a double shot, then waved off my offer of ice. "What do you think Cavazos would think of me drinking his whiskey?" Cam took a long sip.

"I'm pretty sure that's *my* whiskey, considering how insistent he is that this is my apartment."

"Well, then, you have excellent taste." He took a second sip, then set the glass down. "Maybe you should consider staying here occasionally, just for the fringe benefits."

I frowned at him, leaning over the bar. "I'm pretty sure that's exactly why he wants me to stay here."

I let him drink in silence for a few minutes, then I had to nudge. Every moment we wasted was a moment Anne spent without her daughter. A moment Tower could be moving Hadley even farther away from us. "Ideas?" I asked, and he shook his head. "You could always name her after your mother."

Cam nearly choked on a fresh sip. "I think I should probably tell her she's a grandmother—maybe—before I start naming unexpected children after her."

"A valid point." I hesitated, then pushed forward again. "I hate to rush something this important, but we need to move, Cam. What'cha got?"

"Nothing, yet. I don't even know if she's my kid...."

"I know."

"But if she is, I owe her the courtesy of putting a little thought behind a name she's going to be stuck with."

"So pick something pretty."

He scowled at me, as if I'd just suggested he hang his theoretical daughter over the balcony by one foot. "Screw pretty. She needs something safe. Something with several potential nicknames. Something unrelated to me or to her, so it can't be guessed. Something random, but not without some aesthetic value. After all, she *is* a girl."

"That's what I was getting at," I said, both stunned and amused by the level of thought he was putting into it.

"Most people get nine months to think about this…." he complained.

I laughed. "Most girls start naming their future children in junior high." He glanced at me with both brows raised, and I shook my head vehemently. "Not I. But I will admit to putting almost as much thought into picking out the .50 caliber as you're putting into this."

His frown deepened, and his disappointment was almost palpable. "You'd rather have guns than kids?"

"I wouldn't suggest hanging pistols over a crib as a mobile, but other than that, I don't consider the two mutually exclusive." But Cam's expression didn't change. And finally I understood. I slid over onto the chair next to his and pulled his chin up so that our gazes met. "Hadley's not a deal-breaker, Cam. If she's yours, she's mine, too. Not like she's Anne's, of course. But you're not going to get rid of me by accepting paternity."

"Sarafina," he said, and I blinked.

"What?"

"Sarafina. For her middle name."

"That's *my* middle name."

"I know. You said if she's mine, she's yours, too, and this would make that true. Let me name her after you, Liv. I've always thought it was a beautiful name."

I smiled. I couldn't help it; I was all gooey inside from a rare moment of mushiness. "Let's see if it works."

This time when he closed his eyes, it seemed to mean more. I felt intimately connected to the process, and my next breath seemed to hinge on the gravity of the result. And this time, when he opened his eyes and his disappointed gaze met mine, the breath I held felt too heavy to let go of.

"Nothing. She's not mine."

He looked so disappointed that I decided not to mention the other possibility—that Kori had lied about Tower's intentions. That Hadley could be dead. That was too much to think about at the moment.

"This is so stupid." Cam leaned with both elbows on the bar. "I didn't have a daughter yesterday, and I don't have one today. Nothing's changed. So why do I feel so..."

"Empty?" I suggested, and he looked up. He didn't nod, or acknowledge what I'd said, but I could see in his eyes that I was right. And I felt it, too. I'd thought—just for a minute—that he had a daughter, and that she could be like a daughter to me, too. Or maybe more like a niece. Either way, she would be someone small and fragile that I could help keep safe from the world and its iron fists.

But then that moment was over, the fantasy shattered, and I remembered that in real life, I was in love with a man I couldn't survive and bound to a man I couldn't escape. I remembered that I collected guns and counted scars, and that maybe I wouldn't be the best influence on someone as impressionable as Anne's young daughter was sure to be.

"Well, I guess that's that." Cam crushed his empty soda can and screwed the lid back on the bottle of whiskey. "Name-tracking is a no-go, unless Anne has some more accurate information for us."

"How long do you expect her to sleep?" I asked, and he glanced at his watch.

"It's already been almost two hours and I gave her a small dose. She could wake up anytime."

I stood and headed for the bedroom, and he called after me. "Careful. Mama bears wake up cranky." Especially those who wake up missing their cubs. I peeked into the bedroom and found Anne stirring slowly, sluggishly, on the bed. She was waking up.

I sat on the edge of the mattress, and when I put a hand on Anne's arm, she opened her eyes. She blinked several times, then sat up slowly and stared at me, her hair mussed as if she'd slept for days. Her nap obviously hadn't been very restful.

"What happened?" she croaked, eyes still red from crying.

"Cam sedated you."

"Bastard…" she mumbled, pushing tangled hair back from her face. She cleared her throat, then met my gaze again. "Hadley?"

I glanced at my lap, then made myself meet her gaze. "We're still working on it."

"I don't understand. I left Kori a message directly asking her to bring Hadley back. She can't ignore that."

"I know. We don't think she's listening to her messages. Cam thinks she's been ordered not to." I sighed, then plunged into the rest of it. "Cam tried to track her, but…something's off about her name, Anne. Whatever's going on, you need to tell us. We can't find her if we don't have all the information."

"I can't…" She scrubbed both hands over her face, then left them there, shoulders shaking with silent sobs.

I pulled her hands away from her face and made her look at me. "You don't have any choice, Annika. We've tried everything we could think of. Cam tried to track her using Shen's last name, then yours. He even tried his own, but that didn't work, and neither did giving her a middle name. We know she's not his, so whatever you're hiding...well, it can't be worse than that, right?"

Anne frowned, momentarily distracted from her tears by obvious confusion. "What? Why would she be Cam's?"

I watched her expectantly, waiting for comprehension to sink in, and when it didn't, I had to actually say what I'd been avoiding discussing. "Anne, I know about the two of you. At the party. Six years ago." Her eyes widened, and I barreled on. "Kori told me. So, on the off chance that Hadley was his, Cam tried giving her a paternal middle name, then tracking that name. But it didn't work. So we need to know—who is her father? Or at the very least, what's her real name? The whole thing, Anne."

For a moment, she looked as if she was actually going to answer, as hard as that might be. Then she burst into tears instead.

Cam's footsteps echoed in the hall while I tried to calm her down, and when he appeared in the doorway, she saw him and cried even harder. "Anne," he said, as I pulled her gently to her feet and guided her toward the door, "I know you're upset, but we don't have time for this. Actually, we don't know how much time we have. We don't know much of anything, and we're not going to until we find her. So we need you to calm down and tell us everything you know. Everything."

She nodded unsteadily and wiped her face with the tissue I handed her, then glanced back and forth between us, still sniffling. "Okay. But I'm gonna need a drink."

Cam forced a smile. "That, we can do."

In the breakfast nook, I pulled a chair out from the table for Anne while Cam poured two fingers of whiskey over ice. He set the glass on the table in front of her, and Anne traded the box of tissues for her drink. She downed half of it, winced, then held the glass in both hands and stared into it.

"I haven't told you guys the truth about all of this. About any of it, really."

"Yeah, we gathered," I said softly, trying to set her at ease.

"The truth is that I don't know who Hadley's father is. I don't know what her full name is. I couldn't even swear that Hadley is her real first name. All I know for sure is that she isn't five—she's seven. Fortunately, she's kind of small for her age, so no one's really questioned that. They just think she's very bright, which is true. Hell, *she* even thinks she's five."

Damn. I blinked at Cam, relieved that he looked just as speechless and confused as I felt. But before I could formulate some kind of response, Anne went on.

"Hadley turned seven last month. And she's not mine."

Twenty-Three

"Whoa..." Cam stood and stomped toward the kitchen, then turned to face us again, stiff with anger. "You let me think she might be mine, when she isn't even *yours?*"

"I'm sorry," Anne set the glass down and turned in her chair to face him. "It never occurred to me that you'd think that. I honestly haven't thought about... that night—the party—in years, and I hadn't done the math in my head, because... Well, because the math isn't real. She's not really five."

"So...who's her mother?" I asked, while Cam ran cold water into a glass at the sink.

Anne studied my expression, as if she was testing it for sincerity. "You really haven't figured it out?"

"No!" Even as I answered, I was silently grasping at straws, looking for clues I might have missed, fully aware that there were probably some things she couldn't tell me. But I came up empty. "How could we have?"

Anne sighed and picked up her glass again, but just held it, as if she was testing her own willpower. And this time when she looked at me, her damp eyes were bottomless wells of pain mixed with relief. "Olivia, she's Elle's daughter. How can you look at her and not see Noelle?"

Stunned, I sat back in my chair, and on the edge of my vision, I saw Cam slowly lower his glass of water. I hadn't seen it—*we* hadn't seen it—because we weren't looking for it. We hadn't been looking for Noelle.

Cam refilled his glass, then sat down on Anne's other side, across the small table from me. "Why do you have Noelle's daughter? And how did she get a daughter? And where the hell *is* she?"

All valid, important questions, but the rapid-fire succession only added to the chaos. "I think we can deduce how she got a daughter," I said, then returned my attention to Anne. "But as for the rest of it, we're truly in the dark."

"Okay." Anne drained her glass, then slowly swirled the ice standing in the bottom. "A few days after that party—*the* party—a woman showed up on my porch with a baby."

"Seriously?" Cam asked, and Anne nodded.

"Just like she'd stepped out of a movie. She had a baby in a car-seat carrier and a letter from Noelle, asking me—*begging* me—to take care of her. That was it. No time limit. No 'I'll be back for her soon.' Just 'Will you please take care of my baby,' and 'Will you please not tell anyone that she's mine unless it's necessary for her safety.' That, and a list of her vital statistics. And, of course, I had to do it. Not that I would have just left Hadley on the porch, but you know, because of the binding, I didn't have that choice."

I frowned, trying to puzzle through an inconsistency in her story. "But how did she…" And then I understood what probably should have been clear earlier. "You didn't burn the second oath. *Noelle* did."

Anne nodded. "That's the only thing I can figure, anyway. Otherwise, she would never have been able to ask me, even through a letter."

"Why didn't you come to me for help? I could have tracked her!" And maybe I could have prevented all of this…!

"Because I couldn't!" Anne sat straighter, her animated gestures fueled by frustration. "You'd have asked about the baby, and I couldn't tell you she was Elle's! I did try to find her, though. I've hired Tracker after Tracker over the years, and no one's even gotten a single blip on her signature. No sign that she's even alive. And she's not. She can't be. She would have come back for her daughter, if she were still alive."

"Okay, wait," I said, trying to sort through information swirling around my head. "Noelle *gave* you her baby?" It was part question, part repetition of the facts in an attempt to understand them. "She just…what? Sent the babysitter over with her only child? Why?"

"I don't know. The sitter said she was their neighbor and she'd agreed to watch Hadley for a few days, while Elle went home to see her parents. Elle said she hadn't told them about the baby yet, and she wasn't sure how they'd react."

"I thought you said Elle's parents are dead," Cam said, turning to me.

"They are," Anne answered for me, picking up the glass again, staring into it as if she could see the past in the melting ice cubes. They'd died in a wreck our freshman year in college, leaving Elle and her older brother no choice but to sell their house and take out loans for school. "And we spent that whole New Year's weekend with her, and she never told anyone she had a baby." Anne shrugged. "She never told *me,* anyway. I'm assuming you didn't know, either."

"No clue." I admitted. "How did the sitter know to bring the baby to you?"

"That's where it gets weird..."

"I think we're way past weird," Cam said.

"Evidently Elle gave the sitter my address and told her to bring me the baby if she didn't come to pick her up on time. And, of course, Elle never showed up. To my knowledge, she never showed up *anywhere* after the party."

"What about the dad?" Cam poured a shot for himself before passing the whiskey to me. "Did the sitter know the father?"

Anne shook her head, while I debated having a drink. "That was the first thing I asked. The sitter said she'd never seen Elle with a man at all, and Elle never once mentioned the father. A couple of weeks later, the sitter called me and said Noelle was being evicted. So I went to the address she gave me and she watched the baby while I packed up Elle's things. I went through everything, looking for some sign of where she'd gone, or who Hadley's father is, but I found nothing. All her correspondence was from us—none of it recent—and all her old pictures were from high school, except for Hadley's baby pictures. Most of *those* were on her camera or her laptop, and there isn't a man in a single one of them. Just the baby, and a few shots of Elle with her."

"She knew something was going to happen," Cam said silently. And I decided I needed that drink after all. "Elle saw something and knew she wasn't going to be there to raise the baby, so she arranged for you to take care of her."

"Then she went back home to see everyone one last time…." I downed my shot, savored the smoothness of a whiskey I could never afford and poured another. "That's why she told me about you and me when she did—she knew she wasn't going to get another chance."

Anne looked puzzled, but respected our privacy enough not to ask for details.

"So, she knew she was going to die, and she made arrangements for Hadley," I said, eager to redirect the conversation. "But why would she want you to let everyone think the baby was yours?"

"I don't know," Anne said. "I don't know anything, other than what I've already told you. All I know for sure is that she gave me Hadley and asked me to keep her safe, and I've raised her as my own, and I love her more than I've ever loved anyone in my life—including Shen and now she's gone, and I'm not protecting her, and the only thing that hurts worse than my head right now is my heart." Tears filled her eyes and threatened to run over as she pressed one hand to her chest so hard I was sure she was bruising her own ribs. "I'm so scared, and I don't know how to get her back…."

"We're going to get her back." I rubbed Anne's back absently, while my thoughts shot in a thousand different directions at once, then finally settled on one point. "Your head…" Her head hurt because she was no longer actively protecting Hadley, as Elle had asked her to. It would probably hurt worse and lead to systemic shutdown if she wasn't already trying to get Hadley back. "Maybe this will help, at least a little." I dug through my satchel for a bottle of Tylenol while Cam ran cold water into a fresh glass.

"What about the vital statistics?" he said, as Anne swallowed four pills at once. "You said she left you some information about the baby? What was the information?"

"Oh, um…" Anne rubbed her face again, thinking. "Her birthday. February eighth. She was almost eleven months old when I got her, but I had to gradually push her age back by another year to account for the pregnancy I never actually had, before I could get back in contact with anyone I'd known before. Elle also left me her blood type—she's A positive. Her length and weight at birth. And potential allergies—Elle was allergic to penicillin and peaches, so she thought Hadley might be, too. Turned out to be a yea on the peaches, nay on the penicillin, thank goodness."

"What about a birth certificate?" I asked, still hoping for a clue about the father's identity.

"Nope." Anne shook her head slowly, as if she was narrating a memory. "I had to pay for a fake one, just to get her enrolled in school."

"Did Shen know she wasn't yours?"

Anne shook her head again. "No one knew, except my parents, and I swore them to secrecy. I had to kind of back away from everyone I'd known for a while, to avoid questions I couldn't answer, so for a long time, it was just me and Hadley."

I couldn't imagine how alone she must have felt.

Well, yes, I could. I knew all about being alone. But I couldn't imagine being alone with a baby. Especially a baby that came with no warning and no explanation.

And no instructions. Maybe that was why Elle hadn't left her child to me.

Why she hadn't left her with Kori was obvious.

"Okay…" Cam sank onto the chair opposite me, looking more hopeless and frustrated than I'd ever seen him. "So, just to sum up, we need to find and free a missing child, but we have no idea where she is, no blood sample and only her first name to work with. Is that accurate?"

Anne and I glanced at each other, and finally she nodded. "Based on what I know…yes."

"Based on what you know…" Cam mulled that over for a second, then looked up again. "But what do you really know? What do any of us really know? I mean, is Hadley even really her name?"

"Yes. It has to be." Anne's confidence in her statement never wavered.

"Why? Because you've been calling her that all her life? Because Elle told you in a note? What if Elle was lying? She lied to us all, that whole weekend, just by never mentioning the fact that she had a kid." Cam leaned back in his chair, arms crossed over his chest, and the bitter resignation in his eyes scared me. "Maybe she doesn't. Or didn't. We don't know for sure that Hadley's hers, do we? All we have is the written word of a dead woman."

"Hadley *is* Noelle's daughter," Anne insisted, and I recognized the fiery determination sparking behind her calm facade. I recognized it, and I welcomed it. "She had pictures of Hadley dating back to the day she was born. Why would she spend so much time, energy and money on someone else's kid?"

Cam shrugged. "*You* did."

"Yeah, and I'm not done doing it. Because she was Elle's daughter, and now she's my daughter, and her name *is* Hadley."

"You can't be sure of that…." I said softly, when I couldn't find a flaw in Cameron's logic, harsh though it sounded. "Not one hundred percent."

Anne turned on me, and I could practically feel the heat of her anger. "Yes, I can. I am absolutely sure of that because I know how Elle must have felt when she sent her baby to me. She knew she was going to die, and her child was the most precious thing in the world to her, and I've been walking in those exact footprints for the past two days. Tower's men will kill me to get to Hadley—they've already killed Shen—so I've been struggling with the same mental preparation for her future that Elle had to face. And if I know anything at all, it's that no mother would prepare to give her daughter a new life—a life of lies meant to protect her—without leaving her with at least one truth. Hadley doesn't know who her mother really was. She doesn't know who her father is. She doesn't know what Skill she'll inherit, or if she'll ever see her home again. The only truth she has is her real name—one quarter of it, anyway. The name her real mother gave her, and the only thing that can never be taken from her. And Elle would never lie about that."

Cam and I stared at Anne, stunned by the power of her words and her absolute conviction. And finally Cam nodded. "Okay. We have one name to work with. I guess that's better than no name." *But not much.*

He didn't say the last part, but I heard it anyway.

"Okay, here's what I suggest." I stood and started opening kitchen drawers in search of paper and a pen.

"You two sit and think of every possible name Elle could have given her daughter. I'd concentrate mostly on middle names, since we have no idea who the father is, and she probably has his surname." A child's surname was entirely up to the mother to give—it could be hers, the father's or any other random name she chose, though the rest of the world would almost always know the child by his or her father's last name.

"I don't know..." Anne said, as I plucked a black ballpoint pen from a disturbingly neat—and sparsely populated—junk drawer. "She has no pictures of the father, and there wasn't a single mention of him in any of her personal correspondence or official paperwork. I don't think she wants anything to do with him. And if that's the case, why give the baby his name?"

Cam shrugged, and I continued my search for paper. "I think we're skimming right over the most obvious possibility—Hadley's father could be dead."

I shook my head without looking up from the last drawer in the kitchen. "If he were dead, why would she hide his identity? Wouldn't she want her daughter to grow up at least knowing her late father's name?"

"Maybe she was trying to keep Hadley from his family?" Anne suggested. "In the absence of a will, orphaned children go to the next of kin. So maybe she didn't like his family and didn't want them to know about the baby."

"That doesn't fit the timeline," Cam insisted, rounding the peninsula toward the fridge, where he plucked a magnet notepad from the front and handed it to me with a brief grin. "She named the baby eleven months before she died."

I set the notebook and pen in front of Anne on the

table. "So maybe she knew, even then. We have no idea how long she knew she was going to die." And that was the root of the problem—we didn't know what Elle had seen, or how long ago she'd seen it.

"Here." I tapped the notebook for emphasis. "Write down every possible name combination you can think of, and Cam can try them one at a time. Cross them off once you've tried it, otherwise, you'll just repeat your efforts." And I knew from personal experience how frustrating that could be. "Use Elle's family names—her own, her mom's, et cetera—and her friends' names. Try everything you can think of."

"What are you going to do?" Cam called, as I made my way toward the bedroom.

"I'm going to try Kori again." Maybe if she knew what we'd just found out…

That was wishful thinking, and I knew it. We all knew it. But I dialed anyway. And just as I'd expected, I got her anonymous voice-mail message.

"Hey, Kori, it's Liv," I said, sinking onto the king-size bed I'd never slept in. "To be honest, I'm kind of banking on the assumption that you were following orders when you took Hadley, and that if you could have found a way around following that particular order, you would have. If that's not the case, then… well, I guess more has changed over the last few years than I thought. But in case I'm right, there's something you should know." I inhaled deeply…and the machine cut my message off. The dial tone buzzed in my ear.

Damn. So much for a heartfelt message—short and sweet it is.

I called back, and again I got her voice mail. "Okay, I'm gonna keep this short." Because I had no choice.

"Hadley isn't really Anne's daughter. She's Elle's. She's Noelle's *baby,* Korinne. Elle knew she was going to die, so she left her baby with Anne and made her promise to keep it a secret. If any of us have ever meant anything to you—hell, if *Elle* ever meant anything to you— find a way to bring her back. Please, Kori. I'm leaving the bathroom dark for you. Will you please bring her back?"

That time when the machine cut me off, I was ready. I'd said what I had to say, including a direct request for her help, and beneath the mountain of my cynicism, there was a tiny blossom of hope, dying from lack of light, but deeply rooted. Within our four-sided friendship, Elle and Kori had always been best friends, like Anne and I were. Closer friendships within the whole. Even if Kori wasn't willing to risk her job—not to mention her life—for me or Anne, or even for Hadley, she might be willing to do it for Elle.

For Elle's memory.

Assuming she heard the message. But if she were listening to her messages, she would already have brought Hadley back, compelled by Anne's request.

Anne looked up from the notepad when I sank into the chair next to her at the table. "Well?" she said, and the naked longing in her voice nearly killed me. Her hope was raw and obvious. It was her first line of defense, not merely a backup parachute cord, like the one I clung to privately. And when I shook my head in reply, her heartbreak and disappointment were just as raw and obvious.

"I left a message and told her about Elle," I said, glancing at the first page of potential names, crossed off, ripped from the pad and dismissed once they'd been eliminated.

Anne looked up, still clutching the pen. "Try texting her. She'll probably have the text read before it occurs to her that she shouldn't finish it. You can compel her before she even realizes what she's read."

"Anne, that's brilliant!" I said, pulling my phone from my pocket.

She shrugged. "That's how Elle got me in the first place. In writing." She held up the notepad full of names for emphasis.

I was halfway through a short, to-the-point text when Cam suddenly snatched my cell from my hand. "Wait!"

"What?"

"Don't compel her in a text." He backspaced over everything I'd typed. "That'll only compete with her orders from Tower and make her self-destruct."

Anne frowned. "You said her binding to us would supersede her marks from Tower."

"I was wrong." He handed my phone back. "I can't believe I didn't see this before, and I can't elaborate, but her binding to him is just as strong as her binding to you two. That's why she's not listening to her messages. It has to be."

"You said Tower probably told her not to listen to them," I said, flipping my phone open again.

"I was wrong about that, too. He doesn't know about her binding to you guys, remember? Why would he order her not to listen to a request from Anne when he doesn't know Anne can compel her? She's ignoring the messages on her own, because if she hears you make a request in conflict with her current orders, her body will tear itself apart, trying to do both at once. It's a miserable way to die. I've seen it."

"Tower?" I asked, staring at my phone.

He nodded. "Standard sentence for divided loyalty."

My stomach churned in horror. "So what can we do?"

Cam shrugged. "Ask her for help without compelling her to go against Tower's orders."

"Okay…" But that was much easier said than done, considering that I didn't know what orders he'd given her.

I started typing again, and when I was done, I showed Cam.

Hadley isn't Anne's daughter—she's Elle's. Know u can't return her, but we need help. Can't track her w/ no real name or blood.

Cam read it and nodded, so I hit Send. "Now it's up to her." I set my phone on the table and glanced around at the scattered notepad pages. "What'd you guys come up with?"

Cam answered from across the table, while Anne feverishly scribbled more name combinations on a fresh sheet from the pad. "Nothing yet. We've tried every possible pairing of Noelle's name, her mother's name, and yours, Anne's and Kori's. But we don't know everyone's full names, and we don't know for sure that Elle used any of them. If she was smart—and she obviously *was* smart—she probably used a random name, to prevent exactly what we're trying to do."

"That's the problem with having smart friends." I picked up the sheet of eliminated names and glanced over it, trying to think of something they might have missed. But I came up empty.

A moment later, something clattered on the floor in the hall, and we all three spun around in time to see a small pink canvas shoe tumble to a stop in the middle of the living-room floor. But the hall was empty.

Anne was out of her chair in an instant and she had the shoe in hand before either Cam or I reached her. "It's Hadley's," she said, fresh tears forming in her eyes. "Why would she send us Hadley's shoe? Why isn't Hadley wearing it? Is this some kind of warning?"

"Anne, calm down." I took the shoe from her gently and pulled the tongue back with the opening aimed at the light overhead. "There's something inside."

She grabbed the shoe before I could stop her and pulled a folded sheet of plain white printer paper from inside. Cam and I read over her shoulder.

If she's really Elle's, you're going about this all wrong.
    You have to think like Noelle.

That was it. No signature. No introduction. But it was definitely Kori's handwriting. We'd passed dozens of notes—maybe hundreds—in school during my life before cell phones, and her writing hadn't changed since the seventh grade.

"What does that mean?" The note shook in Anne's hand. "Is she taunting us? Why not just call or text?"

"She's probably prohibited," I said, rereading the note for the third time, trying to find more meaning in the sparse wording. "Tower doesn't know she's bound to us, but he does know we're friends."

"She can't make a phone call, but she can throw a shoe down the hall with a note stuffed inside?"

"She's using the loopholes." And the shadows I'd left in the bathroom. I took the shoe from Anne. "It's a given that Tower would ban her from calling or texting us, but who thinks to specifically forbid tossing a shoe with a handwritten note inside it?"

"So what does this mean?" She gestured with the shoe, and I noticed that her hands were still shaking. If I wasn't afraid it would start to fuzzy her logic, I'd offer her more whiskey. "How is thinking like Elle going to help us find Hadley?"

"I think she means we have to think like Noelle to figure out Hadley's name. So we can track her." I shrugged. "She probably heard us talking from the bathroom." Or maybe she just knew we'd try tracking Hadley—it was a logical assumption, considering that two of us were Trackers.

"Okay...so how does—*did*—Elle think?"

"Like a Seer," Cam said. "Elle thought like someone who knew what was going to happen, but not how to prevent it. All she could do was prepare for it, and that's what she was doing when she sent Hadley to you."

"Oh, hell..." I whispered, and my entire body suddenly felt heavy with the weight of a startling understanding. I sank into the nearest chair, trying to wrap my head around the details as they tumbled into place, some more reluctant than others. "It wasn't just that."

"It wasn't just what?" Cam sat on the couch next to my chair, his knees nearly touching mine, and he looked as if he wasn't sure whether to take my temperature or pour me a shot. "What's wrong?"

"It wasn't just sending her baby to Anne. Noelle did much more than that to prepare for this."

"To prepare for what?" Anne dropped onto the couch next to Cam and they watched me like one of those three-dimensional images you have to squint to see just right—as if they couldn't quite bring me into focus.

"I don't know. I don't know what she saw, or how long ago she saw it. Maybe she knew that Tower would someday be selling Skills on the black market, and that he'd want her daughter's blood for his project. Or maybe she just knew that someday someone bad would be after Hadley and that she'd have to be able to ask for help to protect her kid."

"Yeah, we've established that," Cam said gently. "That's why she burned the second oath."

I shook my head. "I think this goes back a lot further than that. How do you think she got the second oath from wherever Kenley hid it in the first place? If Kenley knew it was missing, she would have told us."

"She saw it in a vision?" Anne said, and I shook my head again.

"It doesn't work like that. She's not—she *wasn't*—a psychic metal detector. In fact, she was always losing her own stuff and borrowing ours, remember?" As teenagers, we'd theorized that her head was so full of the future it was hard for her to keep track of the present, and I'd never been more convinced of that than I was in that moment, with Anne and Cam watching me as if they were waiting for me to either start making sense or spontaneously combust. Was this how Elle always felt? As if she could speak until she turned blue, but no one would understand a word?

"What are you saying?" If the lines of confusion in

Anne's forehead grew any deeper, they'd be trenches. "She snatched the second oath a long time ago and didn't tell anyone?"

"Yeah. Probably *years* before she burned it—because she knew someday she'd have to be able to ask you for a favor."

"You're saying that when we were seventeen, while you, Kori and I were daring one another to sneak into frat parties and make out with strangers, Noelle was making plans to protect her future daughter from a Skilled crime lord?"

I took a deep breath and dove in even deeper. "You're gonna think I'm crazy, but I think this goes back even further than that. At least, it does for Elle. Do you remember the day we signed the original oath?"

Anne nodded, clearly impatient for me to get to the point. "I was twelve, not brain dead. That was the night I had my first kiss, at the back-to-school mixer. With Robby Parker. Who then told the entire male half of the seventh grade that my mouth tasted like dog shit smells."

Cam looked as if he wanted to laugh, but he caught my censuring glance just in time and held it in. I turned back to Anne. "And after that?"

"After that, Kori went across the street into the park and filled a paper party napkin with *actual* dog shit, which she then shoved into his mouth in the middle of the gym, in front of the entire school. She got suspended, and I got the last laugh when Robby spewed dog poo all over his friends."

That time Cam did laugh, and even Anne cracked a smile at the memory, in spite of the circumstances necessitating the trip down memory lane.

"And after that…?" I prompted.

"We went back to Kori's house and swore we'd always be there to help one another. Her sister, Kenley, drafted an oath, and we all signed, then stamped in blood. Of course, we had no idea what we were doing—"

"Yes, but whose idea was the oath, do you remember?" I interrupted, when she seemed to be sidestepping my point entirely. "It wasn't Kori's—she's more of a seat-of-the-pants revenge-taker—and it wasn't mine."

And that's when Anne finally understood. She sat up straight and stiff on the couch, her eyes wide, staring at nothing and everything all at once. "Noelle…"

I nodded solemnly. "We were just goofing around—kids high on loyalty and revenge—but she saw what we couldn't. And she must have known about Kenley…."

"Hell, she must have known about us all!" Anne's stunned expression was starting to shift into amazement. "She must have known part of it, anyway."

"Wait a minute." Cam leaned back on the couch, arms crossed over his chest in an obvious display of skepticism. "You're saying that a twelve-year-old kid saw *sixteen years* into the future and not only understood what she saw, but also understood how to *prepare* for it?"

I nodded. "And she knew how to nudge *us* into preparing for it."

Cam's brows rose, and I couldn't tell if he was scared or impressed. Or both. "Well, it's no damn wonder Tower wants her kid, if there's even a chance that she'll develop her mother's Skill. I've never heard of a Seer that powerful in my entire life."

Yeah. But look where it got her. Noelle had spent

half her life planning for her own death and putting us in place to make sure the same thing didn't happen to her daughter.

And we weren't going to let her down.

Twenty-Four

"Okay, so Elle's been planning ahead." Anne leaned back on the couch, one arm over her closed eyes, and I wondered if she was trying to keep the light out or the hope in. "But if she could see so far in advance, wouldn't she know we'd eventually need Hadley's real, full name? Even if she never saw this particular problem coming? Why on earth would she trust me with her child, but not with that child's name?"

"Maybe she did," Cam said, and Anne sat up to frown at him. "But she couldn't just write Hadley's middle and last names down somewhere where anyone might find them."

"An understandable paranoia," I said, waving one hand for him to continue.

"So maybe she hid them."

"Hid them where?" Anne demanded, her voice brittle with frustration. Or maybe that was pain. She was probably miserable by now, considering how long her accidental breach of contract with Noelle had been in effect.

"It would have to be somewhere you'd be sure to see

them, but no one else would notice them." I rubbed my forehead, my brain racing. "They'd have to be in something she gave you. Something she sent with Hadley. Or maybe something she left in her apartment."

Anne shook her head. "I've been through all that!" She ran one hand through her hair in exasperation. "I've been through everything. Over and over. She didn't have an address book—not hard copy, and not digital. There are no names on the backs of her photos except for Hadley, and that's all she ever called her in writing. Just that one name. There was nothing embroidered or written on her clothes, no name tag on her diaper bag or suitcase. It's like Noelle was hiding her before she ever even sent her to me." Another sigh, then Anne met my gaze with an exhausted one of her own. "Besides, she was too careful to leave anything telling in her apartment. What if I hadn't come to clean it out before she was officially evicted? What if someone else came looking for her before her neighbor called me? She couldn't have seen *everything,* Liv. Some things had to be in the shadows, and she wouldn't have taken a risk like that."

"She's right," Cam said, before I could reply. "Elle wouldn't have left sensitive information in the apartment. So it had to have come with the baby. It had to be in or on something she sent with Hadley."

"There wasn't anything!" Anne's eyes watered, and she swiped away the tears angrily. "There was just the baby in her carrier, a diaper bag full of supplies, a stuffed bear, over-the-counter medication and a small suitcase full of clothes. And I went through all of it over and over. I ripped the lining out of the carrier, the diaper bag and the suitcase when I was looking for

Hadley's birth certificate. Hell, I even cut the bear up his rear seam and ripped out the stuffing, then had to sew the damn thing up again by hand. There was nothing. No note. No mysterious P.O. box key. And certainly no X to mark the spot. There was just Hadley and the letter from Elle, asking me to take her."

"The letter…" I glanced at Cam and was both relieved and thrilled to see the same spark of possibility glowing in his eyes. "It had to be somewhere in that letter. In code or something."

"Yeah. Or maybe written in invisible ink." Anne sighed. "Wouldn't that be a bitch. All these years I've been searching for information, and it could've been right there the whole time, written in lemon juice, just waiting to be exposed by a warm lightbulb."

"Anne…" Cam reached for her hand, and with it, he also got teary eye contact. "Do you happen to remember what that letter said? Exactly? I'm assuming you read it several times over the years…?"

"Yeah. You want to see it?"

I blinked, sure I'd heard her wrong. "You have it with you?"

Anne shrugged. "It's in Hadley's memory box, with a few of the baby pictures Noelle wrote notes on the back of—the date and the occasion. Her first steps, stuff like that." She leaned forward and grabbed the backpack she'd brought with her, digging through the contents as she spoke. "They're the only things she has from Elle, and I wasn't going to go on the run without them. Of course, she hasn't seen them yet…"

Because Hadley didn't know anything about her real mother.

Anne pulled an old-fashioned cardboard pencil box

out of the bag. It was pink, hand-decorated with Hadley's name in purple glitter paint and accented with white daisy stickers—clearly Anne's handiwork. She flipped open the lid and pulled out a folded sheet of blue-lined white notebook paper, then set the box on the coffee table and unfolded the letter beside it.

We all leaned forward to read.

As Anne had said, the letter was short and to the point. Just a paragraph long, with no obvious code or pattern in the letters, and no single words which could easily be identified as names.

Below the official request was the list of vital statistics Anne had mentioned, and below that, Hadley's potential allergies. And at the very bottom of the page, there was a small ink sketch of a teddy bear with button eyes and a stitched X for a nose.

"Did Elle draw that?" I asked, and Anne shrugged.

"I guess so. That's the bear that came in the diaper bag—the only toy Elle sent with Hadley. It was her favorite until she started school, and some little prick kindergartner told her only babies carried stuffed animals. After that, she put Harrison up on her shelf and she hasn't taken him down since."

A chill crawled up my spine. "The bear's name was Harrison?"

"Yeah. Harrison Lee."

That first chill spawned an army of baby chills that raised goose bumps as they raced across my skin. "Did you name the bear?"

"No, she named it herself." Anne blinked as the facts clicked into place with the memory. "That was one of only two or three things she could say when I got her. 'More,' 'Pwease' and 'Hawison Wee.'"

I glanced at Cam. "Do babies name their own stuffed animals?"

He could not have looked more surprised by my question. "I know as little about babies as you do. Maybe less."

So I turned to Anne, but she was already frowning. "I don't know. Hadley's the only toddler I've ever spent any time with, and I didn't question it. However he got it, the bear's name was Harrison Lee."

"So, are we all thinking what I'm thinking? That Elle gave the bear Hadley's middle and last names so that—at least subconsciously—she'd always know them? Then she drew the bear at the bottom of the basics-of-parenting cheat sheet as a hint for Annika, complete with an actual X to mark the spot?" The bear's nose, of course.

Anne shrugged. "Nothing has made any more sense than that, so far."

I glanced at Cam and he nodded solemnly. "It's worth a shot." He closed his eyes, and as we watched, he muttered, "Hadley Harrison Lee." His eyes rolled beneath his eyelids, as if he was actually scanning his own private darkness for light on the horizon. I held my breath, my mental fingers crossed, and if wishing for success could have made it happen, we would have found Hadley in that very moment.

But instead, several seconds later, Cam opened his eyes and shook his head. "That's not it."

"Reverse them," Anne said, unwilling to give up. "Try it one more time, in a different order."

While Cam tried again, I flipped open Hadley's memory box and took out the thin, four-by-six-inch photo album, staring at the baby whose picture peeked through the oval frame cut into the cover.

I saw no resemblance to Elle. But then again, I saw no resemblance to the older Hadley, either, except for her green eyes. Everything else had changed, and her hair had lightened several shades, as if she spent most of her time in the sun. Seven-year-old Hadley's hair was much closer in color to Elle's as I remembered it.

Cam mumbled the name again, this time using Hadley as the last name and Harrison as the middle name, and I flipped through the album while Anne watched him intently. Just past the halfway point in the thin album, I found an empty photo sleeve on the left side of the page, opposite a shot of—

I froze with the next page between my fingers, ready to flip before I'd realized what I was looking at.

What the hell?

"Anne...?"

"What?" She turned to see what I was staring at, and Cam whispered again, trying another name combination.

"Is this Hadley?" *It can't be. No way.*

"Yeah, that's one of my favorites. According to the date on the back she was about six months old, and I think she'd just learned to sit up on her own. See?" She flipped the blank page to reveal the picture behind it, then turned back to the one that had sent adrenaline shooting through my heart, strong and fast enough to make it literally skip a beat. "This is the first one where there's no pillow propping her up from behind."

I stared at the picture of baby Hadley in a tiny, solid blue baseball cap, chubby little fingers clutching the corner of the green checkered blanket she sat on, and

I had to will my pulse to slow before my vision went black.

"Where's this one?" I whispered with as much volume as I could manage, tapping the blank page.

"Don't know. That one was empty when I got it. I guess she just skipped a page. I thought about shifting them all down one so I could add a new one at the end, but it just seemed wrong to rearrange something Elle made for her."

I fumbled for my satchel, and Anne caught the album when it slid from my lap. But before she could snap at me to be more careful, Cam exhaled, long and low.

"I got it."

My fingers fell away from my bag and I looked up at him in surprise. "You got it?"

"Yeah. I had to try several variations, accounting for the possible speech difficulties of an eleven-month-old child, but I got it. She's Leah Harrison Hadley." His grin nearly split his face in two. "I'm assuming Harrison is a family name—maybe Elle's dad's?—and Hadley's her *last* name, not her first."

"Harrison is her brother's name," I said.

Cam frowned. "Harrison Maddox?"

I nodded absently, still focused on that missing photo.

"Clever Noelle...!" Anne mumbled, already reaching for the pen and paper to write her daughter's name down. Then she evidently thought better of that and dropped the pen on the end table. "Is the energy signature strong?"

"Strong enough. I think she's still in the city. And she's definitely still alive."

"Great. Let's go." She was halfway to the door before we could stop her.

"Anne, *wait*." Cam lunged forward and grabbed her arm before she could throw open the front door and expose herself to whoever Ruben had watching the apartment. "We need a plan. We need backup. We need…a plan."

She tugged her arm free and frowned at him. "You already said that."

"It's worth repeating." He gestured toward the couch and she sat again, reluctantly. "I know you're eager to get her back, but if we just bust in…" Cam rubbed his forehead, and I wondered if he was getting repercussion pain from working with us, in conflict with his oath to Jake Tower. Or maybe he hadn't actually crossed that line yet and was just anticipating the pain—I could certainly sympathize.

"Actually," he continued, "that's not even possible. I *can't* bust in on Tower's pet project, so it would just be the two of you, and that'd be *beyond* stupid."

"So…what are we going to do?" Hope drained from Anne's face, revealing the fear and worry it had briefly hidden.

"Uh…guys? I hate to complicate things, but…" I set Hadley's photo album open on the coffee table in front of them and tapped the empty page. "We need to talk about this missing picture."

Anne glanced impatiently at the album. "What about it?"

"It's not missing anymore."

"What are you talking about?" she demanded, as I pulled a green plastic binder from my satchel, but Cam only watched in silence as I opened it on my lap.

I flipped to the back of the binder and popped open the three one-inch rings, then removed a clear plastic page protector and handed it to Anne.

She glanced at the photo it held, then blinked and looked again. For a long time. When she finally met my gaze again, her eyes were wide and tear-filled. "Where did you get this?"

I sighed. "I can't tell you that." Then I rushed on before she could argue. "Am I right? Is that Hadley in the photo?"

She pinched the top of the page protector and held her hand over the opening. "May I...?"

"Yeah. That's a copy anyway."

She pulled out the photo and held it inches from her face, as the first tears fell. "Where's the original?"

I thought about that for a second, then decided that answering wouldn't actually breach my contract, though I probably couldn't answer anything *else* she was certain to ask. "The original is in the top drawer of the desk in Ruben Cavazos's home office."

"What...?" Anne glanced from me to Cam, and I looked up to see him leaning with both elbows on his knees, shaking his head slowly. He'd already deduced what I couldn't say. "What the hell is going on here, Olivia?" Anne demanded.

I couldn't answer her, but before that became an issue, Cam spoke up with another question I couldn't answer.

"You're serious? *Hadley* is Cavazos's illegitimate son?" Another painful pause. "That means that Noelle...?"

I shrugged. "Well, obviously Hadley isn't a boy, but beyond that, I can't..." Another shrug, and I had to let them draw their own conclusions. "I'm sorry, Anne. I'm contractually prohibited from discussing most of this."

"Fortunately, I'm not." Cam sighed and twisted on the couch to fully face her. "Liv's spent the last year and a half trying to track Ruben Cavazos's illegitimate son, born by a mistress he had..." Cam's eyes closed as another piece of the puzzle fell into place. "Damn. Eight years ago, or so. That makes sense now."

Scary, beyond-coincidental sense. How much of this had Elle known?

"And you're saying Noelle was this mistress?" Anne said, already shaking her head in denial of what none of us wanted to believe. "But why would he think Hadley's a boy?"

Since I couldn't actually answer that, I lifted Anne's arm by her elbow, placing the photo she still held back at eye level. Cam scooted closer to her so he could see it, and another layer of confusion melted away.

"Because all he had to go on was this picture, and you have to admit, dressed in blue and wearing a baseball cap, she looks like a little boy. And Noelle was obviously in no rush to correct that assumption. If she even brought him the picture in person?" He glanced at me in question, but I couldn't comment, even though his guess was spot on. She'd sent the picture in an envelope with no return address, accompanied only by a note card with one word handwritten on it. *Yours.*

Anne dropped the picture, and it landed facedown in her lap. "You're telling me that my daughter's biological father is Ruben *fucking* Cavazos, whose mortal enemy has kidnapped the daughter he doesn't even know he has?"

"*I'm* not telling you anything. Because I can't. I can

make conjecture about what Elle might have done, but I can't discuss anything Ruben told me. However, what I *can* say—since it doesn't fall under the terms of my contract with her husband—is that Michaela Cavazos had her husband's former mistress killed six years ago and was *not* happy to learn that said mistress might have—" I hesitated, tiptoeing carefully around verbal landmines. "—left a part of herself out there."

"Shit." Anne's breathing quickened, and was starting to sound a little wheezy. "Shit, shit, *shit!*"

"Anne…" Cam said, in a low, soothing voice.

"What am I going to do? What the *hell* am I going to do now?" She turned on me and grabbed my arm before I even saw her hand move. "You can't tell him. Liv, you *can't* tell him about Hadley."

"I *have* to tell him. And I have to tell him very *soon*." My contract was very specific on that point.

"No!" Anne's grip on my arm tightened painfully. "Elle hid her for a reason, and it's obvious now that that reason was Ruben Cavazos! She went to so much trouble to protect her daughter, and you can't just throw that away. You can't just hand Hadley over to him!"

"Anne, think about the facts." I pulled my arm gently from her terrified grip. "If she was afraid of Ruben, she never would have sent that picture. But she knew what I know—he may be a soul-rotting bastard in nearly every other aspect of life, but he would never hurt a kid. Especially his own kid. And she obviously thought he should at least know he was a father. Hadley was his first." I paused a moment to let that sink in, then continued. "Noelle was probably hiding her daughter from Michaela. Not from Ruben."

"Michaela Cavazos—the woman who had Noelle

murdered? If you give Hadley to them, she'll have her killed, too!"

"No." I squeezed her hand, trying to pass along some of my own certainty. "He would never let that happen." Even if he decided not to bring an illegitimate child into his house, he would never let Meika hurt her. "And the truth is that we *need* him to get Hadley back. He has the resources we need to get past Tower's defenses."

"That won't happen without a fight," Cam mumbled, as if withholding volume would make the words any less true.

"Even if he does fight for her—even if he can get her out of there intact—he won't give her back to me, Olivia! He'll take her, and I'll never see her again, and she won't be any better off with him than she is with Tower."

"Okay, you have to calm down." I held her hand tightly when she tried to pull away. "First of all, that's not true. Ruben doesn't want to lock her up and take her blood. Hell, we don't know that he wants her at all. He's expecting a son. He already has a legitimate daughter, and I don't know if he'll consider another one worth the fight, considering the monumental *bitch-fit* Meika's going to throw when she finds out. So...there's a chance he'll let you keep her."

Or...he might ship her off to a boarding school, from where he could control her, but never see her....

Anne frowned. "But if he doesn't want her, why would he help us get her back?"

Cam laughed out loud, a startling sound in the midst of so much tension. But Anne didn't get the joke. "To save face," Cam explained. "There's no way in hell that Cavazos would let Tower get away with kidnapping his kid, even if neither of them knew she was his kid at the time. Cavazos will welcome an excuse to bring the fight to Tower's front door. The real challenge will be getting Hadley out of there without sustaining any collateral damage."

"Maybe Kori…?" Anne suggested.

I shook my head firmly. "She can't. It's not her fault." Not directly, anyway. Though it was her own fault she worked for Tower. "The most she'll be able to do—if we're lucky—is remove herself from the fight. If we're not lucky, she'll be forced to fight against us."

"As will I," Cam said softly, staring at the phone between his feet.

"We're going to find a way around that," I said. "Or else…you can't be there."

"He'll call me in."

"Give me your phone."

Cam managed a small smile as he dug his cell from his pocket, clearly anticipating my next move. He handed me his phone and I set it on the coffee table, then took my boot off to use the heel as a hammer. Three blows later, his phone was obliterated.

"Can't answer a call you don't receive." I would pick up a prepaid phone for him as soon as I got a chance.

"So, how do you want to play this?" Cam scooped the remains of his phone into one broad hand and crossed the room to drop them into the kitchen trash can.

I shrugged. "I'm going to call Ruben over and fill him in. You guys should probably stay out of sight until I've had a chance to…reason with him. If he thinks he's been set up, he'll call in the guard dogs and have us all shot before he even knows what's going on."

"You're going to bring him *here?*" Anne glanced at Cam nervously, then back to me. "You really think that's a good idea?"

"It's better than the alternative. I'm not going back to his place while Michaela's on the warpath. She nearly opened my femoral artery earlier tonight. Besides—" another shrug "—this is his apartment. It's only a matter of time before he shows up anyway—his spies already know I'm here."

"This is his apartment?" Anne demanded. "You were going to hide Hadley in her own father's apartment?"

"Well, obviously I didn't know about their shared DNA when I came up with that plan. But yeah, Ruben owns the whole building. Why? What did you think this was?" I said, spreading my arms to take in Cavazos's would-be love shack.

"I don't know." Anne hugged herself, and the gesture made her look very fragile and naive. "I thought it was a safe house, or something."

I stifled a laugh. "Annika, I'm a one-woman operation, not the fucking FBI. I take what I can get, and this was the only place I could think of where Tower's men couldn't follow us." And it would have worked—if Kori weren't one of Tower's men.

I gave her a minute to absorb the new-to-her facts, then cleared my throat. "Are you two ready for this?"

"Looking forward to it." Cam's firm nod said he was looking for a chance to pick a fight with Cavazos, and the stern look I gave him did nothing to change that.

"As ready as I'm going to be," Anne said, and I was pleased to find determination strengthening her gaze. She was channeling her inner mama lion, and I was relieved to see it.

"Okay." I stood and headed for the front door. "I'll be back in a minute. Stay out of sight and don't come outside, no matter what. Got it?"

Cam nodded, but Anne's agreement was a little shakier. But that was as good as it was going to get.

I patted my holstered gun beneath my jacket, then opened the door and stepped onto the second-floor landing. I jogged down the stairs and had only been standing in the parking lot for a few seconds when an unmarked black sedan rolled to a stop in front of me, and the passenger's side window buzzed as it receded into the door.

"Evenin,' Liv." Gene smiled up at me from beneath the brim of his cowboy hat, faux-Southern gentleman, through and through. "What can we do for you?" I didn't like many of Cavazos's men, but Gene was at the bottom of my list.

"You can get on your phone, or your radio, or whatever toys Ruben's passing out these days and tell him I need to see him. Here. Now."

"Cool your panties." Gene's languorous gaze traveled south of my waist. "He's already on his way."

"I'm not sleeping with him," I snapped, though I don't know why I bothered.

"Right." Gene laughed, and I wished he'd choke on his own disbelief. "You cover the windows and turn on all the lights for privacy so you can get *yourself* off."

Bastard. "Just send him up when he gets here." I jogged back up the stairs and into the apartment without looking back.

My heart thumped painfully when I closed the door and leaned against it. "He's already on the way." Which I might have known, if I hadn't asked Cam to destroy my phone. "It's only a five-minute drive, so you guys should probably head to the bedroom...."

"Do you know what you're going to say?" Cam asked, as Anne started gathering her stuff.

I shrugged and slid my arms around him when he stepped closer, pressing me into the door. "I'm going to tell him the truth. Some of it, anyway." The parts I was obligated to reveal, along with whatever else would help us get Hadley safely out of Tower's grip. "But I'm going to have to spin it. Let him think he's making all the calls."

"What does that mean?" he asked into my hair, while I pressed my face into the side of his neck, breathing him in, dreading the moment when I'd have to trade his presence for Ruben's. "I'm not going to hide in the other room and let him pound on you!"

"I can hold my own."

"You don't have to," he growled, holding me tighter, and a bolt of dread lanced my heart. "I'm not going to let him touch you."

"Cam." I stepped out of his grip and looked up at him, trying to convey the import of what I was about to say. "You have to stay in the bedroom until I call for you. No matter what. Okay?"

"Hell no!"

Outside, a car engine growled to a stop, then died, and my pulse raced. It was Cavazos—it had to be.

"Cameron, *listen* to me." I held him by both arms, but I was pretty sure that didn't have the same impact it had when our positions were reversed—my hands only fit halfway around his biceps. "He's going to be pissed at first, but the important thing here is getting him to help us go after Hadley, and I'm going to do whatever that takes. Anyway, as soon as he hears about his daughter, he'll forget about everything else."

"And if he doesn't?"

Voices spoke outside my window and down one floor, and I recognized Cavazos's cultured rumble among them.

"He will!" I whispered fiercely, already tugging Cam away from the door. "Promise me you'll stay in there with Anne." Who was watching us silently from the bedroom doorway.

"Liv…"

"Swear!" I snapped, whispering because I heard heavy, confident footsteps on the stairs.

Cam scowled. "Fine. I swear." But we both knew that he'd break his word if Cavazos went too far. If I *let* him go too far.

"Thank you," I breathed. Anne stepped back and I used my good arm to push Cam into the room with her. "I'll call you when I'm ready for you." I started to close the door, then noticed that Anne clutched Hadley's photo album to her chest. "Can I take one of those?" I whispered, as the first knock echoed from my front door.

She hesitated, obviously reluctant to alter Elle's handiwork. But then she nodded, and I flipped through the pages hastily until I found the shot I needed: Hadley, still in her blue cap on her green blanket. But this time, Elle was in the frame with her. I had no idea who'd taken the picture—the neighbor/babysitter?—but it suited my purposes perfectly.

"Thanks. I'll bring it back." But at the last minute, I refrained from promising her, because for all I knew,

Ruben would insist on keeping the picture, and I couldn't stop him.

"Olivia!" Cavazos shouted, pounding on the door again. He was pissed, and I wasn't surprised.

"Shh!" I hissed at Cam and Anne as I closed the bedroom door, then I raced down the short hallway and skidded to a stop a foot from the door. *Not yet...*

I slid Anne's photo into an end-table drawer, then jogged into the kitchen and pulled a steak knife from the block on the counter. Just in case. Carefully, I shoved it between the first two couch cushions, then took a moment to catch my breath and slow my pulse.

Then I pulled the front door open to find Ruben Cavazos waiting with his arms crossed over his chest, eyes narrowed in quiet fury—ten times more dangerous than an obvious bluster. "Sorry. I was in the bathroom."

In response, Ruben backhanded me across the face.

Twenty-Five

I stumbled backward and grabbed the back of a chair to keep from falling. Pain exploded in my cheek. But I clenched my teeth and cursed beneath my breath to keep from alerting Cam. *"Motherfucker!"* I lifted one hand to my face to find it flaming against my cool palm.

Ruben stepped inside and pushed the door closed, then met my gaze with infuriating calm, as if hitting me sent him to his mental happy place.

Bastard.

My mental happy place involved him, ropes, nudity, honey and a massive nest of fire ants.

"Why didn't you answer my calls?"

I stomped into the kitchen and he followed while I loaded ice into the center of a clean hand towel. "Regrettably, I am no longer in possession of my phone." I twisted the bulk of the towel around the ice and pressed it to my cheek, but that only made the throbbing worse. "How many times did you call before you figured out I wasn't going to answer?" Taunting him wouldn't help anything, and it wasn't as satisfying as hitting him back. But it was a close second. "Ten?" His scowl deepened, and my smile grew in direct proportion. "Fifteen? Twenty? Did you call me twenty times, Ruben? You know that makes you look desperate, right?"

He stepped closer. "Are you trying to piss me off?"

"Every girl needs a hobby." I tried to step around him, but he grabbed my arm and pushed me into the countertop, standing so close our bodies touched from knee to chest, and I could feel the fury radiating off him like a fever.

"I'm assuming you came here to apologize. And to work toward forgiveness."

"Then you're making an ass out of us both." I shoved him back with one hand and dodged his next grasp.

"If you're not going to play nice, why are you here?" Ruben's grin would have looked natural on a snake. "Did my mark scare Caballero off?" He came closer, and when I backed away, I bumped into the couch.

Anger got in the way of clear reasoning, and for a moment I saw red. "He doesn't give a shit about your mark, and neither do I. And there's nothing you or your joke of a binding can do about it."

"Let's see how you feel about that mark in six months when I own you, head to toe, and everything in between...." His hand slid over the curve of my backside, and I shoved him away again, but he only laughed.

"That's not going to happen."

He actually laughed. "You're no closer to finding my son now than you've ever been, and once you've failed, there'll be nothing stopping me from securing Caballero's services, whatever that takes. Maybe as a signing bonus, I'll let him watch us together, so he can see what a good little girl you've become." Cavazos leaned in closer and my teeth ground together when his lips brushed my ear. "He might even learn something…."

I buried my right fist in his gut and treasured his explosive grunt of pain as I lurched away from him.

For one long moment, Ruben couldn't speak. He couldn't breathe. He could only clutch the top of the couch, hunched over in the spot I'd just vacated, riding out the pain. I wanted to throw another blow. I wanted to kick him while he was almost down. I wanted to *kill* him, and in that moment, I think I could have. He couldn't shout for help with empty lungs, and if he died, my mark would die with him. I would be rid of him. I would be free.

But we needed him. *Hadley* needed him. And I didn't want to have to tell a child who'd already lost her real mother and her adopted father that I'd just killed another of her parents.

So I sucked in a deep breath and backed around the sofa, keeping it between us, and when he straightened, fists clenched in the overstuffed cushions, I knew that playtime was over. It was time to get down to business—before his retaliation drew Cam out of hiding.

"Truce? I need to talk to you, Ruben." I edged toward the end table as he rounded the couch.

"You need to do more than that." He shoved the coffee table out of the way and came two steps closer.

"Look." I opened the drawer and was reaching for Hadley's picture when his next word froze me in place.

"Stop."

I fought the direct order, mentally, but couldn't make my body disobey. I stood, but left the drawer open. "Please just look…."

He lunged forward and grabbed my arm. The room

spun around me, ceiling soaring before my eyes. My back hit the couch and he was on me in an instant, one hand tangled in my hair, pulling my head to the side. "Now. You are going to shut the fuck up and do exactly what I tell you, or I'm going to make you wish you never set foot in this city."

I forced a bitter laugh, rolling my eyes to the side to keep him in sight. "You're a little late for that one. I hate you."

Ruben laughed. "That's why this is so much fun. You and Meika have more in common than you would ever believe. Swear you'll play nice, and I'll let you up."

"Fuck you." I dug between the cushions for my knife, but only wound up pushing it deeper.

He let go of my hair and his hand wrapped around my throat. But I managed three short words before he started to squeeze.

"I found him."

Cavazos's hand loosened, but didn't leave my throat. "What?"

"I found him. Your son."

"You're lying."

I shook my head, and his ring dug into my chin. "Let me up, and I'll tell you."

"You'll tell me anyway."

That was true, and we both knew it. I had to tell him what I knew, but my mark wouldn't die until he was in physical possession of his child. "Fine. Let me up and I won't make you work for the information." It was within my ability to make him fish the information from me question by individual question, which would take forever and piss him off.

Of course, I didn't have that kind of time to waste at the moment, but he didn't know that.

Ruben let go of my throat, and trailed his hand from my neck down the center of my torso as he climbed off of me. I didn't let go of the breath I'd held until he settled into a chair perpendicular to the couch, still within striking distance, but removed from my personal space. "Talk fast."

I pushed myself upright, in spite of the pain in my arm, and took a moment to tug my shirt back into place, determined to reclaim a little dignity before we began the professional portion of the night's festivities. "I found your kid, but he's not exactly…a he."

"Not *exactly* a he? I'm losing patience, Olivia. If I'm going to have to beat the information out of you, we should really get started."

"Okay. Here." I stood, and he was in front of me in an instant, ready to stop me, should I bolt for the door. "Relax. I'm not going anywhere." I couldn't, even if I wanted to. I edged past him and bent to pick up a photo from the floor, where it had fallen when he'd shoved the coffee table.

Ruben didn't sit again until I sat and handed him his own photograph. "This is your picture of Lucio." The middle name he'd given the illegitimate child he'd thought was a boy. "The one you gave me a year and a half ago."

He took the picture and frowned at it while I pulled Anne's photo from the drawer of the end table between us. "Now look at this one. Do they look like the same child to you? Same room? Same outfit? Is that your baby?" And more importantly… "Is that 'Tamara'?"

Ruben gaped at the picture, his eyes growing steadily wider. "Where did you get this?"

"Is that her?"

"Without a doubt." His gaze was glued to Noelle's face, smiling out at us from a moment frozen in time. "Where is she?"

"Dead," I said, and his jaw tightened, the only outward sign of his displeasure, and I was surprised to realize that he still cared about her, even years later. "Your wife had her shot six years ago, about four months after this picture was taken."

Ruben's eyes closed, but he didn't let go of the picture.

"Also, her name wasn't Tamara Parker. It was Noelle Maddox."

"How do you know all this?" he asked, staring at the picture again.

"Michaela told me she had 'Tamara' killed, as a conversational lead-in to her intent to do the same to me. As for the rest of it…I'm getting to that. But first, I really need to know something."

"You're answering questions, not asking them." But for the first time since I'd met him, he sounded neither confrontational, manipulative nor controlling. He wasn't trying to overpower me, make an example of me or get me out of my pants. And oddly enough, melancholy-Ruben was pretty damn creepy.

I could find nothing to blame for the change in him, other than seeing Elle again for the first time in years, and I really needed to understand why one of my best friends in the world would have voluntarily spent so much time with someone as vile and abusive as Ruben Cavazos. So…

"Did you love her? Not like you love Michaela." If their twisted marriage could even be described in such terms. "Did you actually, really love Noelle, more than you love yourself?"

Ruben scowled, as if I was wasting his time. "That's a pointless question."

"It is *not* a pointless question. You cheated on your wife for the first time with Noelle. Surely that means something—your first infidelity. Did you love her?" *Please. I need to know...*

Ruben sat back in his chair, watching me like a shrink with a sadistic streak. "Are you jealous, Olivia?" But this time I recognized his misdirection for what it was—a defense mechanism. He was hiding from the truth.

"Hell no." I bent to pick up the towel I'd dropped and scooped several fuzzy ice cubes back into it. "I'm searching for a shred of humanity in that shriveled tangle of arteries you call a heart."

"Well, stop." His scowl deepened. "It's not there."

But it was. It *had* to be. Elle wouldn't have stuck around long enough to produce another *human being* with him if he didn't treat her better than he treated... anyone else I'd ever seen him with, other than his daughter. But he wasn't going to say it.

"Fine. Did you hit her?" I asked, approaching the issue from another angle. Surely he wouldn't beat on someone he truly loved. And I wanted that to be Elle for more reasons than I could even list. I wanted Elle to have been in love at least once before she died. I wanted to know that Ruben hadn't abused one of my best friends during the last years of her life. I wanted to know that she wouldn't have put up with it, if he'd tried.

She wasn't bound to him. If she had been, she could never have run from him.

"Did I *hit* her?"

"Don't act like that's not a reasonable question." I put the icy towel on my bruised, swollen cheek for emphasis.

Ruben sighed. "Did I hit her...?" And this time he actually seemed to be contemplating the question. "Only once. When she told me she was leaving. I left to cool off and when I came back, she was gone."

"Holy shit. She *hurt* you, so you struck out at her." He *had* loved her. And he *missed* her.

Maybe he'd been different with Elle. Maybe she hadn't even known what he was really like, if she never saw him in his own world. After all, they were together eight years ago. A lot could have changed since then.

That's what I told myself anyway.

"Enough." He glanced at the picture again. "Tell me about my son."

I nodded. In addition to satisfying my curiosity, talking about Elle had put him in a much more malleable mood. "Okay, here's the short version. Your son is actually a daughter. Her name is Hadley, she's seven years old, and she's both smart and beautiful."

Ruben blinked at me. Then he leaned back in the chair and crossed his arms over his chest. "I don't like games, Olivia."

"Yes, you do. But this isn't a game."

Another blink. Then Ruben held up Anne's photo and pointed to the baby. "That is a little boy."

"No, that is a little girl in a blue baseball cap. Evidently gender-specific physical traits aren't so clear at that age. At least, not with the diaper on."

Ruben brought the picture closer to his face and stared at the baby. Then he compared it to the child in his own picture by staring at that one. And finally he met my gaze again. "So…you're serious? I have another daughter?"

"Yes."

"Where is she?"

I hesitated a little longer than I should have, unsure how best to break the rest of the news to him. "That's where this gets complicated. A couple of hours ago, she was in Cam's apartment, but—"

"You brought him in on this? You took *my daughter* to Caballero's apartment, before you even told me you'd found her?"

"No, on both counts. Cam and I were working on something else entirely. We were trying to protect a mutual friend's daughter. But then it turned out that her daughter and your son were the same person. Only she was a little better informed about the child's gender. And location. And name." But not by much.

His forehead furrowed and his voice dropped into the dangerously angry range. "You and Caballero knew Tam—Noelle?"

"I grew up with her. Cam only met her once, through me. But we never knew she had a baby. Elle and I were out of touch the whole time she was with you, and afterward…she didn't tell anyone."

"If Noelle is dead, how did she hire you to protect her daughter from me?"

"We weren't protecting her from you, Ruben. I've

found no indication that she ever thought you'd hurt your own child."

He looked so relieved by that fact—so uncharacteristically human—that I had to press the ice into my battered cheek again to remind myself that he really was a world-class asshole in everyday life.

"And she wasn't the one who hired us. Before Elle was murdered, she sent Hadley to another friend to raise, in the event of her death. Which she obviously knew was coming. You knew about her Skill, right?"

Cavazos nodded and waved that bit of trivia off as unimportant. "Get on with it."

"Anyway, she gave the baby to Anne and forbade her from telling anyone the child wasn't hers. Which is one of the reasons you've had trouble finding her. Well, that, and you thought she was a boy. Clever on Elle's part, huh?"

"I should have expected no less."

"Yeah, well, she's given all of us a bit of a postmortem surprise. But the weirdest part is that I randomly wound up working for you six years after she died, looking for the daughter you never knew you had. It's almost too coincidental to believe."

Ruben brows rose in mild amusement. "It's neither weird nor coincidental, Olivia. It's my Tamara. Your Noelle."

"You think she knew I'd wind up working for you? And that Anne would hire me to protect Hadley in the middle of all that?" I shook my head slowly, trying to wrap my brain around the impossibility.

"I'm saying she *pushed* you into working for me, just like she pushed your friend Anne into raising her child and protecting her from Michaela."

Did he really think we were all trying to protect his illegitimate child from his own psychotic wife? A valid assumption, I guess, but way off base...

"Ruben, I know she was a Seer, which is part of the problem with Hadley, but she couldn't have seen *every-thing*. No one can see everything."

"Is that what you think?" He laughed, as if he hadn't even heard the part about his daughter. "You think she was just a Seer? Tamara—*Noelle*—was so much more than that. She didn't just see the *possibilities* for the future, she saw the strings connecting all those possi-bilities. She could mentally pluck one string and watch how it rippled along all the other lines, changing things. Rearranging them. She pulled my strings, Olivia. It sounds like she pulled yours, too—yours *and* your friends. Hell, I wouldn't be surprised to find out that she pulled the string that put you in the city—in my line of sight—in the first place."

"No." I shook my head, trying not to see all the pieces of the puzzle that was Elle, suddenly falling into place now that he'd revealed the pattern they formed. "I came to the city to get away from Cam." Because Elle had said one of us would kill the other.

Shit!

Ruben laughed at my expression. "It was her, wasn't it? She's the reason you're here?"

"Not just me..." I mumbled, before I realized I wasn't obligated to tell him this part of it, and that if I did, he'd no doubt use it against me someday.

But the unspoken words still echoed in my head. The truth was that Elle hadn't just pulled *my* strings. Cam had followed me to the city and wound up working for the other side—the side that had kidnapped her daughter—and that no longer felt like an unfortunate-but-random occurrence. If Ruben was right about Elle's Skill, she could have put Cam where he was. She'd placed a mole—an insider's set of eyes and ears—into the organization she knew we would someday have to infiltrate.

But she hadn't placed Kori in the Tower syndicate. I was virtually certain of that. She never would have put a friend in the position Kori was in. Kori was a wild card—the one element Noelle, for whatever reason, hadn't been able to account for.

"Oh, wow." I had no other words for it. No wonder Tower wanted her child. He might not even know Hadley was also the daughter of his mortal enemy—knowing she might inherit the kind of serious Skill her mother had was temptation enough to snatch the child while she was still small and helpless, even if there was no proof yet that she'd actually be a Seer.

"Impressive, isn't it?" Cavazos said, and I saw a hint of a nostalgic smile on his face, so out of place it was startling. "She was also impossible to surprise on her birthday. Though I still have no idea what she saw." He spread both arms to take in the whole tangled catastrophe. "Why she did any of this."

"She did it to protect her daughter—*your* daughter—from Jake Tower."

"What?" Cavazos demanded, and in an instant, the calm, almost nostalgic syndicate leader I'd come to tolerate over the past few minutes was gone. In his place sat the Ruben Cavazos of old, but the anger now blazing behind his eyes was fueled by fear and desperation, lending a much more personal—and dangerous—flavor to his rage.

"Olivia, where is my daughter?"

"We're not sure. Exactly. Cam was able to get a read on her name, and he thinks she's still in the city. But Tower has her."

I barely even saw him move. One second he was sitting in the chair to my right. In the next instant, a Ruben-shape blur streaked toward me and an instant after that, I fought to get my feet beneath me as I was dragged across the room by my neck. My back slammed into the front door. Then Ruben was in my face, and I really wished I'd had the forethought to grab the knife I'd hidden in the couch.

"How the *hell* did Jake Tower get my daughter?"

"Spy," I gasped, and he loosened his hold so I could speak. But not by much. "Before we knew Hadley was yours, we called a friend for help—a Traveler—but it turns out she's bound to Tower. She didn't want to take Hadley. She didn't have any choice."

"How long ago?"

I rolled my eyes to the left until I could see the clock mounted on the wall above the kitchen sink. "About two and a half hours ago."

"Jake Tower has had my daughter for two and a half hours, and you're just now telling me?"

"We didn't know she was yours until a few minutes ago—when I told your men to call you."

"So…I hire you to find my child, and instead, you get her kidnapped by a man who's been trying to kill me for the better part of a decade. Give me one reason I shouldn't kill you right now."

His hand tightened around my throat, and I gasped reflexively, trying to drag in air that wouldn't come. I clawed at his hands, but when he whispered for me to let go, my hands fell to my sides of their own accord. Contractually speaking, he couldn't kill me. But he could damn well choke me until I passed out, and then he'd find Cam and Anne in the back room, and without me to mediate, he might very well decide to kill them both before he even realized who Anne was.

I kicked out as hard as I could, and my boot slammed into his shin. Ruben cursed and squeezed tighter.

Desperate and out of ideas, I kicked backward, and my boot heel echoed against the hollow door. I kicked it one more time, before he could order me to stop.

A second later, Cam stepped into my line of sight over Cavazos's shoulder, gun aimed at Ruben's back. "Let go of her now, or I *will* shoot you."

Twenty-Six

Ruben Cavazos turned to face me slowly, one hand still around Liv's neck. I'd only met him once, and I would have hated him then even if his men hadn't just beaten me into a mass of lumps and bruises. Seeing his hands on Liv now... I wanted to kill him. Not just shoot him. Not kick his teeth in. I wanted to squeeze the last breath from his body and watch the life drain from his eyes.

"If you pull that trigger, it'll be the last thing you ever do," Cavazos said, and in that moment, I didn't give a damn. At least he'd be dead and she would be free of him. Until his men burst into the apartment and killed everyone left standing.

So I didn't shoot, but I didn't lower my gun either, and Cavazos turned back to Liv as if I wasn't still pointing a gun at him—an illustration of the arrogance and fearlessness he was known for. And I hated him just a little more.

"What the hell is he doing in my apartment?" he demanded calmly. "Did you fuck him in my bed? Because I'm not sure I could forgive that, Olivia."

"Helping," she gasped, when his grip loosened just enough for her to speak. "He's helping."

"Clearly." His voice deepened with sarcasm. "A gun aimed at my back is always the sign of a helping hand." He turned to me without letting her go. "Put the gun down, or I'll crush her windpipe. Now."

"I don't think you're going to do that," I said, and Olivia's eye widened. "In fact, I think you're contractually prohibited from killing her, and even if I'm wrong, if you kill her, I have no reason not to kill you. Then your men will come in here and kill everyone else, and there'll be no one left to go rescue Hadley. And I don't think you're going to let that happen."

Even if Liv was wrong about his capacity to love a child he'd never met, I *wasn't* wrong about his determination to take her back from Jake Tower, at all costs. Cavazos would never let an insult like that go unpunished.

He nodded, once, curtly, as she sucked in another breath. "We seem to be in a draw."

"No, *you're* at a distinct disadvantage. I have a gun and am willing to kill you, but you have no gun and are not willing to kill her. Ergo, I win."

Cavazos considered that for a moment, then narrowed his gaze at me. "If I let her go, you will put the gun away? Immediately?"

I nodded. "If you swear to leave your men downstairs out of this."

"Done. I swear." He let go of Liv's throat and she half collapsed, gasping for air. He reached for her, as if he'd either help her up or haul her up, but she dodged his grasp before he could wrap a hand around her gunshot wound.

"Don't...touch...me," she growled, her voice as low-pitched and hoarse as I'd ever heard it. Then she stomped past him, headed in my direction. "FYI, Cam, he does have a gun. He *always* has a gun."

"Good to know." I holstered mine, but left it exposed just in case.

"Olivia, you can't trust him," Cavazos said. "He works for Tower."

"Not by choice." In the kitchen, I ran a cold glass of water for Liv and handed it to her across the counter dividing the two rooms. "And if Tower knows I'm here, it's not because I told him. Liv destroyed my phone. We've been operating completely outside both syndicates."

"You really expect me to believe that?" Cavazos scowled at me from across the room through eyes so dark they could have hidden original sin.

"I don't give a shit what you believe."

"Ruben," Liv said, still hoarse from the abuse of her throat. He looked at her as if he wanted to eat her whole, and the urge to rip his heart out with my bare hands grew from fleeting fantasy to finger-twitching compulsion. "Cam's not representing Tower in this. He's telling the truth. And I trust him with my life."

"Then you're a fool," Cavazos snapped. "He'd hand you over with one word from Jake Tower."

"Yeah, and you just threatened to crush my windpipe. The difference is that *you* were acting of your own free will. So shut the hell up so we can start planning. We're going to need your manpower and Cam's knowledge of the Tower syndicate to get her out of there."

"Will someone please tell me why the *hell* Jake Tower took my daughter? Is this a move against me?"

"It has nothing to do with you," Liv said, while I pulled two clean, short glasses from an upper cabinet. "As far as we know, he has no idea she's yours."

"Then what does he want with her? Has he hurt her?"

Liv glanced at the floor, then met his gaze again. "I don't know. But the more time we waste, the less likely she is to be unhurt when we get to her."

I set the bottle of whiskey on the countertop harder than necessary to capture his attention, and when Cavazos looked at me, I poured a fifty-dollar shot into each of two glasses, then handed one to Liv. When I drank the other one myself, he scowled, but made no comment.

"If he's not trying to get to me, why the hell does he want her?"

"He wants her blood," Anne said from the hallway, having ventured out of the bedroom for the first time since I'd told her to stay put, unsure how bad things were going to get. "How are you going to keep him from getting it?"

Cavazos whirled around fast enough I half hoped he'd injured his own neck. "Who the hell are you?"

"This is Anne," Liv said, before Annika could dig herself in any deeper. "She's been raising Hadley since Elle died. Which means you owe her both respect and gratitude."

"Is there anyone else back there?" he demanded from Liv. "Or are you done pulling rabbits from your hat?"

Anne crossed her arms over her chest. "I'm the last," she said, and Cavazos truly looked at her for the first time, studying her from head to toe, and I could see that she wanted to squirm, but wouldn't give him the satisfaction.

"My daughter thinks you're her mother?"

"I *am* her mother," Anne insisted. "The only one she remembers."

"And your husband?" he demanded, glancing pointedly at the wedding ring she still wore. "She thinks your husband is her father?"

"She did." Anne glanced at the ground for a second, silently grasping for composure, then she met his gaze again boldly. "Tower had him killed yesterday, trying to get to Hadley."

"Did your husband treat her well? Did you both?"

Fresh tears shone in her eyes. "As if she were our own."

"Then I am very sorry for your loss. You will be compensated for your care of my daughter."

"I don't want your money!" Anne snapped, cheeks flaming with indignation, fists clenched against injustice. "I just want my daughter back. And she *is* my daughter. She may have your DNA, but she has Elle's heart and my love, and you don't even know her!"

Liv tried to quiet her with one hand on her shoulder, but Anne brushed that hand away and stepped closer to Cavazos, fearless in defense of her daughter. "We could really use your help, but I'd rather go after her all alone than rescue her from one monster only to turn her over to another."

"You think I'm a monster?"

"I *know* you are." She glanced pointedly at Liv's bruised face. "And I won't let you have Hadley, even if you help us get her back."

Cavazos watched her for a moment in silence, evidently waiting for her to take the insult back or soften it with an apology, and when she did neither, his expression broke into a small, genuinely amused smile. "I admire your grit. When this is all over, I'd like to discuss a potential future for you in the syndicate…."

"Go to hell," Anne spat, and Cavazos laughed out loud, turning to Liv. "Are the two of you actually related? Because I think I see the family resemblance."

"Anne…" I tugged her toward the table and motioned for Liv to follow, and with us seated on either side of her, she seemed to calm down. "Why don't we just worry about getting Hadley back for now, and we can sort the rest of this out then. Once she's safe." And finally Anne nodded.

Instead of joining us at the table for a civilized discussion, however, Cavazos leaned against the back of the couch, where he could see the three of us, the front door and the hallway, with nothing more than a glance in one of three directions. "First, the facts," he said, evidently under the impression that he was in charge. Rumor had it he lived his whole life under that delusion. "Why does Tower want my daughter's blood?"

"It's not just hers," Liv said. "He's collecting Skilled blood samples—or maybe Skilled *people,* we're not entirely sure about that—like Noah collecting for the arc. Minus the apocalyptic flood."

"Interesting recruiting technique…" Cavazos said, as if he might consider something similar, and I wanted to punch him. "But taking children is way over the line."

I huffed in disgust. "And enslaving teenagers as prostitutes isn't?"

Cavazos turned to me slowly and the slightly deepened lines on his forehead hinted of caution—not guilt, not regret and certainly not denial—and that pissed me off even more. "I have no moral objection to the skin trade," he said. "If someone wants to sell his or her body, who am I to object? Beyond that, I'm perfectly willing to profit from the sale, should someone wish to use my contacts to establish a reliable customer base. But I neither sanction nor participate in the binding of minors, for a variety of reasons."

"Whether you 'sanction' it or not, it's being done in your name, and you're profiting from it, so don't start talking like the horse you ride is any higher than Tower's when the truth is that neither of you would recognize morality if it punched you in the face."

"Cam…" Liv began, as Cavazos flushed with anger beneath a fragile facade of calm.

"Fine." I held up both hands, palms out. "I'm done." I'd had my say, and pissing him off would only hamper our efforts on Hadley's behalf. "But once this is over, he *will* answer for what he did to Van and those other girls."

"And when will you answer for what *you* did to them?" Cavazos returned, infuriatingly calm and smug, and for one long moment, I was at a loss for words, caught somewhere between guilt and righteous anger. "I know you killed my Binder, and the only reason you survived such an affront is that I wanted your services. Though I must say I've benefited from Olivia's offer of an exchange."

She bristled over his invasive gaze, and my own anger flared hotter. But Cavazos wasn't done. "You didn't free those poor girls from indentured servitude. You merely exchanged one master for another."

"I was following orders—I had no choice. But they

did. I didn't make them sign, and none of those who did were underage," I insisted, drowning in my own guilt even as I tried to justify my actions, speared by the disgust clear on Anne's face.

She hadn't known what I'd done.

"I didn't solicit their services, nor did I seal their bindings," Cavazos said. "I didn't even know some of them were bound as minors until the report came in that *you'd* recruited them for Tower." He paused to let that hang in the air, and I couldn't even deny the accusation. "When you get the chance, please extend my apologies to your friend Vanessa and assure her that the men who conscripted her have since met with a rather prolonged and painful end, befitting their crimes."

"Do *not* say her name." Names were power, and that bastard had no right to wield any power over Van—not ever again.

"Okay..." Liv stepped between us, as if she'd play mediator, and I read tension in every taut line in her body. "If we could get back to the point, the fact is that Tower's not recruiting. He's kidnapping people and stealing their blood, then selling it in the form of transfusions, to give temporary Skills to previous unSkilled people. For profit. For a *huge* profit, presumably."

Cavazos blinked. Then he blinked again, and I found his complete ignorance of the issue incredibly satisfying. Especially considering I'd been in the same position only hours before.

He crossed his arms over his chest, and the effect was like watching a spring coil tighter, knowing it would soon explode from the tension. "Are you telling me that Jake Tower is selling Skills? To the general populace?"

"Yes." I took almost perverse pleasure in confirming that. "And he's obviously decided that your daughter's blood should be part of his inventory."

"What's her Skill? I assume she's either a Seer or a Binder?"

"We don't know yet." Anne played nervously with the cap from a bottle of water. "She's only seven. Most people don't know their Skill until closer to puberty."

"But for Hadley, that may not be the case," I pointed out. "Elle knew much earlier, right?"

"How could Tower know that?" Liv asked, and they all three turned to me.

I sighed and crossed my arms over my chest. "You said Elle's brother's name is Harrison, right?" I asked, and Anne nodded. "Well, there's a Sonny Maddox working for Tower. One chain link—he's about three years in. If Sonny is actually Harrison, my guess is that he's how Tower found out about Elle and Hadley."

"That son of a bitch!" Anne shouted.

I shrugged. "He may not have had any choice."

"You know, I'm getting kind of tired of hearing that excuse tossed around," she snapped, and I couldn't blame her for her anger, even though it stung. I'd had nothing to do with Hadley being taken. "There are ways around most orders. You've all shown me that."

"Unfortunately, she's right," Cavazos said. "And beyond that, people can't be made to do anything if they never commit to a binding in the first place. So there's plenty of blame to go around." He blinked, obviously dismissing the topic entirely, then glanced at each of us. "What else do you know? Where is this project being run? Where are they housing the blood donors?

Are they all involuntary, or are people actually willingly selling their blood?"

"Surely not..." Anne said, clearly horrified by the idea, but Liv only shrugged.

"I assume it pays slightly better than donating plasma...."

"But the risk! Having your blood on file..." Anne actually shuddered at the thought. "Tower could bind you, or find you at will. No amount of money is worth that kind of risk."

"Money is a very powerful motivator," Cavazos said. "Almost as effective as fear..."

I chose not to comment on that.

"Look..." I ran one hand through my hair, fighting exhaustion and drowning in frustration. "I don't know anything about the blood-transfusion project. I didn't even know Tower was involved in it until Kori told us, so I'm no help to you there. But I can track Hadley. In fact, I can probably track her better now that we have her entire real name."

Cavazos, presumably, would be willing to reveal the middle name he'd given her, if it would help us find her.

"But once we get there, I'll be largely useless. I can't fight against the Tower syndicate any more than your men can fight your organization," I said, holding Cavazos's gaze pointedly. "We're going to need your men and your weapons for that. And we're going to need them fast." I lifted both brows at him in challenge when he scowled at me. "Is that going to be a problem?"

"My men will be the solution, not the problem. You find her, and I'll take care of the rest."

"Good. Once I've found her, we'll call you with an address, and you can trot out your toy soldiers."

"Fine." Cavazos pulled his phone from his pocket and tossed it to Liv. "Program your new number. I assume you remember mine?"

"You really have to stop assuming things…." She hesitated for a moment, obviously reluctant, then dug out her own new phone and tossed it to him. While they exchanged numbers, I pulled Anne aside.

"I don't trust him," I whispered, pulling a bottle of water from the fridge, just to look busy. "How's he rating on the truth meter?"

She shrugged. "He hasn't outright lied yet." Which meant he was telling the truth about Van's underage binding—not that that absolved him of anything. "But I don't trust him, either."

"Good. I need you to stay with him while Liv and I Track Hadley. Text me if he says anything that doesn't ring true."

"No." She shook her head vehemently while I stuffed the water into the bag Liv had packed for me. "I am not staying here alone with him. Take me and leave Liv here with Cavazos."

"You saw what he did to her! I'm never leaving her alone with him again." I zipped the bag and dropped it into a chair at the table.

Her eyes widened. "But you're willing to leave *me* with him? Don't you think it'd be easier for him to just kill me now, rather than fight me for Hadley?"

I coughed to disguise the half smile I couldn't quite hide. "Anne, he doesn't need to kill you to get custody of Hadley, legally or otherwise—a single DNA test will prove he's her father and the courts will give her to him if he wants her." She started to argue, and this time I spoke over her. "And before you say he'll never submit to a test, it's done through a cheek swab—no blood involved."

And that was assuming he even bothered with the courts, but I wasn't going to scare her any worse by admitting he'd probably just take Hadley the minute we found her. "But my point is that he's not going to hurt you. And you can have my gun, just in case."

But Anne only crossed her arms over her chest, digging in for the long haul. "I'm not staying alone with him. Liv can handle herself, Cam. She's survived him for the past year and a half, all on her own. She'll be fine. I'm coming with you."

I started to argue again, but this time Liv cut me off, and I realized she'd heard at least the last part of our discussion. "Take her. I'll be fine here."

"Liv…" I began, but she cut me off with a look.

"You're wasting time. *Hadley's* time," she pointed out, as Anne shoved my bag into my arms. "You'll have to take my car back to your apartment." Because I couldn't drive hers through enemy territory. But then she really would be stuck there with Cavazos.

"Fine." But he watched me over her shoulder, hands in the pockets of his suit pants, as petty and obviously satisfied as the cat who ate a whole fucking *nest* of canaries.

I pulled Liv toward the door with me, whispering on the way, trying not to see how swollen and blue her left cheek was. "Don't drink with him. And don't let him out of your sight, even to go to the bathroom. And call me if he—"

She cut me off with a kiss, grim amusement sparking in her eyes. "I got this, Cam."

"Caballero," Cavazos called from across the room.

"If it'll set your mind at ease, you have my word that she'll still be breathing when you get back."

I glanced at him over her shoulder. "Your word? That's a joke, right? Why don't you give me a real laugh and swear on your honor?"

"Okay..." Liv pulled open the front door and pushed me onto the landing ahead of her. "Time to go." Anne followed me out, and Liv gave me another kiss, so long and deep I got lost in it, and almost couldn't find my way back. Then a soft click from below brought me back to the real world and I glanced down to find two of Cavazos's men aiming guns at my head.

"It's okay," Cavazos said from the doorway, making a subtle lower-your-weapons gesture with one hand. "Caballero has agreed to do a little job for me, and service has its rewards...." He made another, less subtle gesture toward Liv, as if he was *lending* her to me, and my temper flared so bright and hot that for a moment the world seemed to glow around the edges.

Obviously furious, Liv muttered several profanities at him, then turned back to me. "Be careful," she whispered, and I nodded. Then she backed into the apartment after Cavazos while I escorted Anne down the steps.

We ignored Cavazos's men on the way to Liv's car, and twenty minutes later we pulled into the parking lot of my own building and transferred all our stuff to my car. I let Anne drive so I could concentrate on Tracking.

I closed my eyes while she drove, repeating the three-quarters I knew of Hadley's name over and over in my head, peeking out at the city occasionally to suggest a side road or see what part of town we were in.

After about fifteen minutes, we turned left and the pull from Hadley's name—so strong I could feel it buzzing on the surface of my skin—finally matched the direction of the road we were on. I opened my eyes one final time and a sudden jolt of alarm drove Hadley's name right out of my head. Not that it mattered by then.

I knew the neighborhood. I knew where we were headed, even without tracking Hadley the final eighth of a mile.

We were nowhere near the industrial district where I'd expected Tower to house his new project. We were also nowhere near the commercial district where he owned several large, unused office spaces that might have worked, if his "donors" weren't prone to loud disturbances that might alert the neighbors.

Instead, we were in a residential neighborhood. A very nice, very expensive residential neighborhood I'd been called to several times a year since I'd signed with the syndicate.

"No, no, no…" I mumbled, staring out the glass, transfixed as the estate looming ahead grew larger and larger through the windshield.

"What?" Anne glanced at me, then back at the road, which ended ahead in a massive circle drive serving just one residence. "Are we almost there?"

I nodded, still staring at what little I could see of the house through the tall iron gate.

"Which way?"

"Straight."

She frowned, following my gaze. "But the road ends… Ohhh." She pulled onto the side of the road in front of a patch of wooded-but-manicured land belonging to another property, out of sight from the house itself. "Is she in there?" Anne stared at the property ahead, and I nodded, my mind already buzzing with the complications this new information would mean for the rescue mission.

"Whose house is that?" Anne demanded, but I couldn't answer. "You can't tell me, can you?" she guessed, and I nodded. "That means it's his, doesn't it? That's Tower's house? He's keeping her in his own house? Why the hell would he do that?"

I couldn't answer any of her questions, and I didn't even *have* an answer to the last one. Yes, the syndicates often reaped the benefits of having influential police officers, politicians and government officials bound into their ranks—secretly, of course—but this was still quite a risk. A man had been murdered—a civilian, unconnected to the syndicate—and his wife and daughter had subsequently disappeared. If the public found out about that...

But they wouldn't. Tower wouldn't keep her in his own home unless he was absolutely sure he could keep the whole thing from both the press and the officials.

What he obviously didn't realize, however, was that the child he'd stolen and hoped to hide from the world would actually shine some very unwanted attention on Tower's private life—and lead his biggest enemy right to the front door.

Twenty-Seven

"Well, then, wake him up," Ruben snapped into his cell phone, pacing back and forth behind the couch fast enough to make me dizzy. "I want everyone ready to go in half an hour." I couldn't make out the response over the line, but Ruben scowled and stopped pacing to listen. "Fine. Get Tatum ready just in case, but keep tracking Wilson and call me if you find him. Or if you hear anything." He pressed a button to end the call, then slid his cell into his pocket and turned to face me, where I sat at the table.

His table. In his apartment. Deep in his syndicate's territory, with two of his armed men keeping watch outside.

I'd never felt more caged in my entire life.

"Missing another man?" I asked, as he slid into the chair across from me at the table.

"My best Blinder dropped off the face of the planet two days ago."

"Well, hell." Any other day of the year, I would have been thrilled to hear about Cavazos's staffing problems, but Hadley deserved the very best of his resources, and a world-class Blinder would have come in very handy. Blinders can suck all the light out of a room, effectively leaving everyone in that room blind. Thus the name.

Good Blinders can darken an entire house or small building. Great Blinders can darken an entire sky-scraper, mall or office complex. I'd even heard once about a Blinder who could create his own patch of darkness outside, in broad daylight. But surely that was just an urban legend.

"Anyone else?" I asked, and at first, I didn't think he'd answer. The inner workings of his criminal empire were none of my business.

But then he leaned back in his chair and crossed his arms over his chest. "I *may* be missing a Jammer."

"May? I guess he's hard to keep tabs on, since he can't be tracked?" Because something about a Jammer's personal electromagnetic field scrambled his own energy signature, as well as those of anyone near him.

"She," Ruben corrected. "And yes. Which is why she's required to check in with her supervisor every night with a progress report on each project."

Speaking of checking in... I set my phone on the table and stared at it, still waiting on word from Cam and Anne. "I take it she stopped checking in?"

"And stopped answering her phone. And if she's been back to her apartment, we can't tell it."

"So why is she only *maybe* missing?"

"She requested some personal time off and isn't due to check in for four more days. And since she can't be tracked and has obviously managed to destroy her phone, there's nothing we can do but wait for her to come back."

"You know Tower has her, right? Along with your

missing Blinder and probably the Binder who disappeared with the contracts he was working on." And suddenly I realized we'd been alone together for at least twenty minutes without a single punch thrown. That had to be some kind of record.

He nodded. "That does seem to be the obvious conclusion. Tower's gone entirely too far this time."

I rolled my eyes. "Because *you've* never kidnapped anyone or bound someone against his or her will, or stolen blood for illicit purposes, or..."

He met my gaze unflinchingly. "Business decisions, all of them. But there are lines even I won't cross, and selling Skills to the general populace is one of those."

"Because it violates your personal moral code, or because you're jealous that you didn't think of it first?"

Ruben's scowl deepened. "Passing out Skills to people who don't know how to use them will lower the value of those with legitimate Skills to market, which—you may have noticed—is my bread and butter. And yours."

Before I could figure out how to respond, his phone buzzed on the table. He picked it up, and in the second and a half that it took him to read the text message, his expression cycled through amusement and anger to... was that contemplation? He was considering something. Something I wasn't going to like, based on the look of anticipation he turned my way when he slid his phone into his pocket and stood.

"We've got company."

Before I could request details—before he could even get to the door—footsteps pounded up the stairs outside, light and fast, and the front door flew open. Michaela Cavazos stood in the doorway, knife in hand, beautiful mouth pressed into a thin, pale line, eyes *blazing* in fury.

Damn it. I did *not* have time for another catfight.

I stood and pulled my gun, but pointed it at the floor with the safety on—I could aim faster than she could cross the room, no contest.

"I told you to stay away from my husband." She took two steps into the apartment and kicked the door closed.

"It's kind of hard to stay away from him when he keeps following me." I glanced at Cavazos to see him leaning against the kitchen peninsula, arms crossed over his chest, watching us with obvious amusement.

She came closer, and I raised the gun, aiming for her leg. "Don't make me shoot you, Meika."

"He won't let you kill me." She laughed, and the sound held an edge of madness. He'd pushed her a little too far, a little too often—and he probably didn't even know it.

I shrugged. "Murder's a lot easier than divorce. And he *can't* divorce you, can he?"

Ruben laughed out loud, and I couldn't quite make myself regret the warm note of satisfaction winding up my spine.

"Whore!" She came three steps closer, and I disengaged the safety. I didn't want to kill her, but I wouldn't hesitate to put a bullet in her thigh. Would he let this go that far?

"Ruben, tell her we aren't sleeping together."

He lifted one brow at me. "What you and I do together is none of Michaela's business."

I gaped at him. "She's your *wife*."

He nodded calmly. "And the details of my marital contract are none of *your* business."

"Fine," I said, relieved to see that Meika was as frustrated with his lack of cooperation as I was. "If you like the spheres of your life kept separate, tell her to go home. She's the last thing we need to deal with right now."

"Actually, she's exactly what we need right now. Michaela, tell her what your Skill is."

Meika scowled, but had no choice but to comply. "I'm a Traveler."

"Congratulations. Go home and get a cookie." I turned back to Ruben. "We don't need her, and she doesn't want to help anyway."

"We *do* need her, and she will help whether she wants to or not."

"Help with what?" Meika asked, obviously thrown off by the fact that neither of us had stripped naked to flaunt our nonexistent sexual relationship in front of her. When no one answered, she took a closer look at her husband and I could almost see the lightbulb blink to life over her head. "You found him." She stomped toward him, brandishing the knife. "You will *not* bring that little bastard into my house."

Cavazos grabbed her wrist and squeezed. Meika gasped, and the knife fell to the floor. She glared up at him, and he stared back without releasing her or easing his grip. "Do not ever speak like that about my child again." He let her go, and she rubbed her wrist, but resisted the obvious urge to back away from him. "The child, as it turns out, is a girl. And Jake Tower has taken her. Olivia is going to help me get her back."

"Tower? Why?" Meika glanced at me, and I nodded

to confirm what he'd said, though my version might have gone a little differently.

"That's what this is about, Michaela. There's no affair." I'd been trying to tell her that, but she'd always refused to listen, and I wasn't allowed to give specifics about my work for Ruben. But since he'd disclosed our business, I could finally speak about it in front of her. "There's just a scared, probably traumatized little girl, only a couple of years older than Isabel."

Her eyes flashed angrily. "Do *not* say my daughter's name. You don't get to talk about her."

"Fine." I could understand that. Names are power and family is sacred, and I wasn't a part of her family. I didn't want to be. "But Ruben's right. We probably will need a Traveler."

"Go to hell," she snapped. "I won't help you bring back the product of his infidelity."

Ruben rolled his eyes, finally tiring of the theatrics. "Michaela, sit on the couch and shut up."

She went—she had no other choice—and I was impressed that she managed to slink across the room instead of stomping like a pissed-off toddler. Meika dropped onto the couch sideways, so she could still see us both, and I would have bet a year's rent that she was *really* regretting the *oboedientia* part of her marriage oath.

"She's just going to get us all killed," I said, meeting Michaela's hateful gaze boldly, though I spoke to her husband. *Including Hadley.*

"She will do as she's told," he insisted. "And make my life miserable in return, no doubt." Cavazos glanced at his watch. "My men should be ready to go in a few minutes. All we need is a location. Call Caballero and find out what's taking so long."

I pulled my phone from my pocket, irritated by the order, yet unable to resist it, but before I could even flip it open, it buzzed in my hand and a message appeared on-screen. From Cam's phone.

"Shit..." I mumbled, and scanned the text again, to make sure I'd read it right. "Tell your men to go home," I said, and Cavazos lifted both brows in question. "A sledgehammer won't work for this one. We're gonna have to use a scalpel."

"What the hell is she doing here?" Cam asked with one glance at Michaela, before he'd even closed the front door.

"Spewing venom with every word." I thoroughly enjoyed the angry look she shot at me. Its effectiveness had worn off about fifty heated glances ago.

"I came to kill my husband's whore," she snapped.

Cam laughed, which pissed her off even more. "How'd that work out for you?"

I stifled a smile and wrapped one arm around his waist. "You know, I thought she'd be happy to find out I'm not sleeping with her husband, but instead, she seems to have...I don't know...lost her purpose. It's like neutering a cat—now she just sits there and licks herself."

"She killed Elle?" Anne asked, and I sobered instantly at the reminder. Michaela might have been neutered for the moment, but she knew how to work the loopholes every bit as well as I did, and she was the reason we were all here. Killing Elle had set this whole catastrophe in motion.

"Elle?" Meika frowned, obviously trying to place the name.

"Tamara Parker was really Noelle Maddox," I explained, my voice so cold I could practically see my own breath. "One of our best friends."

Meika shrugged. "Your friend was fucking my husband."

"Then why didn't you kill *him?*" Anne shouted, and Cam led her past the couch, drawing her away from the temporarily caged psychopath.

"If I could kill him, the little brat would be an orphan, rather than a bastard," Meika mumbled. I wasn't sure anyone else heard her, but I did, and I'd had enough.

"All right, bitch, listen up…" I dropped onto the couch next to Michaela and felt carefully between the cushions for the knife I couldn't believe I'd forgotten about. Even empty-handed, she was fierce, and when she got in my face, ready to shout, like I'd known she would, I pressed the tip of my reclaimed knife into her stomach, just hard enough that she could feel the point.

Meika froze, and I followed her frightened-deer glance to find Ruben watching us in interest. But making no move to intervene.

Michaela blinked, and her breathing quickened, but she closed her mouth and stared into my eyes from about four inches away.

"I'm not sleeping with your husband," I whispered, where only she could hear. "But someone is. Several someones, at my last count. If you have a problem with that, maybe you should have tattooed *fidelitas* on *his* arm." For emphasis, I flicked the loose short sleeve covering her own marriage vows. "But since it's a little late for that, you're going to have to learn to live with his games. Or better yet, beat him at them. But leave me and my friends out of it. Or else I'll make sure you have plenty of time to think about your mistakes, while you're recovering from whatever damage I manage to inflict before Ruben decides to pull me off of you. Got it?"

With that, I marched into the kitchen and returned the steak knife to the block while everyone else gathered around the table. Without Michaela, who wasn't allowed to join the group until she learned to play nice —an ironic declaration, coming from her husband.

"Why the hell would he take her to his own home?" Cavazos demanded, jumping right to the point. Which I appreciated.

Cam shrugged. "To keep her close? Maybe even to keep her happy. She's not old enough to use as a donor yet—I don't think he *can*, until her Skill manifests—so maybe he's planning to keep her there until it does."

"In his house? Like a part of his family?" Cavazos scowled, and I realized that for him, the fight had just gotten a little more personal. It pissed him off that his mortal enemy had spent more time with Hadley than he had.

Cam stared at the table, obviously trying to figure out how to answer without breaching his service oath. "I can't say much about Tower's home or his family, but I can say that he doesn't run things quite the same way you do."

"And how do I run things?" Ruben was accustomed to dealing with people who couldn't freely give information and he knew how to ask the right questions.

"From the outside looking in, you seem to keep your

family separate from your business. Tonight being the unfortunate exception," Cam said, with a backward glance at Michaela. "Some people don't mind mixing the two. Some homes don't house only family."

"His employees live with him?" I asked. Like most people, I'd heard a lot of rumors about Jake Tower, but that wasn't one of them.

"Some people have *some* employees they trust as much or more than they trust their own family, and it's helpful to have them close at all hours," Cam said, hiding behind a thin but effective shield of vagueness.

"Evidently one of those employees is a Jammer," Anne added, and Cam looked relieved to let her take over, saying what he clearly couldn't. "The pull from Hadley's name died before we even drove off."

"Maybe he moved her," Michaela said, obviously interested in spite of affectations to the contrary.

"No," Anne insisted. "The pull died all at once. It was there one minute, then just gone. If they'd moved her, it would have faded or at least changed direction. She's being Jammed."

"That's going to make her hard to find once we get in," I said.

"The real problem is getting in," Cavazos said, and I nodded. Cam looked as if he wanted to say something, but there wouldn't be much he could contribute to a conversation about breaking into his boss's home.

"Cam…" I began, and he stood. He already knew what I was getting at.

"I'll be in the bedroom with my headphones on…."

"Why?" Anne asked, and I answered for him, as he trudged down the hall, disappointment clear in the slump of his shoulders.

"Because if he actually hears our plans to breach the Tower syndicate, he'll have to report it."

"He already knows we're going after Hadley. Won't he have to report that, too?" she asked.

"If he had to, he'd have already done it," I assured her. "But I suspect he's found a loophole for that one— he hasn't officially been notified of Tower's new business venture, so he's not obligated to defend it."

"Oh." Anne smiled. "Ironic, isn't it? Tower's trying to keep things top secret, but by leaving Cam out of the loop, he's letting us into his house."

"I doubt it'll be as easy as 'letting us in,'" Cavazos said, and suddenly I regretted discussing contract loopholes in front of him—I didn't want to give him any pointers on how to narrow the inevitable gaps in his own boilerplate. "If his home security is set up anything like mine, there will be armed guards at every entrance, and those guards may be Blinders, so if you try breaking in the old-fashioned way, you'll find yourself shot and bleeding out in absolute darkness."

For a moment, I was surprised that he'd reveal so much about his own security measures. But he wasn't saying anything I didn't already know, and unless he was willing to completely cut Anne out of Hadley's life—and he wouldn't be; it wouldn't be in his daughter's best interest—Anne would likely soon be spending some time at the Cavazos estate.

"Okay, but your wife's a Traveler, right?" Anne said, and I was pleased that she'd been paying attention, even when she'd looked too distraught to focus. "Surely she can get us in. One at a time is risky, but it's better than not at all."

"It won't be that simple," Michaela said, twisting to

fully face us from the couch, no longer even feigning disinterest. Either she'd decided she really would rather make Ruben's life hell afterward, or she was actually anticipating the job we were about to pull—the boldest, most dangerous breach of a syndicate's inner defenses I'd ever heard of. And for the first time, I wondered what she'd done before she married Cavazos. Before she became a wife and a mother, and let someone seal the oath *oboedientia* on her arm. Was she active in the syndicate—an employee of her future husband? Was it possible that she now missed the action, and that part of her obvious personality disorder was the result of being effectively shelved away from the action?

Or was I giving her too much credit?

"Why not?" Anne asked, and Cavazos deferred to his wife with one outstretched hand.

"Do I get to sit at the grown-up table now?" Michaela snapped. And when he nodded mutely, she stood and directed her explanation to Anne, though most of what she said was new to me, too.

"You can not just shadow-walk into any of Tower's buildings, including his house. I'd bet my life on it. You certainly can't get into any of *ours* that way. All the closets are kept lit. The beds have storage beneath them. Tables have glass tops. Showers and cabinets have glass doors."

"What about at night?" Anne asked. "I tried to leave the lights on all night once and nearly lost my mind. I couldn't sleep, even with my sleeping mask."

Michaela actually laughed—she didn't seem the least bit threatened by Anne, for which I was profoundly grateful. "An overhead infrared grid is the cornerstone of any good security setup."

Anne frowned. "What does that mean?"

"It's exactly what it sounds like." Meika leaned against the back of the couch, and her accent lent an exotic flavor to what was already an interesting explanation. "Every room in the house has lighting recessed into the ceiling. A grid of them, placed at precise intervals. They look like normal accent lights, but the bulbs are all infrared, and there are no switches. They're on all the time, though they can be turned off at the master control in the security room. Even though you can't see the light they shed, it covers nearly every square inch of the house, leaving no shadow big enough to walk through—unless you are a toddler."

"But how does that help?" Anne asked, and I listened as closely for the answer as she did—we were way beyond my understanding of shadow-walking. "Infrared light isn't visible to the naked eye. So there would still be shadows where the visible light doesn't fall."

"Yes, but shadows that don't penetrate the infrared spectrum are very...shallow, for lack of a better term. They're not deep enough to walk through for something like ninety-nine percent of shadow walkers. With the infrared grid, the room is actually completely lit and impenetrable for virtually all Travelers, even if you see shadows in the visible spectrum."

"Wow, that sounds complicated. And expensive," Anne said, and I could see the wheels in her head turning. If comprehensive infrared lighting was the only way to protect her daughter, she wouldn't be able to *afford* to house Hadley.

"They can afford it," I assured her.

"We can't afford *not* to have it," Cavazos said. "My

enemies are…numerous, and we've foiled two abduction attempts on Isabel this year alone."

Anne paled and suddenly looked as if she might vomit. "They want money?"

"For Isa," Michaela said. "Most of them just want Ruben dead."

I laughed out loud, and for once, Meika didn't look as if she'd like to rip my head off.

"So you're saying there's no way to shadow-walk into Tower's house? What about emergencies? What if someone does get in and Tower needs help? He's not going to call the police…." A safe assumption, considering how much of his business was illegal. "So how would he get his men there in a hurry?"

Michaela shrugged. "I'm sure he has at least one darkroom. We have three of them, in different parts of the house."

"Darkroom? Like photographers use?" This part of Cavazos's life was all new to me—I'd never been allowed to roam free in their house.

"No, more like a closet. Darkrooms are special entrances and exits for Travelers to use. There is no infrared light. Just one standard overhead light, which is kept off unless you need to lock the house down for some reason. I use ours all the time, and if you have staff, or close friends or family who are Travelers, they can use it, too." Like we were using the bathroom, keeping it dark for Kori, just in case. "Some of the wealthier families even keep full-time Travelers as chauffeurs."

Figures. I could barely afford my own car, and Tower was probably paying someone to take his wife shopping without ever stepping outside.

"Great." I shrugged. "If you're pretty sure Tower has one or two of these darkrooms, you can just bring us in one at a time, right?"

"Assuming I had any desire to touch you without a blade in my other hand…yeah." She shrugged, but the reminder that we'd never be friends came through loud and clear. "I could get you into his darkroom, unless it's locked down. But you'd have nowhere to go from there. The typical darkroom has a steel door with concealed hinges and a dead bolt thicker than my wrist. If you try to cut through it, you'll trigger the alarm, which will then trigger a lockdown. The light will come on and you'll be trapped in that fucking closet until his men come in and get you. Or just gas you through the vents."

I turned to Cavazos, trying not to sound any more dazed than I hopefully looked. "Is she serious?"

He lifted one dark brow. "Our darkrooms are currently equipped for both tear gas and carbon monoxide."

"Daaamn." Maybe I didn't want to wander around in his house after all…. "So, how do the locks work? Fingerprint? Retinal scan? Voice recognition?"

"Voice recognition is an inferior technology," Cavazos said. "We tried it for a while, but I got locked out of the house every time I got a cold. And most syndicate members aren't willing to have their fingerprints on file anywhere." For obvious reasons. "Retinal scanners are still prohibitively expensive for most people, even considering the benefits." He shrugged. "We had three of them installed last month. However, I have it on good authority that Tower has yet to make the switch."

I frowned. "How the hell do you know that?"

"I took a Reader with me when we went to price the units we just had installed, to make sure we were getting the best possible deal on the best possible equipment. At that time, Tower hadn't placed an order from any of the top three manufacturers. And even if he's placed an order since then, he hasn't had time to get them delivered and installed."

"So how do you unlock his darkrooms?" Anne asked, clearly fascinated.

Another shrug. "He's probably still using key cards, like the system we just replaced. The digital code is changed every morning, and there's a card coder right outside each darkroom. You just run a fresh card through the coder before you leave, and it's good for that day."

"What about an employee coming in for the first time that day?"

"He would have to use the intercom," Michaela said. "There's a button by the door, and when you press it, the lockdown light comes on so the security camera can see who's there. Say your name into the speaker, and if you are approved, the guard will unlock the door, and you can grab a key card in the hall. If you're not approved..." She shrugged. "Start holding your breath."

The possibilities tumbled around in my head. "So... we need a key card. Preferably one less than a day old..."

Anne sighed and ran one hand through her hair. "We have to get into his house to get a key card. But if we could get into his house, we wouldn't need the damn card in the first place. What's that called? A paradox?"

"It is called good security," Michaela said.

"Wait a minute..." My pulse jumped a little in reaction to my new idea—not a certainty, but certainly a possibility. "Why don't we just have the key delivered, by someone who would definitely have one, if there's actually a key to be had?"

"Kori?" Anne's brows rose over the possibility, and I nodded slowly. "She's not just going to hand her key over. Assuming she has one."

"No, and if we take it from her, we can't let her go back and report to Tower."

"Who the hell is Kori?" Meika asked, and I could swear I saw the fingers of her right hand clench around air, as if she were wishing for the blade Ruben had confiscated.

"Another friend of..." At the last moment, I decided not to mention Elle. Surely that would have been the fastest way to bring Meika's inner bitch roaring back to the surface. "Ours," I finished lamely. "She's one of Tower's Travelers."

Michaela's expression darkened like a cloud had just rolled across the sky. "How many friends do you *have* on the west side of town?"

I shrugged. "I didn't know I had any, until today. But the point is that I think I can get her here. I might need some help subduing her—" which I hated to do at all, considering she probably *wanted* to help us "—but after that, keeping her here should be as easy as tying her to a chair and leaving the lights on." I met Cavazos's gaze steadily, hoping he wouldn't decide this was one of those times I was fun to mess with. "But you have to swear you won't let anyone hurt her."

"Why would I want her hurt?" he asked, not even trying to look innocent.

"Because she works for Tower? Because she took

your daughter to him? Because she's a beautiful woman who does really interesting things when she's mad? Take your pick. Just swear you won't let anyone hurt her."

"What will I get in return?" he asked, his voice low and intimate enough to make his wife scowl.

"Your daughter," I snapped.

Finally he nodded. "I swear I won't let anyone hurt her if she plays nice."

Unfortunately, *nice* wasn't a descriptor I'd ever heard used in reference to Kori. But that was the best I was going to get. "Fine." I sighed, then gulped the last of the water from my bottle. "She'll be traveling into the bathroom, so I'll text her there." Because otherwise, she could show up before we got into place. Or...she could make us wait in the dark for an hour. "I'll need some help."

Michaela shrugged and stood, but I shook my head. No way was I going to stand alone in the dark with her. Not after she'd nearly nicked my femoral artery the last time. She couldn't have changed *that* much in the past hour.

I glanced at Anne and sighed again. She couldn't do it. She may be able to shoot a stranger in immediate defense of her daughter's life, but she couldn't hit a friend when no one was in right-this-minute mortal peril. And, honestly, I kind of liked that about her. It was nice to finally have someone in my life who balked at the idea of killing someone.

Cam was out of the question, of course, so that only left...Cavazos, who stood waiting for me to come to that realization. "After you." He gestured toward the hall, and I sucked in a deep breath, then reluctantly led the way into the shadows.

Twenty-Eight

In the dark, with the door closed, I sat on the edge of the tub holding a roll of duct tape in one hand and my phone in the other. Cam had left the tape on the counter when we'd taped up the window earlier. "Here." I handed the roll to Ruben when he sat on the tub next to me, his thigh and shoulder touching mine. "Tear off a strip to go over her mouth." That way she couldn't ask me or Anne for help, which would ruin our entire plan.

"My pleasure." His voice resonated with sincerity, and I hated him a little more, having heard it. "If she's smart, she won't come," he said, as he ripped a length of tape from the roll. "Tower will kill her for this, when he finds out."

"She doesn't know what we're planning," I whispered. "But she'd come even if she did, if she could possibly find a way. She feels bad enough about giving Hadley to Tower, and she wants to make it right."

"That sounds more like you than Kori."

"You don't even know her!" I snapped, my thumb hovering over the text-message icon on the disposable cell phone I'd borrowed from Cam. I couldn't use mine, because I'd already texted from it, and she'd recognize my number.

"But I know you."

I looked up at him, wishing he could see in the dark so he'd know how thoroughly pissed off I was. "You don't know me. Don't *ever* think you know me. The only things you know about me are the things you made me do, and that illustrates your character, not mine."

Cavazos laughed softly. "I didn't make you take the mark on your thigh. That bond was *your* idea, to free Caballero. And I didn't make you risk my anger and your own life by bringing your friends here, even before you knew Hadley was mine. You did that on your own, to help a child you barely know."

"Shut up." I didn't want to hear his assessment of my character.

"Your hard shell protects some very soft innards, Olivia. That's what makes you so much fun to play with. If that shell had cracked, even just once, I might have been done with you then and there. Well, I would have fucked you first, *then* I would have been done with you. But the more I poke at your armor, the stronger it gets. Just like Michaela. Only there might be just a *bit* too much pressure on her shell," he admitted, finally.

"I don't think you give a shit what's behind my 'shell,' Ruben. I think you just want to crack it for your own amusement."

He laughed again. "Isn't that what I said?"

I closed my eyes, trying to mentally block him out and concentrate on the task at hand. Then I opened my eyes and started typing, which was a real pain in the ass in the dark, on the new phone's numeric-only keyboard.

It's Cam. New phone. Need to see you at Liv's love nest. now.

I'd hesitated to tell her Cam got a new phone, even though I was impersonating him on my own, because she might have to tell Tower that before she came over. But then I realized Tower had probably already figured that out, when Cam stopped answering his old number, which had surely been called after Kori brought Hadley in.

"Not sure how long this'll take," I said, flipping the phone closed, suddenly acutely aware of how cold and hard the tub was. But that was better than Ruben's evil warmth any day.

"Olivia—" he began, and he sounded so serious I was sure I wouldn't want to hear whatever he had to say.

"Shh. If she hears us talking when she gets here, she'll just walk straight back through the shadow and we'll be screwed."

Cavazos made no reply, and I attributed his uncharacteristic moment of cooperation to the fact that he wanted his daughter back.

We sat like that in silence for several minutes and by the time my eyes adjusted to the tiny crack of light bleeding beneath the door from the hallway, each breath either of us took sounded like the hiss from a closed air vent—intrusive, harsh and obvious. The wait was excruciating.

Then, all at once the air felt different. A silhouette

stepped into existence right in front of us—a darker, human-shape among the shadows. Tall and slim, long hair that would have been pale and straight in the light. Definitely Kori—as if I'd had any doubt.

Cavazos was off the tub before I even knew he was going to move. He grabbed her arms and Kori grunted in surprise as I lunged past them both to flip the light switch on the wall. When I turned, Cavazos held her from behind by both elbows. White-blond hair had fallen over her face, but her dark-eyed gaze was still piercing through the pale strands of hair.

"We got her!" I pulled open the bathroom door, belatedly hoping that Cam hadn't heard me through whatever music he was playing. He needed plausible deniability, or he'd have to turn himself in to Tower. And probably take Kori with him.

"Liv, what the *fuck?*" Kori demanded, tossing her hair to clear her line of sight.

"I'm sorry." I snatched the strip of tape Ruben had left hanging from the counter and slapped it over her mouth, catching a strand of hair in the process. Then I reached for her front pocket as footsteps headed toward us from the hall. Yelling something unintelligible from behind her gag, Kori threw her hips back to avoid my hand and nearly knocked Cavazos off balance, but he recovered quickly and tightened his grip on her arms. Kori groaned when he wrenched her shoulders, glaring at me wordlessly.

Anne stared at us from the doorway and Kori continued to buck while I pulled her gun from her shoulder holster, then dug into her pocket for her phone.

Kori's eyes went wide when she saw Anne, and though I couldn't understand her individual words, her inarticulate demand to be released came through loud and clear.

"Sorry, Kor," Anne whispered. "You shouldn't have taken Hadley." Then Anne headed into the living room, cradling her own stomach, as if seeing Kori gagged and restrained actually nauseated her.

"Let's put her in a chair," I said, pocketing Kori's phone. I checked the safety on her gun, then stepped into the hall, where Michaela stood waiting like a child about to meet Santa.

"Better search her first," she suggested, a creepy but confident light dancing behind her eyes. "That'll be harder once she's strapped down."

Kori's brows rose in wordless question and she craned her neck for a better look at Meika, obviously trying to place the face. When Cavazos ordered his wife out of the way, Kori stiffened visibly and I realized she'd thought Cam was holding her.

Ruben forced her down the hall and into the living room with a series of short shoves, and she stared at Michaela the whole time, still clearly trying to identify her. Then, finally, her eyes widened again, and she started shouting behind the tape. She'd recognized Meika.

Kori twisted viciously in Ruben's grip to face me, wordlessly demanding an explanation even as he jerked her around again.

"Hadley's his daughter." I reached between her backside and his pelvis—*not* a pleasant place to be— to search her pockets, while she shouted inarticulately, and this time I thought I heard her say, "Elle."

"Yeah, she's Elle's, too. I know it's weird." But that was all the explanation I had time for. Her left pocket was empty, except for a convenience-store receipt for an overpriced pint of ice cream.

Kori fought Ruben's grip even harder, kicking the air, trying to throw us all off balance as I slid my hand into her right back pocket. She understood now—I could hear it in her voice, feel it in her struggles. She knew she'd brought the two most powerful syndicates in the country into a head-on conflict. And that her boss had no idea it was coming.

Finally, I pulled a blank white plastic key card from her right back pocket and held it up for everyone else to see. Anne looked relieved, and Meika looked... aroused—a fact I decided not to focus on.

I handed Kori's gun to Anne—couldn't risk Meika picking it up—and searched Kori myself, because I didn't trust either Ruben or his wife not to find a way around his promise not to hurt her. But when my gaze met hers, she finally stopped struggling and just blinked at me. Then said what might have been "please" behind her duct-tape gag. There was something she needed to say. Maybe something I needed to hear.

I exhaled slowly, trying to decide. "If you ask me or Anne for anything, I'm going to let Ruben knock you out. Do you understand?"

Kori nodded eagerly. So I peeled the tape from her mouth.

"Liv, please— " She stopped suddenly, biting off an instinctive request, then started over with a rephrase. "You can't do this," she said, as I removed a knife from the sheath strapped to her belt. "If I don't go back, he'll take it out on someone else."

"Hadley?" Cavazos jerked her arms hard enough that Kori grunted in pain.

"No. She's fine. Playing video games on a fuckin' sixty-inch flat screen. He doesn't want to hurt her, I swear."

I removed two more blades from Kori's boots—electing to ignore the hungry look Meika eyed them with—and gestured toward the chair Anne had pulled out from the table.

"We need cuffs. Or rope," Meika said, eyeing her husband. "Bedside table drawer?"

Cavazos nodded, and my stomach churned with sudden nausea at the thought of...whatever he'd had planned for the two of us in that bedroom. "There may be a ball-gag."

"You're sick," I spat, as Anne edged closer to me and farther from him.

Ruben chuckled. "That's a matter of perspective. Fear and adrenaline heighten other physical sensations, you know."

I palmed Kori's largest blade, getting a feel for the weight. "They just make me want to kill someone."

He shrugged. "I'm not taking anything off the table."

A minute later, Meika returned from the bedroom, accompanied by inarticulate sounds of surprise and disgust from Cam. "Just swear they're not for Liv!" he shouted down the hall.

Kori heard him and opened her mouth to shout, but Ruben slapped one hand over it.

"No, I'm fine!" I called back.

"'Kay. Carry on," Cam said, then the door closed and—presumably—he put his headphones back on.

"He's kinda hot when he blushes," Meika said, glancing back toward the bedroom.

"Bitch!" Cavazos snapped, and for a moment I

thought he was talking to his wife, until I looked up to find him shaking his right hand, flinging small drops of blood all over the pale Berber. Kori grinned and licked a single remaining drop from her upper lip.

"Is it just me, or does blood always seem to fall on white carpet?" Meika said, ripping a long strip of duct tape from the roll.

"I'll clean it in a second." Cavazos shoved Kori into a chair and secured her hands at her back with the handcuffs Meika had set on the floor at his feet. They were the real kind—no fuzz or padding. Not what I'd choose for play. If I were to choose such a thing for play.

Meika shoved Kori's ankle against the leg of the chair and reached up for the strip of tape her husband held ready. Kori's free foot shot up. The toe of her boot slammed into Meika's chin. Meika fell backward with an "oof" of pain, then rolled onto her knees holding her jaw, eyes flashing in fury. *"Puta!"*

She stood, fist pulled back for a blow, and I stepped in front of Kori, hoping she wouldn't kick me, too. "Meika, back off! You'd do the same thing in her position."

"I *will* go through you to get to her."

"No, you won't," Cavazos said, and when Anne gasped, I glanced up to find him holding a knife to Kori's throat, her chin gripped tightly in his other hand. I didn't *think* he'd really kill her, but he'd definitely cut her if he had to. The boat had sailed on "playing nice." "Tape her legs and keep your hands to yourself."

"Liv, what's your plan?" Kori asked while Meika taped her to the chair, her words kind of mushed together by Ruben's grip on her face. "If you go in guns ablazin', they'll mow you down."

"They'll never know we've been there until Hadley's back with her mom. After that—" I glanced at Cavazos and he released Kori's head while I threaded a second holster onto my shoulder harness at the table "—I don't care what you do to Tower. Stomp him into the ground. Just don't touch the kids."

"No!" Kori shouted. "You can't kill Tower!" she insisted, and the thin thread of panic in her voice rang a harmonic note in me. I glanced up to find her eyes swimming in fear as she strained against the chair she was taped to.

"Oh, I assure you I can." Cavazos knelt in front of her, hands on her knees for balance. Or maybe just because he wanted them there. "And I plan to enjoy it."

Kori craned her neck to see me around him. "Liv, if Tower dies, his bindings will all be transferred to someone else. To his successor."

Oh, shit. I hesitated and lost count of the 9mm rounds I'd been counting. I'd thought that if Cavazos killed his longtime rival, all Tower's people would be free of their bonds. Including both Kori and Cam.

"Clever," Ruben said, and I could practically see the gears turning in his head. No doubt his team of lawyers would soon have a new clause to draft. "Who's his successor?"

Kori looked at him as if he'd just asked her who shot Kennedy. "I couldn't tell you even if I wanted to." She dismissed him again and her gaze pleaded with me as I loaded an extra clip. "Liv, if you let him kill Tower, I'll wind up…in a very bad position. And so will Cam."

"A bad position? Like…working for someone you hate?" With a glance at Cavazos, I dropped the clip from my gun and slid a fresh one into place until it clicked home.

"Married to someone you want to kill?" Meika suggested.

Kori actually rolled her eyes. "No, much fuckin' worse than those."

"Like missing your daughter?" Anne asked softly, and the entire room fell silent.

Kori slumped against her bindings, as Ruben knelt to clean up his own spilled blood. "Yes, actually. Kinda like that. Only I don't have a daughter," she added, before any of us could ask. Then she turned to me again. "You may think you and Cam are star-crossed now, but if you kill Tower, things will be worse for the two of you than you can even fucking imagine."

I dropped the newly loaded gun into my left holster. "I have a pretty good imagination." Which was why the drawer full of ropes and handcuffs bothered me.

"Olivia. Nothing good will happen if Tower dies." She closed her eyes, then met my gaze again. "Take Hadley home—I'd help you if I could. But don't kill Jake Tower. You have to trust me on this."

And the funny thing was that I did. I believed her.

"Okay," I said finally, dropping the second pistol into the holster beneath my right arm, and Meika propped both hands on her hips, scowling at me.

"*Niña,* I don't think you understand how this works. *La puta* in the chair doesn't get to say how things go."

"Neither does the bitch who killed Hadley's mother," I snapped, and Kori glanced at Meika in surprise, which morphed quickly into fury.

"Is there anything else we should know? Anything you can tell us?" I asked

"Yes, and no," Kori said. "In that order."

"Great." I pulled my jacket on over the shoulder holsters and grabbed my smallest duffel, then glanced at the others. "Let's go."

"Olivia!" Kori called, as I headed toward the brightly lit hall, Cavazos close at my back. I stopped, but didn't turn. "What?"

"He'll kill you if he catches you."

"Oh, good," I said, already walking again, as Anne slapped another piece of tape over Kori's mouth. "No one's tried to kill me in hours."

Twenty-Nine

In the hall, I turned to make a *shh* gesture to Ruben, Meika and Anne, then pushed the bedroom door open. The motion caught Cam's eye and he took his head-phones off, but didn't rise from the edge of the bed, the only piece of furniture in the room.

"I need you to stay here," I said, when he shot me a nervous, questioning look.

He nodded reluctantly and took his cell back when I handed it to him. "You know I wish I could help with… whatever you're doing."

"I know." I also knew that it took a very trusting man to turn his back on the kind of job I was about to pull and believe that everything would be okay just because I said it would. I touched his cheek, letting the stubble scratch my palm, desperately hoping this job wouldn't make a liar of me. I needed to survive the night, even if I might one day die at his hand. At least we'd have the years between, and I had to believe that a few short years with him were better than a lifetime without him.

"I don't want to do this without you…" I began, but he shook his head.

"Don't say anything else. I can't know what *this* is," he said, and I nodded. "But I don't want you to do it without me, either."

If all went well, what we were about to do would rescue Hadley and free me from Cavazos. But Kori and Cam would be screwed. Hell, they probably already were. Cam and I would have to run. Forever. But I could handle that, as long as we were together.

"Be careful," he said, and I nodded, then I put his headphones back over his ears. I kissed him, letting the moment linger, in case it was our last, while the ache in my chest swelled and threatened to devour me. Then I backed into the hall without breaking eye contact until Cavazos closed the door and stepped in front of it to capture my attention.

"I need your word that you won't kill Tower," I said. Ruben shook his head slowly, and I crossed my arms over my chest. "We're not leaving until I have your word."

Cavazos nodded firmly. "Fine. We don't need you to get into Tower's house."

"But you need me for backup, and you sure as hell need me to find Hadley. What do you think the chances are that he's keeping her anywhere near one of the darkrooms?" When he didn't answer, I turned to Michaela. "How close is Isabel's room to any of the exits?"

She didn't reply, but I could see the answer in her face. Isa was more closely guarded than the president. It would be no different for Tower's kids, and we had every reason to suspect Hadley was being kept very near them. Maybe even *with* them.

"Hadley won't come with you," Anne added, sounding very much like that mother lion again. "She doesn't know you. She's never even seen you. And she knows to scream if a stranger ever tries to take her."

"You don't want to traumatize your own daughter, do you?" I asked, and Meika glared at me, clearly pissed over the reminder of her husband's infidelity. But she didn't try to stab anyone. Maybe my little talk had gotten through to her.

"Beyond that," Anne added, "if you want her to trust you—ever—you're going to need my help."

I was so proud of her I almost smiled, in spite of the circumstances.

"Fine," Cavazos said at last, and I could see that eagerness was eating at him, too. "You have my word."

But without his blood to seal the deal, his word was worth no more than the unrealized ideals tattooed across my own back. Fortunately, as soon as I'd united him with his daughter—however temporary—the mark on my thigh would die and I would no longer have to obey his orders. Which meant I'd be free to stop him from killing Tower. Or to die trying.

"Okay..." I turned back to Meika. "Take me first, then Anne, then Ruben." That way she couldn't just disappear with her husband and leave us behind. "Once we're there, I'll take point." Because I'd be tracking. Or trying to, just in case the Jammer moved far enough from Hadley for me to get a read on her. "Ready?"

The others nodded. Cavazos looked distinctly uncomfortable with following someone else's lead, but he didn't openly object.

All four of us piled into the bathroom and Meika stood in the middle of the floor. "It'll take me a minute to find his darkrooms," she said, and I pictured her closing her eyes in concentration, though I couldn't see

Rachel Vincent

a single detail of her face in the darkness. "Okay..." she said finally. "I can feel two of them. Two cool, dark spots in a raging inferno of light."

That was an elaborate description coming from the woman who usually referred to me as *"la puta blanca."* I decided that meant it was accurate.

Meika fumbled for my hand in the dark and I gave it to her reluctantly. "Take a couple of steps forward, when I squeeze your hand," she said, and for once I felt no urge to argue. "Stop when I squeeze again."

Before I could acknowledge the directions, she squeezed my hand hard enough to grind my knuckles together, then jerked me forward into the darkness.

I stumbled into obscurity, then righted myself in the artificial night of a cold room I'd never been in before. I was sure of that, even though I couldn't see my own fingers in front of my face.

Meika dropped my hand as if it was made of fire, and in the next instant, I felt her absence like a safety net dropped from beneath me, leaving me flailing. I reached into the dark, and in the cold, still silence, panic gave rise to the thought that I'd given her too much credit. She'd probably dropped me in a bank vault, or a museum, or something like that.

But if she had, the joke was on her, because I still had Kori's key card. They weren't getting into Tower's house without me.

Fortunately, two steps later my outstretched hand landed on a cold, smooth, featureless wall, and I decided I was where I was supposed to be. And that if I wasn't, panicking would do no good.

After a couple more seconds in absolute darkness, doubts simmering on my mental back burner, the feel of the air around me changed and something collided with my back, shoving me forward.

Anne gasped, and I exhaled with relief so deep I almost cried. They'd nearly materialized right over me.

"Move over, *puta!*" Meika snapped in a harsh whisper. Then she was gone again, and I pulled Anne closer and backed up until my spine hit the wall. I had no idea how big the darkroom was, but it felt small enough to be claustrophobic, if I could have seen my surroundings.

Less than a minute later, the air felt different again—a change in pressure?—and I recognized the sound of Cavazos breathing less than a foot in front of me.

"Everyone ready?" I whispered, and got three hushed replies in the affirmative. "Okay, here goes…" I felt my way along the wall, then around the room until I felt the door, flush with the wall itself. Heart pounding in my ears, I dug my phone out of my pocket and flipped it open for the bare minimum of light. But after several minutes in absolute darkness, the dim glow of my cell display was blinding. It took a second for my eyes to adjust, then I glanced around briefly—trying not to see the ominous-looking air vent built into the ceiling—before sliding Kori's key card into the scanner next to the door.

A small LED light flashed green, then metal whispered against metal as the dead bolt—obviously huge—slid back. And that was it. No hiss of released air pressure. No alarm announcing our home invasion. No computerized voice welcoming me into the future.

It was kind of anticlimactic, really.

I verified that my phone was on Silent, then slid it back into my pocket and pressed down on the lever-style door handle. I pushed the door open. The rubber weather seal squealed softly against the floor and I froze, holding my breath, certain someone had heard, and the entire Tower arsenal was now being sent to intercept us. To *eliminate* us.

But the slice of hallway I could see was dark and quiet. And still. If we'd been detected, the squad coming to kill us was *really* good.

Carefully, I pushed the door the rest of the way open and stepped into the hall. The others followed, and Cavazos let the door close slowly behind us—lit only by the flashing glow from a television somewhere down the hall.

We were upstairs—I could see the corner of a rail overlooking the first floor at one end of the hall—and there were at least a dozen doors opening on either side of the hallway ahead. Before choosing a direction, I closed my eyes and said Hadley's full name in my head, vaguely aware that for the moment at least, I was the only one in the world who knew the entire thing. I felt for the pull of her energy signature—I *searched* for it—but came up with nothing. She was still too close to the Jammer to be detected. We'd have to find her the old-fashioned way.

I glanced at the railing one more time, then took off in the opposite direction, walking carefully, glad my boots were too well-worn to squeak on the tile. The others followed me, and we paused in front of every door to make sure no one inside would see us pass.

The third room on the left held the flashing television, but no sound. Leaning against the wall next to the open door, I pulled Cam's silencer from my pocket and screwed it onto the end of the gun I'd borrowed from him. I peeked into the room slowly and carefully, gun aimed at the floor several feet ahead, safety off. Then I exhaled silently and slid the safety back into place.

The room was a bedroom with an attached bathroom, set up a bit like a motel suite. The occupant—a slightly thickening man in his mid-fifties—was sound asleep in his recliner, head flopped forward, chin dragging his chest.

I led the others past the open door quietly, and when we were clear, Cavazos stepped close to whisper into my ear. "Ray Bailey," he said, gesturing over his shoulder to the room we'd just passed. "Tower's best Blinder."

Unwilling to speak, I gave him a questioning look, and he shrugged. "I do my homework. Tower probably knows who you and Meika are, too."

Which meant we'd be shot on sight. Of the four of us, Anne was the only one who might survive discovery, because if Tower had done his own homework, he'd know she'd raised Hadley and had no affiliation with the Cavazos syndicate. And that she was no threat to him.

"Olivia, we can't leave him," Ruben whispered, and Anne and Meika turned back to watch us, Anne visibly antsy. "If this goes wrong, he'll be used against us. We'll be blinded and vulnerable." Ruben pulled his gun and started to step into the bedroom, but I put one arm out to stop him.

"You can't shoot him—he hasn't done anything."

"Everyone's guilty of something." He pushed my arm out of the way and stepped silently into Bailey's room, over my whispered protest.

"Wait!" I grabbed his arm, but Cavazos shoved me

back and pulled the trigger without hesitation. His gun *thwupped,* and the far side of Bailey's head exploded in a shower of red droplets.

I blinked through my own shock and Ruben hauled me out of the room by my good arm, whispering fiercely in my ear. "It was us or him. If you don't have the balls to do what needs to be done, then stay the hell out of my way."

In the hall again, scrambling for composure, I realized that the Bailey's own television had covered the sound of his murder. Anne hadn't seen or heard, thank goodness.

"What happened?" she asked, but I only shook my head and led us farther down the hall, hating Ruben a little more with each step.

We passed several more closed doors until there was only one room left—open and spilling light into the hall—before a ninety-degree turn to the right. Pressed against the wall, I listened for sound from inside the room, but heard nothing.

So I peeked.

And froze at what I saw. A bed, unmade, with blankets spilling over the edge. A chair, clothes tossed over the back. And a dresser, two drawers open and spilling jeans like a denim spider had tried to crawl out. I might have assumed the room had been searched— in a hurry—if not for the framed photo standing on the dresser. Kori, around fourteen years old, one arm around her younger sister, Kenley, the other around their older brother's waist.

Kori's room had been a mess as long as I'd known her. That much clearly hadn't changed.

"Those were his employees' rooms," I whispered as

we rounded the corner into another empty hall. "All of them." We'd shadow-walked into the wrong wing of the house.

The hall ahead held rooms full of books, theater seating and a projection screen, or collections of couches. One room held a pool table and an oak bar. But they were all empty, and at the end of that hall was another right-hand turn, leading to more rooms. This hall was different, though. I could feel it. This hall was populated, and that could only mean one thing.

"The family wing," Cavazos whispered, and I nodded, having come to the same conclusion.

At the end of this new hall was another set of stairs and a rail presumably overlooking the same great room we'd glimpsed before. And between were six doors on one side of the hall, half open, half closed, and one grand, double set on the other side obviously the master suite. Closed, thankfully.

We snuck down the hall, on pins and needles, fully aware that any sound could trigger a lockdown and get us all killed. Pulse roaring in my ears, I glanced carefully into each room we passed—most were unused guest rooms—and discovered that Michaela had been right. What looked like normal, if opulent family quarters was actually more of a fortress. The windows each bore decorative but functional iron bars. The ceiling was dotted with recessed lighting—an entire grid of infrared bulbs, no doubt blazing in the nonvisible spectrum of light. And the walls, I'd bet anything, were solid concrete beneath expensive paneling.

Two of the rooms obviously belonged to children—privileged, overindulged children—but both beds were empty. Which I found odd, until a couple of doors later, when I peeked into a playroom lined with shelves full of toys and carpeted in thick rubber mats.

In the center of the room was a big pile of pillows and giant beanbags, illuminated by a huge flat-screen television—was that sixty inches?—glowing with the solid blue screen that shows up after the DVD has run its course. In front of the television, a little boy slept sprawled half over a beanbag three times his size and half over his sister's tiny legs. They were out cold.

Not ten feet away, a woman slept curled up on a plush leather couch, facing both the kids and the television, a novel open on the floor beneath her outstretched arm.

"Slumber party?" I whispered to Anne, and she nodded.

"Probably in Hadley's honor."

"That's Katherine George," Meika whispered, pointing to the woman asleep on the couch. "We tried to get her for Isa, but Tower got to her first. Jammer nannies are in high demand among the wealthy."

Ohhhh. The nanny was the Jammer. No wonder she lived with Tower—she had to be near his children. And while she was Jamming their energy signatures, she'd been Jamming Hadley's, too. But...

"Where's Hadley?" Anne asked. There was a third beanbag half-draped with a fuzzy pink blanket, but she wasn't in it.

Before I could answer, the rush of running water sounded from inside the room, and a moment later, a door squealed open, backlighting a small form in the bathroom doorway. Hadley froze with one look at us, and the blue light from the television lit her face as it cycled through surprise, fear, then blessed recognition. Thank goodness we'd brought Anne.

Thank goodness neither of the other children had to pee.

Hadley opened her mouth, but Anne put one finger to her lips and waved her daughter forward silently, miming tiptoed walking. Hadley nodded, then tiptoed across the room without even a glance at the sleeping nanny. Anne pulled her out of the doorway, then wrapped her in a hug, and even in the dimly lit hallway, I could see the tears in her eyes.

"Are you okay?" Anne whispered, and Hadley nodded, eyes wide and still sleepy. "Good." Anne hugged her again. "Let's go home."

"Who are they?" Hadley whispered, staring up at Ruben and Michaela as we tiptoed back down the hall, and I wondered if she thought this whole thing was a dream. I wondered if she could keep thinking that, and wake up in the morning completely untraumatized.

Then Hadley noticed my gun, extra-long and intimidating with the silencer, and I realized that a *little* trauma was inevitable. Survival was the goal.

"They're..." Anne began, as I hid the gun behind my leg, and I watched her struggle for words. It wasn't the time to explain about Hadley's parentage and Cavazos and his wife could hardly be called friends. "They're helping us," she finally explained, and Hadley only stared up at Ruben—who stared back, openly curious—then squatted to be on her level and stuck one hand out for her to shake.

"Hi. My name is Ruben."

Hadley took his hand hesitantly and shook it until Anne started tugging her gently down the hall.

Ruben rose and as we retreated, as silently and carefully as we'd come, a spot on my inner thigh began to burn—a tiny ring of fire—and I smiled through the minor pain. My mark had just died. I was no longer bound to Ruben Cavazos.

I hadn't truly believed it would happen until that moment. In the back of my mind, I'd always assumed something would go wrong. I'd fail to actually physically hand the child to her father, or to jump through whatever crazy hoop I didn't remember from the contract I'd signed. Or—Heaven forbid—Hadley would get caught in the cross fire and die before she'd officially been returned to her father.

But now that was all over. I was unbound. I was free of Ruben. Free to be with Cam. And *cedo nulli* had regained its meaning for me. All that was left was to lead our little expedition safely out of enemy territory, and I could start trying to free Cam from his binding, so we could live the rest of our lives however the hell we wanted.

We turned the corner onto the hallway connecting the two wings and with Hadley's hand in Anne's and that fresh, blissful burn on my thigh, I was feeling cautiously optimistic for the first time in a year and a half. Thanks to Elle's foresight, Kori's unwitting but heartfelt assistance and Anne's determination to get her daughter back, I'd done the impossible—I'd found the child with no name and rescued a friend's daughter. I felt invincible.

Right up until the alarm started shrieking all around us.

"Shit!" Meika shouted, but I could hardly hear her over the high-pitched screeching pouring from overhead. Hadley started crying, and Anne pulled her daughter close, eyes wide with terror, trying to see everywhere all at once.

Cavazos drew his gun and pressed his back against the wall, motioning for the rest of us to do the same. Then he leaned closer to be heard over the alarm. "Lockdown!" he shouted into my ear, and my head swam from the cacophony. Gone was his typical look of amused schadenfreude, and in its place I found an even scarier mercenary determination. "The darkrooms won't work now. We'll have to find an exit and make a run for it."

But less than a second later, Kori stepped around the corner ahead, a gun in one hand, a handheld radio in the other. She aimed the gun in our general direction—a wordless order to stop where we were—and shouted something I couldn't hear into the radio. A second after that, the alarm died, but its screeching echo lived on in my head.

"Found them!" I heard Kori shout into her radio, once the ringing in my ears had mostly faded. "They're in the back hall. Four adults and the girl."

I turned to head back the other way and a steel panel slid out from one side of the wall and slammed into the other, a security measure out of some over-the-top spy movie, meant to divorce the family living quarters from the danger. It worked. We were cut off from both sides.

"Who do we have?" a staticky voice demanded over the radio, while Ruben and I aimed at the floor near Kori's feet. I was starting to wish we'd given Meika a gun.

"Anne Liang," Kori said through clenched teeth, staring at me in some intense combination of anger and remorse. "Olivia Warren. Ruben Cavazos and his wife, Michaela."

"Cavazos? What the hell is he doing here?" the radio voice asked, and as the last of the ringing faded from my ears, I recognized the voice as Tower's. The man himself was on the way.

"The girl is Cavazos's daughter, sir."

"Son of a *bitch*," Tower roared, and we all breathed through a single moment of tense silence while he recovered from the shock. "Get the girl. Kill the rest."

Hadley screamed and Anne pushed her between us, trying to guard her from all sides, while Ruben stepped in front of us all, drawing Kori's aim and ready to fire in return.

Kori's jaw tensed and her forehead crinkled with obvious pain. "Can't, sir. Contractual conflict with two of the intruders." Her voice was taut with the conflict, and for one brief moment, I thought it might all work out okay. She couldn't kill me or Anne—at the very least, that should give us a few extra seconds to work with.

Then Tower's voice crackled from the radio again. "Fine. Shoot those you can. Caballero, kill the rest."

I froze in shock as Cam stepped around the corner to stand next to Kori, aiming an unfamiliar .45 in our direction. "I'm so sorry, Liv," he said, so softly I could barely hear him. "Tower called my new phone. I had to answer."

Fuck! That was my fault. I'd called Kori from Cam's new number. She'd obviously given it to Tower before she walked into our trap—she'd probably had no choice.

"Liv, help us." Anne squeezed my arm and I pulled

it from her grip to keep from compromising my own aim.

And in that moment, all of Elle's planning swirled around in my head, winding rapidly toward a single point of darkness that was this specific instant in time. She'd seen this. Me and Cam, guns pointed at each other across the gulf of our divided loyalty.

He'd kill me because he had to.

I'd kill him to protect Anne. Because I had to. I'd have to even if I weren't bound to her, because she was innocent, and so was Hadley.

Light flashed from the end of Kori's gun, and an instant later I heard the *thwup*. Anne and I lunged in front of Hadley. Cavazos threw Meika against the wall, covering her with his own body, even as he returned fire. Kori's bullet split the air between me and Ruben. He fired again. Kori screamed and lurched to one side, then grabbed her left shoulder. Blood poured between her fingers and over the grip of the gun she still clutched.

Cam still held his gun, his aim wavering as his hands shook. He was fighting the order. But he couldn't last.

"In there!" I hauled Ruben off his wife and pointed at the open billiard room across the hall. Meika shoved Anne aside and dove into the dark room just as a third figure stepped into sight around the corner ahead, bringing yet another gun to the party. We were officially outgunned, and I recognized Jake Tower in spite of the indignity of addressing his nemesis in nothing but a pair of pajama pants.

"Shoot Liang in the leg," he ordered, and Cam's face was a violent collision of guilt, remorse and bitter obligation. But that order was too specific and direct to fight. He hesitated for one long moment, then roared with frustration as he squeezed the trigger.

Anne screamed and collapsed to the floor, blood pouring between her fingers from the hole in her thigh. Hadley's sobs became wrenching gasps for air between tear-strangled cries, and she backed away from us all.

"Hadley," Tower called across the chaos of guns drawn and blood spilled, and she watched him through her tears. "Your mom's hurt, but if you come to me now, I'll call for a doctor. She'll be fine. You can save your mother. You want to be a hero, don't you?"

Hadley glanced at her mother, then back at Tower, and she started to step forward. "No!" Anne shouted through her own pain, and I put a hand on the child's shoulder to stop her, my own gun aimed at Tower's head now. But I couldn't pull the trigger, even if I'd been sure I could hit him from that distance with almost no light. I didn't know what his default, preprogrammed orders might be upon his death.

And I didn't know who his successor was.

Cavazos was also aiming at Tower, and the only thing keeping him from shooting—as far as I could tell—was the reluctance to subject his daughter to any more bloodshed than necessary.

So instead of shooting, I glanced into the billiard room where I could barely see Meika watching us in the dark, her arms tense at her sides, eyes wide with fear. "Take her!" I snapped, nodding at Anne, who sat just inches from the doorway, but wouldn't crawl out of the line of fire without her daughter.

"No!" Anne screamed again, when Meika grabbed her arms from behind and hauled her into the dark. A

bullet shot past where her head had been an instant earlier. Hadley screamed, but she was too scared to move.

"Bust up the grid and get her out of here!" I shouted
to Meika, and after a second to process what I'd said,
her dark silhouette climbed onto the pool table with a
pool cue in hand. She jammed the thick end into the
ceiling, and glass shattered, then fell all around her, re-
flecting the little available visible light.

"Shoot them, now!" Tower ordered, when he realized what Meika was doing.

Obviously reluctant to shoot me as long as they
had a choice, Cam and Kori both fired on Cavazos,
who returned two shots as he lunged toward Hadley
and hauled her into the unlit billiard room. I was right
behind them, and more bullets thunked into the door-
jamb as I passed it.

Peppered with glinting broken glass, Meika's silhouette had Anne's limping silhouette around the waist,
presumably standing in an infrared shadow she could
feel much better than I could see. "Go!" I shouted, and
Meika stepped into oblivion, dragging Anne with her
in spite of sobbing protests.

I pulled Hadley away from the door as footsteps
pounded down the hall toward us. But they stopped
just out of sight. "Don't shoot, you can't see in there!"
Kori yelled, and I could feel the blood she was still
dripping—I could practically smell it. "You might hit
the girl."

"We don't even know if she's still in there," Tower
pointed out. "Caballero?"

"She's there," he said, and I could hear the reluctance
in his voice as he tracked her from only feet away.

"The others?" Tower asked.

"Just Cavazos and Warren."

"Shit!" Tower shouted, and I spared a moment to thoroughly enjoy his anger.

A moment later, the air changed and I turned to see Meika's dark form in the spot she'd disappeared from a minute earlier. I pushed Hadley toward her and Cavazos glanced at them both, then returned his attention and aim to the doorway, even as he whispered to his wife, "Take her to our house and lock the place down."

"But then how will you...?" Meika began, but her husband cut her off.

"Go! And don't come back!"

Because without Hadley there, they would open fire on us. Plain and simple.

An instant later, Meika and Hadley were gone, and that time Tower must have felt the shift in air pressure. "Caballero?" he said, still just out of sight, and I ran for the window farthest from the open doorway.

"Hadley's gone."

I pounded on the glass, but it didn't even rattle. It was thicker than my thumb and probably bulletproof.

"Motherfucker!" Tower shouted, ripping the word right out of my own mouth. We were trapped. "Open fire."

"I can't," Kori insisted, her words half sobs of obvious agony. "I might hit Liv."

Tower swore again. "Caballero, kill them."

Cam thundered a wordless sound of rage and pain. I held my breath, gun aimed, heart pounding fiercely. Cam opened fire.

Cavazos glanced at me as the first bullets punched through the air, inches away, and thunked into the walls at my back. I raced farther into the room, away from the door. Anne was no longer in danger, which meant I couldn't shoot Cam. I *wouldn't*. Not even to save myself. But Cavazos wouldn't hold his fire—he wasn't willing to die for me.

Ruben stepped into the doorway, already returning fire at Cam. I rammed him from the side, as Cam fired again.

Pain ripped through my stomach and I fell against the wall, fighting to breathe. Cavazos crashed into the door frame, still shooting.

A grunt of pain echoed from the hall, and Jake Tower fell to the tile, half blocking the doorway. "No!" I shouted, as Kori dropped to his side to feel for a pulse, still bleeding from her own wound.

Cam rushed into the billiard room and pulled the duffel from my shoulder, already digging inside. He pulled out a cloth diaper—the best for absorption—and pressed it to the explosion of agony my stomach had become, to keep my blood from dripping on the floor.

"He's alive," Kori called. "But he can't give orders while he's unconscious. Let's get you out of here." She holstered her gun and stepped into the billiard room, one hand covering her bullet wound, as she squinted into the dark, feeling for the hole Meika had hammered into the infrared grid.

Cam put one arm around me and led me toward Kori and the scattering of broken glass. "Wait! Anne's blood!" I cried, wobbling as a newer, more personal darkness washed over me. I was going to pass out.

No, I was going to die. Elle had been right all along.

"I'll get it later. I swear," Kori promised. "Let's get you out of here before I have to sterilize yours, too."

"I'm not leaving here while her blood's viable," I

gasped, scared to realize that my voice was unsteady and sounded kind of hollow. But I wasn't going to be there to protect Anne anymore. The least I could do was make sure Tower didn't have her blood.

Kori groaned, still clutching her shoulder. Cam handed her my duffel and she dug inside, one-handed, until she found my squirt bottle of bleach and dumped the whole thing on the small pool of blood Anne had left behind. Then she pressed another diaper to her own shoulder.

"Now, let's go!" We could already hear footsteps pounding our way from the hall. Kori took me from Cam and the world tilted around me as we crunched on broken glass.

"Take her to my place," Cavazos insisted. "The house is locked down, but the gazebo in back has infrared shadows. Meika will have already called in my staff doctor for Anne."

I think Cam nodded, but that could have been a trick of the light as the shadows closed in on me. And then I couldn't feel my legs. The dark room spun around me, and suddenly I was looking up at Cam. He was shouting something, but I couldn't hear him over the rush of my own pulse.

Then that stopped, too, and the last thing I felt was the warmth of his lips on mine.

Then there was nothing.

Nothing at all.

Thirty

Bright lights. Flashes of pain. Glimpses of faces I should have known, but couldn't place.

Then more silence. Numbness. And the blessed, blessed darkness.

The cold came first. Then the smooth touch of expensive sheets against my skin. By the time I opened my eyes, I'd decided I was either dreaming or in Heaven, and I didn't really care which.

Blinking, I turned my head to the left and saw Cam slumped over in a recliner, sound asleep. I tried to sit up, and fire shot through my center. My gasp of pain woke Cam and he sat up, startled.

Then he saw me, and he smiled, and an instant later he was perched on the edge of the bed next to me.

"Am I dead?" I asked, surprised when my voice creaked like a frog's.

"Not anymore."

I blinked. "You actually killed me, you son of a bitch."

Cam flinched. "Yeah. I'll spend the rest of both of our lives trying to make up for that."

I laughed, then flinched when the pain resurfaced. "I'll let you." I cleared my throat. "Where are we?"

"Casa Cavazos."

"No..." I winced when protesting tugged at the muscles in my stomach. "Cam, I can't be here. This isn't free." I waved one arm carefully to indicate the dubious nature of Ruben's hospitality. "Nothing from him is ever free." *Nothing except the bruises...* "Just because he hasn't killed us yet doesn't mean he won't." Or worse.

"I worked it out." Cam's smile was too bright. Like a mask, hiding something ugly. "It's going to be fine."

"Worked it out?" My pulse spiked painfully. "What have you worked out? What did you do?"

He shrugged. "We'll talk about it later. Anne's in the next room."

Anne... "How is she?"

"Better than you." Cam smiled. "Her heart never stopped. She's fucking *pissed* at me, though."

"Women get like that when you shoot them."

He frowned. "So I noticed."

"Hadley? Is she here?" I listened, but if there were any voices coming from Anne's room, I couldn't hear them.

"Down the hall, playing with Isabel. She seems to like having a little sister. Don't worry, though," he said, before I could ask. "Cavazos is sending her home with Anne, as soon as she's well enough to go. Michaela agreed to finally let his affair with Elle go, if he'd agree not to press for full custody of Hadley."

"I hope he got that in writing...." I mumbled, wondering just how much drama I'd slept through.

"You know he did. He's having Anne's house retrofitted with an infrared grid and assigning full-time security to them both."

"Wow." Anne probably wasn't happy about the 24/7 guard, but she wouldn't turn down anything that would help keep Hadley safe. I wondered if she'd had any idea what she was getting into that day in junior high, when she introduced Noelle to me and Kori.

She couldn't have. None of us could have. Except maybe Elle.

"Cam, how long was I out?" I'd evidently missed quite a bit.

He glanced at the comforter and only looked up when I took his hand, and that's when I noticed the dark bags beneath his eyes. "Four days," he admitted at last. "Cavazos wasn't sure you were going to wake up, but I never doubted it." His smile, that time, was wistful. "You survived me killing you, so I knew you could beat some stupid coma."

Death. Coma. A sick room at the Cavazos estate. I couldn't decide which was worse. And all of it less than a week since I'd first found Cam leaning against my car in the middle of the night.

"This can't have been cheap." I refused to let go of his hand when he tried to pull it away. Private doctor. Operation to remove the bullet. Maybe another to stop the bleeding or repair the damage. Aftercare. Antibiotics. Medical supplies and equipment. Room and board.

The bill would easily run mid-five figures at any public hospital. Here, it was probably more.

I didn't have money.

Cam didn't have *that* kind of money.

"What do we owe him, Cam?"

"You don't owe him anything," he insisted, meeting my gaze steadily. "I covered it."

"No." I shook my head, and darkness crept in on the edges of my vision. "*No.* You can get out of it, whatever it is." I threw back the covers and winced at the pain in my stomach when I tried to move my legs. Then I moved them anyway. "We're leaving, and you're going to get out of this if I have to kill the Binder myself."

"Olivia, stop." Cam gently lifted my legs back into the bed. "It's done."

"No!" I shouted, and the tears were part physical pain, part denial. "I signed with him in the first place to keep you away from him, and it was all for nothing!" I swiped angrily at my cheeks. "It *can't* be for nothing." I was free from Ruben, and in four years—less, if possible—Cam would be free from Tower, and we'd both survived Elle's prediction. We were supposed to have our forever, damn it, and I wasn't going to let Ruben take that away!

"It wasn't for nothing, Liv. It was for you." Cam held me by my shoulders, and I didn't know whether to shove him away or pull him closer. "I killed you. Your heart stopped on Cavazos's front yard. I couldn't just let it end like that. I couldn't let you die."

"What did you do?" I ran my hand slowly up his arm to the edge of his left sleeve and lifted the material with my eyes closed. It couldn't be true. He couldn't serve Cavazos. He was bound to Tower, and he'd signed a noncompetition clause.

My fingers brushed smooth medical tape, then the rough grid of a gauze bandage. I opened my eyes, and there it was. Proof of the price he'd paid for my life.

I peeled back the bandage and blinked away more tears. The black chain links were a faded, lifeless gray. Dead marks, all three of them.

Below them were three freshly inked, black interlocking rings.

Three rings at once. Five years each. Cam had committed to fifteen years up front, waiving his right to decline reenlistment after each of the first two terms. He'd paid for my life with fifteen years of his own.

Ruben, you hell-spawn son of a bitch.

"How?" I demanded, and my voice carried almost no sound. "What about Tower?"

"Cavazos bought my contract."

"No." I shook my head, insistent. That made no sense. "Tower would never sell you. Not after what went down in his house. He'd want your head, and Ruben's, too."

Cam shrugged. "I don't know how he did it. All I know is that he bought out my contract with Tower and saved your life. All for three little black rings."

And fifteen years of service and abuse.

Muneris. Oboedientia.

Fucking *fidelitas.*

Hell. No.

I sucked in a deep breath, and Cam realized what I was going to do an instant too late. "Ruben!" I shouted, but my bellow ended sooner than I'd intended. I was shocked silent by the agony in my abdomen. I drew in another shaky breath, but my next words held little strength. "Ruben, get your ass in here."

"Liv, whatever you're about to do…don't," Cam insisted, already backing toward the door.

"Ruben!" I shouted again, in spite of the pain.

Cam tried to close the door, but it bounced off a shiny black dress shoe.

Cavazos leaned against the door facing and gave me a slimy smile. "You rang?"

I turned to Cam. "Get out."

"I'm not going anywh—"

"Wait in the hall," Cavazos said softly, and Cam scowled, then turned and stepped into the hallway. Because he had no choice. The binding had already been sealed. Cam leaned against the wall opposite my room, arms crossed over his chest, face flushed and fists clenched with anger.

"Take it back," I said, as Cavazos settled onto the side of my bed.

"No."

"You son of a bitch. I found your daughter. I got her out Tower's house. You fucking owe me."

"You were paid up front for your services." He put one hand on my knee, like a doctor trying to calm his patient, and I jerked free from his touch. He'd lost that right. "Cam Caballero went free—you served in his place."

I tried to back away from him, but there was nowhere to go. "Then you turned around and signed him for fifteen years!"

"As was my legal right. You should be thanking me—I saved his life. Tower was ready to kill him, and your friend Kori, too."

Kori. She'd helped us, in spite of her loyalty to Tower, and probably paid for it with resistance pain far beyond her gunshot wound. "Is she okay?"

"Caballero says she's alive and still in the city, though I can't imagine why Tower let her live. I wouldn't have." He shrugged. "Still, I'm sure she's far from comfortable at the moment." Cavazos cleared his throat and leaned closer, lowering his voice so Cam wouldn't hear. "Do you have any idea how hard it was to buy out Caballero's contract? I had to give Tower another Seer to replace Hadley, and they're not exactly a dime a dozen."

"You sold someone else to Tower? You supplemented his blood-donor project?" I hadn't just slept through drama, I'd slept through the end of the world as I knew it!

"I traded Caballero's contract for one I already held, and I let Tower keep the Blinder, Jammer and Binder he'd already taken from me, as a sort of peace offering. Unrest between his syndicate and mine is the last thing this city needs right now, don't you agree?"

"*You* are the last thing this city needs."

"That is a matter of opinion, Olivia. But because

I like you—because you *did* serve me faithfully and find my missing daughter—I'm going to make you an offer I wouldn't make for anyone else." Cavazos opened his suit jacket and pulled out a thick stack of papers, folded in half. His other hand produced a pen from some unseen pocket, and my blood pressure spiked at just the sight of him wielding that particular weapon.

"Caballero signed away fifteen years of his life. For you. Are you going to let him serve it alone? Or will you share his burden?"

I exhaled slowly and hated myself for what I was about to ask. "What are you offering?"

"You take half his time. Seven and a half years, from the day you sign. You can serve together and watch Hadley grow up. Then you can leave, if that's what you want. Together."

I looked at Cam and found him watching us both from the hall, but Cavazos was angled away from him. Cam couldn't see the contract or the pen. He stood stiff and angry—already mentally fighting Ruben's orders. Serving Tower had been hard for him, but submitting to Cavazos would be hell. Ruben wouldn't just employ him—he'd humiliate and exploit Cam for his personal entertainment. And Cam would fight, because he couldn't not fight. And when he couldn't be bent, Ruben would break him. Or kill him. Either way, the Cam I knew and loved would be destroyed.

Or I could join him. I could take half of his pain and humiliation. Serve half his time. We could be each other's lifeline in a sea of misery. We could suffer together, then be free together. But for a price I'd sworn never to pay again.

I thought about Cam, and the life I wanted with him.

I thought about the words tattooed on my back—the words I wanted to live by.

Cavazos watched me closely. Then he held out the pen.

* * * * *

Coming soon is
SHADOW BOUND
by Rachel Vincent

Acknowledgments

Thanks first and foremost to my husband, my #1 fan, for listening to all the crazy brainstorming that went into this book without betraying any hint that the author may be as crazy as the ideas. You're the most wonderful sounding board ever.

Thanks as always to Rinda Elliott, my longtime critique partner and the first to see every book I write. You're my second pair of eyes, and I always appreciate the fresh viewpoint.

Thanks to my editor, Mary-Theresa Hussey, for guidance and patience. And for pronouncing this manuscript "twisted," then liking it anyway.

And thanks to everyone at MIRA Books, who made it all happen. There are so many more of you behind me than I would ever have guessed when I was first starting out, and I sometimes think books should get credit reels, like movies.